I

Secrets from a Stranger

SECRETS
from a
STRANGER

Fame and beauty are a deadly combination

Even people who have everything want to change their lives.

Juliette, famous for winning a gold medal in the 1936 Olympics at the age of 17, is living peacefully in the South of France when a stranger arrives and expresses interest in her daughter Camille.

David N.O. Newton Dunn

Printed in the United States of America
First Printing, 2021

ISBN: 979-8-9851201-1-0
Library of Congress Control Number: 2021921522
Published by: David N.O. Newton Dunn
Miami,
Florida,

Website: www.davidnewtondunn.com
Email: kidwelly@icloud.com

I'm not upset that you lied to me.
I'm upset that from now on I can't believe you.

Friedrich Nietzsche

TABLE OF CONTENTS

CHAPTER	TITLE	PAGE

Chapter 1

PROVENCE, SUMMER 1967

WHAT IF HE'S DEAD? The thought struck her as she drove by splashes of red poppies in the orchards and olive groves, and the yellow fields of wheat. He was very pale and hadn't moved. He looked as if he was sleeping, and there were no signs of blood. Better try the garage when she reached Marseille and call the police if there's no reply.

❧

"I found Walter dead yesterday," Camille said.

Juliette was sitting at her dressing table, studying an old photograph of herself in a silver frame. It was one of many pre-war photographs in silver frames on the walls and small tables around the room, all taken thirty years ago when the media was at her feet; newspapers, magazines, radio. Even television, and Pathé News. She was tall, slim and stylish, and her silk, eau-de-nil peignoir went perfectly with the soft oyster-grey of the walls.

As Camille waited, she watched the dust float lazily in the sunlight streaming through the windows and eyed her mother sourly. She lowered her gaze for a moment, then looked up at her mother again. Juliette put down the silver frame and sighed; one of her normal, everyday, leave-me-alone sighs.

Without turning around, she said: "Yes, Camille, what is it? What do you want? I am very busy."

Camille sighed too, though her sigh was deeper and less audible.

"I said, I found Walter dead yesterday."

"Who's Walter?"

"Walter. Walter Clément, you know, the owner of the village garage. I found him dead."

"Goodness. Where did you find him?" said Juliette, her back to Camille.

"Sitting in a car at his garage."

"It was bound to happen one day. He was a heavy drinker," said Juliette indifferently.

"I thought you should know."

Juliette glanced up at her daughter's reflection in the mirror and thanked her.

Downstairs in the kitchen, Nadia, Juliette's best friend and companion, was preparing lunch as Camille came through the door.

"Shouldn't you be at work, sweetheart? Not working today?"

"No work today," said Camille. "I called at the garage on my way to work yesterday and found Walter Clément asleep in a car. At least I thought he was asleep, but I couldn't wake him up. So, I called the police when I got to work. They phoned me this morning and told me he was dead—and they want to talk to me."

"Oh, for goodness sake. Walter dead? That's awful, but why do the police want to talk to you?"

"I have no idea. I hope they don't think I did it. I didn't even know he was dead till they called me."

"Of course, they don't think you did it! But that's so sad, though he did drink like a fish, poor old man, and never seemed happy. Maybe he drank his heart out." Nadia looked up sympathetically at Camille.

"Could be. All I know is that I got there at eight to fill my car and there he was, sitting in a car. Not moving."

"Did you try and wake him?"

"Of course, I did. I shouted and banged on the window."

"Perhaps he had a heart attack?"

"Maybe," said Camille as someone knocked at the door.

"Good morning, Mademoiselle," said an overweight man in his fifties who was wearing a light-coloured suit and a flat cap. "I am Chief Inspector Paquet of the local brigade of intelligence and criminal investigations of the Bouches-du-Rhône."

The inspector took off his cap.

"Mademoiselle Dumont?"

"Yes, please come in Chief Inspector." Camille showed the policeman into the hall. "I presume this is about Monsieur Clément. We can talk in the kitchen if you like. I don't have much to tell you."

Camille pulled out a chair for the inspector.

"I went to the garage to fill up my car and couldn't wake him. That's all there is to it. I didn't know he was dead."

"Don't worry, Mademoiselle," said Paquet smiling as he sat down, "my visit is only a formality. In every case of unexplained death, we have to go through this. Witness statements, autopsy, you know how it is. All I need is for you to fill in this form and write in your words what you saw to the best of your knowledge and belief. A paragraph will do unless you noticed something out of place."

"So," Camille asked as she filled out the form, "do you know what he died of? A heart attack do you think?"

"It's too early to tell, but it's an unexplained death. He was sixty-nine and had worked at the garage for twenty-seven years. It could have been a natural death; it could have been suicide; it could even have been murder. We don't know yet. Did you notice anything unusual?"

"Nothing. I just knocked on the car window and tried to wake him up. I thought he was asleep. I only called you when I got to work in case he wasn't well."

"You were right there. He wasn't well, not at all well. Do you remember if the car windows were up?"

"I'm sure of it. And the driver's door was locked. I know because I tried it."

"Did you touch anything else?" Paquet opened his notebook.

"No, just the driver's window and the door handle."

"Did you check inside the car at all? Did you see anything inside?"

"I couldn't open the door, and I couldn't see much through the windows. Only Monsieur Clément. I thought he was sleeping. His face was very pale."

"That, Mademoiselle, is known as pallor mortis. We think Monsieur Clément had been dead for a while when you saw him, possibly several hours. Did you notice if the car engine was running?"

"No, the engine wasn't running, I am sure of that."

"And you didn't notice a hose attached to the exhaust pipe?"

"No, I didn't."

"Because there was one. It was sticking through a rear window of the car, the ignition was on, and the tank was empty."

"Oh no! That's awful. That does sound like suicide, doesn't it?"

"It would seem so, except the first reports suggest he didn't die of carbon monoxide poisoning, which is strange. We arrived soon after you called, and the car engine was still warm. Our engineers think it had only stopped an hour earlier."

Nadia and Camille looked at the inspector.

"So, what did he die of?" They said in unison.

"It's too early to reach a conclusion. We are certain he absorbed some carbon-monoxide, but not enough to kill him. So, something else, a heart condition or alcohol must have caused his death."

Two months later, August 10, 1967
"I'm sorry, Maman, but my car is… I was wondering if…"

"If what? If you could borrow my car? You know perfectly well Camille, I don't like anybody driving my car." Juliette replied sharply, visibly irritated.

Camille smiled ruefully to herself, or at least she thought she smiled, but her reflection in the mirror on her mother's dressing table confirmed that her eyes were not smiling, and her mouth and lips had not moved.

Why won't she lend me her car? It wasn't much to ask.

Yes, the scarlet Alfa Romeo Giulietta convertible had been an anniversary present from Bernard, but that was ten years ago, for God's sake.

"No, Maman, I shall be going into Aix this morning, and I was wondering if you need me to pick up anything while I am there. That's all."

That was not all, nor was it what she had planned to say. She frowned and bit her lip. For a moment she hesitated, as if about to add something else, and then the cicadas began their noisy symphony, promising another blistering summer's day. Through the tall windows behind her mother, the morning sun had reached the line of stately linden trees that swept up the drive, past the cottage and the pool.

She would ask Nadia.

The wicker basket bounced over the front wheel of the old Raleigh bicycle, and the worn leather seat was small and hard as Camille set out on the eight miles to Aix-en-Provence. Nadia had needed her car. She rang the small bell on the handlebar, wobbled as she turned right out of the chateau gates, and cycled along the tree-lined Avenue de Victor Hugo before reaching the Route de Berre, the D10 road to Aix.

In the distance to the north, beyond the mottled greens of the vineyards and the dark, imperious cypress trees, the violet tips of the Alps were clearly visible, a sure sign that the Mistral was starting to blow. It would blow for three days, six, or even nine. It always did. It was a maddening wind. It was said that if a man killed his woman when the Mistral was blowing, a judge would have mercy on him. Nobody said what would happen if a woman killed her man.

Pedalling was hard work. And though there were few inclines and the road was tarred and smooth, Camille's legs ached, and the perspiration stung her eyes. Yet the thought of the man she was going to meet pushed her forward. It was disquieting and a little exciting: she had made a spontaneous decision that she hoped she would not regret. It would not be her first bad decision.

She winced as an image of Leo came to mind and slowed in the shade of a canopy of plane trees alongside the road.

It was Saturday, and there was less traffic than usual. Mostly small trucks, some laden, some empty, toiling their way to and from the market, plus a few cars scuttling by with thin beeps and the metallic clatter of stressed engines. An occasional cyclist, hunched over drop handlebars, pressed by in the heat, but no-one was a match for the motorised *Solex* two-wheelers of the women of Aix. In black print dresses and flashes of petticoats, they whizzed by with baguettes and courgettes protruding from baskets at the front and the back of their bikes.

Close to an hour later, she rode unsteadily into the ancient capital of Provence, bouncing along the cobblestones of the Boulevard de la République and on to the Avenue Napoléon Bonaparte. She stopped by the old Casino Municipal, a stone's throw from the Place de la Rotonde at the bottom of the Cours Mirabeau. Flushed and out of breath, Camille propped her bicycle against the casino wall and checked her watch. She was early.

Breathing deeply, she gazed at the grand fountain in the Place de la Rotonde guarded by the three imposing statues incarnating Justice, Agriculture and the Arts. For a while, she watched the cool water gushing and tumbling from the water jets, then turned and studied her reflection in the dark window of the casino. She shook her head, ran her fingers through her hair, and brushed down the wrinkles in her dress before she wheeled her bike across to the *Bar de la Paix* on the Place Jeanne d'Arc.

Camille pushed open the heavy bar doors and was blinded for a moment by the change in light. She shaded her eyes and scanned the room to see old men playing cards by the windows, wreathed in cigarette smoke, and framed by sunlight spilling through the dusty glass. They paused, lifted their heads, looked her up and down, and turned back to their cards.

Max smoked too at a small table at the back on the left of the long zinc bar. He wore jeans, a white shirt and a leather jacket, and was better dressed than the first time she had seen him at the village garage a week ago when he had said her pretty eyes reminded him of a cat. Nobody had ever said that before. He had been wearing overalls then, as he was three days later when she called at the garage to ask about a noise her car was making. And they had talked a while before he playfully asked her if she would be offended if a working man like him offered to buy her a drink. Would she accept? That had put her on the spot and made her laugh and, not wishing to be rude, she had heard herself reply: "Of course, why not?"

Max stood up, put down his cigarette, smiled broadly, and stretched out his hand as she approached.

"Ah bonjour, Mademoiselle, how are you?" Max spoke affably and Camille was pleased when he pulled out the other chair from the table for her to sit. "I'm surprised to see you. I wasn't sure you'd come. So, now that you are here, may I buy you something to drink?"

Camille seated herself confidently and laughed as she replied. "I need something strong after cycling all this way and I don't normally drink alcohol before lunch. But I'll have a Scotch, please, a Ballantine's and soda. Fifty-fifty with a little ice."

"You cycled here?" said Max astonished. "That's quite a ride."

He turned to attract the waiter's attention and she had her first good chance to study him. He was certainly attractive, and strikingly masculine in a rugged country way, with sunburnt skin and deep lines around his black eyes. He was clean-shaven and his dark hair was long and lank, and his teeth were straight and white. He looks Italian, she decided. I wonder how old he is. Late thirties, early forties at most. One thing was certain: her mother would not like him.

"Yes, Max, I cycled. You have my car, remember?"

Max snorted with laughter and exhaled a wreath of smoke that curled and danced in a shaft of sunlight reflecting off the glass behind the bar.

"Oh no, your car, Mademoiselle de Vaucluse. I'm so sorry. I forgot I still have your Renault Dauphine. But it's nearly ready. There was nothing much wrong with it, just a loose engine mounting. That's what that noise you kept hearing was. *Kerbang, kerbang, kerbang.* The engine was trying to get out of the car!"

Max grinned good-naturedly.

"Come around this afternoon. I'll make sure it's all set—or I can leave it on the forecourt for you to collect if you wish."

The status and respect accorded to her parents in the region made Camille ill at ease. She was unused to, and uncomfortable with being addressed as Mademoiselle de Vaucluse. Since childhood, she had witnessed her parents' constant and unremitting social life but had never wanted to be part of it. She did not share their values and had always preferred the company of simpler, less-conventional people.

"Please don't call me Mademoiselle de Vaucluse. Call me Camille. And for that matter, my family name is not de Vaucluse."

Max leaned forward, as if he didn't understand.

"But I thought you were… Don't you live at the chateau with Monsieur Bernard and Madame Juliette de Vaucluse?"

"Yes, I do, but de Vaucluse is not my family name. Juliette de Vaucluse is my mother, but Bernard de Vaucluse is not my father." Her voice died away; she wished he had been.

Why did she have to blurt that out straightaway? It was true, though. She had been to a private Catholic school and tutored by nuns before going to the girls only Lycée of Aix-en-Provence at sixteen, where she had mixed with less-fortunate people for the first time. She had been proud to carry her mother's maiden name, Dumont. Everybody had heard of Juliette Dumont. But only then did she realise her parents used a different name.

"But your mother, Juliette de Vaucluse, is Juliette Dumont, is she not? The famous swimmer?" Max stared intently at her, as if inspecting her. "At least let me introduce myself. I am Max Berger, son of Michel and Chantal Berger from the Auvergne. My parents are farmers, and we have nobody famous in my family as far as I know," he added gracefully.

So, he is not Italian. There are no Italians in the Auvergne, just low mountains and forests, cattle, dried sausage and cheese.

"The Auvergne? You surprise me. So why are you called Max?" Camille asked, keeping her voice light. "Max is a Provençal name. Wouldn't Gaspard be more typical of the Auvergne?"

"Hey, wait a minute! Gaspard? I am pleased they didn't call me Gaspard! No, it was my father's idea to call me Max. He had a soft spot for Provence; something to do with an old girlfriend." Max chuckled. "So, Camille, what's your story? Who are you?"

Camille may not have been as stunningly beautiful as her mother, but she had learned her lessons and knew a little mystery would not be amiss.

"You already know my name is Camille, and my mother is the famous swimmer. And that, for now, is all I am going to tell you." Camille teased.

François the waiter, arrived with the Scotch and a glass of pastis for Max, who gave him a crumpled banknote that disappeared into a black waistcoat pocket that already bulged with notes. The cuffs on his white shirt were frayed and there were stains on his lapels. He fumbled in the pocket that sagged with coins.

Camille was pleased when Max said: "Forget it, François. Keep the change."

Max slowly, deliberately, stubbed out his filter-less cigarette and ground it into the ashtray before looking at Camille.

"It's a strange thing, but I thought you would be standoffish, more aloof; yet you seem quite normal to me. I have to say, I am enjoying spending time with you. As a rule, I don't like rich girls very much—which is probably just as well because they don't like me either."

Max contemplated his glass of pastis.

Camille was unsure what to make of him. His directness was disconcerting.

"Oh really? So, I am a rich girl, but I seem normal to you? Am I supposed to take that as a compliment?"

Without waiting for a reply, she continued. "Don't judge me, Max; I am who I am, and I don't like labels. And it may surprise you to know that I don't usually accept random invitations from men I hardly know. Believe it or not, I don't need people very much, and normally I choose people I spend time with more carefully. I prefer my own company and quite enjoy being alone."

Max leaned back and smiled. "Well, that's good, isn't it? If you're lonely when you're alone, you're in bad company."

"Clever, but not original," said Camille, impressed and surprised. "Jean-Paul Sartre said that before you."

"I know. I thought you'd like that." Max said as he pulled a soft blue and white pack of Gitanes cigarettes from his shirt pocket.

Camille had not expected this verbal sparring but found it disarming and oddly refreshing. It was unsettling to feel drawn to a man she could not measure. Though neither polished nor presumably well educated, he came across as confident and knowledgeable, and exuded a rough charm.

"So how do you like our village, Ventabren? You heard what happened to your predecessor?"

"Old Monsieur Clément?" Max looked down at his drink. "Yes, I heard. He committed suicide, didn't he? Poor old codger."

"It was either suicide or murder. Or natural causes. The police can't decide."

"Oh, I'm sure it was suicide. I met his wife and she told me they were married for thirty years. I'm sure he decided thirty years with her were enough."

Camille laughed. "Oh, come on, she's not that bad. But you never met him, did you? He was a grumpy old sod but very sweet once you got to know him. She was lucky to find you so quickly."

"Yes, I suppose so. I read about his death in the newspaper and applied for the job immediately. I've always wanted to live in this part of Provence."

"So, where were you before Ventabren?" Camille asked.

"West of here, in the Languedoc," Max continued. "But that's a long story. I came to get away and start a new life."

"Get away from what?"

"My wife died." Max said quietly lowering his eyes, "I lost my wife to breast cancer. It happened very quickly, only six months after being diagnosed."

"Oh, I'm so sorry. I didn't mean to pry." Camille reached over and touched his arm. "Please forgive me."

"Don't feel sorry for me," said Max, "that was a year ago. We had ten great years together. And we didn't have children, which made things easier. Still, it's hard to lose your best friend."

"I know," said Camille. "I lost my best friend too, a year ago."

There was a moment's silence, before she continued.

"To change the subject, tell me about life on a farm. I am more of a city girl. I lived in London for six years."

"Then you speak English?" said Max with interest. "I've always wanted to learn another language, but I never had a chance where I came from."

"Yes, I can speak English. In fact, I teach English at a school near Marseille. But you were telling me what it's like to live on a farm?"

Max inhaled deeply on his cigarette. "You know, I don't think you'd find it very interesting. That was many years ago, and I don't think about it very much. The past is only interesting in that it explains why people become who they become. I only find my past interesting for what it taught me."

"All right, so what did your past teach you?" Camille put her Scotch down.

"About nature, about life," Max said, thoughtfully. "For one thing, living in the past is futile, whether your memories are good or bad. Good memories tend to make you nostalgic and complacent. Bad memories are painful, though they can—or at least they should—serve as lessons and make you stronger. I've known good times, and I've known bad."

"That's true for everybody," Camille thinking back to London.

"Yes, but there are degrees of good and bad. And with your upbringing, I'm betting your good memories are better than mine, and my bad memories are worse than yours."

"Possibly, but Max, it's all relative. Life isn't a competition. I've had some bad times too. Everybody has. But I'll say this for you: most people in this part of the world would jump at an opportunity to talk about themselves, even if they've never done anything."

Max grinned. "All the same, I'm sure you would have found growing up on a farm boring; I spent most of my time alone and only had my cows to talk to."

"Yes," agreed Camille, "I can see that could get old very quickly, talking to cows all day."

"Talking to the cows wasn't so bad." Max took a sip of his drink. "The bad thing was they didn't listen—though the good thing was they didn't interrupt."

It was Camille's turn to laugh.

He's anchored and intelligent, thought Camille. What Bernard would call without malice, one of nature's gentlemen—someone without education but level-headed and with a good grasp on life. Anyway, he is refreshingly different from all the other emotionally stunted men around here.

Camille later scolded herself for prejudging him. He was deeper, and more interesting than she had expected. It's true: you can't judge people by their appearances. She had not sought the attention of any man since returning to Provence, and she didn't take herself to task; Max was an unusual man and surprisingly attractive. And the pleasure of the clandestine rendezvous was made all the sweeter by the cast-iron certainty of her mother's disapproval.

※

The following morning Camille woke early and lay listening to the Mistral sighing as it ruffled the leaves on the linden trees. For once, the cicadas were silent, and the splashing of her mother doing laps in the pool and the fresh smell of Colombian coffee ready on the terrace drifted through the open window. Camille loved Sundays, especially in the summer. But there was something special, something almost exquisite about today. And then she remembered Max.

Dumont. Ever since school, Camille had wanted to change her name from Dumont to de Vaucluse, Bernard's family name. At fourteen, Camille had understood that Bernard was not her biological father and asked who her real father was, and Juliette had told her that he had been a professor at the famous Sorbonne University on the Left Bank in Paris. And then she had done the math and understood that her mother had been very young, only eighteen when Camille was born; hardly a year after winning her gold medal for swimming in the Berlin Olympics of 1936.

Camille had no memories of those early years, though from photographs she knew that her father had been around for the first few years of her life. Somehow, they had never married, and Camille had been brought up by her mother and her best friend, Nadia Beausoleil. And with Bernard's help after he married Juliette in 1943. But being called Dumont was a constant reminder that Camille was illegitimate. She would have so much preferred the name de Vaucluse, like her parents. But it was Juliette, not Bernard, who had objected virulently. What difference would it make to her?

She slipped out of bed, stretched, and walked across to the window. Much of her childhood, she had lived in this cottage separated from the big house by the terrace and the pool. And if it was true that she had been sad when Nadia—Bobo as she called her affectionately—left to live in the big house, she liked living here by herself now. For as long as she could remember, she had watched her mother's weekend guests through this window and thrilled to see Nadia coming with a tray of canapés the moment the guests went inside. Camille was not interested, nor ever had been, in her mother's socialite friends. Nor, she suspected, was Nadia.

She leaned through the window and called to her mother, who was towelling herself dry by the pool.

"Bonjour Maman, looks like the Mistral will be back today!"

"Good morning, little one. Yes, it looks like it. Come and have some coffee with me."

As Camille turned to dress, she paused before a large black-and-white photo that Leo had taken of her when they first met, a bittersweet souvenir of London. She slipped on a cotton dress and padded barefoot across to where Juliette sat in a grey towelling robe with her hair slicked back, tilting her head to the right. She shook the water from her ear and clipped on a pearl earring.

Camille pulled up a deck chair beside her mother, conscious of how different they were. Juliette, nearly forty-nine, still looked every inch the athlete she was: tall, trim and slightly tanned, like a model from the pages of French Vogue or a German catalogue of Aryan women. She had hardly changed since the photograph of her receiving her gold medal in 1936 had swept the world. All of France went wild for her that year and the adulation still echoed, albeit more faintly, to this day.

Camille lowered her gaze and studied her own tanned hands and slender fingers.

"What are you thinking about, chérie?" asked Juliette.

"Oh nothing, Maman, nothing important." Camille hesitated before she continued. "It's ridiculous, I know, but sometimes I wish my hair was more blonde and that I had taken more after you."

Camille half-smiled as she watched her mother expectantly, unsure how she would take the compliment. The thought had crossed her mind frequently.

Juliette took a sip of coffee. "I've been meaning to tell you, Camille; in two weeks, Bernard and I are going to Switzerland for a seminar organised by the International Olympics Committee. We shall be gone for a week, so make sure you have everything you need. Nadia will be here as usual, of course."

For a moment, Camille felt herself flush with resentment, censured like a child. Why was her mother so cold and brittle? Could she not be kinder and gentle? In the same instant, she rebuked herself for being oversensitive and vowed not to confide in her again. It had always been like this, so why expect anything different? And why did it matter so much?

After Juliette left, Camille slipped off her dress and dived naked into the pool. Like her mother, she was a good swimmer, but had never pursued it as a sport.

Chapter 2

BERLIN, SUMMER 1936

J ULIETTE HAD NEVER BEEN TO BERLIN before, and she was excited. Not that she was interested in, nor knew anything about that country of lieder and cream cakes, rules and uniforms, sausages and brass bands.

Everybody had heard of Adolf Hitler, but at seventeen, Juliette knew little and cared less about him. She did not see how he affected her. In the small, enclosed world of French swimming, she was a star, and she had been selected to represent her country at the Olympic Games. The prospect of fame and glory was what excited her, much more than the prospect of visiting Germany.

The French team was made up of ten members, six men and four women, plus the non-swimming captain, Bernard de Vaucluse, who had represented France in the 1928 Amsterdam Olympics. He was tall, suave and rich, and all the girls adored him, though Juliette felt certain he had a special place for her in his heart. He had already told her she was good enough to win the gold medal in the 100-metre breaststroke.

He was not alone in his praise for her; everybody told her how athletic she was, how tall and elegant, and how much she resembled Greta Garbo. And it was her film-star appeal that whipped the French press into a tumult for whom she epitomised *La Belle France*, personified *Marianne* herself, and embodied the *Triomphe de la République*. All France would be cheering for her.

Two days before they were due to leave for Berlin, Bernard called a meeting after team training at the Piscine des Tourelles in the 20th *arrondissement* in Paris.

"Now listen everybody, this is important," said Bernard as he looked around the meeting room.

"The Ministre des Affaires Étrangères [Minister of Foreign Affairs] has prepared a short brief for us on the state of Germany today, and I have copies here for everyone. It contains a list of useful German words and phrases, so you don't make fools of yourselves."

Somebody giggled.

"Seriously, the eyes of all France and the world's press will be on you, and there are things you need to know. So, briefly, this is a short history lesson."

A collective groan was followed by more laughter.

"Firstly, you must understand that, like us, the Germans are a proud people, and they've been through some extremely hard times. Of course, we suffered too, but after the Great War, the Treaty of Versailles forced Germany to accept responsibility for starting the war and to reimburse us for its cost—us being the Western Allies. And as you may imagine, Germany was not happy about that.

"The Allies were asking for a great deal of money from a country that was already materially and psychologically on its knees, so the new Reich, or government—what we know as the Weimar Republic—decided to print money to repay its debts. And as most of you know, the result was catastrophic hyperinflation. The Deutsche mark came to be worth so little that people spent their cash immediately, so as not to see it devalued the next day."

Bernard paused.

"The situation improved somewhat when a new currency, the Reichsmark, was introduced, but it was clear—and this is the key point—that the misery, followed by the spending frenzy, had unleashed a cynical, fatalistic way of thinking. Escapism. Life is short. Let's have fun. And no doubt you'll see some of that during your time in Berlin."

Bernard looked at the expectant faces, and Juliette caught his eye.

"Today in Paris, there is nothing unusual about young women wearing makeup, smoking cigarettes and wearing their hair short—or even dressing like a man and wearing a monocle. But all that began in Germany more than ten years ago. In Paris, jazz is fashionable today, but in the 1920s, jazz was even more popular in Germany than in the USA. The Germans took to it because they needed joy in their lives—so they had fun any way they could, experimenting in dress, in art, in architecture, in morals, in music and in life. And in many ways, they still are.

"You may get a chance to see some of the cabarets and nightclubs that Berlin is famous for, but if you do, you'll need to be on your best behaviour. You will be representing your country."

Juliette glanced at Bernard quizzically; the other team members nodded their approval.

"Now, about the Nazi Party. Some of you may be wondering about Monsieur Hitler and how the Nazis will affect you. This is serious and something you should understand.

"The Wall Street crash in 1929 sparked off terrible unemployment and money problems in the United States, and American banks recalled their loans to Germany, which was still very weak. No money meant countless German companies and factories had to close, and that led to unrest and soaring unemployment. In France, we were affected too, but it was worse, much worse in Germany. Things are better now, but three years ago over one third of the workforce was still unemployed, and the German people were impoverished, hungry and depressed. And that's when Adolf Hitler and the Nazi party came to power with a promise to restore the pride of Germany and make her strong again.

"The international community wants to see Germany on its feet, but some countries are concerned by the nationalistic nature of the Nazi rhetoric. A year ago, we learned of Nazis plans to ban Jews, Gypsies and Black people from competing in the Games: and it was only the threat of a boycott by France, Great Britain, the USA and other nations that made them change their minds. We can be proud of that, but we are not here to judge or take political sides, we are here to represent our country and win medals for France. And the minister, Monsieur Delbos, has made it clear that we are not to rock the boat! So, best behaviour, everyone! Read the briefing carefully; there is more than what I said."

Bernard distributed the copies of the political briefing, along with maps of Berlin and a French-German dictionary.

"Now team, are there any questions? Remember, we will be on our way in two days."

Juliette raised her hand.

"If there are so many problems, why are the Olympic Games being held in Germany?" she asked.

"Good question, Juliette. All that is in the Minister's briefing, but basically it was a goodwill gesture. The Olympic Games were created in a spirit of altruism, and they were awarded to Germany in 1931 because the world wanted to welcome her back. But that was before Hitler came to power and, frankly, blind eyes were turned towards potential problems."

Juliette nodded. Coming as she did from a rural corner of Southern France, she had encountered very few people of different nationalities. An Italian or two and a Spaniard. And Desirée, a clever black girl from Senegal who was rumoured to be a princess, a thin boy from Morocco, and two other Algerian children whose faces she could barely remember. As far as she knew she had never met a Jewish person.

After the meeting, Bernard walked back with Juliette to the spacious apartment of Monsieur Drigny, a former swimmer and now Secretary of the FFN, la *Féderation Française de Natation* [French Swimming Federation]. He had a spare room, and he and his wife had been only too pleased to have Juliette stay with them.

"You know, Juliette," said Bernard as they neared her lodgings, "we are all looking forward to it, but Berlin can be a dangerous place."

Juliette glanced up at Bernard.

"You are still very young, and you won't be alone, so there will be nothing for you to worry about. I'll make sure of that."

"What do you mean, Berlin can be a dangerous place?" asked Juliette. "In what way?"

"Let me put it this way. All that excess, the hedonism I described earlier, has made the city a hotbed of loose morals. It's dangerous for everybody, especially young girls. But also for wives who don't keep an eye on their husbands, and husbands who don't keep an eye on their wives."

"Sounds like fun to me," said Juliette glancing at Bernard again.

"Fun maybe, but the problem is not loose morals. Those risqué nightclubs with their husky-voiced singers may sound glamorous, but clubs are where people let down their guard. We have been told there will be spies everywhere listening for loose tongues, searching for enemies of the Nazis. Gypsies and Jews especially, but also communists and homosexuals: anyone who doesn't toe the line. As participants we have nothing to fear, unless someone is compromised, or gets drunk and misbehaves."

Bernard looked down and paused.

"Lord knows I have complete confidence in you and your abilities, but you've never been out of France before. Berlin and Paris are very different. You'll see. We will have to be on our guard."

As they walked in the warm light of early evening, Juliette slipped her hand into the hand of the handsome man beside her, but he pulled his away.

"Juliette, you're adorable. I am very flattered, but you are my charge, my responsibility. I'm the team captain, and I take my responsibilities very seriously."

※

At six P.M. on Sunday, July 19, Bernard collected Juliette from the Drigny's apartment and hailed a taxi, and they headed for the Gare de l'Est, Paris's eastern railway station.

The huge terminus was pulsating with activity and the sound of steam-engines shunting, clanking and hissing, raising pressure in their boilers before departure. At the far end of the concourse, black fumes curled up the ribbed vaults of the glass roof, where wisps of grey smoke blended with white plumes of steam.

A man's voice boomed over the public address system. "Passengers for the Northern Express for Warsaw are informed that the train will depart from Platform Three at nineteen hours and fifteen minutes, with stops at Ostend, Cologne, Hamburg and Berlin, arriving at Warsaw at seventeen hours and thirty-five minutes on Monday, the twentieth of July."

They made their way over to Platform Three, towards the shouts of porters and the flurry of activity around ten luxurious sleeper cars, each with a uniformed Wagons-Lit attendant checking tickets and directing porters where to put the luggage.

Juliette was first to spot the team gathered by carriage Number Eight, marked by a sign "Reserved for the Swimming and Fencing teams." Porters were already heaving their leather suitcases through the windows of the car.

"Thank goodness," Juliette said breathlessly, "we cut it fine."

A corridor ran the length of each carriage, allowing access to eleven compartments for two people, with upper and lower berths, washbasins and private lavatories. For Bernard's small team of eleven, six cabins were reserved. Three for the six men, and two for the four girls. The team captain slept alone.

At precisely seven-fifteen P.M., the blast of a shrill whistle announced the departure, open doors slammed shut, and the great train sighed, clanked, and shuddered and gradually began to move.

The team leaned from the windows to wave to the handful of press and spectators and Juliette said excitedly: "Did you notice the dining car? Dinner on the train. How romantic!"

"Yes, but no wine for you; you're too young," said Renée tartly, who had recently turned eighteen.

"No wine for anyone until the Games are over." Bernard returned.

After a simple dinner, the movement of the train and rhythm of the noise soon rocked Juliette to sleep, and it was only when the train stopped again that she woke up. Lying in the pitch dark and profound silence, she pulled back the edge of the curtain to see a dimly lit platform and a sign saying Köln.

She glanced at the luminous dial of her watch. It was one forty-five A.M. and she lay in the dark and listened to distant footsteps and men speaking

German in low voices until a door slammed, the guard blew a whistle, the train clanked and jerked and started moving again.

Shortly after seven A.M., there was a tap on the cabin door, and the attendant called out. "Good morning, ladies. It is seven o'clock. Breakfast is being served in the restaurant car."

At eight fifty-seven precisely, the train pulled into the grand Lehrter Bahnhof station in the centre of Berlin to a German military welcoming committee, including a small brass band, the French consul, and a contingent of the press.

"This is it, team," said Bernard. "This is where it gets serious. Big smiles, everybody."

The visiting French athletes, the swimmers, gymnasts and the fencing team, were formally welcomed by the committee with typical German courtesy before a French-speaking guide and the brass band led them to their green-and-white bus.

A guide, a thin blond youth with round spectacles, smiled broadly and introduced himself, speaking clipped French slowly with a strong German accent. "Good morning, ladies and gentlemen! I hope you are not too tired after your long train ride. My name is Hans."

As the bus got underway, Hans shouted: "Welcome to Berlin! I will be looking after you during your stay in our beautiful city, and you may ask me any questions you wish.

"Our first stop will take us to the Friesenhaus at the German University of Physical Education, where we have arranged accommodation for all three hundred and thirty-one lady athletes. It is, as you will soon see, very close to the Olympic Stadium.

"Then our bus will proceed to our own special Olympic Village where the three thousand, six hundred and thirty-two male athletes will be accommodated! It is nineteen kilometres away from the ladies to make sure there is no mischief."

Hans paused and inspected his audience with a smile. "But you will find it very comfortable." It sounded like an order.

"At the village, you will find French-speaking stewards to take care of you, and we have taken national preferences for food into account, so your food will be prepared by a real French chef!"

Hans spoke with a broad smile that he theatrically collapsed into a frown. "But I am sorry to tell you, alcohol is banned for all athletes."

Hans glumly contemplated the faces of his small audience.

"Don't look so worried!" he continued, "I am teasing you. Alcohol is not banned! It was banned until the French and Italians told us that wine is part of your way of life—and the Belgians and Dutch said they could not compete without beer! So it's okay now! You can all drink!"

The members of the French contingent smiled weakly.

"Many other teams are also arriving today, and Berlin is proud to welcome them," said Hans pointing to the Olympic flags and the black-white-red banners of the Nazi party flying side by side throughout the city.

"Tomorrow morning, after you have settled in, there will be a special press event and reception at the Rathaus, what you call your Hôtel de Ville, or City Hall. This bus will collect the gentlemen at nine-thirty hours, and ladies, please be ready at ten! I must tell you, and we are very proud of this, that for the first time in history, twenty-eight television viewing rooms have been set up around the city where events can be watched live and free of charge. German know-how! *Wissen der Deutschen angewiesen*!"

With a triumphant smile, Hans scrutinised his small audience.

The bus crossed the river Spree and eased through the Tiergarten as it headed west towards Charlottenburg. Juliette had imagined the city grey and dingy and had not expected long avenues of newly planted trees, green parks and flowers everywhere. And like her co-athletes, she was surprised by the fresh coats of paint and impressive new buildings that lined the streets. In the bright morning light, Berlin positively gleamed.

Even the trees had a little number attached to each trunk so—said Hans with a heavy wink—the birds would know where they lived. He grinned a prepared grin and forced an odd, high-pitched laugh.

In less than twenty minutes, the bus approached the Adolf-Hitler-Platz, and Hans gestured with his hands excitedly and said: "On your left now, you will see our version of the Eiffel Tower! It is a little smaller than yours, and we call it the Funkturm, and it is from there that we transmit our radio and live television pictures."

The bus proceeded up the Reichsstrasse and pulled up outside the German Sports Forum in the northeast corner of the Olympic Park.

"The Friesenhaus building," Hans announced authoritatively. "This is where the ladies will be staying. All ladies, please descend here!"

Hans helped Juliette and the others with their cases as far as the reception desk, where a tall lady of a certain age welcomed them and introduced herself as Baroness von Wangenheim.

"Welcome to the Friesenhaus," she said. "I am the *Direktor*. Heidi will show you to your room."

Heidi, wearing an official uniform, bowed and shook the hand of each one of them in turn, and showed them to a large room with twelve beds on the second floor with a fine view of the Olympic stadium.

"There are four swimmers, that is right? And three fencers? Please select your beds. The other beds are for your field athletes, who arrive tomorrow. All females of the French teams will stay in this room."

Of the twelve French competitors, Juliette was the youngest at seventeen, though she was not the youngest competitor at the Friesenhaus by any means. There were plenty of other young gymnasts and swimmers, including twelve-year-old Inge Sorensen from Denmark and fourteen-year-old Martha Genenger of Germany, both breaststroke specialists like Juliette, and the thirteen-year-old springboard diver Marjorie Gestring of the United States.

As for her rivals, twenty-four-year-old Hideko Maehata of Japan was expected to win the 200-metre gold medal for breaststroke as the reigning world champion, though Juliette expected to do well in the 100-metre competition against Hideko's younger sister Miyoko.

"You are built for speed, not for stamina," Bernard had told her when she asked if she could compete in the 200-metre event as well.

Juliette had joined the French team in Paris at the impressionable age of fifteen. And as she matured in the austere environment of team training, she had become slowly aware of the magnetic effect she had on men—and on women. Everybody called her stunning, gorgeous, or beautiful and the constant praise, together with the rigours and discipline of training, only fuelled her belief in herself. It had not escaped her attention that even Hans's watery blue eyes had lingered lasciviously in her direction.

By the approach of the Games, she had unashamedly concluded that she was not only breath-taking to look at, but also uncommonly gifted and athletic. And her boundless self-assurance was reflected in her languorous, graceful way of walking, and in the way she tossed her head to move her hair to the side.

The second evening in Berlin was July 21, and Bernard had arranged a relaxed soirée for all the members of his team with an old friend who lived close to the Olympic Stadium off the Reichsstrasse.

The bus pulled up outside the large stone villa, and Juliette followed Bernard and the troupe up the steps to a sturdy front door where they were greeted by a beaming Alfons Piękny-Słońce, a tall, aesthetic man who had studied at the Sorbonne with Bernard in the 1920s.

"Welcome," he cried with open arms. "Herzlich willkommen! Soyez les bienvenus!"

Alfons was from Poland and nicknamed Sunbeam, Bernard explained in the bus, because his family name was so difficult to pronounce. Happily, in addition to Polish, German and English, he also spoke impeccable French.

A maid dressed in black with a white pinafore and her hair in braids showed them through double French doors to a large reception room. Beneath a window on the left stood a grand piano with a silver candelabra and six candles. On the far wall, a comfortable sofa flanked by upholstered armchairs fronted an illuminated *Wintergarten* brimming with pots of red and pink cyclamen.

"Come on," said Alfons, laughing his welcome. "Follow me."

He led the way over to a long table where candlelight cast a soft glow over numerous plates of German specialties. "I know how fussy you French are about eating, so we've prepared a few Berlin favourites for you," said Alfons hospitably.

"Here on the left, we have *Eierkuchen*, the most delectable potato pancakes; then *Spargel* and *Königsberger Klopse*—asparagus and meatballs to you. In these dishes next to them are *Schnitzel* and *Bratwurst*, which you know already, and over here, we have my personal favourites *Eisbein* and *Sauerkraut*: pickled pigs' knuckles and fermented cabbage. Delicious! And naturally, we have plenty of German cheeses, beers and wine."

Alfons, his eyes sparkling, was obviously delighted to play host and speak French again.

Carrying a silver platter laden with glasses of Sekt sparkling white wine, the maid passed smoothly amongst the guests.

"I don't believe it! You're not drinking!" Alfons said to Juliette early in the evening. "I thought all French girls liked champagne."

"Well, don't forget I am very young and on my best behaviour," she replied coquettishly, lowering her gaze. "Anyway," she added looking up, "Bernard told us all to be careful and to avoid drinking alcohol. We are in training, don't forget. Let me guess. You're obviously not an athlete, are you?"

"An athlete? Anything but!" said Alfons roaring with laughter. "Come on, let me introduce you to Nadia, my young sister; she'll soon liven you up."

Alfons's sister Nadia was a few months younger than Juliette and though not as tall, nor classically beautiful, her liveliness and sense of mischief, wide eyes and ready smile made an immediate impression on Juliette.

"I don't suppose you're an athlete either, are you?" asked Juliette as they kissed each other on both cheeks.

"The truth? Not at all," replied Nadia, adding with mock sincerity, "though I love to play games. Does that count?"

"Goodness, your French is excellent! Where did you learn?"

"We Germans have to learn French and English in school. Besides, I have a soft spot for France. That's my brother's fault; he never stops telling me how wonderful Paris is."

As the evening progressed, Alfons proved to be the perfect host. To everyone's delight, he sat down at the piano and played a medley of popular songs to which many of the team members knew the words. Among them were Maurice Chevalier's *Livin' in the Sunlight, Lovin' in the Moonlight*, and *Parlez-moi d'Amour* that Alfons sang in a passably good imitation of Lucien Boyer. Everybody joined in, linking arms and swaying to the rhythm of the music.

All too quickly, the evening was over.

"Come on team, time to head back," said Bernard as he reminded them of their responsibilities and the scrutiny of the press. Their special bus was waiting outside, and it had attracted the attention of passers-by.

"You know Juliette, there is a wonderful private club near here; it would be a perfect place for you to relax, to get away from prying eyes," pleaded Nadia before they left. "Please do come with me; I go every afternoon. And they have a swimming pool."

"That sounds fun. Yes please," said Juliette, "I would love to join you. We train in the morning and have time off in the afternoon. Would Thursday be a good day?"

Two days later, the girls left Nadia's house and sauntered arm-in-arm down the Reichsstrasse, skirted the Adolf-Hitler-Platz and strolled under the trees in Thuringer Allee to a security post where two uniformed guards manned a gate marked *Privatgelände. Berliner Schlittschuhclub. Nur für Mitglieder* [Private. Berlin Ice-Skating Club. Members only].

"Schönen Tag," said Nadia brightly, showing her membership card.

The club was as attractive and secluded as Nadia held it to be.

"See those tennis courts?" asked Nadia as they strolled towards the club-house. "They spray water on the clay in the winter to turn them into skating rinks. That's why it's called the Ice-Skating Club. There's a bar and restaurant in the clubhouse. and a five-piece band plays every evening at cocktail hour. At weekends there's dancing until midnight."

"How wonderful, so romantic! I hope I get a chance to try it out," said Juliette.

"You never know!" Nadia said, laughing.

Beyond the impressive clubhouse was a large, open-air swimming pool surrounded by sunbathers lounging on deckchairs, reading, or talking quietly, and sipping cool drinks served by waiters.

The two pretty girls attracted a good deal of attention from the sophisticated young men at the club. Juliette had never met such stylish suitors and was captivated by their charm and good manners. At least until Bernard decided she needed to be protected from herself and her admirers and resolved to accompany the two girls to the club until the Games were over.

From then on, every morning Juliette and the team trained in the practice pool near the stadium, after which Juliette and Bernard rode the U-Bahn one stop to the Adolf-Hitler-Platz and walked four minutes to the club. Sometimes, Bernard walked Juliette all the way, past the tall, grey apartment buildings of the Reichsstrasse and the countless Kaffee and Bierkeller, flower shops and hair salons. Juliette enjoyed being recognised by Berliners and tourists lingering at the multiple souvenir stalls and carts of hot Wursts.

They were precious times together, and Juliette loved having Bernard to herself.

⁂

The 1936 Berlin Olympic Games opened on Saturday, August 1 at exactly one P.M. when the East Gate of the stadium swung open, and the crowds surged in.

At the other end of the stadium, outside the West Gate, the athletes had arrived in a vast holding area called the Maifeld, bounded by the Olympic Bell Tower on one side and the Olympic Stadium on the other. They had been directed to line up nation by nation in alphabetical order before they paraded through the stadium behind their flags. Some teams wore folkloric versions of their national costumes, though most wore smart casual uniforms: the French chose dark-blue blazers and white-flannel trousers or skirts, topped with traditional berets. The Americans were dressed similarly but wore white boater hats.

Juliette glanced around at the other teams as they searched for their markers and collected in lines. She was inches taller than most of the women and as tall as many of the men. And, while there were many other attractive girls here and there, not one was in the same league as her.

As the teams took their places and formed up in rows, orchestral music drifted from the stadium and mingled with the rumble of excited crowds. By the Bell Tower on the other side of the Maifeld, an honour guard was forming near a military detachment when everyone turned to marvel at a vast silver shape in the sky. The massive eight-hundred-foot-long Hindenburg airship was flying slowly towards the stadium with *XI Olympiade Berlin 1936* painted on its side. An enormous Olympic flag fluttered from its gondola.

Minutes later, a string of official limousines drew up at the Bell Tower and a dozen uniformed officers and high-ranking dignitaries descended. They were followed shortly by a convoy of open Mercedes-Benz cabriolets escorted by motorcycles with yellow flags.

Adolf Hitler, the Chancellor of Germany, the Führer, had arrived.

A fanfare of military trumpets sent a frisson racing through the Maifeld, and a potent blend of curiosity and apprehension engulfed athletes and officials alike. Everyone, including Juliette, was on edge as they turned to watch the German leader leave the third car wearing his distinctive brown military officer's cap, brown double-breasted uniform and brown jackboots.

He's small, she thought, I imagined him taller. He doesn't look the least bit frightening to me. Yet like everybody else, Juliette remained riveted and watched him proceed with interminable handshakes, kowtowing, saluting and heel-clicking with multiple dignitaries and decorated officials. Finally, after inspecting the honour guard, Hitler turned and walked towards the stadium, a gaggle of officials one step behind.

As he neared the West Gate, he passed the rows of athletes, and Juliette had a better chance to see him.

She stared hard, hoping he would notice her, but he reached the steps to the stadium without even glancing her way. For a moment, Hitler and the small group with him paused, motionless, at the top of the stairs: then the clock struck four, and a military band struck up *Huldigungsmarch*, the March of Homage by Richard Wagner. And the Führer began a measured descent into the vast arena.

Juliette shivered as a thunderous ovation erupted from the stadium.

"*Sieg Heil*! *Sieg Heil*! *Sieg Heil*!"

Five minutes passed of more applause and cheering before the Olympic bell tolled and the athletes saw their national flags rise simultaneously on poles all around the perimeter of the stadium.

It was time for the athletes to appear.

As the creators of the Olympic movement, the Greeks led the way behind a tall blond German student dressed in white from the *Nazi Bildungseinrichtung* holding up a sign saying Griechenland. Behind him, an athlete carried the Greek flag, followed by team officials, the female participants, and finally the men, all marching to the tune of a military band. Every team had been instructed to pay tribute to the Führer as they passed his special box, and the Greeks gave the customary Olympic salute with right arms outstretched to the side. Mistaking it for the Nazi salute, the crowd howled with delight.

The French, eighteenth in line, waited patiently if a little nervously, with the female athletes in two rows of six. Juliette was on the right of the front row. When their turn came, she was so excited that she held her head high and grinned broadly as she marched, and when the team reached Hitler, they all clicked their heads to the right to give the Olympic salute. Juliette was sure the crowd noticed her and certain they were cheering for her. And, in a playful excess of enthusiasm, she even wiggled her outstretched hand at Hitler, and heard the crowd shout for joy.

The Germans, as the hosts, were the last team to appear and predictably got the warmest welcome of all before they took their place with the other athletes in the grass oval in the centre. As the crowd hushed, the recorded voice of the ailing founder of the modern Olympic movement, Baron Pierre de Coubertin, boomed out over loudspeakers with a message in French.

"The important thing in life is not the triumph but the struggle; the essential thing is not to have conquered but to have fought well."

All eyes turn to Hitler's box, and the German Chancellor solemnly declared the Games open.

It was the moment everyone had been waiting for. A booming artillery salute from guns on the Maifeld made sure the world knew, and twenty thousand pigeons were released to hesitate and swirl over the top of the crowds before scattering into the early evening sky.

A choir of thousands sang the Olympic Hymn, and a lone blond German athlete entered the stadium holding a flaming torch and ran along the track towards the West Gate and the Olympic cauldron. Bounding up the steps, he set the cauldron alight to more raucous cheers and explosive applause from the crowd.

"Will this be over soon?" Juliette whispered to Renée beside her. "Please?"

"Dear heavens, I hope so," her friend replied, "nature is calling."

They both giggled.

Ten minutes later, after yet another speech and the swearing of the Olympic Oath, the chorus sang the Hallelujah Chorus from Handel's Messiah and much of the crowd joined in. At last, at five forty-five P.M., the teams were ordered to march out the way they had come in, through the tunnel under the West Gate.

Hitler stood to salute the athletes as they left.

"Oh, Good Lord, it's over." exclaimed Juliette. "Wasn't that amazing?"

It was as exhausting as it was impressive.

The following day, every newspaper carried myriad photographs of the Games' opening, including many of Juliette smiling and waving at the Führer. The German Press nominated her the prettiest foreign athlete: *der kleiner französischer Liebling* they called her, the little French treasure, and she felt as if she had already won a medal.

❦

One week later, the swimming competition began in the eight-lane, 50-metre Olympic pool perpendicular to the main Olympic Stadium.

When the time came for the first of the three heats of the women's 100-metre breaststroke, Juliette stepped onto the starting block feeling and looking better than ever. She had drawn lane seven, not her favourite, but fashionably suntanned from her afternoons at the club, if the competition had been judged on glamour alone, she would have been awarded the gold medal on the spot.

To her right in lane six, was nineteen-year-old Miyoko Maehata, the younger sister of the 200-metre world record holder, Hideko Maehata. Though not as tall as Juliette, the broad-shouldered sisters were formidable competitors and thought to be from a family of Japanese pearl divers because they were rumoured to hold their breaths for the entire length of the 100-metre race. In lane eight to her left stood the tall, blonde and impossibly young-looking Dane, Inge Sorenson, who was only twelve years old.

On a platform behind the swimmers, an official raised his starting pistol and the swimmers strained on their starting blocks, leaning forward, legs bent, arms pointing back. The crowd cheered wildly.

"*Auf die Plätze …*" cried the official. "*Fertig… los!*"

At the crack of the pistol, Juliette launched herself into the blue pool, momentarily surprised by the temperature, a chilly 20° Celsius [68° F], as ordained by the doctors of the Olympic committee. She pulled her way through the water, kicking out her legs in perfect synchrony with the sweep of her arms, and by the end of the first lap, she was ahead of the Japanese girl. Forty seconds later it was over, and Juliette had won by a touch from the Dane.

The crowd cheered her wildly as she pulled herself gracefully out of the pool and paused to be photographed, posing and waving to the crowd with a broad smile.

The three fastest swimmers of each heat and the next two fastest swimmers overall advanced to the semi-finals to be held the next day. Juliette was elated to have won her first heat, but in the debriefing that followed, Bernard had to tell her he wasn't pleased.

"Yes, you did well, and everybody is proud of you. But you can do better. Do you realise that Martha Genenger's winning time in the second heat was a second and a half faster than yours? You are going to have to up your game if you are to win the gold medal."

Juliette took his words to heart and improved her time to win her semi-final, but she was chastened to learn that Martha had also won her semi-final and been nearly a second faster.

⁂

Two days later, on August 11, the four fastest swimmers in the two semi-finals lined up to compete in the final of the 100-metre breaststroke. By then, the spirit of the Olympics and excitement of the rivalry between nations had built to a fervent crescendo, so if the crowds had been enthusiastic for the two races, by the finals, they were positively fanatical.

Usually sure of herself and level-headed, Juliette was intimidated by the applause and wild cheering of the spectators, and not just the French but her German fans, too. Nor was she used to the constant presence of throngs of journalists and photographers, or the intrusive camera of Leni Riefenstahl, the celebrated filmmaker instructed to capture evidence of German victories and prove that Aryan race was superior. To say nothing of the multitude of commentators, radio microphones, and colossal television cameras there to beam the event live across the city.

The swimmers were seeded according to their semi-final times; the fastest were allocated the central lanes of the pool, the slowest the outer ones. As the fastest in her semi-final, Juliette was assigned number four, her favourite lane, next to Martha in lane five and Inge in lane three. With a quiet confidence and a fierce determination underpinned by intense training and a God-given natural talent, Juliette climbed onto her starting block, all but oblivious of the cheers and yells of encouragement.

"*Auf die Plätze* ...," cried the starter. "*Fertig... los!*"

At the gun, Juliette flung her arms forward and pushed off the block with all her strength. She soared through the air, her chin tucked into her chest, her back arched, her hands and her feet outstretched, and she reached the water inches ahead of her rivals. Ferociously, she swept the water back as she pulled her head up to snatch a deep breath, then plunged her head down and kicked back mightily with her legs, propelling herself forward as she shot out her arms to sweep back the water again.

Keep the rhythm. Breathe deeply, expel quickly, pull, kick. Keep the rhythm. She was only conscious of the sounds of her own breathing and the clatter of the water rushing by.

By the 50-metre mark turn, she and Martha were level, with Inge only an inch or so behind. Juliette had never wanted anything as much as she craved the gold medal. Her flip turn was perfect, and she pushed off underwater like a rocket with a furious thrust of her legs to propel herself back to the surface. Keep the rhythm. Breathe deeply, expel quickly, pull, kick. Keep the rhythm.

All she could feel was the chill of the chlorinated water and the air rushing into her lungs, and all she could hear was the crowd cheering and the pounding of her heart. Her determination turned to anger and her anger to rage, and when seconds later, she touched the bar, her rage collapsed to tears. Gasping for breath as the crowd cheered deliriously, she turned towards lane number five. Martha was already there.

Crestfallen, she climbed out of the water to be greeted by a storm of excited photographers and officials. She had touched the bar a fraction before the German and won by two tenths of a second, and she, Juliette, was the winner of the Olympic Gold medal and could rejoice before the world's press. She raised her arms victoriously as the tears streamed down her cheeks, and she threw back her head and screamed for joy. Never would she achieve such adulation again.

Juliette was the only member of the French swimming contingent to win a medal that year, and since their part in the Games were over, the team was expected to return to France on Friday. However, Alfons and Nadia persuaded Bernard and Juliette to stay a little longer, and on Saturday evening, the four of them went out together to celebrate Juliette's victory.

"I can't possibly let you go home without a little taste of Berlin," Alfons implored, "and I know the perfect place. It's not as wild as it was before our friend the *Gefreiter*, our little Bohemian corporal came to power, but it's still a lot of fun."

Alfons's perfect place turned out to be a luxurious restaurant and dancehall known to Berliners as the Resi. Founded in 1908, by 1936 it had become synonymous with satirical cabaret, showgirls, flirtation and dancing. It was some thirty minutes away by taxi, near the Alexanderplatz, the heart of Berlin nightlife.

A smartly dressed doorman welcomed them, and they stepped into a plush, Bauhaus interior buzzing with a crush of high-spirited, gowned and black-tied acolytes of the beau monde. It was a more decadent version of the only other nightclub Juliette had visited, the cavernous restaurant-dancehall, La

Coupole, in Paris.

Under a vast glass ceiling to the left, a spectacular Art Deco bar beckoned them with a U-shaped, chrome and glass top reflecting countless bottles of liquor arranged by colour on mirrored shelves. Beyond it was an expansive dance floor surrounded by small tables for two occupied by glamorous young couples. Dozens of guests were already dancing to the music of a thirty-strong orchestra wearing white tuxedos, as an androgynous figure carried out a sinuous impression of Fred Astaire singing *A Fine Romance* in German. And on each side of the orchestra along the walls, coloured water fountains danced in rhythm to the music.

A hostess directed them towards one of a hundred dining tables on the right arranged in tiers, each furnished with a telephone and a curved tube ending in a snakehead. A tall red lamp displayed the number of each table.

"Oh, my goodness, this is beautiful!" exclaimed Juliette, "and why are there telephones on the tables? For calling the waiter? And the weird snakes on the tables?"

Alfons laughed.

"No, my dear, the telephones are not for calling the waiter! People use them to call other tables and flirt," he winked at Bernard. "And the snakeheads are pneumatic tubes, *Rohrpost*, for sending little messages and gifts.

"Now, over there on the other side of the dance floor, to the right of the band. Do you see that little row of vendors? They sell all kinds of things over there, from cigars to rings and jewellery to cigarette lighters—even novelties and… er… other more suggestive things… Bernard knows what I mean." He laughed again.

The hostess showed them to table number seventy-seven, up a few steps and with a good view of the dance floor. Most of the other tables were already full of happy customers and within moments, a pretty waitress with generous cleavage weaved through the tables towards them, carrying a silver tray with four glasses of champagne.

"No," said Juliette, "not for me, thank you, I don't drink."

Both Alfons and Nadia roared with laughter and Nadia said: "But you must! You are not in training now, and besides, you have something to celebrate! We all do!"

Juliette looked quizzically at Bernard, who smiled and said gently, "It's over. You worked hard; you won a gold medal. Juliette my dear, you are on holiday, of course you can have a drink if you wish."

She glanced around her as if for approval. Though not yet eighteen, she did not feel out of place in this club full of beautiful women and handsome men.

"In that case, yes please," she said. "I would love some champagne."

"Good girl," Bernard whispered tenderly before murmuring, "by the way, I have to say, I love what you are wearing tonight."

Juliette was wearing a grey, crepe-de-chine dress with a soft, blouson bodice and a red Bakelite barrette in her short blonde hair, accessorised with red patent leather shoes and a matching red clutch bag. Nadia was dressed in black with flared silk trousers and a black blouse with crisp white frills around the collars and cuffs. She wore her dark hair in a generous demi-wave with finger curls.

Like many of the men in the club, both Alfons and Bernard were dressed in single-breasted black dinner jackets, starched white shirts with stiff, detachable wing collars, white silk waistcoats, and single-end bow ties. Both carried white gloves and wore long, white silk scarves.

"Yes, I know we have something to celebrate," said Juliette raising her glass. And one by one, they clinked their glasses and cried "Prost!" in unison and all of them laughed with delight.

At that moment, the red telephone on the table rang and Nadia grabbed it.

Laughing, she turned to Juliette. "It's for you! You have an admirer!"

Nadia passed Juliette the telephone, but Alfons reached over and took it, and told the caller firmly in German, "We aren't accepting calls for the moment, but thank you anyway."

At that moment, the band began playing *Sing Sing Sing* in the style of Benny Goodman, and Juliette spun around excitedly as couples moved to the dance floor.

"I can't believe it. Look at me. I won a gold medal, and I am at a nightclub with Bernard, Alfons and Nadia. I love Berlin. I've never been so happy."

"Yes," said Alfons, "there are many wonderful things here in Berlin, but we are on our best behaviour, you know. May I offer you a cigarette?"

Alfons held out a silver cigarette case to the two girls and Bernard. Only Nadia accepted.

"Things are not all that they seem," Alfons went on, tilting his head as he cupped his hands to light his cigarette.

Instinctively he lowered his voice. "We certainly know how to have fun and put on a good show, but we are secretly very worried and ill at ease."

"Worried?" echoed Juliette. "Worried about what?"

"All right, since our time together is coming to an end, I shall tell you. I don't want to put a damper on the evening, but there are things you should know…"

Once again, the telephone interrupted, and Juliette grabbed it.

"*Bist du der kleine französischer Schatz*?" said a voice.

"Here Alfons, you take it, I have no idea what he's saying."

She handed him the phone. His face darkened as he replied in rapid German and replaced the receiver.

"I am afraid, but it was to be expected. You've been recognised Juliette, and sadly not by a gentleman but a drunk."

"Honestly?" said Juliette. "Where is he? Which one is he?" She scanned the enormous club, but there were so many people talking on the phone it was impossible to pick him out.

"Please continue, Alfons," said Bernard, "what should we know?"

"All right. You may have noticed that the band is playing American songs, but the singer is singing them in German? Unfortunately, he is not singing a direct translation, but a version approved by the Ministry of Propaganda. As you know, Germany is becoming very nationalistic and few of us are comfortable with that. Our family is originally from Poland, and last year the National Socialist Party, the Nazis, announced a new citizenship law For the Protection of German Blood denying German citizenship and political rights to certain groups."

"Yes," said Bernard, "we heard about that."

"You may not have heard that half-Jews, even quarter-Jews are no longer citizens of this country? That's why so many are leaving Germany and going to live in France. You may have seen them in Paris."

"Yes, we've seen plenty of them, hungry and homeless, with no possessions. The Marais is full of them. They don't even speak French, poor devils. Dreadful."

"Dreadful yes," continued Alfons, "and dreadful for Nadia and me too…"

"Why?" said Juliette, "why dreadful for you? You're not Jewish, are you?"

"That's the point," said Alfons leaning forward, holding his cigarette to one side so that smoke did not go in her face. "Our parents were Polish, and that's almost as bad in Berlin. Added to that, our mother may have been Jewish. She denied it and was brought up as a Catholic, but if it were true, Nadia and I would be half-Jewish. According to the new law, we would not qualify as German. Even now, we aren't full citizens officially, just subjects of the state."

"I had no idea," said Bernard. "You never mentioned it in Paris."

"Why would I? It wasn't an issue then, and it means nothing to me. Even if I do happen to be half-Jewish, it's an accident of history. In Poland, we were brought up as Catholics like our parents. It is only here in Berlin that race has become important."

"So, what will you do?" asked Bernard, putting a hand out to comfort Nadia.

"This is my home. I love it here. We both do," said Alfons. "But after what happened to our parents, I am certain we are under surveillance. There are spies and informers everywhere, and things will only get worse. As a matter of fact, if we have to, we may leave and go to America. We have cousins over there."

"I won't," said Nadia quickly, "I shall go to Paris and study at the Sorbonne, as you did, Alfons."

"What happened to your parents, Alfons?" Bernard asked gently.

Alfons and Nadia exchanged a harrowed look.

"You wouldn't know. How could you?" Alfons inhaled deeply on his cigarette. "When the Nazis came to power three years ago, they were determined to eliminate their political opponents. Our father was Mayor of Köpenick, a suburb of Berlin, and in the March 1933 elections, he won Köpenick for the SDP, the Social Democratic Party."

"Anyway," broke in Nadia, "it's a long, sad story. I'm sure they don't want to hear it."

"Please continue, Alfons," said Bernard, "we need to hear it."

"I'll keep it short," said Alfons.

"You've probably never heard of the *Köpenicker Blutwoche*? That means Köpenick Bloody Week. Three months after the elections, our parents disappeared in a crackdown on opponents of the Nazis. Their bodies—with twenty-one others—were found in the Oder-Spree canal. There were no official investigations, but everybody knew it was the work of the SA, the Brownshirts, the paramilitary wing of the Nazi party."

"My God, that's terrible, awful," said Bernard. "I had no idea."

"It is important people know what's going on here in Germany."

The telephone rang again, and this time Nadia answered.

For a minute or so, she talked playfully in German until she turned to Juliette and said, "It's your drunk friend again, Juliette. This time he says you are the most beautiful woman he has ever seen, and he wants to buy you a present. I asked where he was sitting, and he said at table sixty-two behind us."

All four of them turned to see a large middle-aged man with a crew cut and a pleasant, if lived-in face with a nose as red as a dogwood. He was beaming at them.

"*Schatzi*," he called out. "*Mein französischer Schatz!*"

Diners at the nearby tables watched with amusement when they saw him leave his three companions and struggle unsteadily to his feet to make his way over to Alfons's table.

"Oh! *Schatzi*," he called out again. "*Mein französischer Schatz* !"

At once, Alfons and Bernard stood up to intercept him and protect Juliette, but there was no need. Two burly waiters were already on their way, and they quickly hustled her inebriated admirer away. At the same moment, a fellow diner, a tall, distinguished man of around fifty, appeared beside Juliette.

"*Fräulein Dumont*," he said as he clicked his heels and bowed. "I know who you are, and it is an honour to have you in our country. Please excuse this gentleman. I presume his enthusiasm for your good looks and—to all appearances—alcohol has made him forget his manners. He will not bother you again."

With that, he handed out visiting cards to all four of them. "Should you need anything at all during your stay in our city, please do not hesitate to contact me."

The cards read:

> Generalmajor Ernst von Schaumburg,
> Kommandant von Berlin,
> Reichskriegsministerium,
> Bendlerstrasse 11-13
> 10785 Berlin
> Tel: Tiergarten 47433

In excellent, if accented, French he turned to Juliette and added: "Enjoy your stay Mademoiselle, and congratulations on winning your gold medal. I was there, and I saw you win it. You were magnificent."

He bowed his head, clicked his heels again, and returned to his table.

"Good God, do you know who that was?" said Alfons, studying the card. "That's General von Schaumburg, the Army Commander. He's head of the army in Berlin. Keep that card. Keep it in a very safe place. The way things are these days, you never know when it might be useful."

Above the dance floor, a hundred mirrored globes opened and closed to the rhythm of the music, and Juliette suddenly wanted to dance. "Bernard, won't you dance with me, please?"

As Bernard took her hand, the table telephone rang again.

"I'll tell them they've got the wrong number," called Nadia as they made their way to the dance floor.

The band was playing Falling in Love Again, and a Marlene Dietrich look-alike sheathed in a shimmering gown sang the words, *Ich bin von Kopf bis Fuß auf Liebe eingestellt...* in a husky voice; 'I am ready for love from my head to my toes...'

Juliette closed her eyes in bliss as Bernard's strong arms folded around her.

Chapter 3

CAMILLE AND MAX

T WAS SIX DAYS BEFORE THE MISTRAL stopped blowing and the cicadas began to sing again, and another week before Camille called at the garage to refill her car. She had driven by a few times on her way to work without seeing Max.

This time, however, he was there and pleased to see her.

"So, where have you been hiding, *minou* [kitten]. Have you been unfaithful to me? Have you been filling your car somewhere else?"

Max wagged a finger at her and laughed his loud laugh.

"Excuse me?" she said defensively. "I've been filling my car here for years. I certainly don't come here just to see you."

"Forgive me, Camille," he said and hung his head, "I didn't mean to offend you. I was trying to be funny. But seriously, I was hoping you would stop by." Max smiled apologetically. "I'm not sure if it's your kind of thing, but there is a party in the village tonight. Is there a chance I might see you there? There is a bar by the church where I plan to be around seven. I would love it if you joined me."

There are immutable moments in life that seem scripted, preordained somehow, when everything slips into place and for Camille, this was such a moment.

"All right," said Camille, "that sounds like fun. Of course, I know the bar. It's called *au Bon Accueil* [the Good Welcome]. I'll see you there tonight."

🐚

The Chateau de Vaucluse was on the northern edge of Ventabren, and the Bon Accueil pub was in the village square at the top, closer to the fountain than the church. Camille knew it well.

Although her parents were not churchgoers, every Sunday between the ages of six and sixteen, Nadia had taken her up the endless flights of stone steps, past the timeless cottages with window boxes full of geraniums and lavender, across the square to the church. The *Place du Village* continued northwest past the *boulangerie* [bakery] and the B.O.F. [butter, eggs and cheese shop], and the Bon Accueil was after the fountain, closer to a parapet that overlooked the valley.

It was with pleasant memories that Camille climbed the steep stairs, worn smooth by centuries of tired feet before her, up to the glorious aromas of barbecue that wafted down to greet her. Spicy *merguez* lamb sausages and fat pork *saucisses de Toulouse*, vegetables roasted with olive oil, lamb chops grilled with rosemary and thyme, and liberal quantities of garlic, fried peppers and onions.

When she finally reached the top, it was almost seven thirty P.M. and most of the village's inhabitants and a good many people from surrounding communities were talking and laughing at long trestle tables set up for the occasion.

By now, the sun had begun its leisurely descent and the long shadows of the parasol pines stretched as far as the church. The cicadas were silent for a change, either intimidated by the crowd or listening to a group of boys and young men surrounding three youths with guitars singing Beatles' songs inaccurately but enthusiastically.

At the other end of the square near the drinks, the village elders, perched around clusters of foldaway chairs and tables, were playing cards or talking earnestly, all with a glass of aniseed-flavoured pastis, beer, or red wine in their hands.

The young girls of the village, with back-combed hair and pretty cotton dresses with pinched-in waists, made up a third group. They were close enough to eye the boys and hear the Beatles, but not far enough to escape the gaze of their purse-lipped mothers, who made up a fourth, smaller group in the middle, overseeing the food and keeping an eye on the money, their husbands and their children. And over loudspeakers, the recorded songs of Edith Piaf and Georges Brassens quavered out a quintessential Frenchness to anybody who cared to listen.

Camille nodded and smiled at the villagers she had known all her life as she made her way towards the bar. She was recognised and liked by all, despite an unspoken reticence and quiet deference to the inhabitants of chateaux that history had drilled into the French people. Liberté and Fraternité, by all means, but not yet Egalité, despite the French Revolution nearly two hundred years earlier.

Camille saw Max standing outside the Bon Accueil by the fountain. He was wearing a blue shirt and talking to an older man who she didn't recognise. She hesitated, surprised to feel her heart skip a beat. She checked her dress, ran her fingers through her hair, and walked confidently over to him.

"Hello Max, I like your shirt. That colour blue suits you well."

"Hi Camille, how are you? Meet my friend Pierre. Camille, this is Pierre Paglioni."

"*Enchantée*," said Camille, allowing herself to be kissed on each cheek, "delighted to meet you."

With a name like Paglioni, he had to be Corsican.

Pierre was an older version of Max: medium height, powerfully built, and burned by the sun. While Max's eyes were burnt umber, almost black, Pierre's were surprisingly blue.

There were others there too, men and women who Pierre knew, and as the sun went down, the garland of lights around the square grew brighter, the drinks flowed more freely, the laughter became more raucous, and the music grew louder. Only it was no longer local youths playing Beatles' songs badly and tinny thin versions of French classics. Now it was a local rock band called Les Blousons Noirs with drums and amplified guitars blaring the music of France's latest pop idol, twenty-four-year-old Johnny Hallyday, born Jean-Philippe Smet, the nearest thing France had to its own Elvis Presley or Mick Jagger.

The young were jiving to the latest dance, girls with girls and boys with boys. It would not have been that way but for the mothers watching them from a distance through narrowed, disapproving eyes, sipping white wine through puckered lips.

It was challenging to hold a conversation above the noise. The blood-red sky was fading to black, and Camille wondered why she had never taken part in the village fête before, though knew the answer the same instant. There was a profound simplicity, an indubitable down-to-earth authenticity to these people that excluded the pretentious from the secrets of happiness: laughter, spontaneity and kindness, music and friends. No need to impress, no need for jewels or smart cars, big houses, or swanky friends. Never had she seen her parents enjoy themselves as much as this.

She looked at Max tenderly and saw he was looking back at her. And knew he understood

Camille slept poorly that night as unsettling emotions swirled through her mind: revelations one moment, nonsense the next. Images of Max laughing with his long dark hair and white teeth, Nadia singing in the church, the village fête. And Leo, always Leo.

✹

The next morning was Sunday, and Max called her near midday. What was she doing that afternoon? Would she care to go for a walk?

"There's a restaurant I like called *Chez Thomé* over in Le Tholonet. Let's have lunch there and go for a walk afterward," Camille said.

She was not ready to invite him to the house.

"Good idea," said Max. "I'll find it. Shall we meet in an hour?"

Camille's heart soared, and she rushed to the mirror to see what he found so attractive. Her shoulder length hair was cut in a layered bob and bleached a little by the sun, her skin was tanned and the alluring blue grey eyes that looked back at her were soft and appealing. "Not too bad," she said to herself, "though why do I remind him of a cat? At least its's better than reminding him of a pig." She laughed.

Camille turned the ignition key, and the engine sprang to life. She had always loved the bark of the Alfa Romeo, and it had a lot more power than her Renault. She put down the top and accelerated hard up the road to Aix. Tires squealing, she rounded the fountain on the Place de la Rotonde and zoomed up the Cours Mirabeau to join the narrow D17, savouring the growl of the exhaust as it echoed off the stone buildings. It did the car good to be stretched. Italian tuning Bernard called it. She smiled broadly to herself. Juliette would be furious, but she would never know.

Le Tholonet was less than four miles east of Aix-en-Provence in the shadow of the mountain of Sainte-Victoire. It was one of Camille's favourite places, yet as she neared the village, she felt uneasy and wondered if meeting Max was a good idea. They had so little in common, yet she did like him; he intrigued her, perhaps because they had so little in common. But then again, he was the first attractive man she had met since returning from London, and quite unlike other men around here—other men who her mother no doubt would deem suitable, but Camille found pretentious, small-minded and dull. After leaving school, she had not known what to do, only what she did not want to do: and that was to be like other girls from wealthy families in Provence and become a bored young mother and a housewife.

❀

Camille arrived at Chez Thomé before Max and chose a table for two and watched several grizzled old men playing a game of boules in the dirt below the terrace. One, with a mane of white hair and a berry-brown face creased like a walnut, took a heavy steel boule in one hand, spat on it, took off his beret and used it as a polishing rag. The others laughed when he kissed his boule and took aim at the little *cochonnet*, piglet, a few metres away and surrounded by the other players' boules. The old man's boule sailed into the air, hung for a moment, then plunged vertically onto the boule nearest the piglet, hitting it with a resounding metallic smack and blasting it out of the way.

"Oh là là !!!" came the simultaneous cry from all four men, followed by much hilarity.

At that moment, Max drove up behind them in a 1959 maroon Peugeot 403 shooting brake, which he parked beside the red Alfa Romeo.

"Here already, Camille? I didn't see your car," said Max as he bounded up the steps to the terrace, rubbing his hands. He sat down opposite Camille. "Don't tell me you cycled here."

Before Camille could answer, a waitress came over to the table.

"So, what's good today?" Max asked.

"Rabbit in a cream and mustard sauce is the dish of the day," came the reply. "Served with ratatouille."

"Perfect! I love rabbit! Okay with you, Camille?"

Camille nodded.

"Very well, two please."

As he inspected the wine list, Camille inspected him. She liked his strength and decisiveness. And if he had raised his head, he would have seen her a thoughtful look on her face as she studied him.

He ordered a bottle of Chateau Simone, the best local red wine; tasted it; and poured a glass for Camille before pouring some for himself.

He may come from a simple background, but he knows about wine and has manners. But can he talk about politics or theatre, and does he know about music, history or art? Camille decided to mention that Cézanne used to come to Le Tholonet and see if he had heard of Cézanne.

"I am sure you know Cézanne's paintings?" she asked finally.

"Cézanne? Of course, I do!" said Max with a smile.

"Then you know his paintings of Sainte-Victoire?"

"Oh, Camille, obviously, even if I'm not from around here."

"I'm sorry. I didn't mean to be patronising; it's just that I love his work and wondered if you knew he used to come here sometimes, to Le Tholonet, on his way to paint the mountain?"

"I could have guessed," said Max. "There's a restaurant around the corner called le Relais Cézanne."

Camille laughed.

"Yes, that's true. It used to be called le Berne. After having lunch there, he'd go up to the quarry in his donkey-cart."

Camille pointed towards the mountain. "What amazes me is that he painted Sainte-Victoire so many times. At least fifty. They said he was trying to capture its nature on canvas, to simplify it, so he could understand."

"I could have saved him some time," replied Max. "Nobody can capture nature; it's alive, Camille, it's wild, it changes all the time."

Camille was about to reply when the waitress arrived with a basket of fresh bread and the dish of the day, topped up their wine glasses, and returned to the kitchen.

Max bent over and inspected his plate, sniffed it, and leaned towards Camille and said quietly: "I don't think this is rabbit. I think it's marmot," and looking up at her, he added, "and I should know."

They both burst out laughing.

"I don't even know what a marmot is," said Camille, inspecting her plate.

"Don't you have them around here? It's like a big fat squirrel. They are all over the place in the Auvergne. But don't worry. I was joking. I am pretty sure this is rabbit."

For a while, they ate in silence.

"Have you been up here before? To the lake?" asked Camille.

"To the lake? There's a lake up there?" Max took a sip of his wine.

"There are two," replied Camille. "The oldest one is the smallest and the closest. It's called Lac Zola and was created over a hundred years ago by Emile's father as a reservoir for the city, for Aix."

"And Emile would be who?" asked Max, as he scraped his plate.

"Emile Zola? The writer?" Camille was surprised that Max had never heard of him. "Come on, I'll show you the dam if you want. A walk after lunch will do us good."

They turned left out of the restaurant onto the D17, past the old Chateau du Tholonet before turning right onto the Chemin de la Paroisse, the narrow path that Cézanne used to take to the quarry.

"We stay on this path for five minutes and take another path on the right that will take us up to Lac Zola," Camille said.

They made slow progress in the heat, breathing heavily as they climbed. Thick green pines and evergreen oaks bordered the red earthen path and the further they climbed, the rockier the terrain became. The heavy scent of wild jasmine, rosemary and thyme hung in the air, and from the trees high above, the strident trill of cicadas came in waves.

"Yes, Emile Zola was a close friend of Cézanne's," Camille said slowly as she caught her breath. "They went to school together in Aix. You must remember how he defended the Jews in the Dreyfus affair? Everyone learns that at school."

She wanted to tell him more about Zola, about his books, his friendship with Cézanne, and his untimely death. But Max said nothing, and she sensed she was making him uncomfortable.

They continued to climb in the dry heat without talking until they reached the Barrage Zola, the old stone dam across the valley. For a while they stood on top of the curved wall, looking east at the green water framed by sheer slopes of granite to the north and pine covered hills to the south. Little grew between the trees, and the dark reflections made the water look rank and murky. Behind them, the dam wall plunged down to the riverbed where a stream gushed into a narrow gorge.

"So, this is Lac Zola. It's small, smaller than I expected," said Max.

"Don't forget, it's over a hundred years old, and Aix had fewer people in those days. Today they only use it as an emergency overflow from the *Lac du Bimont*, the main reservoir farther up. That's a lot wider and deeper. It's bigger in every way." Camille said.

Max stared fixedly at the water.

"I bet that water's cold."

Camille laughed.

"I am sure it's cold. It's fed by the river Cause flowing from Lac du Bimont. It's essentially melted snow from the Alps."

They stayed for a while watching the still water, Max hunched over, searching for signs of fish.

"This water's deep, there'll be some good-sized pike in there," said Max at last as they both became aware of how quiet their surroundings had become.

"Silence. The cicadas have stopped," he said softly. "That's nature's way of warning you. I don't like this place. Let's go back."

❧

Two days passed without news from Max, and Camille wondered if she would hear from him again. On Wednesday morning he called.

"I know you said your parents are coming home this weekend. Is there a chance we could see each other before then? We could always meet at the Bon Accueil if you wish. Or I could come to your house, where you live?"

Camille hesitated. She had expected this, and wanted to show him the house, yet she dreaded the thought of a lecture from her mother about how unsuitable Max was. Nadia was easy-going and would not care, but she and Juliette told each other everything. Sooner or later, Juliette would find out.

She decided to risk it.

"Well," said Camille slowly, "I could cook dinner for you tomorrow. Come around after work, not before seven-thirty."

She would tell Nadia that she was having a friend to dinner and count on her discretion, though it was infuriating to feel a need to explain. Six years ago, she had left for London because she suffocated like this. Now Juliette was becoming her jailer again.

Juliette had never been a loving mother, but Camille's need for reassurance as a teenager had turned into a slow-burning resentment against her mother's indifference. And if things were better now, it was because since coming back, she had gone out of her way to avoid confrontation. It was infinitely preferable, she discovered, to bide her time, keep herself to herself, and do what was expected of her until she could sort out her life again.

※

The next day, on her way home from Marseille, Camille stopped to buy some entrecôte steak, bread and two local cheeses: *Banon* made from goat's milk, and some cow's milk *Beaufort d'Alpage*. After parking her car, she passed through the kitchen garden, and chose some ripe tomatoes and romaine lettuce to make a salad with oil and vinegar, garlic, fresh herbs, and pine nuts. She already had a good bottle of Rhone wine, a 1955 Côte Rotie.

Camille showered quickly, changed into a pretty, navy cotton dress with red flowers she had bought in London, and raced around preparing. She was unsure what to offer him to drink before dinner. Gin and tonic? Unlikely. Her parents and their friends drank whisky. Champagne? Too pretentious. Red wine? No doubt, but she had only one bottle for dinner. Beer? Possibly. Or pastis? Of course he drank pastis. All men in this part of the world drink pastis.

She dashed to the big house and returned with a bottle of Ricard, an ice bucket and two tumblers. She placed them, with a jug of water, on the side table and added a ramekin of olives and a dried sausage before she lit the barbecue. She had suggested he walk the mile or so from the garage, and at seven-thirty sharp, he saw him striding self-consciously up the drive. She came out to greet him as he approached.

"Welcome to my house. Though it's not my house of course, it's my parent's house. Mine is the cottage, the little house by the pool."

Max made as if to shake her hand, but Camille leaned forward and offered him her right cheek, and he kissed her firmly as an old friend would, and she kissed him on the cheek, too. Then she turned her face to offer him the other cheek, and they kissed again. He smelt of soap and brown tobacco.

Max was wearing a grey, crumpled linen jacket and dark slacks, and Camille was surprised and touched that he wore a shirt and tie.

"My, you are handsome! And I like you in shirt and tie."

"Thanks, Camille. I may come from a mountain in the Auvergne, but I am not a complete peasant, you know," said Max with a good-natured grin.

He pulled a loose cigarette from inside his jacket and lit it.

"Now come and sit down," said Camille, adding, "I hope you drink pastis?"

Max nodded as she poured him a glass of the yellow-green liquid and handed it to him.

"Please add your own water," Camille said. "There's ice in the bucket if you need some."

"No ice, just water, thank you," said Max as he sat down in her mother's favourite chair. Camille made a mental note to clean it thoroughly later. He stretched across to pick up the dried sausage, pulled a folding knife out of his pocket and cut several thin slices.

"I like your knife," said Camille bending to inspect it as she reached for the wine.

Max held it up. "This knife? I've had it for years. It used to be my grandfather's. We have a tradition in the Auvergne that if you give someone a knife, you cut your friendship with them, so I gave him a centime for it." Max ran his forefinger down the blade. "Don't you know these knives? They're from the village of Laguiole in the Aveyron. This brass fly on the top is the symbol of the village."

He unhooked the knife from its lanyard and passed it over to her.

"I like knives as objects but to be honest they scare me," said Camille, cradling it, "though this one is particularly beautiful. What's the handle made of? Bone?"

"Not bone, no. It's made of horn; cow horn and brass."

Max watched Camille holding the knife.

"It's old. Very old. I know my grandfather had it for years before he gave it to me. It's my most important possession and never leaves my side. It's kept me alive many times, in fact I owe my life to it."

Camille inspected the knife with interest, before cutting a slice of dried sausage for herself. "I'm impressed. I can see why you like it and keep it sharp."

She passed it back to him.

"What impresses me is your parents' house," said Max. "This is quite a place. It's the first time I have been to a real chateau,"

"Oh, this is not a real chateau. It's neither enormous nor particularly old, little more than two hundred years. A real chateau, in the historical sense, was built to be defended, not to impress. Have you been up to the ruins of Queen Jeanne's Chateau overlooking the church?"

Camille turned her head in the direction of the village. "That would have been a real chateau, built a thousand years ago. Too bad it was destroyed in the Revolution."

"Yes, I've been up there, but there's not much to see, other than an arch or two and piles of old stones," said Max. "Your place is more interesting. I don't suppose you'd show me around?"

Camille wavered for a moment, knowing that there was nothing her mother hated more than strangers being shown around her home. Nadia had left to have dinner with a friend and there was little chance anyone would know. She unhooked a large key from behind her cottage door and they walked across the gravel to the big house.

The heavy door swung open to reveal a high-ceilinged, eighteenth-century hall with a worn, black and white marble floor. Along the wall to the left were two grand double-doors, two small chairs and a table: to the right, another double-door stood beside a limestone, L-shaped staircase. On the olive-painted walls hung several dark portraits in gilded frames, and on the far wall above the second flight of stairs, was a large, threadbare tapestry. Below the stairs, straight-ahead, a battered dinner-gong guarded a leather-covered door with a circular window, opposite a clutch of canes and walking sticks in an empty elephant's foot. The entire scene was bathed in the diffused evening light streaming through the mullioned windows above and on each side of the entrance.

Max said nothing as he took it all in.

"This is spectacular," he whispered finally, "very impressive. Like a museum."

Camille laughed.

"Oh, you don't have to whisper! There's nobody here. It's all a bit dilapidated, but we like it that way. My stepfather's family has lived here forever." She turned towards the double-door on the right. "He uses this room as his study and bedroom. It used to be the library."

Camille eased the door open, and light streamed into a darkened room from another age with tightly drawn curtains and floor-to-ceiling bookshelves. On a bold-patterned oriental rug, stood a heavy-looking desk strewn with papers and a large glass paperweight that glinted in the light. On the floor, behind the desk, lay an old safe partly obscured by a chair, and in the shadows at the back, sat a massive, oak four-poster bed.

Max let out a low whistle and stepped into the room to look around. "This is some bedroom," he said. "Where's the light?"

"You are not going in there," said Camille as she grabbed his jacket and pulled him back. She closed the door quickly and guided him to an identical door on the other side of the hall.

"This is our formal drawing-room, though we never use it. At least I never use it, and my parents only use it for parties."

Camille opened the door a crack to reveal another large room, much like Bernard's, but with yellow silk chinoiserie panels on the walls and display cabinets between the tall windows. Numerous small tables and armchairs matched two large sofas perpendicular to a marble fireplace on the far wall.

She closed the door.

"This place really is like a museum," Max repeated in a hushed voice. "Can we see upstairs?"

Camille hesitated.

"My mother would kill me."

"Please?"

"All right, but very quickly."

The warm evening light bounced thin, multicoloured rays off the crystal chandelier as they climbed the stairs. To the left, a corridor with a balustrade ran to the front of the house, with three doors leading off it. They walked past the doors and turned left again towards a more imposing door guarded by a white marble column and the bust of a Roman emperor.

"This is my mother's bedroom," Camille said, as she reached for a key behind the marble bust. "It's above my stepfather's room, so the same size. The other doors lead to smaller bedrooms."

"Your mother keeps her bedroom locked?" asked Max.

"You don't know my mother!"

Camille laughed as she pushed the door open a little to reveal the soft grey walls and multiple photos in silver frames. Positioned squarely in the centre of the room was Juliette's elegant, oversized bed, underneath a grey silk canopy.

"I daren't let you go in," she said, and a moment later, she closed and relocked the door.

"Was that your mother's Olympic medal?" asked Max.

"You saw it? The medal on the wall? Well spotted. Yes, that's the gold medal she won for the 100-metre breaststroke in the 1936 Olympics. My stepfather was captain of the swimming team. That's how they met."

"Mon Dieu, that's interesting," said Max. "Any chance you'd let me see it?"

"Absolutely none," replied Camille taking his arm. "That's more than my life is worth."

As they descended the stairs and reached the hall, Max asked Camille what was behind the other doors off the hall.

"You saw the one on the left, it's the drawing-room. The other one is a dining room we rarely use. The leather door under the stairs leads to the kitchen. It used to be the servants' quarters, but since we don't have servants anymore, my mother had the rooms converted into an apartment and an office. Here, I'll show you."

Camille pushed open the leather door to reveal a short hallway leading to a large, old-fashioned kitchen with a flagstone floor and a yawning fireplace. To the right, a passage led to a clinically modern office-cum-sitting room furnished in the Art Deco style, complete with a small gymnasium and a marble bathroom.

"Whew," whistled Max, "so this is how the other half lives."

"We'd better get out of here," said Camille in a low voice, "because my mother would murder me if she knew I'd brought you in here."

Back by the pool, Camille began to relax. "Now you know everything about me. Tell me something I don't know about you," she said as she dressed the salad.

"You know Camille," said Max, still using the formal French *vous*, "we are very different, you and me. I already told you I come from a simple family farm high up on Mont-Dore in the Auvergne." Max looked searchingly at Camille. "You probably know mountain farms are the poorest because the land in the valleys is where the water is. But the poor farms are often the oldest."

He paused to take out a soft pack of Gitanes from his shirt pocket, and two spilled out. He picked them both up and offered one to Camille. She shook her head.

"Our farm is probably three hundred years old, even older than this place, and as far as I know, our family has always lived there."

He put the packet and the loose cigarette back into his pocket and dangled the other one from his lower lip as he felt for his lighter. Cupping his hands to shield the flame, he set fire to the cigarette, illuminating his rugged features for a moment in the bright yellow light. It was an oddly masculine gesture, at once familiar and reassuring.

"In the winter, it was my job to take the cows down to the valley, to pastures we rented from the monastery. When the weather allowed it, we would stay there overnight, and I would sleep in a tras—a hole in the ground lined with sheepskins and covered by branches. But when the weather was bad, I'd have to walk the cows back up to the farm and that could take hours."

"How did you know when bad weather was coming? Is there some special secret, like all the cows start lying down in the same direction?"

"To keep their patch dry? No! You really are a city girl, aren't you?" Max laughed. "Like you and me, cows lie down when they are tired or after eating, though it's true they often lie facing north. But that doesn't have anything to do with the weather."

Max took a sip of his drink.

"Actually, changes in the weather are easy to predict—a brusque change in the wind, for example. A wind from the east brings bad weather, and if the wind drops suddenly, that's the calm before the storm. I used to watch the shadows of the Red Kites."

"And what's a Red Kite?"

"A raptor, a bird of prey. Like a big buzzard with a forked tail."

"What could you tell from the shadows?"

"It's all to do with pressure. In fine weather the birds fly higher, and if you notice their shadows getting larger, it means the pressure is dropping and bad weather is on the way."

"Aren't you a fountain of knowledge!" Camille laughed, taking a sip of her wine. "I suppose things were much harder in the winter?"

"Yes, they were. The winters can get very cold in the Auvergne. We'd graze the cows in the valley until the snow began to melt in March, then start moving them up the hillside. By September, we would be near the top and work our way down to the valley again before the snow came. That was my job. Every day, from seven until I was sixteen. I spent a lot of time alone in those days, but the cows were good company. They each had their own personality."

Max smiled and took a deep sip of his drink. "As a matter of fact, bad weather bothered me more than them."

"So, you really did spend the whole time alone with cows. What on earth did you do all day?"

"Oh, I wasn't alone," said Max said readily. "I always had a dog, my dog Coco, with me."

Camille laughed. "Coco? That's a great name. What kind of dog was he?"

"A Labrit, a Pyrenean sheepdog. They're a bit small for a sheepdog but very alive, very bright. Being smaller than a sheep, they jump on their backs to get a good view, and then jump from sheep to sheep to keep the flock together.

We had cows, so he couldn't do that, but he kept them in order by nipping at their legs."

"Yes, but Max, what did you actually do by yourself all day long?"

"I worked, Camille! A lot goes on in the hills. I had to keep an eye on the cows in case of accidents and sickness, and make sure they didn't stray. And watch out for predators. There were wolves and bears in the region in those days. Not many, but I saw them." Max paused. "And we had to eat. I would hunt with Coco, and when we caught something—a hare or a rabbit—I'd gut it in the river with this knife."

Max held his knife up.

"Fish are attracted by blood, so they swarm over and are easy to catch. I'd catch eels and brown trout mostly, salmon and pike now and then. And afterward, I would light a fire and cook whatever I caught."

Max paused and stretched the fingers of his hands, as if remembering.

"Did you catch other animals?"

"You know Camille, that's rich volcanic land up there, and those mountains are teeming with wildlife. I did this for years, long before the war, and caught most things—rabbits and hares, and small deer now and then. There were loads of wild animals around in those days and we were never short of something to eat. And if I caught something big, like a deer for example, I'd put it on a cow's back and bring it back to the farm. Then we'd cook it in blood with eau-de-vie, ginger and cream. And chestnuts or mushrooms when we had them."

"It sounds like another world to me," said Camille.

"It was another world, like your aristocratic life in a chateau is another world to me."

"We're not aristocrats, Max," replied Camille quickly. "Though I suppose you could call my parents bourgeois or upper middle-class. But we are not aristocrats."

Max picked up his drink.

"Listen," he said seriously, "in your world, the richer people are—aristocrats or bourgeois, I don't care—the further they are removed from nature, and that makes them weak. The rich have no idea about nature, how animals are killed and processed. They don't care as long as their *filet mignon* doesn't look like a piece of a dead animal."

Max paused to sip his drink.

"I think everybody should be made to visit farms and abattoirs to see what animals go through. Where we lived, everybody respected animals. We ate what we killed, so we knew what we were eating. We wasted nothing, Camille. And let me tell you, everything tasted good."

Max folded his arms and stared at the ground, as if nostalgic.

"Even marmots?" Camille teased, changing the tone.

"Marmots?" Max looked up and laughed. "Seriously, they don't taste that bad, though I never caught one deliberately. I always decided in advance what I wanted to catch and set my trap accordingly. Every animal is different, Camille, but they are all worriers. They think contingently, short-term, like people. Where is my next meal going to come from? What's around the corner? Where's the danger? Their weakness is they don't think ahead. So hunters decide what they want to catch and prepare a suitable trap. It's that simple."

Max stopped to light another cigarette.

"I caught a wild boar piglet once and bent over to pick him up and when he squealed, Coco started barking, and I turned around in time to see the mother charging at me. She tossed me in the air but went after Coco when he chased her other piglets." Max shook his head. "We got out of there fast and stayed in a shelter until she went away. She left the piglet, and I cooked it on a spit and shared it with the dog."

Max inhaled deeply from his cigarette and stretched out his fingers.

"I learned everything in that valley. And not just about nature. About how the world works, about life," he said intently. "And people's strengths and weaknesses."

Max was silent for a moment and then put his finger to his lips and whispered. "Ssshhh, listen."

"Listen? Listen to what?" Camille whispered back.

"Look, over there!" Max pointed across the pool to a linden tree. "There! Can you hear that? Did you see the leaves move?"

"Where? It's almost dark, Max. I don't know where I am supposed to be looking, and I can't hear anything." Camille stared vainly in the direction of Max's finger. "I can't see a thing."

"The leaves are moving; that means the cicadas are laying their eggs. Did you hear the twig fall? And see those twigs beneath the tree?"

Camille saw and heard nothing.

Max walked around the pool to the tree and picked up a twig.

"See these little cuts in the wood? Inside these cuts, there are eggs. Before long, they'll turn into larvae and burrow in the ground. In a year or two, they'll reappear and crawl up a tree, shed their skin and become cicadas."

Camille had lived in Provence most of her life and had never given cicadas a second thought other than as rowdy harbingers of hot summer days.

"You know why they make all that noise?"

"Don't tell me. Let me guess. Because they get a buzz out of it?" suggested Camille.

"Very funny, Camille," Max said without laughing. "The noise is to scare the birds away. It's a defence mechanism."

"Is there anything you don't know?" Camille asked blithely.

She was not bored but uneasy. All this talk of nature was fascinating in a way, but it was also disconcerting because the conversation was so one-sided. Usually sure of herself intellectually, Camille found herself on shaky ground. What Max said was neither deep nor complicated, but he had skewed the gist of their conversation to make her feel as if everything she knew or said was trite and unimportant. It was not so, she knew that, but with some uncanny sleight of hand, he had cast a spell and brought her into his world, and his field of expertise. And in doing so, she had lost her landmarks and begun to doubt the fundamentals of her own way of thinking.

As she grilled the steaks, Max described a world that was so unlike her own, with no telephone, no electricity and no running water. She heard how his father smoked pigs and fish in the chimney while his mother made butter and cheese to barter for salt and flour to make bread. He told her how a weasel will mesmerise a rabbit before biting it on the neck, and how to steal the rabbit from the weasel.

As she listened, Camille found herself identifying with the poor, mesmerised rabbit, and unable to dispel an image of her mother in a silk dress, complaining about a ladder in her stocking.

"What about school? Didn't you go to school?"

"School?" Max laughed. "School? Where we lived, the nearest school was two hours away, besides, I was needed on the farm. No, I didn't go to school, Camille. My mother taught me to read and write using old newspapers."

Max drained his glass. "Don't feel sorry for me. We were poor, even destitute from your point of view because we had no money. But we were rich in other ways, and I swear, I wouldn't change it for anything."

For a while, neither of them talked. The light had faded fast, and the dark of the warm night had crept upon them. The only light now came from the stars, the two candles and the muted glow of the barbecue. Camille and Max sat in silence with their thoughts, half-listening to the water lapping in the pool and the tuneless croaking of frogs in the kitchen garden. In the distance, a dog barked.

"It is beautiful here, isn't it?" said Max. "You are a lucky girl, you know."

"Yes, I am lucky. I realise that." Camille looked coyly at Max.

"Being here tonight is special. The dinner, the wine, this beautiful pool. I can't resist it. Would you mind if I have a swim?"

Without waiting for a reply, Max stood up, slipped off his jacket and unbuttoned his shirt to reveal, as far as Camille could see in the low light, a trim, muscular torso and thick, strong arms. She watched spellbound, alarmed and a little excited as he kicked off his shoes, slid off his trousers, and walked naked to the far end of the pool. With his back still to her, he slipped noiselessly into the pool.

With a start, Camille realised that she could neither see nor hear Max anymore. A minute passed, then two. Where was he? Abruptly, without a sound, his face emerged from the dark water beside her, and he called to her softly. "Come and swim with me, Camille. The water's lovely."

Intoxicated by the warm air, the rich food and fine wine, and the romance of the night, Camille got up and walked softly to the farthest, darkest end of the pool, quietly removed her clothes and lowered herself naked into the water.

Since the moment earlier that evening, she had first seen Max walking up the drive, since their first kiss hello, since well before their first glass of wine, Camille had that feeling again, as if she was powerless, inconsequential and out of control. And she knew it wasn't her decision to sleep with him tonight. It had already been decided, and she was glad.

❧

When Camille woke the next morning, she was both happy and uneasy to find herself naked in Max's muscular arms.

"Max, Max." She shook him. "Max, wake up. You must get up. It's ten to seven. You're going to have to go soon."

Max opened one eye and smiled at her. "Good morning, minou. Don't look so alarmed. Nobody will see me."

Camille grabbed a towel to cover herself and ran to the bathroom and closed the door behind her. She glanced at herself in the mirror and laughed aloud when her reflection grinned back at her. She felt jubilant, reenergised as if she had needed that, the first time since London. A quick trip to heaven, or was it a little death? At least she was a member of the human race again, someone who could love and be loved.

Hurriedly she brushed her teeth and called out to Max. "Do you want to take your shower first?"

There was no reply.

"Max, do you want to take your shower now?"

Camille opened the door. The bed was empty.

"Max?" she said quietly. "Max, are you there?"

She moved to the window in time to see him walking quickly through the grass towards the front gates. She hoped he would sense her watching, but he neither turned nor waved and was gone.

Damn. She turned on the shower. He could have said goodbye.

It felt good to rise early and have time to reflect. The evening had sped by and been more enjoyable than she had expected, and if Max was not perfect, it had not mattered a bit; he was congenial, attractive, and very different. And then she remembered Leo quoting Timothy Leary in London: everyone carries a piece of the puzzle. Nobody comes into your life by mere coincidence.

So which piece of the puzzle was Max carrying? He was unlike anyone she had ever met. More in tune with nature than society, he lived life on his own terms with no need for other people. He was his own man, a free spirit and it made him mysterious and exciting.

In retrospect, she regretted showing him around the house, especially her mother's apartment and her bedroom. At least he would never need to see the house again. Throughout the day, her thoughts kept returning to him, and she wanted to hear his voice. She knew the number of the garage and considered calling him, and towards five o'clock, she did.

"Max? Is that you?"

"Nobody else works here, minou. How are you? I was hoping you'd call."

"You know my parents get back tomorrow, and I was wondering…"

"I am so sorry, but I can't see you tonight. I wish I could. But now I know where your bedroom is, I can come and see you in the week, no?"

"NO, no and no! Absolutely not, Max. My parents would kill me and then kill you. It is out of the question."

"Camille, you are forgetting. Nobody will know or see me if I come after dark. Believe me."

"No, Max, it's impossible. You must not come."

"Relax, Camille. I shall come and see you next week." And with that, he put down the phone.

Camille stood and stared in disbelief at the receiver in her hand.

How could he? Surely, he wouldn't dare. Would he? He must not, not here. It would be too risky. Yet the thought of him coming to her in the night was thrilling, and another reason she found him so attractive: he dared.

By the time Bernard and Juliette returned from Switzerland, Camille had the giddy feeling she might fall in love, though that was the last thing she needed after London. For the first time since coming home, she was alive again, the clouds had lifted, her mother's grip had loosened, and her confidence had flooded back.

It would be easy to be discreet because Juliette never noticed when Camille was out in the evenings or away at weekends. And never set foot in Camille's cottage.

Chapter 4

MUDDLED THOUGHTS

J ULIETTE AND BERNARD arrived back from Switzerland late on Saturday after catching the slow train from Geneva to Lyon, where they changed to the first-class only, Trans-Europe-Express to Marseille. A driver waited at Saint Charles railway station to sweep them to Ventabren.

Each time they came back from Switzerland, Juliette would gush about the famous guests they had dined with at their luxurious hotel, the Beau Rivage Palace on the shores of Lake Geneva in the shadow of the Jura Mountains. And preach about the respect accorded Bernard as a high-ranking member of the International Olympics Committee.

"Every morning, a chauffeur-driven Mercedes-Benz arrived to whisk us to the I.O.C. Headquarters in the *Villa Mon Repos*—you know, the old home of Baron Pierre de Coubertin, the founder of the Olympic movement?"

That evening, all four had dinner together informally in the kitchen. Nadia had prepared a *Tagine* lamb dish with preserved lemons and saffron couscous, Bernard's favourite, and inevitably, the conversation revolved around their trip.

Camille had heard all the stories before, but she listened politely as her mother recounted details of the sumptuous lunches that followed the morning meetings attended by Bernard, succeeded by smaller committee get-togethers to discuss matters such as *How to Keep the Games Amateur* and *Ensuring the Gentlemanly Nature of the Olympic Movement*.

Juliette could hardly contain herself when describing the glamorous parties hosted at the villa every evening by countries vying to influence the committee, each more extravagant and luxurious than the last. She had been in her element.

Bernard leaned closer to Camille and said under his breath, "*Entre nous*, your mother likes socialising much more than I do."

Camille smiled connivingly. "I'm sure, but I thought you loved the I.O.C.?"

"Oh, I do, and I used to enjoy the meetings, but they've become ruthless affairs. One would have thought—hoped—they would be guided by esoteric principles and goodwill, but unfortunately inter-nation rivalry has become part of the Olympic movement."

Bernard looked disenchanted.

"The consequences are that our committee discussions nearly always deteriorate into petty arguments about pecking order, prestige and political influence—all of which are now associated with hosting the Olympics." He shook his head. "Baron de Coubertin, would turn in his grave if he could listen in. He's been dead for thirty years, and many of us feel that his visionary ideas become more tarnished every year."

Camille always enjoyed talking to Bernard and tried to concentrate on what he was saying. Both he and idealism were close to her heart, but closer still was Max.

"Are you listening?" asked Juliette. "Bernard's talking to you. What's the matter with you?"

"Nothing, Maman. I'm so sorry, I was far away," spluttered Camille. "Please go on."

"You look different, Camille. What have you done to yourself?"

"Nothing, absolutely nothing."

Camille frowned and tried to pay more attention.

❀

For the next few days, life returned to pre-Switzerland normal: at seven-thirty in the morning, Juliette would swim in the pool and take her coffee on the terrace, and Camille would bring her a copy of the local newspaper, La Provence, and kiss her goodbye before leaving for work. As ever, Bernard remained at his desk.

❦

When Camille arrived home the following Wednesday, she parked her car by the stables, walked through the kitchen garden, and entered the big house through the kitchen.

"Hello everybody," she called. "I'm home."

"There you are, Camille," came the dry reply, and Camille knew immediately that something was wrong.

Juliette came out of her office holding a pair of scissors and some flowers. "Do you have something to say to me, Camille? Something you want to tell me? Do you?"

Camille reddened and looked at her mother with her eyes wide. "What on earth do you mean, Maman?"

"I think you know very well what I mean."

Juliette put down the flowers on the kitchen table and stared down at her daughter with her hands on her hips.

"I do not, Maman. I have no idea what you are talking about."

Camille searched her mind frantically. This could not be about Max; she had cleaned up very carefully after his visit and was certain she had left no trace.

"Camille, I cannot bear lies. Bernard found this in his room by the door. Would you tell me what it was doing there?"

She fished in the pocket of her kitchen apron and produced a single, slightly bent, Gitanes cigarette.

Camille recoiled as if struck by a blow to the head and felt the blood drain from her face.

"Well... I can..." was all she managed to say.

"Bernard doesn't smoke, Nadia doesn't smoke, and I don't smoke, and as far as I know, you don't smoke, Camille. So, whose cigarette is it, and how did it get there?"

Nobody would have called Juliette beautiful now. Her eyes had narrowed, her lips were curled; she could have passed for some heinous animal closing in for the kill.

"Camille," she snarled. "I am waiting."

Camille had always been more comfortable telling the truth. "Maman, I'm sorry. I had friends over to dinner when you were away, and they wanted to see the house."

"You have a house of your own Camille," retorted Juliette. "You have no business showing other people my house. Have you no respect for my privacy? Besides, who were these people, these friends of yours?" she paused, before adding, "I wasn't aware that you had any friends."

Camille looked at Nadia and saw that she knew, but Juliette's insult gave her strength. She swallowed hard and took a deep breath.

"Maman, I am grown up. I am thirty years old, for God's sake. I do have friends and without meaning to be rude, my friends are my business. I admit I was wrong to..."

"Wrong? Your business? I'll give you wrong, young lady," Juliette was almost spitting with rage. "I want to hear you promise me that you will NEVER, EVER show any of your friends, male or female, my house again! Do you hear me? I said, do you hear me? Who are these friends, anyway?"

So far, it had not been as bad as it might have been. This was only bluster.

Camille gathered her courage and told her. "You won't approve, Maman, I know—you never do. But my friend's name is Max, and he's from the Auvergne. He's just a friend," said Camille triumphantly, taking a step forward, astonished at her bravery and proud she had defended him.

"Is that true?" said Juliette turning to Nadia. "Do you know this Max person who smokes cigarettes?"

"No, I don't know him," said Nadia. "But I think you're a little hard on her, Juliette. It's not as if anybody stole anything. Camille is proud of this house and wanted to show it to her friend."

Juliette glared at Nadia.

"Camille, you can go now. But I will not forget. I will not have you EVER showing strangers around my house again. I will not stand for it. Go on now, go! Go!"

Camille did not wait to be told a second time. Brought up in the shadow of her mother's bad temper and imperious authoritarianism, she was surprised to get off so lightly. She was lucky Juliette had not asked which other rooms she had showed Max.

❧

The following day, Camille phoned Max at the garage to tell him that Bernard had found a cigarette in his room by the door. And that her mother was furious.

"Dear God," exclaimed Max. "I hope you didn't tell her it was mine, did you? I hope you didn't mention me?"

"I did. What else could I have said? Anyway, I don't like lying and have nothing to be ashamed of. I simply told them you were a friend called Max who came to dinner and wanted to see the house."

"Who's them? Who's the other person? Your stepfather?"

"No, my mother's friend, Nadia Beausoleil."

"Camille, that's bad. I'm not happy about that. You shouldn't have told them. Can we meet later tonight? I can come to your place. Nobody will see me."

"No, absolutely not. I forbid you to come to the house. We can meet in the Bar de la Paix in Aix if you like, where we met the first time? But I don't understand why you're so bothered about it."

Max paused as if he had to think about it. "All right," he said finally. "I'll see you there at seven tonight."

Camille put down the phone and stood motionless for a minute, worried by Max's reaction.

❦

The Bar de la Paix was more crowded and noisier than the last time they were there, and Camille had to push her way through to Max. He was frowning and appeared subdued, but he stood up quickly and embraced her.

"Camille, I must tell you how sorry I am. It was stupid of me. I should have been more careful. What do they know about me?"

"Not much. Only your first name."

"Do they know that I work at the garage?"

"No. I don't think they have the least idea you work at the garage, although they'll probably find out sooner or later. But why does it matter?" asked Camille. "It doesn't bother me. I don't see what difference it makes."

"I don't think your mother should know anything about me, though it's a bit late now. So, who's your mother's friend? You didn't mention her before."

"Nadia Beausoleil, my mother's companion. She lives with us," Camille replied. "They've known each other all their lives."

"Lives with you? I didn't know anyone else lived in that house."

"Well, she does, and she has all my life. She's cared for me since we lived in Paris before the war and came with us when we moved to Provence."

"When did you move to Provence?"

"In the summer of 1942."

"So, you were in Provence before the Germans occupied the south." It was a statement, not a question.

"Yes, I suppose so," said Camille. "I was too young to know what was going on."

"Do you know why your mother left Paris?"

"I'm not sure what all this has to do with anything, but the war changed after the Americans joined it, and life in Paris became more dangerous. The Germans started rounding up and executing people, not only foreigners and Jews."

"So she left Paris because the Germans were rounding up foreigners and Jews? Why did she care so much about the Jews?"

"I don't mean that at all. Things were getting dangerous for everybody in Paris, not just the Jews. Anyway, Bernard lived here, and he wanted us to come down and join him."

"And Madame Beausoleil came down with you?"

"I already told you she came with us. What is the point of all this? Why is all this so important to you?"

"People had secrets in the war... And if I learned anything from those days, it was never to take anyone or anything for granted."

Max paused and tapped the ash from his cigarette. "I know your mother was famous, and I understand why she lived in Paris. She knew the right people. But I can't help wondering how this Madame Beausoleil fitted in. What did she do to survive in Paris? Was she rich? Did she collaborate? What was her secret? Was she a member of the Resistance?"

"Stop it, Max! No way! She was at university in Paris before the war, living with my mother. When the war came, she helped my mother care for me, for God's sake. That was a full-time job; I was too small to be left alone. I'm sure she didn't collaborate."

Max took both Camille's hands in his.

"It was all relative. Anyone who bought a chicken on the black market was a criminal theoretically, and lots of people collaborated in one way or another; it was common sense. Everybody hid something in those days, and everyone had to beg, lie and steal to survive. Nobody trusted anybody."

Max stared into Camille's eyes. "All I want is to know who I am dealing with."

"Dealing with?" Camille asked incredulously. "What do you mean by dealing with? What's all this about Max?'"

"Knowledge is power. If your mother decides she doesn't like me and wants to keep me away from you, I must find something on her. I need leverage. Everybody had secrets in the war, and I want to know hers. There must have been something shady about their life in Paris."

Max lit another cigarette. "The secrets were always one of four things: buying or selling on the black market, collaborating with the Germans, being involved with the Resistance. Or something to do with the Jews—though the last two were basically the same thing."

Camille sat up and shivered. "I've lost you. What do you mean? The Resistance and the Jews were the same thing? You are talking in riddles."

"Nothing, Camille, nothing," said Max. "It's not important; let's change the subject."

With that, he took her hand and squeezed it. "Don't worry, minou. Don't be alarmed. There's nothing to worry about. And as for your mother knowing about me, I don't want a confrontation. I'll have to be more careful."

As Camille drove home from Aix, she went over the conversation in her mind. Why was Max so concerned, and what had Nadia got to do with anything?

There is more to Max than meets the eye.

When Camille awoke, the sky was a bitter shade of blue, and the Mistral growled in a way that presaged trouble. Hunching her shoulders and squinting against the dust, she made her way to the stables to collect her car.

As she passed the kitchen, she pushed open the door and called out, "Good morning, Maman. I am going to work now."

There was no reply.

By the time Camille returned that evening, the Mistral had slackened to a breeze, as it did at the end of the day. She parked her car in the usual place and saw that the Alfa Romeo was missing. She went through the empty kitchen to Bernard's room and knocked on his door.

"Come in," said Bernard.

Camille put her head around the door without entering the room.

"Is Maman all right? Her car isn't in the stable."

Bernard was sitting at his desk reading the newspaper. He looked up at her over his glasses.

"There's no doubt she's all right. She had an appointment somewhere, I have no idea where. I'm sure she'll be back soon."

Camille came into the room and stood before Bernard. She played with her hands and spread out her fingers, admiring the intertwined gold rings she was wearing on the middle finger of her right hand.

Bernard continued reading.

"Bernard," said Camille hesitantly, "may I ask you something?"

Not waiting for an answer, she went on: "Why did we all leave Paris in 1942? Are there any exciting family secrets I should know about? Like being on the run from the Gestapo, or smuggling escaped pilots to Spain?"

Bernard laughed and looked up from his paper. "Wouldn't that be fun? No, no secrets, good or bad, that I'm aware of, Camille."

"None? How about being in trouble with the Germans for buying chicken in the black market? Or Juliette being in cohorts with the Jews?"

Bernard's smiled faded. He frowned and stood up, towering over Camille. "In cohorts with the Jews? What on earth makes you say that?"

"No reason at all. I was playing."

"Juliette isn't Jewish, and neither are you. We're Catholic, and so is Nadia. But would it matter if we were Jewish? What difference would it make?"

Bernard peered at her over his half-moon reading glasses.

"None I suppose, "replied Camille softly. "I was wondering, that's all."

Camille returned to her room deep in thought, wondering why Max had asked all those questions. They had brought back dim, unsettling memories of Paris when she was a small child. The two-room apartment on the Ile Saint-Louis and that dark, curling staircase to the seventh floor, the cramped room she shared with Nadia under the roof with its sloping ceiling and tiny window.

She thought of the strange lights and noises in the night. Especially the noises. Distant bangs, shouts in the street, raised voices in the passageways, doors slamming, boots on the stairs. Even gunfire. And the muted sobs from the old lady next door who was always crying.

Nadia cried too. She sometimes curled up in a ball on her bed weeping, the tears tumbling down her cheeks. And then her mother would come home as it began to get light and start to talk, and she would hear Nadia whisper, "Ssshhh! You'll wake Camille."

She had been too young to understand, but she still remembered the fear that came with the cold in the small hours of the night.

On her fifth birthday, after they left Paris for the south, her mother produced a small birthday cake for her, the first she had ever had, and Nadia gave her a doll with real hair and eyes that opened and closed. But when Camille took off its clothes, Nadia had got upset and told Camille that it was a German bisque doll and very special, and she had to take better care of it. She had hardly played with it after that.

Her mind was troubled as she climbed into bed, and vague memories trickled back of being rocked to sleep in Nadia's arms as she sung the Brahms lullaby in German. How did it go again? She still knew it by heart.

Guten Abend, gut' Nacht, mit Rosen bedacht, mit Näglein besteckt, schlüpf unter die Deck. [Good evening, good night, with roses covered, with lilies adorned, slip under the covers].

Camille turned over and hummed the tune, but sleep would not come. For a while, she lay on her back with her hands behind her head, staring at the ceiling and listening to the silence of the night, the blackness hiding but not muffling the dull, repetitive croaks of bullfrogs and the thin rhythmic chirp of a million insects. Sometimes, the nocturnal drone faded to a distant hum before swelling softly to a dull buzz. Then silence again, broken only by the melancholic call of an owl. Max could hoot like an owl. There it was again. Could Max be signalling to her? Wait, it was nearer now. It was Max; it had to be. Had something happened? Had he come to tell her something?

Camille got out of bed, pulled back the curtain, and stood motionless, staring at the black trees silhouetted against the sky. Was that a shadow moving, there, by that tree? Camille shivered with fear and excitement. Max! She watched intently for ten minutes but she never saw the shadow again.

She returned half-heartedly and nearly fell over with surprise to find Max sitting on her bed, cross-legged, with his face impossibly creased with a grin.

"Max! Max, what are you doing here? How on earth did you get in?"

"I've been here for five minutes watching you watching me," he said with a laugh, uncrossing his legs and leaning back against the pillows and putting his hands behind his head.

"Now, come here. You should close that kitchen window at night, you know."

"You're not a man, you're a cat! How could you get in without me noticing?"

Max looked pleased with himself. "You people, you make me laugh. You live in a cocoon. You couldn't exist without hot water, electricity and supermarkets, could you? You've lost touch with your senses, Camille."

"No lectures, please! Cats don't lecture people."

Camille laughed and came over to the bed and kissed him. It did not matter that he smelled so strongly of tobacco and alcohol; she gave herself to him with a ferocious passion that she hadn't known she could feel. When at last they lay quietly in each other's arms, Camille drifted to sleep, but she did not dream of Max. There was no need. Instead, she dreamed of Paris and the war. But this time, the soldiers were laughing and singing as they marched, and everybody was cheering.

When Camille awoke early the next morning, Max had already gone. It was better that way. For a while, she relived the night until finally, she climbed out of bed to shower and luxuriate in the hot water.

Max is right. I definitely could not live without electricity and hot water.

Secrets from a Stranger

64

Chapter 5

PARIS, JULY 1942

T WAS EARLY MORNING. On the far side of the road, the birds in the trees of the Jardin des Tuileries were barely awake and only a few arid beaks emitted sporadic chirrups, tuneless precursors of the dawn chorus. Way beyond the Tuileries gardens and the river Seine, masked by the steep mansard roofs of the Louvre, a corner of the night sky was teasing the darkness to pink. The air was cool and fresh; crisp but not cold.

Juliette pulled on her gloves, tugged down her hat, and gathered a grey silk shawl around her shoulders as she came out of the entrance of the grand Hotel Meurice onto the Rue de Rivoli. The sentries on each side of the door snapped to attention and saluted her, and one of them smiled and called out in accented French "Bonjour, Madame." She nodded her head without acknowledging them, slung the large bag onto her shoulder, and glanced to her left and her right.

The five A.M. curfew was over, dawn had broken, and up the street to the right, a detachment of field-grey soldiers tramped from the Place de la Concorde down the Rue de Rivoli towards the barricaded checkpoint on the intersection with the Rue de Castiglione. The guard was about to be changed.

Juliette turned left and hurried away under the darkened arches towards the Louvre. She kept her head low and her eyes to the ground as she walked quickly under cover of the arcades. It was not a good idea to attract the attention of anybody, let alone a police patrol so early in the morning. Her *Sonderausweis* special pass allowed her to go anywhere, but the patrols were French, and it was better not to arouse their curiosity as to why she was all dressed up at five in the morning or give them an excuse to inspect her bag.

The immense black, red and white Nazi flags hung limply on their poles all along the Rue de Rivoli, and only the fading stomp of the soldiers' leather boots and the sharp click of her own wooden heels on the stone pavement broke the stillness of the morning.

When she reached the Rue des Pyramides, she crossed the road to walk in the shadow of the Palais du Louvre, conscious of and comforted by the mass of its faded glory. She cherished the bleak history and timeless strength of the old palace, despite it suffering the indignity of its glorious art collections being scattered all over France at the approach of war. Worse, it was now said to be bursting with confiscated private collections, many of them Jewish, that had been 'safe-guarded' on the orders of Otto Abetz, Ribbentrop's two-faced friend and Hitler's acting ambassador to France. The Louvre had lived through bad times before. Both it and she would survive.

As she walked past the still shuttered Grands Magasins du Louvre on the other side, she noticed the line at the boulangerie on the corner of the Rue de l'Oratoire. All women. Like yesterday, the day before and the day before that. The bread they were queuing for was flat, coarse and grey and made from wheat flour cut with whatever the baker could find—corn, barley, potatoes, beans, rice. Even sawdust some people said. It was rationed at one baguette per adult, four days a week, if there were any loaves left by the time your turn came.

Food was always on everybody's minds, and there were frequent demonstrations for more, although they were always derided by the press as 'anti-patriotic conspiracies designed to sow dissent.'

Juliette kept her head down and switched her bag to the other shoulder. It was not that she didn't care about other people suffering, but life was grim for everybody. She, too, was hungry from time to time and she too had to queue for bread, but if she managed to gain luxuries once in a while, it was because she was prepared to take risks.

Like everybody else, Juliette had ration cards: category A [adult] and a category J1 [juvenile] for Camille though they only covered the basics. All kinds of other good things were available if you had the money: from fine wines and champagne to butter and coffee, olive oil and beef, smoked ham and fish. Even caviar. Anything could be bought on the black market, and everything had a price.

She walked straight on past the empty windows of La Samaritaine, avoiding the unsavoury cluster of dilapidated houses and medieval streets leading down to the river until she reached the crossroads at the Rue Saint-Denis. It was busy here, with people pouring onto the streets after the curfew and rushing to the central food market at Les Halles, where restaurateurs and shopkeepers battled with mothers and wives, fraudsters and conmen, thieves and scavengers for anything they could find.

Everybody knew demand exceeded supply: hence the bribery and kick-backs, the undeclared produce, and the animals raised in secret. And everyone knew that the problem was created by the Germans sending French farm produce straight to Germany. Juliette did what everybody else did and had to do: compete, argue and fight over the little available.

At the Rue Saint-Denis, Juliette turned right, past La Cabane, a *Maison de Tolérance* reserved for the Wehrmacht, where girls and their clients stood in small groups on the pavement, smoking cigarettes after a night of laughter, sex and cheap champagne. It was tempting to paint all the girls with the same brush, but many were desperate mothers with small children to feed, and others had sick or infirm family members. It was perilous work, not only because of the intrinsic risks, but because sleeping with the enemy was deemed traitorous, and the French police kept a register of their names.

There were plenty of other pretty girls at the Hotel Meurice each night, doing what they could to survive. German officers were not immune to the charms of French girls, especially with their wives far away. Sleeping with the French was formally forbidden in the luxurious hotel staffed solely by the military, but sleeping with French girls was permitted, off-the-record, for officers. Although Juliette felt safe under the protection of her General, it upset her to see other girls endanger themselves to stay alive.

Juliette remembered her father encouraging her to move to Paris when she was selected by the FFN eight years ago to train for the swimming team.

"You must go," he had said. "Pretty girls don't stay in villages, you know that. There aren't any pretty girls around here over eighteen. When girls are pretty, they move to the city, and when they are as pretty as you are, they move straight to Paris."

And he had been right. All the prettiest girls live in Paris.

Then came the glory of the 1936 Olympics and the gold medal: the celebrations, the cameras, the adulation, nationwide fame and recognition in the streets. Overnight she had become famous, *Championne de France* ! As she walked, Juliette reminisced about the constant attention.

Everything had been so effortless on her return, with interviews and photo shoots, contracts for modelling, celebrity appearances and endless parties and invitations to important occasions. She had money then and thank God she had bought her apartment on the Ile Saint-Louis while she could.

Things will get better again. Wars do not last forever.

She skirted the Théâtre du Chatelet to avoid two blue-clad workmen unfurling a giant poster announcing in French, 'Vienna Waltzes, an Operetta in two acts by Johann Strauss, father and son.' She turned left when she reached the Quai des Gesvres and followed the river past melancholy shapes hunched over fishing rods, motionless on the cold stones.

A long black barge, low in the river, pushed against the current, and the slow muffled chug of its engine echoed off the walls of the old hospital Hôtel Dieu, built by the river and close to Notre Dame to facilitate physical and spiritual cleanliness. It had been scorching this summer and later today it would be hot again and people would swim in the dark water.

Ever since her first evening at the Hotel Meurice, Juliette had felt ill at ease: stared at, ogled and lusted after. This evening had been no different, except this time the officers had worn dress uniforms with medals and swords, and ornate daggers in a symphony of black, grey, red and silver. It had appeared to be a special occasion of some kind, and so it proved after the usual heel-clicking, small talk and drinks.

After a preliminary address by Ambassador Otto Abetz, General Ernst von Schaumburg, distinguished and handsome in his grey *Waffenrock* tunic, medals, silver epaulets and dress dagger, had stepped onto the podium and taken the microphone.

He had begun by heaping praise on the senior SS officer Reinhard Heydrich, recently assassinated in Prague, before denouncing America's support for Britain and the immorality of Britain's thousand bomber raids on German cities. But as proof that the war was going Germany's way, he announced that Field Marshal Rommel had recently crushed the British Eighth Army in North Africa and captured forty-two thousand troops.

After the cheers and applause had died down, the hotel staff were asked to leave, and Juliette and the other girls were given a glass of champagne and instructed to wait in another room. And although they were not supposed to listen, the General's amplified voice was still audible and the French girls' command of German good enough for them to understand everything the General said.

They listened horrified as he announced Operation Spring Breeze, the imminent arrest a further twenty-eight thousand foreign Jews with the help of the French police. The arrests were to start on July 16 and taking part in the round-up would be the French fascist, pro-German youth movement, the JPF *Jeunesses Populaires Françaises*, [the French Popular Youth].

The address ended with the Nazi salute, answered by a shouted *Sieg Heil* from everyone present. Juliette had found the speech extremely disturbing, and the longer the evening wore on, the more boisterous it turned out to be and the more anxious she became to escape and go home.

Quite as troubling had been the sight of Pierre Bony and Henri Laffont among the crowd. She had recognised them immediately as leaders of the Carlingue, the French branch of the Gestapo. Bony was wearing traditional evening wear, but Laffont was dressed in the black uniform of a captain in the SS. Everybody knew they had been common criminals before the war who had ingratiated themselves with the Nazis in 1940—and that Laffont had brazenly taken German nationality.

All the French were terrified of them. They did the Germans' dirty work, specialising in spying on, blackmailing, stealing from, torturing and even murdering Parisians who had something to hide. Jews, homosexuals, the weak, the rich and the elderly. And they did it all with the tacit approval of the German authorities. They had frightened her when they smiled and wished her a good evening. They knew very well who she was.

Juliette had been shocked when France and Great Britain declared war on Germany on September 3, 1939. Everybody had been. But for the next eight months, little changed in Paris, and everybody carried on blithely with their lives unaware that outside France the Germans were furiously preparing for a real war, and when that awful reality reached the city, it arrived very swiftly.

On June 3, 1940, one hundred and fifty German bombers attacked the western suburbs of Paris, demolishing buildings and killing more than two hundred and fifty people. Within eight days, the Germans had trapped the French army in the north, and the government had fled west to Bordeaux, closely followed by two million Parisians fleeing any way they could: by train, bus, car, horse, or bicycle. Even on foot, carrying their most precious possessions in wheelbarrows.

Three days later, on June 14, German soldiers marched down the Champs Élysées to the music of military bands, Nazi swastikas replaced French tri-colour flags, and signposts in German materialised overnight in every main street in the city. Juliette had seen them arrive. Through circumstance rather than courage, she had stayed. She had little money saved and no family nearby and dared not abandon her apartment. Within days, all the city's clocks were reset to German time, and posters in French cropped up every-where:

ABANDONED POPULATIONS
Have Confidence in the German Soldier!

Paris was lost, and so was Juliette. And although the terror receded, it never entirely went away: dulled in the day by the need to survive, it always came back in the night. The Germans did not want trouble, but they wanted acquiescence and for the first few months, the German soldiers followed orders to charm the Parisians with exaggerated courtesy and good German manners—despite imposing constant curfews and the presence of twenty thousand troops. Yet within weeks, Parisians were being arrested for shaking their fists at the Wehrmacht or refusing to obey orders. Others were shot for vandalising posters or slashing tires. However, most of the invading soldiers had never been to any city before, let alone Paris, and the Parisian young from the better-off, bourgeois families were soon poking fun at the unsophisticated invaders.

They called themselves the Zazous and styled themselves as a satirical version of the British with rolled-up umbrellas, small moustaches and long, slicked-back hair, while the girls, parodying 1930s film stars, sported bleached blond hair with scarlet lips and smoky eyes behind large dark glasses. They flooded the terraces of the cafés on the Champs-Élysées and the Latin quarter to talk loudly and provocatively in fake British accents in the presence of German soldiers—or just as good, the socially-deprived though equally vocal, pro-German JPF. They trod a fine line and there were frequent clashes between the Zazous and the JPF.

Juliette was too conventional, too frightened and too recognisable to be a Zazou. Besides, she needed money to survive, and was thankful to find a job in an antique shop in the Rue Jacob on the Left Bank. Kept afloat by the rich with money to place and by collectors needing cash, it continued to flourish in fashionable Saint-Germain-des-Prés.

One day, in early October 1940, an expected customer arrived: it was General Ernst von Schaumburg from the nightclub in Berlin. Recently appointed Commander of Greater Paris, the General recognised Juliette at once, and that evening they had dinner together at the Brasserie Lipp on Boulevard Saint-Germain. He found her grace and beauty irresistible; she fell for his power and sophistication and within days she was his mistress, and her life became glamorous again.

Juliette's thoughts turned back to the Meurice, and she heaved her bag to the other shoulder. These dazzling evenings were momentary escapes from reality, as much for the Germans as for her. She knew she needed Ernst more than he would ever need her. He was sixty-two with a wife in Germany, kept a mansion on the Avenue Raphael, had a horse to ride every morning in the Bois de Boulogne, and a chauffeur to bring him to work. Juliette was twenty-three, single and walked home alone to a small child and a tiny apartment. She was his danseuse, and he could, might, and probably would discard her at any minute.

By the time Juliette passed the Rue du Pont Louis-Philippe, the weight of her bag was slowing her down. She switched shoulders once again and crossed over the Pont Marie bridge towards the Ile Saint-Louis where she lived. The sky was brighter, and the grey had turned yellow, promising a beautiful day. And then she stopped dead in her tracks.

Straight ahead, there was a disturbance of some kind. A crowd had gathered around a contingent of police outside the *Fondation Fernand Halphen*, a low-rent shelter for newly arrived, foreign Jews with large families. Those poor Jews. Chased from their own countries without possessions, very few could speak any French, and now they were forced to wear yellow stars. Juliette winced as she recalled the outrage a year ago when three thousand seven hundred Czech and Polish Jews went to police stations to have their status verified, only to be arrested and sent to the camps.

She was about to turn left towards her apartment on the Quai d'Anjou, when someone tapped on her shoulder. She was startled to see two police officers, Gardiens de la Paix, standing behind her.

"Good morning, Madame," said the older of the two as they touched the peaks of their kepis. "That's a heavy bag for a young lady like you. May we see inside?"

Juliette froze. Her first instinct was to scold them. How dare you! Don't you know who I am? I have friends in high places. Instead, she took the bag off her shoulder and opened it for them to examine.

"I've been to the market, to do some shopping," she said as brightly and charmingly as she was able, despite the pounding of her heart.

"You bought all this? With a ration card?" asked the officer, unconvinced.

"Good Lord no," said Juliette pulling out her Sonderausweis special pass as confidently as she could. "You can't get bread like this at a normal boulangerie."

The older officer took the pass and looked at it suspiciously, scrutinising it to see if it was counterfeit.

"Now that's a name to conjure with," he said, turning to the younger officer. "Guess who we've got here. Juliette Dumont. Mademoiselle Dumont won a gold medal for us in the '36 Olympics! It's an honour meet you, M'selle… But I have to ask where you got these groceries? And this early in the morning? Certainly not from a market around here."

Juliette took a deep breath and remembered how her father had taught her to be polite to men in uniform. A uniform gives a man courage he had said, and it makes a man feel invincible.

"I completely understand, officer, but I am just on my way home from visiting some friends on the Rue de Rivoli, and they gave me this bag as a gift."

The officer paused. "Is that so? They must be quite some friends who have a party that ends at this time in the morning and give out gifts like that. You know very well that none of this food is available through the normal channels and our job is to catch black marketeers. I am going to ask you again where you got this food from, or are we going to have to confiscate it and take you to the station for questioning?"

Juliette blanched but stood her ground. "I wouldn't do that if I were you," she said. "I don't think my friends would like that if I tell them. If you don't believe me, why don't you ask them yourselves?"

With that she produced a visiting card that read:

> Général Ernst von Schaumburg,
> Gouverneur Militaire du Grand Paris,
> 228 rue de Rivoli,
> Paris 1er.

The officers exchanged glances and paused. "In that case, Madame," said the older officer showing greater respect, "I don't think we need to take this matter any further."

"I would prefer that," said Juliette. "And to say thank you for your understanding, please take this home to your wife."

She reached into the bag for a saucisson sec, a dry-cured sausage and gave it to them.

"Thank you, thank you very much. Much appreciated, Madame. Sorry to have troubled you," enthused the officer as he took the sausage. They both snapped to attention and saluted.

It had taken her thirty-five minutes to reach 33 Quai d'Anjou.

Wearily, she pushed the heavy door and entered a diminutive courtyard lined with pots of tomatoes, lettuce, courgettes and potato plants, and wooden cages containing rabbits and chickens. A small door to the right opened onto a flight of spiral stone stairs, each step scooped and worn by the ages. She tiptoed past the grill of the concierge's window and began the long slog up to her apartment on the seventh floor.

As she trudged up the stairs step by step, she reflected anxiously on the commotion downstairs and what she had learned tonight—that thousands more Jews who had sought shelter in France were about to be arrested, and that French Jews were about to be banned from theatres and cafés.

Things were getting worse by the day, and she needed to decide what to do. Should she hope the Germans win, and that things turn out for the best? But what if they lose? In two years, she had seen attitudes in the Hotel Meurice change from supreme confidence in German superiority to doubt, anger, and stress. The truth was inescapable. Times were changing, and the bellicose episode at the Meurice tonight had scared her.

She was exhausted by the time she reached her apartment, but at least she knew what to do. It was time to face reality and join Bernard. She turned the key silently in the lock. Nadia's bedroom door was open, and Juliette put her head in.

"Good morning, Nadia," she whispered. "Awake already?"

Nadia was lying propped up by pillows on her simple brass bed, reading by the early morning light streaming from the window in the sloping roof. Next to her, Camille lay sleeping in a small child's bed.

"Good morning," breathed Nadia. "So how was it? How was your evening? Can we talk in your room? Did you bring anything?"

Nadia slid off the bed and they moved silently to the kitchen.

"I brought all sorts of things," said Juliette. "I did well tonight."

She opened her bag and pulled out a full loaf of country bread, a pound of butter, a bottle of olive oil, twelve eggs, a full-fat Camembert cheese, two bags of lentils, a bottle of milk and a small carton of cream.

"And I brought this for us," Juliette said, grinning as she pulled out a fine bottle of wine from the Loire.

"A feast! That should keep us going for ages," said Nadia in a low voice. "You are amazing."

"I'm not amazing. The kitchen staff is amazing, though it is going to have to keep us going for a while because the time is coming to make changes. Nadia, I've been thinking. We need to leave Paris. Every day at the Meurice, it's getting worse, and I am becoming scared."

Nadia looked up from Juliette's haul with wide eyes. "This is very sudden, isn't it? Where are we going? And what about papers? The only papers I have are an out-of-date *carte-de-séjour* from before the war and my German passport."

Juliette held Nadia in her arms and pulled her close. "My love, there is nothing to worry about. We are going to join Bernard in the south, and when I told Ernst about it, he didn't even blink. More than anybody, he knows that changes are coming, and the war is ramping up. He even asked how he could help. He's been a real gentleman about it, Nadia. He remembers you from the Resi in 1936 and knows we live together. He's even promised to get us travel permits and authorise the issue of an ID card in the name of Nadine Beausoleil."

A wave of relief swept over Nadia's face.

"We must get rid of your German passport and your carte-de-séjour as soon as possible. From now on, you are changing your name officially and are going to be one-hundred percent French."

Juliette gazed into Nadia's large eyes with a pang of guilt. Despite not leaving the small apartment for nearly two years, Nadia had always remained positive, and never complained. But how tired and thin her face was. Then she saw the tears running down Nadia's face.

"Please don't cry, Nadia," she said. "We have to remain strong."

"These are tears of happiness, you imbecile," said Nadia wiping away the tears with her hand. "Let's do it, let's leave Paris, let's go down to the South. I want to find a way to make myself useful, instead of staying cooped up here, in this little flat."

Chapter 6

QUESTIONS

···

WITH THE DAWNING OF A NEW DAY, the Mistral was no more than a caress, and yesterday's worries had faded with Max and the night. Juliette was in the pool, and she even waved and called out: "Good morning, little one."

For the next few days, everything was normal again, and Camille took coffee with her mother before going to work and kissed her in the evening when she came home. But on Saturday morning at ten to nine, dark clouds rolled in again.

"Camille, I want to see you in Bernard's office in five minutes, please."

Juliette was standing at the door of Camille's cottage, and Camille recoiled at her narrow eyes and flushed cheeks. She bit her lip and held her head in her hands. What now? Could this be about Max again? With her head held high, she made her way to the main house, knocked on Bernard's door and entered.

Bernard sat behind his desk with his arms folded across his chest, stiff and ill-at-ease. Juliette stood behind him to his left, her right hand on his shoulder, and she motioned Camille to sit down in the straight-backed, armless chair in front of them.

"Camille, you know I have many friends in the area. Since we last spoke about your cigarette-smoking friend, it has come to my notice that everybody in Provence, except Bernard, Nadia and me apparently, knows about your relationship with him. That is your business. Yes, you are grown-up, and you have the right to choose your friends. But I want to ask you this."

Juliette's lips were so tightly pursed, the words had difficulty escaping from her mouth, and her voice was harsh and thin.

Leaning in towards Camille, she said: "How much do you know about your friend Max? Do you know, for example, that he was convicted of stealing a car?" She wagged a finger and leaned closer to Camille. "Do you know that he spent two years in prison in Clermont Ferrand for his part in a bank robbery?"

She leaned back, fiery with triumph.

Juliette had done it again. Camille gripped her chair with both hands, about to faint. She opened her mouth to speak, but no words came, just a low moan.

"You may wonder how I know, and if it's true?" Juliette leaned forward again. "I have friends, Camille, friends in important places, high-powered friends, people of note. For your information, the Prefect of Provence is a good friend of mine, and I asked him to make inquiries about your garage attendant friend—yes, I know he works at the garage—and this is what he told me: this person, I cannot bring myself to say his name, is known to the police as a petty criminal. Not only that, but he is a pauper and a peasant, and recorded as only having had one year of school. He is a criminal, Camille, a useless, uneducated criminal."

Juliette folded her arms as Bernard unfolded his. He leaned forward and put his elbows on his desk and held his cheeks in his hands.

"And," she continued, "let me make this clear. I forbid you to EVER invite him to the house again, for my sake and yours. I cannot prevent you from seeing him, but should you choose to do so, you should know this: you will risk not only my disapproval but also that of Bernard. And your inheritance."

She turned to Bernard, who looked up and nodded silently.

Camille shook her head silently, her cheeks streaked with tears. With no defence and nothing else to say, she glared at her mother and said defiantly: "Is that it? May I go now?"

She returned to her room in a daze. She had been eyes-shut happy in London with Leo, neither wanting, nor expecting to meet anyone else. Even here in Provence, she had been happy enough in an undemanding, low-key way until the day Max had invited her for a drink.

This was all too much. For ten minutes, she lay despairingly on her bed until anger replaced self-pity. Damn Max. Despite her better instincts, she had lowered her guard. Damn him. She strode to the bathroom to shower and wash away the tears. Max would be at the garage, and she would go and confront him and straighten this out.

Camille changed into a white, knee-length, sleeveless cotton dress and hurried to collect her car, taking care to keep out of sight as she passed the kitchen window. Max's garage was only minutes away, and immediately she saw him standing on the forecourt, she could see he was alone. She glanced at herself in the rear-view mirror and ruffled her hair with her hands.

Damn, damn, damn.

Switching off the engine, she ran over to where he stood, wiping his hands with a rag.

"Max, I have to talk to you urgently. Now."

She was surprised and gratified that the tone of her voice made Max's eyes widen with alarm. "By all means, Camille, what is it? What's the matter? We can talk here."

Max, his hands on his hips, listened attentively as Camille recounted everything her mother had told her.

"Is it true, Max? Please tell me. You have to tell the truth."

Max put down the oily rag.

"Come with me into the office. We can sit down and talk more freely. Yes, every word is true, Camille. I did take a car when I was sixteen, almost seventeen. It was abandoned during the war, and I found it in a shed covered in dirt and managed to get it going. A policeman saw me driving it around and accused me of stealing it. I tried to explain it was abandoned, but of course I got reprimanded. And the story about the safe? Yes, that's true too. Some friends of mine found an old safe and asked me to help them open it. I'm good at that sort of thing, with locks and things. What they didn't tell me was that they'd found the safe in a bank."

Max pulled a loose Gitanes from his blue overalls and cupped his hands to light it. He inhaled deeply and continued. "Anyway, I was accused with them of bank robbery and sent to prison for a while. But, most importantly, what your mother didn't tell you, is that I joined the French Foreign Legion after that."

The hint of a smile crossed his face as he exhaled a thin cloud of smoke.

"Why?" he continued. "You've probably heard that anyone can join the Foreign Legion anonymously with no questions asked. And anyone means anyone, whatever your nationality, religion, education, or criminal history. It means you can start your life again and, if you serve your time and haven't murdered anyone, your crimes can be removed from the written record. So, I started my life again."

Camille's anger flooded away as she listened to him. "So, does that mean you do, or you don't have a criminal record?"

"Camille, it means I don't, and whoever told your mother I do is in the wrong. And there must be records of my service in the legion to prove it."

Camille put her arms around him and pulled his face to hers. "I knew it," she said, kissing him firmly on the mouth. "I am so relieved. Why did you never mention the Foreign Legion before? That's amazing, so romantic. Or was it horrible?" she added gently.

"Put it this way," said Max, "it was not a picnic. I was in the First Parachute Regiment, and there were three times as many Germans as Frenchmen in those days. The Legion was practically made up of ex-Wehrmacht. They weren't allowed to join the German army of course, and it was the only job they could find after the war."

"Germans in the French Foreign Legion?"

"Absolutely! That's the point of the Foreign Legion. It was created to allow foreigners to join the French Army, so we had people from all over. British, Spanish, Algerian. Even some Americans. Though many of the Wehrmacht were *Malgré-Nous*, you know, French-speaking lads from Alsace who had joined the German army."

Max paused. "There were other, real Germans too, but everybody was checked for tattoos."

"Tattoos?"

"To weed out the *Waffen-SS*. They couldn't join because they were too violent. Most soldiers had tattoos of one kind or another, but the SS had their blood type tattooed under their arms. They wore them like a badge of honour."

Camille's eyes shone as she listened and as if seeing Max in a new light.

"You know my mother ordered me never to see you again? Damn her. She'll never believe me if I tell her what you said."

Max took her hand and led her from the small office and put his hands on her shoulders. "Camille, now listen to me. You are old enough to make up your own mind. She can't tell you what to do."

"I know, but she does, Max. At least she tries to. What is more, she has threatened to disinherit me if I keep seeing you."

Max's black eyes became darker still. "In that case, she is never going to know. Now go home and stop worrying. I'll take care of everything."

Back in her cottage by the pool, Camille felt safe again and more attracted to him than ever. He was so strong, and whatever her mother thought of him, Max did not have a criminal record. But if they were to continue seeing each other, they would have to be discreet.

※

Ten long days passed before Camille saw Max again at the Bar de la Paix in Aix. As she walked to their usual table at the back, he stood up when he saw her and quickly drained his glass. He smiled broadly as she approached and pushed his long hair back with his hands and leaned forward to kiss her.

"Ah Camille, I've missed you. I'm so pleased to see you."

"Hello Max, You're excited. What's going on?"

"I have some news that may interest you about your mother." Max signalled to the waiter. "I, too, have friends who know people, and I have been doing a little digging of my own. Your mother was in a rush to leave Paris."

François arrived to take their order, and Camille asked for a coffee. Max ordered a second *fée verte*.

"A green fairy? What kind of drink is a green fairy?" asked Camille with a laugh, "that doesn't sound very manly!"

"Oh Camille! What a protected life you've led. It's slang for pastis. That's what they called absinthe before the Great War. The green fairy. You haven't lived Camille if you don't know what a fée verte is!"

"Are you serious? You're drinking pastis at ten in the morning?"

Max composure changed a shade, and a fleeting trace of pique crossed his face. "I'm celebrating Camille! And please don't interrupt me. I was telling you, your mother left Paris in a hurry."

"I know she left Paris in a hurry, I told you that. She left because she was getting scared and wanted to join Bernard."

Max shook his head. "I know, but the point is your mother was famous. Everybody noticed her. She turned a lot of heads after winning her gold medal. She was very young, but she was also very beautiful. But what did she do in Paris? How did she survive? When the Germans arrived in June 1940, most Parisians fled to the country, and the few who didn't, only stayed because they had nowhere to go."

"My mother stayed because that's where her friends were, and that was where her apartment was. Besides, she had nowhere to go either. What are you saying, Max?"

"Your mother was not only famous in France; she was famous in Germany. The last Olympic games were in Berlin, remember, and she was very young and exceptionally pretty."

"Yes, I know all this. What are you trying to say?"

Max leaned forward towards Camille and lowered his voice.

"You remember me telling you that there were German soldiers with me in the Foreign Legion? Well, Pierre—you met him in the Bon Accueil—was in the Legion, too, which was where I met him. Anyway, he has a Wehrmacht friend called Otto who remembers Juliette Dumont very well. He speaks French, so was chosen to work at the Hotel Meurice in the Rue de Rivoli in Paris, where the German Kommandantur for Greater Paris was headquartered."

Max leaned in closer. "According to Otto, your mother used to go to the Meurice quite a lot and was friendly with some German officers."

"I don't believe it. How does he know it was my mother?"

"She was famous, for God's sake. Everybody knew who she was. She wasn't exactly inconspicuous. She used to come to the hotel all the time."

Camille stared at him, unable to think clearly. "And you think this is true?"

Max leaned back in his chair and lit a cigarette as François arrived with a small circular tray carrying the glass of clear green pastis, a carafe of water and Camille's coffee.

"Absolutely, it's true. Otto has no reason to lie or make it up. Your mother was not only well-known, but she was also exceptionally beautiful, and young men don't forget beautiful young women. Especially famous ones who visit German officers in the night."

"Wait a minute! What are you insinuating?"

"I'm not sure yet. All I know, Camille, is that your mother spent a lot of time at the Hotel Meurice. More than a young French girl should, and I intend to find out why."

"So basically, you're suggesting my mother was sleeping with a German officer?" Camille spoke testily in a low voice, though could not help but be intrigued.

"I don't know, Camille. But what else was she doing at the Meurice? She must have had reasons to go there. They wouldn't let anyone into the headquarters of the German army without a good reason. My guess is that she was having an affair with a German officer in the hotel, and that had something to do with the fact that she left Paris when she did. Why? I don't know yet. Maybe she came to the notice of the Resistance and was fingered as a collaborator."

"My mother, a collaborator? I doubt that. She is very much a patriot. She must have had a purpose to go there. Anyway, what's the point? What's the point of finding out more? The war's been over for more than twenty years, for pity's sake."

"Camille, I'm sure you know that they called sleeping with a German collaboration *horizontale*. I am not saying she was a traitor. Most collaborators were only trying to stay alive, so she probably never even thought about the politics. I don't believe your mother was pro-German for a second, but we can't take anything for granted."

Max looked hard into Camille's eyes and her concern must have been easy to read. "People crossed all kinds of lines to survive."

It was unsettling for Camille to hear such things about her mother but enthralling all the same. They agreed that Max should continue to make inquiries, and the Bar de la Paix would be their meeting place. Nobody in the bar knew who they were, and it was unlikely that either Juliette, Bernard, or any of their friends would ever frequent such a working-class place.

❧

The following Tuesday they were at the Bar de la Paix again, after the garage closed.

"So, what's your news? How have you been?" Max stood up to kiss her hello.

"Missing you. It's been hell at the house. Bernard has been diagnosed with cancer of the prostate. It's in the early stages, so we don't know how serious it is yet. But you can imagine my mother: she's going crazy, convinced he's going to die any minute."

Max held her chair for her as she sat down. "That's not good, cancer. You should be careful not to catch it, too."

"I beg your pardon," said Camille, trying not to laugh. "First, women don't have a prostate; and secondly, you can't catch cancer."

"Oh please, have an open mind, Camille. You think you know everything. Just do what I say," said Max. "Tell your mother to be sure to put a bowl of rendered fat in his room."

"Do what?" asked Camille and burst into laughter.

"That makes you laugh? You bloody people with your money and education; you think you know it all. But Camille, let me tell you this, it works! Country people have known this for centuries. It won't cure him, but if you make sure there's a bowl of fat in the room with him, nobody else will catch the cancer."

"Well, my mother's not afraid of catching cancer: she's scared he'll die, and she'll never see him again. She doesn't believe in God, so we've been talking about the afterlife."

"The afterlife? Don't tell me you believe in life after death?"

"Yes, I do. At least I think I do. I was brought up a Catholic, remember."

"Dear God, Camille, you are so bourgeoise. So how about my dog, Coco? You think I'll see him again when I am dead?"

"I doubt it, Max. Only humans have souls."

"All humans, or only rich ones and good ones? What about the poor ones and the bad ones? For example, do you think Hitler had a soul?"

Camille was surprised and disappointed by his antagonism. "Poor humans, bad humans, all humans have souls," she said softly. "The point is we all have to account for our lives."

"And what about half-wits? Those born with half a brain like my little brother. I didn't tell you about him, did I? He was incapable of doing anything and lay there like a vegetable until he died at twelve. Does he have an afterlife, too?"

"Yes, Christian teaching says we are all God's children."

Max tipped back in his chair, cupped his hands and lit a cigarette. He scrutinised the ceiling, then looked at Camille.

"Back in the Auvergne, I spent a lot of time thinking, watching life every day, and I can tell you I never saw a sign of God in the mountains or the valleys. Or any sign of life after death. All I saw was a never-ending battle between life and death. Life bursting out everywhere and death just waiting for it, determined to snuff it out."

Max gazed into his pastis and contemplated the cloudy liquid.

"I was amazed by how driven life is. I still am. It never gives up, Camille. It keeps on adapting, and reinventing itself, doing anything and everything to cheat death. But death is always there in the shadows, darkly waiting, thinking up new ways to smother life."

Max took a sip of pastis.

"I used to think I was watching an evenly matched battle. Life against death, and death against life: a desperate instinct to survive competing with a brutal instinct to kill. But then it hit me: it's not an evenly matched battle at all."

Max moved a little closer to Camille, his eyes narrowed, his gaze unequivocal.

"Camille, death always wins. The more interesting battle is life against life, when life-forms fight other forms of life, each adapting desperately to avoid death. Think about it. Different forms of life never help each other live longer or stand shoulder to shoulder against death. They may tolerate the existence of another life form, until their own interests are compromised—or food gets scarce. Then every living thing will compete against every other living thing and won't hesitate to kill others to survive. It's all about survival, at any cost."

Camille sat in silence as she listened to him, bitter and despairing, as if his conclusions disheartened him and he had reached them reluctantly.

"You know," Max continued, "today, the thought of death doesn't bother me anymore. I don't even think about it. Life and death are facts of life, like my pastis or your coffee. Our glasses were full once; now they're half-empty. I am alive now, so I'll die one day. The life-death struggle will go on forever until one side wins. Death will either wipe all forms of life from this earth, or we'll find the secret to immortality. In both cases, God will be irrelevant."

Camille waved a cloud of blue smoke away from her face. "I hate to hear you talk like that. It's cynical and depressing. So, you don't believe in a greater power—or life after death at all?"

"I wish I did Camille, but it's dog eat dog. And that's the way it is."

Camille was silent for a moment. She could never accept such a depressing view of existence and wondered if she could convince this strange, unusual man of the transformative power of belief. Max's thoughts, muddled or not, were based on reasoning, on philosophy.

"You are missing out on life, Max. All that time, talking to yourself in the mountains has made you think one-dimensionally, only about what affects you. Did you never stare at the night sky and wonder about the mystery of the infinite? But I suppose it's good that at least you think about it," she said gently, almost to herself, "like Peter Abelard…"

"Peter who?"

"Peter Abelard. He was a medieval priest and philosopher, a teacher at the Sorbonne who had trouble with a basic precept of Christianity; you have to believe before you can understand. He rejected that and said that he had to understand before he could believe. Doubting is good because by doubting, you ask questions, and by questioning, you arrive at the truth."

Max grinned.

"I agree with Peter! That's what I do," he said. "I question everything."

Camille laughed. "I think you really would like him; he was a rebel like you. He said people should take intentions into account when judging consequences, not just the letter of the law. I believe that too."

"Camille, that's the difference between us—you learned everything from books and other people. I learned everything from nature, by myself. Yet somehow we reach the same conclusions."

Camille smiled. "Yes, we do, don't we? So, did you learn anything else about my mother?"

"I did. Otto contacted one of his friends who worked at the Meurice with him, and he remembered her too. And Pierre found out something else. During the war, he worked as an informer for the police and still has contacts there. Now get this: the French police had a dossier on your famous mother, and they knew she was highly thought of by the Germans and the mistress of a senior German officer."

Camille had never wondered how her mother, a single mother from a simple family, had managed for money during the war.

"So, if the French police had a dossier on her, you can bet the Germans, the Carlingue and the Resistance all had dossiers on her too. It's even possible they all wanted her to work for them, which is why she got scared and decided to leave Paris. You can't blame her, that's a lot of pressure. Especially knowing what the Resistance did to collaborators."

"A collaborator? That word again. I suppose she was in a way. What a thought."

"Life was hard. She had you to feed, and it wasn't so rare to collaborate. Lots of people thought the Germans were better than the Communists or the Americans. And some liked the idea of a new European Order after the decadence of the 1920s and '30s."

Max tossed his head back and finished the last of his drink.

"Let's not judge her," said Camille. "If the Resistance had really thought she was a traitor, they would have killed her, because after August '44, they hunted down and executed traitors."

"All right, that's true. So, let's assume they didn't classify her as a traitor as such, though that makes her very lucky because many other women who slept with Germans were humiliated. We all know lots of women were paraded in public and had their heads shaved. And some were tarred and feathered," said Max signalling to François.

"By the way, did you ever see the film *Les Enfants du Paradis* starring Arletty?"

"I think everybody has, haven't they?" replied Camille.

"Like your mother, Arletty was famous, but she was arrested in 1945 for an affair with a German officer. Do you know what she said in her defence?"

"No, but I have a feeling you're about to tell me," Camille leaned forward.

"She said 'my heart is French, but my ass is international.' Don't you love it?"

"I do! I love it!" Camille said, throwing back her head and laughing. "That I did not know. Whatever happened to her?"

"She was imprisoned for a while, had her head shaved and was paraded through the streets… Less funny."

Both were silent and when Camille looked up, Max was staring at her. "I hope I haven't upset you, about your mother."

"No, that's all right, but I can see why she never talks about the war. I don't know what, or if anything ever happened to her. Nobody in the house ever mentions the war, though Bernard probably knows."

"One person who is sure to know is Madame Beausoleil. You said they lived together and are the same age. What's going on there? You say she never married and was living with your mother before the war. Do you think they're hiding something? Did she go to the Meurice, too?"

"Max, you're forgetting. I've already told you many times, Nadia's job was to care for me. Why are you so interested in her?"

"Camille, she's like a ghost. Neither Otto nor Pierre can find anything in the records about her. The only trace is an identity card issued in July '42 and a German travel authorisation from Paris to Marseille dated August 2, accompanying you and your mother. No birth certificate, no ration card, nothing before 1942. She came out of nowhere."

"Max, what's the point of this? I really don't care."

"In those days, secrets could mean life or death. Camille, your mother doesn't like me, so I need to know these things. But I will tell you this: when she knows that I know everything, she'll change her attitude to me."

"Oh, so you plan to tell her?"

"Tell her? Lord no! Not even blackmail her." Max laughed as he lit another cigarette. "I don't want anything from her, just to be treated normally and allowed to see you. That's all I want."

"You don't let go, do you?" said Camille. "You're like a dog with a bone." She leaned in to kiss him.

"But a wickedly attractive one."

❧

When Camille arrived home, she was elated. Her mother was not so perfect after all, and Max was right: knowledge is power. She poured herself a larger than usual glass of wine.

Camille and Max saw each other more frequently after that, though always on his terms and at her place.

"Listen, Camille. You live in a chateau. I sleep in a little room above the garage. I don't feel comfortable you coming to my place."

So, the preferred once or twice-a-week places of liaison became Camille's house for secret trysts late at night, and the Bar de la Paix for meetings after work. And, inexplicably, Juliette did become kinder to Camille, perhaps because she concluded that she and Max no longer saw each other. Or because Max had been able to reach her and tell her what he knew. In any case, the subject of Max never came up at the Chateau de Vaucluse, and life on the surface reverted to the dull routine of pre-Max days.

❧

On Thursday, November 16, 1967, a curious incident occurred.

At sixty-one, Bernard had been progressively slowing down since being diagnosed with cancer. The debilitating effects of systemic hormonal therapy to lower his testosterone levels caused shortness of breath and cardiovascular problems. On top of which, he had to swallow large doses of oestrogen as a form of chemical castration. Consequently, Bernard spent most of his time not feeling well in his bedroom, either in bed or sitting at his desk.

One day, sorting through his papers, he discovered that a sealed envelope in which he kept his will had been opened and resealed. It was at once a mystery. How could someone have entered his room, opened the safe, and gone through the will without him noticing?

Juliette thought she knew the answer. "Camille, I know you've just got back from work, but I want to see you in Bernard's room now, please."

Camille's hackles rose, but she followed her mother from the kitchen into the hall and left into Bernard's room. Bernard was sitting up in bed, pale and unshaven.

"Camille," began Juliette, standing with her arms folded, "you know that I have done my best to bring you up with a sense of honour, to take account of other people's feelings and never to steal or tell a lie?"

"Yes, I know that." Camille said quietly.

"Bernard has brought it to my attention that someone has been going through his papers. Worse, that someone has opened the envelope containing Bernard's will and resealed it very clumsily. Now, only four people know the combination number of the safe: I know it, Nadia knows it, Bernard knows it, and you know it."

"So naturally, you think it was me?" asked Camille, her voice rising.

"Well, I don't know who else it could have been!"

With a start, Camille thought of Max, amazed that her mother had not mentioned him. Max knew how to open safes. Was it him? She needed to calm the situation.

"Maman, you said yourself that you brought me up to always tell the truth. I promise you that I did no such thing. How could I have? How could anyone? Bernard is here in his room all day and all night, aren't you, Bernard? You would have seen or heard someone coming into your room, wouldn't you?"

Bernard nodded. Juliette was staring at Camille, poker-faced.

"Don't you think it is possible," Camille went on, "that this didn't happen recently, but some time ago and you've only just noticed it? Could you, Bernard, have opened and resealed the envelope a long time ago? Surely, someone else opening it would have resealed it more carefully so nobody would notice?"

"I don't know," said Bernard weakly, "but that makes sense. It might be possible. My memory isn't as good as it used to be."

Juliette stood silently, her arms still folded, taken aback by the argument and Camille's strength in refuting her accusation.

"I have my doubts," said Juliette and her expression showed how dubious she remained. "You may go now, Camille."

On her way back to her cottage, Camille collected some bread from the kitchen and picked some fresh basil from the kitchen garden. Once home, she poured herself a glass of rosé and made some *pistou* sauce with cloves of garlic, fresh basil and olive oil, crushing and mixing the ingredients with a mortar and pestle.

Was it possible that Max broke in to check the will? If anybody could do it, Max could. But why? To make sure they had not disinherited her? Yet surely he would have resealed the envelope more carefully. She decided the most plausible explanation was the one she had given Juliette, and unless Max gave her some other reason not to trust to him, she would not mention the incident.

Chapter 7

LONDON, JULY 1963

"**C**OME ON, CAMILLE, GET ON WITH IT. SPEED IT UP," yelled David.

Camille smiled to herself. Yes, David, get on with it. Speed it up. And forgave him.

Everybody knew he was a perfectionist and became overstressed when cooking, which was another reason the food was so damn good, and the place had a reputation as one of the best French restaurants in London. And it was always busy.

Camille grabbed the hot plates and whisked them over to a couple sitting by the window.

"Sorry to keep you waiting," she said, putting the young woman's dish down first.

"*Caneton à l'orange à ma façon*, for you, Mademoiselle," she said, and turning to the young man, she placed the second dish in front of him. "And *Steak au poivre*, with a peppercorn, cognac and cream sauce for Monsieur."

Camille had lived in London for close to two years, working the lunch shift at *Mon Plaisir* and attending evening classes at the Regent Street Polytechnic School of Photography. She had concluded that her interest lay in counterculture and the arts. Yet, her parents knew no one creative, and Ventabren was a cultural backwater. The nearest thing in the village to anything faintly artistic was graffiti on a wall by the church: *créer, c'est vivre deux fois* [to create is to live twice].

This was the second time she had worked as a waitress since leaving school, the first being at a family restaurant in Aix. After six months, she had found a better job in a bookshop on the Cours Mirabeau, specialising in international literature, fine art and travel. It was there she came across the work of French photographer Henri Cartier-Bresson and learned that he had become fluent in English studying at Cambridge University. It had been a revelation, and she began to think about learning English and moving to London or New York. And the more she thought about it, the more convinced she became that she should do it. She had to leave this sheltered corner of Provence or risk ending up like her parents.

"Miss, please, Miss," the young man was calling her. "May we have some more wine, please?"

Camille awoke from her thoughts and went over to the table.

"Another of the same, please?" The young man smiled at her amiably, holding up the empty bottle. "You're new here, aren't you? I haven't seen you here before."

Camille smiled back at him. God, the British drink a lot. A bottle each?

"No, I'm not new here, though this is my first time working in the evening." She filled the water glasses as she spoke. "I've been serving lunch here for years."

"I should have been coming here for lunch then!" said the young man flirtatiously. "I love your accent, by the way! Oh là là, so chic!"

He laughed.

A week later, he was back at the restaurant again, sitting at a table by himself.

"Hello, french girl," he said, "remember me? I've been thinking about you. I'm Leo. Leo Foster."

Camille nodded. "Yes, I remember you."

"So, what's your name?" Leo asked.

"You can guess it if you want," she replied coyly, "but let me take your order first. May I get you a drink while you decide?"

By the end of the evening, they knew each other's names, and he was openly flirting with her. And when Camille mentioned that she studied photography at the Regent, his face lit up.

"Get away! That's amazing! That's what I do! I'm a photographer. I take photographs for agencies and magazines, doing advertising and fashion work."

Camille turned away towards the kitchen as if she wasn't interested.

"We're always on the lookout for new talent. Would you like me to take some test shots of you?"

"Test shots of me? I could never afford it on what I earn." Camille said. "Anyway, I'm more interested in being behind the camera than in front of it…"

Leo burst out laughing. "Why behind the camera? I love the way you look. I won't charge you anything. TMP. Time For Prints. I'll give you copies. No charge. What do you say?"

His honest, boyish face was framed by long blond hair, and his smiling eyes were green. And he exuded the unselfconscious sincerity of someone she could trust.

"You are very sweet and persuasive, but there is one thing I actually would like to do." She hesitated. "I would love to see your cameras and your studio?"

"Of course! It would be my pleasure!" Leo enthused. "Here, take my business card, and come and see me next week. My studio is around the corner in Neal's Yard. Come around on Monday morning at ten if you can. That would be best. I'll expect you."

Camille took the card. His studio was minutes from the restaurant.

"Thank you," she said quietly. "Monday works for me. I'll see you then."

Camille loved the freedom she had in London to be who she wanted to be without reference to background, convention, or etiquette. She could say anything, wear anything and do anything she wanted to do. She could be herself. Simply French.

At first, everything had been dauntingly unfamiliar; the language, the foreign money and driving on the left. The taxi fare from the station had been £1/2s/6d, however much that was. All she knew was that twelve pence made one shilling, twenty shillings made a pound, and one pound was worth about forty French francs. And all those coins! Half-crowns, florins, shillings, sixpences, threepenny pieces, pennies, half-pennies and farthings.

The accents of Londoners were hard to understand, though she soon came to love their kindness and good nature, and dry, self-deprecating sense of humour. The young were more liberated and worldly than they were in her corner of France, where the dark clouds of prejudice and post-war gloom still held people back. Here people expressed themselves freely, grew beards, dyed their hair and dressed provocatively. New boutiques and coffee bars were opening everywhere, and everybody was obsessed by the Beatles or the Rolling Stones, owned a transistor radio, used the words trendy, dig and gear, and played or wanted to learn to play an electric guitar.

London, indeed the whole country, was engaged in a social revolution. Self-expression and experimentation were breaking out everywhere as people discarded convention and opted to become an artist or a poet, a philosopher or a musician. The beatniks and rock and roll from America supplied the spark, and the arrival of the birth control pill and the end of national service in the United Kingdom did the rest. Creativity bred more creativity, and London positively pulsated with optimism and new ideas, and Camille was thrilled to be part of it. She could feel it in Notting Hill Gate, a once-grand area where she lived in a bedsitter on Westbourne Grove, a broad street lined with restaurants and shops selling old paintings and bric-a-brac, a short walk from the flamboyant Portobello Road market.

Of the six rooms in the house rented as bed-sitters, Camille's room was the largest with two tall windows overlooking the road. After Provence, it felt not only strange, but disconcerting on all levels to be living in a single rented room on a noisy street in a foreign country. And it took time to get used to the coin-operated meters controlling the electricity and gas—and sharing a bathroom with five other fellow renters. Once a week Camille telephoned her parents from a phone booth tucked beneath the stairs.

"Just put in some coins," a tenant told her, "dial your number, and press button 'A' when the other person answers. That makes the coins drop. If no one answers, press button 'B' and you get your money back."

Camille soon learned it was simpler to book a long-distance call in advance through the operator; and reverse the charges.

❧

Neal's Yard was a cobblestoned maze of warehouses and workshops serving the nearby fruit and vegetable market of Covent Garden, and the Leo Foster Studio consisted of an old stable and a warehouse converted into a high-ceilinged workplace, complete with darkroom and office. It made for a spacious photographer's studio in a picturesque courtyard, flanked by an importer of fruit on one side and a cheese storeroom on the other. And every morning when the local market closed, an army of cleaners swept the narrow streets to clear spills and refuse and keep the vermin away.

Mon Plaisir was a two-minute walk away in adjoining Monmouth Street.

"Oh! Perfect! I love it," enthused Leo. "Hold it right there. Yes, yes, keep it like that!"

Camille had been unable to resist Leo's charm and he had persuaded her to let him photograph her wearing one of his studio props: a long white dress, flowing and diaphanous.

"You're a dancer, Camille. I see you as a dancer, like Isadora Duncan," he cried. "So let me see you dance! Your body is your soul! Dance, Camille, dance! Don't be tame. Be wild!"

The champagne he had insisted on serving helped shed her inhibitions, and to the pounding sounds of the Beatles' first album Please Please Me, Camille danced and twirled and posed in various stages of undress, jumping up, falling down, leaning back and bending forward, her eyes fixed on Leo's lens.

Leo was on the floor one moment, up a ladder the next, feverishly clicking and turning the handle on his Hasselblad camera, an assistant supplying him with preloaded film backs when he needed them. Every now and then, a makeup artist shouted, "Stop" and rushed forward to adjust Camille's hair or her makeup.

"Oh, yes! You're perfect, oh yes, yes! You're a natural!" he kept calling out, "Oh là là... I love it!"

At last, the pops of the flashes ceased, and Camille collapsed, exhausted.

"You were wonderful," said Leo. "The prints will be ready by Friday."

⊱

On Friday, Camille stopped at Leo's studio on her way to work.

"How are they? How did the photos turn out?" she asked anxiously.

"I'll let you decide, though I have to say I love them. Come and see."

Camille followed Leo through to the meeting room where twenty large prints of her were pinned to the wall.

"Well, what do you think? Don't you love them? I am going to show them to all my clients."

Camille stood in shock and said nothing. She had never thought of herself as particularly glamorous nor seen professional photos of herself.

"Leo, *mon ami*, I am lost for words. These are amazing, incredible. I can hardly believe they are me. Thank you, thank you so much!" and she stood on the tips of her toes to kiss him on the cheek.

"My pleasure," said Leo beaming, and handed her a large envelope. "Here are some copies for you."

Within days, they were sleeping together, and when it turned out she was not the new face his clients were looking for, he asked if she would consider working for him.

"I am not sure that's a good idea, Leo. Doing what?" Camille hesitated.

"Of course, it's a good idea! Please, say yes, Camille! I want you around me to help with my clients. Besides, you can always help in the darkroom, developing and making prints. You know all that from your classes at the Regent. Please? See how you like it, and we'll take it from there."

Camille gazed back at his appealing, sweet face and brightened up. "All right, I accept, but it will have to be part time at first. I can't leave my job straightaway."

It did not take long for Camille to understand what an extraordinary opportunity it was to work in a studio such as Leo's. Within a week, she had handed in her notice at the restaurant and started working side by side with him as his principal assistant, arranging shoots with advertising agencies and famous fashion magazines. She soon learned that Leo was immensely popular and very good at what he did, and not only did his clients find him charismatic and easy-going, but Camille did too. And without protest, she found herself falling more deeply by the day for his charms.

It was three months after meeting Leo, a week before Christmas 1963, that Camille moved from her lodgings in Notting Hill to Leo's small house in Colbeck Mews in South Kensington. And although he was as congenial and charming at home as he was at work, before long Camille learned that he was also a worrier and less sure of himself than he appeared. And if he was irresponsible from time to time, that too was part of his attraction.

Neither Camille nor Leo smoked cigarettes, but Leo had a weakness for fine wines, especially for his favourite Bordeaux, Chateau de Beychevelle.

"It's one of only ten *Quatrièmes Cru* wines in the Official Classification of 1855," he told Camille, pouring her a glass. "It's expensive, but so damn succulent and silkier than red velvet. I can't resist it."

Drinking wine, however, did nothing to help his insomnia, and every night he took two or three Vesparax to help him sleep. Camille was fond of red wine too, and as the months slipped by, they became ever closer as friends and lovers. Gregarious by nature, Leo introduced her to a galaxy of interesting people, including fashion icons and designers, publishers and playwrights, pop singers and playboys. Even David Bowie once and a very famous, lecherous politician.

It was a wild, golden time, and they frequented jazz clubs and late-night dives where people wore dark glasses and clicked their fingers to the music, discussed Andy Warhol and Carnaby Street, transcendental meditation and French fashion.

They haunted the Victoria & Albert Museum at the weekends, and Ronnie Scott's jazz club at night. And spent hours debating the merits of the Beach Boys versus the Beatles and the Rolling Stones, world politics, the Vietnam war and what the authors really meant in Beckett's Waiting for Godot and Osbourne's Look back in Anger.

Early Tuesday morning, May 17, 1966:
Today was a special day. The previous evening, Camille and Leo had bought several large green plants, which they kept cool in the garage overnight.

"You take the car with the plants," said Camille. "There is not enough room for me. I'll take the tube and see you there."

Camille closed the door quietly and walked down the cobbled mews towards Gloucester Road Underground station. She paused before an antique dealer's window, attracted by a landscape that reminded her of the south of France. But she could not stop; an Italian film director was due at the studio this morning in search of a location to shoot a film.

Thirty minutes later, Camille walked up to the studio in time to see Leo arrive in his sapphire-blue Aston Martin DB4, which he parked strategically in front of the studio.

"Not trying to impress anybody, are we, Leo?" Camille called out.

"Of course I am," laughed Leo. "It's the name of the game."

"I picked this up on the way," said Camille waving a copy of Time magazine's latest issue. "Go through it when you get a minute. It's all about London. They're calling it The Swinging City."

Michelangelo Antonioni was searching for a spacious, attractive, London photographer's studio to feature in his new film, Blow Up. He had already visited the studios of several of London's top photographers, who included David Bailey, Terence Donovan, Brian Duffy and Jon Cowan. The Leo Foster Studio was the last.

Leo was proud of his studio and badly wanted Antonioni to choose it. He, Camille, and his assistants had done everything to make it look its best. From cleaning the tall windows to repainting the walls, buying plants and new lights, and prettying up the courtyard. The word was that the director would need the studio for up to three months and that the film had a generous budget.

When the taxi approached soon after eleven, Leo and Camille were waiting outside the studio, both fashionably dressed.

"Do you speak any Italian?" Leo whispered urgently to Camille.

"A little," replied Camille. "Just say *benvenuti signori, buon giorno*, smile and shake their hands."

"I can't begin to say that," Leo said laughing. "I hope they speak English."

Leo stepped forward to open the taxi door, and they both shook the hands of the dapper Italians, who immediately impressed them with their fluent English, elegance and charm. A second taxi pulled up shortly with the English writers of his screenplay and Donald Toms, the Production Manager.

The visitors gave every impression of being enchanted by Leo's studio and gushed all kinds of compliments. Especially Toms, who spent a lot of time taking notes, photographing and measuring everything as Antonioni and his Director of Photography checked access and camera angles.

"Donald told me that Antonioni likes metaphors and abhors logic," Leo whispered to Camille. "What on earth does that mean?"

"If he likes metaphors, he should love our place: an Aston Martin and a swanky studio in a picturesque working-class street," Camille whispered back.

"He plans to make three films in English," retorted Leo, "and Blow Up will be his first. So, keep your fingers crossed."

The five men stayed for the best part of an hour, attracted by the unusual surroundings, and when the time came to leave, the Italian director thanked Leo profusely. "Thank you, signor Foster. We like it. You have a beautiful studio *fotografico*. Thank you for sparing the time. We will let you know by the end of the month at the latest."

Leo was over the moon. He was sure Antonioni would choose his studio, but two weeks later, came the disappointing news. The film director preferred Jon Cowan's studio in Notting Hill because it had better access, was quieter, and slightly larger. Leo took the disappointment badly. The money would have been welcome, and to be featured in Antonioni's new film would have been prestigious and wonderful publicity.

❧

One evening a month later, Camille was preparing dinner at their home in Colbeck Mews as Leo rolled a joint.

"Camille, I am worried," he said quietly talking to his glass. "There is something I haven't told you… And it's bad."

"What's bad?" Camille walked over and took his hand.

"Money." Leo gazed up at her with marijuana eyes and a crooked smile. "We are out of it, darling. We have no money. Nothing, not a bean. I haven't run the business very well."

He paused, took a drag on his joint, and added softly, "I owe the bank money, tons of it, and they want it back."

"Oh, Leo, why didn't you tell me earlier? Have you checked how many people owe you money? I'll go through the invoices tomorrow. I am sure we can sort it out."

"It's because we didn't get Blow Up. We really needed that money," said Leo glumly.

They both knew that requests for photographs from fashion magazines and advertising agencies had been slowing recently, but when Camille went through the unpaid invoices, she quickly saw that the problem was cash flow.

"You have loads of invoices outstanding. I'll chase up the people who owe you money. I'm good at that."

🍂

Two months later, Leo was his old self again, the studio was solvent, and Camille was in charge of the accounts.

"Let's have dinner at Mon Plaisir tonight," Leo said. "We haven't been there for months. Please? We can afford it, can't we?"

"Of course, we can!" Camille laughed.

Alain, the head waiter, welcomed Camille and Leo enthusiastically and showed them to a table by the window.

"Shall I bring a bottle of Beychevelle straightaway?"

"You know me well." Leo laughed and turned to Camille, asking: "You know who Timothy Leary is, don't you?"

"Timothy Leery? Uh oh, he sounds untrustworthy to me. No, I've never heard of him," joked Camille. "Who is he?"

"Very funny. LEARY, not LEERY!" Leo laughed. "He's a Harvard psychologist, or at least he used to be. I've been reading about him in Playboy. He thinks you can treat psychological disorders with hallucinogenic drugs the way South American Indians use mushrooms."

"Yes," replied Camille, "I do remember reading about somebody giving drugs to Harvard students."

"Okay, that was Timothy Leary." Leo picked up his wine. "They sacked him for that. Then he started experimenting on himself because he's convinced that LSD can expand consciousness, and help people find their true potential and deeper meaning in life."

Leo took a sip. "Anyway, now all kinds of people are taking it. It's now totally with it to take LSD. Camille, they say it's amazing," he continued. "And I know someone who can get us some…"

"Leo, wait a minute," said Camille. "Stop. That's not a good idea."

"Hey, baby, there's nothing to worry about! It's not dangerous at all. Read the article. There are tons of people who've taken it hundreds of times without ill effects. It releases the inner you, the real you."

Leo took Camille's hand. "Our spirits are suffocated by the stress of being inside our bodies, and LSD reawakens the spiritual insights we disregarded when we adapted to the physical world. Please? Let's take it together; it will expand our minds and help us think more imaginatively."

After dinner, they took the Piccadilly Line tube to back Gloucester Road station and walked to Leo's home.

"I have a surprise at home for you. I bet you can't guess."

"Let me see." Camille pretended to think. "Is it animal, vegetable, or mineral?"

Leo flung open the door and walked Camille over to his latest prize possession, a Leak stereo hi-fi system with a Thorens turntable and Rogers speakers.

"Ta-da! I bought a new hi-fi for us, and I, my sweet fifi, am about to blow your mind," he said. "But first, we must light a joint."

"Here," Leo handed her the joint and a pair of stereo headphones. "Now take a drag and put these on."

They sat on the sofa, and Leo helped her adjust the headphones and went over to the hi-fi to select a record.

"Now open your ears to this new Stones number, Paint It Black. Listen to it, I mean really listen to it, to the music and the words. We have to try new things, Camille, and open our minds."

Camille inhaled deeply and listened intently. She had never used stereo headphones before and was astonished by how different the Rolling Stones sounded. The music was vibrant and spacey, ethereal and three-dimensional. And the joint made her laugh with delight.

"This is out of sight! It's like being in the room with the Stones!"

For the rest of that evening, they smoked, drank wine and made love to music of The Who. And from that evening on, they drew even closer with their easy-going natures, shared sense of humour and passions for photography, wine and smoking pot.

The summer that year was cold and wet, and Camille missed the bright light of Provence. Even Leo complained when the few sunny days fell in the middle of the week, but a damp August gave way to a dry, sunny September before the skies above London reverted to their winter monochromes of three shades of grey. By early November, the rain was relentless, and Camille and Leo spent the evenings lying in each other's arms in Leo's house, smoking dope, listening to music and sharing bottles of Beychevelle Saint Julien wine.

On the evening of November 9, Camille arrived home after Leo who met her at the door.

"I have news for you, bambino," he said smugly. "First, I am going to play you this unbelievable new forty-five record by the Beach Boys called Good Vibrations which I am crazy about, and I know you will be too. Secondly, I've bought you your very own… wait for it…"

Leo read carefully from the box, "Koss Easy Listening Headphones with Pneumalite Ear-Cups."

Leo and Camille burst out laughing.

"But better still, take a gander at this!" Leo held up two simple white sugar cubes triumphantly.

"Sugar cubes? Leo, seriously?" Camille laughed too.

"Tonight, my little French cabbage, we are going to take a trip! These innocent-looking sugar cubes contain Lysergic acid, LSD to you, and tonight we are going to expand our tiny minds! As Leary says, we are going to turn on, tune in, and drop out!"

"Well, I suppose it had to happen," said Camille through the wine. "You've wanted to do this for a long time, so lay it on me. Let's do it. Let's tune in! But we have to be comfortable to have a good trip, so let me plump up the cushions before we drop out!"

"Right on, I'll refill our glasses," said Leo, laughing. "Pass me yours."

"No, really, Leo, I can't drink anymore. I've had enough. You have more if you want to."

"Yes, I do, and I already have. Now for the big moment. I'll go first," said Leo. "Watch this! They say the trick is to let it dissolve slowly in your mouth."

With a wide grin, he picked up a sugar cube with two fingers, tipped his head back, and placed it in his mouth with a slow, exaggerated gesture. "Delicious. Now it's your turn, Camille."

Camille laughed as she picked up the other sugar cube and crunched it as Leo put on Good Vibrations and switched it to repeat.

"Quick," he said, "put on your headphones."

For a while, they lay entwined on the sofa, enthralled by the soaring arpeggios and complex harmonies. Twenty minutes later, they were still lying there, eyes closed, lost in the music, sighing in unison at each key change.

Leo removed his headphones and tapped Camille on the shoulder.

"Do you feel anything yet?" he asked.

"Yes, yes, I have been watching that row of little lights on the amplifier. Watch them with me, I've never seen colours like that. They're actually jumping, pulsating. And now they're changing colour."

"Oh my God. Our stereo has a brain. The system is alive!"

They both exploded with laughter.

Leo pressed his wine glass to his right eye and peered at Camille through the dark liquid.

"Wow!" he exclaimed. "This is incredible, surreal. I can see you in there. I can see another red Camille."

"And now watch the candles!" cried Camille. "They are dancing, swaying to the music. Look, Leo, look!"

Leo roared with laughter. "Hang on tightly, baby. We are going for a ride!"

The following morning Camille was the first to wake. She lay on her back for a while with her hands beneath her head, staring at the ceiling. Finally, she propped herself up and noticed the clock. It was after midday. She stood up unsteadily and sat down again. She was stark naked, and her clothes were strewn around the floor.

"Leo? Where are you? I am starving," she called. No answer. They had spent most of the night listening to the Beach Boys' latest album Pet Sound drinking wine, making love and drinking more wine—or at least Leo did until there was no more left.

"That's enough, Leo. Please, you've drunk enough." Camille had told him in the night. She feared more alcohol would dull his senses: she felt so lucid, so insightful, so curiously sensible despite or because of her heightened awareness.

All in all, her first LSD trip had been an exhilarating voyage to an intense world of bright lights, insights, love and understanding in an ever-changing kaleidoscope of beautiful colours and cursive shapes. She had seen Juliette and Nadia laughing and singing, floating in the air like gossamer nymphs. And she saw Bernard too, laughing, dancing, impossibly young and handsome. There had been no bad moments at all.

She stood up again, grabbed some sunglasses, pulled a towel around her, and headed for the kitchen through the sitting room past Leo, who was lying on his side on the sofa, his right arm covering his eyes.

Still a little light-headed, she made a pot of coffee, cooked some scrambled eggs on toast and prepared a tray for Leo.

"Come on, Leo the lion, time for brunch! Eggs and coffee. Leo! Time to get up!"

Camille put the tray down and approached him gently, but her blood turned to ice before she even touched him. She screamed when she pulled his arm from his head. His face was a waxy blue and his bloodshot eyes stared at nothing through pupils so dilated that they looked like black holes. And vomit was trickling from a corner of his mouth.

"Leo! Leo! Oh Jesus, oh my God, NO!!! My Leo!" she screamed and leaped back in shock.

He was not sleeping. He was dead. Camille fell to her knees and howled.

Ten days later Camille learned the conclusions of the autopsy.

"Leo Edward Foster of 6, Colbeck Mews, London SW7 died accidentally on November 10, 1966, between five A.M and nine A.M., his death being attributed to an inadequate uptake of oxygen by the body's tissues caused by a pulmonary oedema and asphyxia brought about by a loss of consciousness following an excessive consummation of alcohol, combined with the ingestion of immoderate amounts of barbiturates and antihistamines in the form of Vesparax."

Or put another way, Leo had suffocated on his own vomit. Nobody mentioned LSD, and Camille chose not to mention it either.

Chapter 8

PROVENCE, DECEMBER 1967

HUDDLED BY THE WINDOW, Camille hugged her knees tightly to her chest and watched the sky darken with the storm. It made her think of London. It would be darker and colder over there, with buses and taxis splashing through the streets, and red and white lights blinking in the rain. And swarms of black umbrellas propelled by wet legs weaving to the pubs where everybody would be laughing loudly and talking at once. Except Leo. It was over a year since he died.

To have stayed in London without Leo would have been unthinkable. Yet it was a mistake to have rushed home; she should have taken a deep breath, paused, and thought it through carefully. Because now she was back where she started: living in Provence with her parents.

Six years ago, she had embarked on a new adventure. Like one of Max's cicadas, she had crawled out of Provence, shed her skin and become a new creature in London. England had transformed her, altered everything. Leo had shown her new ways to approach, interpret and understand life. If it had been a good idea to leave six years ago, it would be a better idea to leave now. But where could she go and what would she do? She should make use of what she learned in London, but how? She liked English and spoke it fluently, but teaching would never be enough. Photography? It had lost its appeal since Leo died.

Meeting Leo had been like running into an old friend. She could read his mind and felt at ease straight away. There was nothing complicated, duplicitous or disingenuous about him. And if he was a little lightweight and sometimes irresponsible, he was also entertaining, delightful, charming, sophisticated and often surprising.

Max was harder to read. Like a complex tome about nature in an unfamiliar dialect; some parts of him fascinated, other parts were difficult to understand. He was complicated and challenging. But magnetic in his own way.

How different they were. Leo smooth, light-hearted and carefree. Even effeminate. You could never call Max effeminate by any stretch of the imagination. Masculine, mysterious, sensual, rough around the edges. Unconventional men had always attracted her she thought wryly. They were not conventional, which was why she liked them.

❧

The following Sunday, as they were walking along the Route du Tholonet outside Aix, the timing was propitious. Max told Camille he did not enjoy working at the garage.

"Camille," said Max, "I've been thinking. There is a town west of here, towards the river Rhone and the Languedoc…" Max hesitated. "And a friend of mine tells me there's a village house with a vineyard for sale for less than thirty thousand francs."

Camille kept walking as she listened. "What are you saying, Max? What's on your mind?"

"I don't have any savings. My job at the garage pays very little, and I thought that, well, if you had a little money put aside, we could buy a place together, and I could pay you back?"

Max turned to look expectantly at Camille.

"But Max, what do you know about vineyards and making wine? They don't make wine in the Auvergne as far as I know." Camille laughed.

"No, they don't make wine in the Auvergne. What you don't know is that after the Foreign Legion, I lived in the Languedoc, and all they do there is grow vines. It's too dry to grow anything else. I worked in a vineyard doing everything: weeding, picking grapes, pruning the vines. And later, I worked in the warehouse, pressed the grapes and oversaw the fermentation. I even know about clarifying and bottling. There is nothing I don't know about making wine."

Camille believed him. There was nothing that this man did not know how to do. She put her arm around him and whispered. "I do have a little money saved. So where is this place? Near the Languedoc? Would you like to take a drive over there?"

Camille knew the area slightly. With friends years ago, she had taken a boated down the Rhone from Lyon as far as Arles, and had fond memories of the vineyards, small towns and castles that border the river and separate the Languedoc from Provence.

The drive from Ventabren took an hour and a half in Max's old Peugeot. West on the D10 as far as Les Bons Enfants, then northwest past Lançon-Provence, through dusty plains rife with cypress trees and parasol pines, past vineyards and twisted olive trees, along a straight, quiet road under limestone peaks through the picturesque village of Mouriès. Then north up a steep hill to Maussane and over the low mountains of the Alpilles [the little Alps] to weave downhill towards Saint-Rémy-de-Provence.

"Are you serious about buying a place? Do you have thirty thousand?" asked Max, turning to look at her.

"Serious, I am not sure, but yes, I definitely have thirty thousand francs," replied Camille, adding playfully, "perhaps even a little more."

"And if we decide to buy, would you agree to the house being in joint names? I could have a legal document drawn up and pay you back over time."

"Let's visit the house first. If we like it, we'll work something out."

Camille looked over tenderly at her man dressed in blue, driving with his elbow on the sill, the warm air ruffling his long hair.

"No, Camille, I want to be clear about that before we get there. If we like it and decide to buy, we'll need to protect your money and I know a lawyer who can do it."

"This is Saint-Rémy coming up, isn't it? Is the house near here? I've been here before; it's charming."

"Yes, we are close. The house is the other side of Saint-Rémy," said Max.

Camille leaned forward as they approached. "Van Gogh was interned in an asylum near here after cutting off his ear in Arles."

"You know more about art than I do," said Max, "but we just passed an asylum, on the right by some Roman ruins as we came down the hill. L'Asile Saint-Paul, the sign said."

Camille twisted her head and looked back. "That must be it. Do you know the story? Gauguin tried to tell him how to paint, which Van Gogh didn't like, and they had a fight. Van Gogh—who was pretty fragile mentally— then cut off his left ear and took it to a girl in a brothel; and predictably she called the police. Anyway, he painted The Starry Night from his window in that asylum."

"Sounds like it was a good thing they locked him up," laughed Max.

Within minutes, they turned off the D5 onto the Boulevard Victor Hugo and continued on the ring road around the town under avenues of tall plane trees until they reached Avenue Fauconnet.

"Almost there," said Max, "first right and then onto Rue Roger Salengro, and it's at the far end."

The house that Max and Camille had come to see stood back from the road behind a brick wall next to a rundown barn with massive wooden doors. Max parked the car and they walked over to a gate.

"Locked," said Camille. "Let's try the barn door."

The huge wooden doors peeled dark-green paint and were crudely fastened by a rope twisted around a peg. Once loosened, the door on the right creaked and swung open at first push, letting the bright light shimmer across the dirt floor.

"Goodness, it's enormous in here," said Camille walking cautiously as her eyes got used to the light filtering in from two small windows high on the far wall. "Have you seen all this old farm machinery? And over there, those giant wooden vats?"

Max walked around a dust-covered, pre-war Percheron tractor and went over to examine two six-foot-tall wooden barrels and a massive oak press at the back.

"Mon Dieu, these are old. I've never seen so many cobwebs. They haven't been used for years," he said. "We can't make wine in these. We'll have to update everything if we buy."

At that moment, an old lady with snow-white hair wearing a simple blue dress and white apron came in from the road.

"Good afternoon, messieurs-dames! I am Madame Genet, from next door. Are you the people the agent sent who are interested in Monsieur Dupin's house?"

"We're not those people, no, but we are searching for a place to buy," said Camille. "And we'd love to see the property if we may; the house and the land?"

The old lady pushed open a smaller door in the rear wall of the barn and took them into a courtyard.

"This is adorable," Camille whispered to Max.

On the left of the yard was a smaller, more modern barn that doubled as a storeroom and a winery.

"This is where they make the wine these days," said the old lady pointing to three large square vats with small metal doors on the bottom. "They're full of last year's harvest."

"That's more like it," said Max. "Concrete vats and almost new. Much better than those old, wooden ones."

"The old, wooden vats in the barn?" The old lady turned and laughed with an odd, high-pitched giggle. "Those old things haven't been used since well before the Great War. They must be over two hundred years old. As for the land, the vineyard is not attached to the house, so you'll have to take the Chemin da la Combette behind the house," Madame Genet said, gesturing. "It's on the outskirts of the village off the Vieux Chemin d'Arles. About ten minutes by car from here."

An hour later, Max and Camille had seen the land, visited the house, and completed an inventory of the machinery that came with the sale.

"What do you think? Shall we do it?" whispered Camille. "The house has potential, though it needs work, but there's plenty of room. I'm leaning towards buying, aren't you?"

On the drive back, Camille played with the rings on her finger, and tried hard to contain her excitement. "We have to think this thing through carefully. If we decide to buy, I'll have to get another job. It's way too far from Marseille."

"Camille, one step at a time. The old lady said the vats are full of last year's harvest, so if we buy the place, we can sell the wine to the local cooperative, if it's any good."

Max reached over and took Camille's hand. "Listen. The vineyard needs money spent on it, but the vines are all healthy, and that's the important thing. Personally, I think we should buy, and not worry about you getting a job. You'll have plenty to keep you busy. If you want me to, I'll see a lawyer and get a contract drawn up to protect your money."

"So, you think we should do it? Oh my God," exclaimed Camille, "it means leaving Ventabren, and I'll have to tell my mother. I hadn't even thought of that!"

She shouted with laughter. Max threw back his head and laughed loudly too.

That evening Camille could not decide whether to be worried or excited. Had they been too hasty? Certainly. They had only seen one house. And could she count on Max? She chose not to dwell on that. The thought of getting away from Ventabren was overpowering. She could have her own studio and darkroom and start taking photographs again. This would be the new beginning she was looking for and knew Leo would agree. She could hear him quoting Leary again: Trust your instincts. Do the unexpected.

❧

The following weekend, the Mistral was blowing softly, teasing the leaves from the trees. She parked her little Renault on the Cours Mirabeau in Aix and strolled down past the cafés and around the great fountain to the Bar de la Paix. She pushed open the heavy door and was surprised to see Max's friend Pierre Paglioni sitting at a table with a glass in one hand and a cigarette in the other.

"Hello, Pierre," said Camille, "what are you doing here?"

"Good morning, Camille," said Pierre rising to his feet to kiss her on both cheeks. "Max asked me to come and meet you. Apparently, there are papers to sign, and you need a witness?"

"I suppose we do. I hadn't thought of that."

As Pierre pulled up a chair for Camille, Max arrived and broke into a grin. "Salut, minou," he said, kissing Camille on her neck. "Here it is, the document we were waiting for."

Dragging an empty chair noisily to the table, he sat down and continued, "Everything's here. The initial statement of intent on the house and the contract to safeguard your money."

Camille looked at him expectantly. "May I read it?" she asked.

"Of course, go ahead, Camille," said Max leafing through the contract. "Basically, it says that if we buy the house and vineyard, they will be yours and will remain yours until I pay you half the purchase price, after which they'll be officially ours, fifty-fifty. Here read it."

Max passed the document to Camille, and she began to read.

After a while she looked up said, "I've never understood why legal documents can't be written in the vernacular. All this archaic, highfalutin legalese. I understand that my loan to you is protected by the value of the house and land—which is what I care about. That's straightforward enough. Where do I sign?"

Putting down his cigarette in a yellow Ricard ashtray, Pierre signed his name as a witness to Camille's signature and François, the waiter, witnessed Max's.

"Now this," said Max grinning broadly, "calls for a celebration."

Camille took a deep breath, conscious of having made an important decision. She had done the unexpected and knew which part of the puzzle Max carried: he was the key to a new beginning.

François brought over four shallow crystal glasses and filled them with *Veuve Clicquot Brut*, the best champagne in the bar, and the four of them raised their glasses.

"Santé, good health!" they all said as they clinked, and Camille was touched to see Max more relaxed and happier than she had ever seen him. He saw her looking at him and winked.

*

Camille found it easy to put off mentioning she would soon be moving out, though it constantly weighed on her mind. Partly out of sympathy for Bernard, whose sickness dulled and dominated conversations, and repressed all notions of joy. But principally because she dreaded the questions, the tears and raised voices.

She was very fond of Bernard but not close to him, and not just because she had been away. They had drawn apart as she passed from infancy to adult-hood, and respect and admiration described her feelings for him now. He was a gentle, honourable man who had never been good at expressing his emotions and she felt strangely guilty that his life was drawing to an end as hers was about to soar. More than anything else, she would miss his kindness and dry sense of humour.

Despite his illness, Bernard still liked to drink, which endeared him to Nadia and Camille. And most evenings they would join him in a Ballantine's with ice, though they would drink more than he did. Christmas came and went, and even when the temperature dropped to a record -12° Celsius [10.4° F] on January 1, nobody noticed or minded. Everyone in the house spoke in hushed voices and worried about Bernard.

In mid-February came the first signs of spring, and buds began to form on the trees and the vines. Max was anxious to take possession of the vineyard and start pruning. In a few short weeks, growth would accelerate, and the almond and cherry trees would blossom.

As February neared its end, Bernard, despite his pale face and translucent skin, began to recover. Though the doctors were pleased, they warned the family not to expect a miracle, but at least there was hope.

❧

On Tuesday, February 27, 1968, Camille left the house at the usual time but did not drive to Marseille. Instead, she drove directly to Aix, parked her car in the Place de Verdun by the Palais de Justice, and took the shortcut through the Passage Agard to come out by the *Café de Deux Garçons* on the Cours Mirabeau. She and Max had agreed to meet for breakfast before a nine o'clock appointment to sign the final documents at the offices of Maître Chapuis, the lawyer recommended by Max.

Max was already in the Deux Garçons, sitting by the window and, to her astonishment, wearing a dark navy suit, white shirt and a blue and red striped tie. He rose to his feet as he saw her coming, smiling self-consciously.

"Max, bonjour! You look magnificent!" she said, putting her right hand around his neck and reaching up to kiss his lips.

"Well, it's a big day."

Thirty minutes later, after a celebratory breakfast of freshly squeezed orange juice, butter croissants dipped in black coffee, and a shared *pain-au-chocolat*,

Max and Camille walked across the street to the lawyer's offices, climbed the limestone staircase hand in hand, and knocked softly on a door marked with the number twelve.

"Good morning," said a mousy, middle-aged woman in a business suit too small for her. "Maître Chapuis will be right with you. Please take a seat."

Moments later, a door opened, and the lawyer appeared with a sheaf of papers. He was shorter and younger than Camille had expected.

"I need both your signatures on this bill of sale and a check from you, Madame Dumont, for twenty-eight thousand, three hundred and fifty-two francs. That includes the property's purchase price, the land tax, the stamp duty and my fee, less the ten percent deposit paid in December."

It wasn't long before they jubilantly descended the stone stairs. The old house on the corner of the Rue Roger Salengro in Saint-Rémy-de-Provence was theirs. And as she drove to her school in Marseille, Camille knew the time had come to tell Juliette. She could not put it off any longer.

❧

Camille parked her car as usual by the stables and walked past the kitchen garden, gathering her courage for the coming confrontation: even the garlic and leeks trembled empathically. She breathed in deeply and put on a determined face. This was not going to be easy.

Juliette was in the kitchen bending over the oven.

"Hello, Maman," said Camille brightly. "Goodness, it's cold today. It doesn't feel the least like spring. How's Bernard?"

"Hello, little one," said Juliette turning around, and Camille was struck by how tired she looked. "He's much the same honestly but thank you for asking. He says he feels better, though I am still sick with worry. I wish he wouldn't lie there and stare at the wall. He has lost all interest in reading and hardly listens to the radio now the Winter Olympics are over. The only things that interest him are the anti-Vietnam War protests—as you know, he lived in Vietnam as a child. That's all he talks about these days, his childhood. It's all very sad."

"Yes, that's so sad," agreed Camille.

At that moment, Nadia came into the kitchen.

"Can you believe it? He's asking for a glass of wine now!"

All three women laughed, and Camille seized her moment. "Maman, Nadia, I don't know how to say this, and you may find the timing bad, but I've bought a house."

The two older women swung round to fix her with slack jaws and wide eyes. They stared at each other, then stared at Camille.

Juliette was the first to speak. "Camille, what are you saying? You've bought a house? Why? You already have a house. What does this mean? You are not moving out, are you? Where, where is this house of yours?"

Camille closed her eyes and took a deep breath. "Yes, Maman, I do plan to move out. Friday will be my last day at work, and I shall be moving to Saint-Rémy-de-Provence next week."

"But why?" breathed Nadia crestfallen. "What is there in Saint-Rémy that you haven't got here?"

Camille wanted to laugh. She walked over to the open bottle of red wine and poured herself a glass. She took a mouthful and spun around to confront them.

"Maman, Nadia, I am grown up for Pete's sake. I'm thirty years old. Did you think I would stay here all my life? I know you always worried I'd never find a man. Well, let me tell you that I have found someone, and his name is Max, and yes, he is the same Max who dropped the cigarette Bernard found. Don't look so shocked, Maman! It's true. He's not rich, but he's not the criminal your prefect friend told you he was. He was sixteen when that happened and began his life in the middle of a war. He didn't steal a car. He found an abandoned car, got it going and was accused of stealing it. And he didn't rob a bank either. He's good with his hands and opened an old safe for some people as a favour. He had no idea that they had robbed a bank. And besides, he had his so-called criminal record expunged by serving in the Foreign Legion, so he doesn't have a criminal record!"

It felt good to unburden herself, but a tear ran down her cheek and gave her feelings away. Why did she feel the need to justify herself? Her life was her business, but she knew she had talked too fast, and her voice had been too loud and shrill.

"Camille," said Juliette, "I think I've heard enough. You can go to your room now. Saint-Rémy, indeed. I've hardly even heard of the place. Nobody lives in Saint-Rémy."

Camille wiped her cheek with her hand, spun around, and walked out of the kitchen, furious with herself. And as she ran across the gravel to her cottage, the wind whistled and taunted her from the trees. Alone in her bedroom, she sat by the window and watched the darkness chase the colours from the sky, the yellow to orange and the crimson to night. She sensed Leo with her and was comforted, and certain he approved.

Sleep came quickly that night. Until two days ago, the decision to move in with Max had been a thought, a notion, a dream. Today she had signed the papers, bought a house, given up her job and told her mother she was moving out. There was no backing out now, and if it was a scary, it was also exciting.

In the morning, there was no wind, the sun was warm, and Juliette was muted and curiously acquiescent. Everything had fallen into place.

Chapter 9

SAINT-RÉMY-DE-PROVENCE

O
N MONDAY MORNING, Max and Pierre pulled up to Camille's cottage in a large moving van. It was eight in the morning.

"This is huge," said Camille. "It's way too big. I don't have that much furniture. Unless you have a lot, Max."

"My stuff is already in there."

"Is that all? Just a suitcase?"

"That's it, Camille, one suitcase. Some of us don't live in chateaux," said Max with a wry laugh.

"I'm sorry, I didn't mean it that way. I don't have that much either."

Although what she did have included a double bed, a wardrobe, a sofa, two armchairs, a coffee table, a small dining table and four chairs, four boxes of books, a hi-fi system with two boxes of LP records, the contents of her kitchen, and three leather suitcases full of clothes. She also brought along Leo's photos of her, carefully rolled in a tube.

The move to Saint-Rémy was straightforward, and by eleven the two men had carried Camille's bed through the front door across the small entrance hall and up the stairs to a landing where a corridor led to one large bedroom, two smaller ones and a simple bathroom. Downstairs, to the left of the hall, Camille had busied herself with the large kitchen, cleaning the French doors to the courtyard and the windows overlooking the front and the side. On the far side of the hall, the good-sized sitting room was already full of the rest of her belongings.

Despite being brought up in a wealthy household, the hardships everybody had witnessed in post-war France meant that she had little hesitation and no pretensions about getting her hands dirty. She filled a zinc bucket with soapy water and scrubbed the old flagstones on the kitchen floor. Max had discovered a basement below ground level reached by stone stairs from a door beneath the main staircase.

"Max, I need hot water. Do we have hot water yet?" she called down to him.

"There will be soon, minou," came the reply. "I've only just lit the furnace. I had to clean it out first—there was a mummified cat stuck behind it. Must have been there for years."

The basement was all that remained of an earlier, much older house, and it consisted of two small rooms with vaulted ceilings. One contained a pre-war, wood-burning furnace that had seen better days; the other had been used to store logs and had a simple half-window at ground level that opened onto a small kitchen garden at the back.

"Hey Camille," he called out, "there's an old sign over the door down here which says, *Dieu paye tard, mais paye largement* [God pays late but pays generously]".

Camille laughed. "I should hope so! As long as he pays in the end. There's one over the kitchen door up here too: *Soupes et Amours, les premières sont les meilleures* [Soups and Loves, the first ones are the best]".

Max's answering chuckle lifted her spirits. On her knees, scrubbing the stone floor with both hands, Camille reflected on the past eight months. What a long way they had come, and now, here they were, about to start a life together. It was exciting. She would buy a new camera, set up a darkroom and start taking photographs again. She sang softly to herself, humming the tune of Sheila's Adios Amor, a chart-topping hit from the previous summer.

The water from the old brass tap was cold, and it dribbled and coughed into the thick, porcelain sink. In the crudely built cupboard underneath was a propane gas tank and cleaning materials long past being of use. And piled beside them were yellowing copies of the La Provence newspaper. Many were over twenty years old so someone, presumably Monsieur Dupin or his wife, had saved them for a purpose, and Camille put them to the side to look through later.

As the day gave way to dusk and the temperature began to drop, Camille was pleased to notice how effectively the stone walls insulated the house, and how well the old furnace in the basement worked. In the kitchen, an unprepossessing gas stove with three rings had replaced a large fireplace long since blocked, and immediately above the stove, on the side of the chimney breast, was a metal grill with a tab.

Camille leaned forward and stood on the tips of her toes to pull down the tab, to allow warm air to escape into the kitchen. As she did so, she became aware that Max was watching her, leaning against the wall by the doorway to the hall, his hands in his pockets, a Gitanes cigarette dangling from his lower lip.

Embarrassed, she swung around.

"How long have you been there, and what are you staring at?" she asked, hands on hips.

"I was admiring your body," said Max with a smile and narrowed eyes. "You would make someone a good wife."

"Now, what the hell is that supposed to mean?" She was hurt at first but could see that Max was laughing, and she laughed with him. She walked over and pushed him in the chest with her hands.

"I suppose that's the closest to a compliment I'll ever get from you."

Soon after seven, Max and Camille sat down together at the kitchen table on the chairs that Camille had brought from her cottage. As Max eased the cork out of a bottle of unlabelled red wine, Camille served a simple dinner of andouillette sausage and flageolet beans with a tomato salad, along with fresh bread from the boulangerie up the road.

"Hey, Camille," said Max, "guess where this wine comes from? It's our wine, from our vats. Our new neighbour, Monsieur Genet, gave it to me. What's more, it's not bad at all. You know what else he told me? It's good because the old goat who lived here never bottled wine during a full moon. He said it makes the wine sour and brings bad luck."

Max laughed and took another swig. "Who knows? I'll remember that."

"Now that is something to celebrate!" said Camille tasting the wine. "You're right, it's not bad at all. I can't believe that less than a year ago, I didn't even know you existed, and now here we are living together, in our own home, drinking wine from our own vineyard. Come here, kiss me."

Camille pulled him forward to kiss him on the mouth. She had grown used to him smelling of cigarettes and alcohol. Max put his strong arms around her, and they embraced.

"We've done well, haven't we?" he said. "We still have a ton of work to do, but it's exciting, isn't it?"

"Yes, yes and yes, my love. We've worked hard," said Camille. "Now let's relax. Did you see these old copies of La Provence I found?"

Camille put the pile of newspapers on the table beside Max.

"Go on, have a look. See if there is anything interesting."

They each took several papers and started to turn the pages.

"Nothing exciting that I can see," said Max after a while. "They liked General de Gaulle a lot, and there are several marked articles about Algeria and Vietnam... here's one from May 1954 about the battle of Dien Bien Phu." He paused. "Dear God, that I didn't know. Eight thousand French soldiers died in that battle, and a quarter of them were Legionnaires. Lucky I'd left by then or I would have been sent to Vietnam."

Camille laughed. "Hey! Here's one for you. An advert from the Minister of Health warning that Drinking More than Three Litres of Wine a Day is Bad for You. That's four bottles. Even you don't drink that much."

"On good days I do," Max laughed as he took a gulp of wine. "And here's an article about President Kennedy's assassination in 1963."

There was silence for a while as the two of them continued reading.

"Oh, here's a sad story," said Camille looking up at Max. "It's about a young girl who got lost in the Cévennes and disappeared. They found her body a year later, or what remained of it, in a ravine off the path. She had a broken leg and had starved to death."

"Here, let me see that," said Max. "Gabriac-en-Lozère? Yes, I know that area; it's rugged up there. What's a girl doing up there by herself in the first place? A tourist of course, which explains it. An idiot, obviously."

Max passed the newspaper back to Camille and took another mouthful of wine.

"Come now, Max, she wasn't an idiot. She was with her family on holiday nearby and had gone for a walk. She was the daughter of an actress who lived in Paris, from a good family."

"A good family? What the hell does a good family mean? A family with money, you mean?" Max had that angry, guarded look. "That makes my family a bad family, I suppose?"

"By no means! It's just an expression. It doesn't mean a thing. Goodness, you are grumpy."

Camille leaned forward to take his hand.

"Not grumpy Camille, tired," said Max. "I have been down in that basement and cleaning out the barn all day."

"I know. I'm tired too. I've made the bed upstairs, so let's have an early night. You go upstairs while I clear up down here."

Max picked up his glass and leaned back in his chair to drain it, stood up and wiped his mouth with his hand. "This wine isn't bad," he said. "In fact, it's pretty damn good. Genet told me that the guy who runs the cooperative has already said that they'd be interested. Isn't that great? We have almost twelve thousand litres, so if they like it, that means we'll have money coming in straightaway."

"Shoo, off you go upstairs. We'll talk about that tomorrow."

Camille slept deeply that night until the pale morning light spilled through the curtain-less window and pried the sleep from her eyes. She propped herself up on one elbow to see the time and watch Max sleep for a while, his long dark hair even blacker against the white cotton pillowcase, his rhythmic breathing slow and powerful.

After a while, she slipped noiselessly out of bed and went downstairs to prepare some coffee. Barely two minutes passed before Max came running down the stairs, already dressed and pulling on a heavy white sweater.

"Where are you going in such a hurry?" asked Camille.

"Good morning, minou." He grinned. "No time for coffee, I have work to do! The sun is up, and I want to get samples together of our wine for the cooperative."

Camille had a lot to do too. After making coffee, she started work and by the end of the day, had finished painting their bedroom and begun work on another room. She barely caught a glimpse of Max and was anxious for news when he came into the kitchen after seven to pour himself a drink.

"What news of the cooperative?" asked Camille. "Did they like our wine?"

"Yes, they did!" replied Max with a smile. "They are coming with a tanker next week to empty the vats and will pay us twenty-six centimes a litre. That means we'll get over three thousand francs. And with any luck, we'll make double that next year."

Over the next week, Camille saw little of Max as he plunged into the business of making wine. The neighbour, Monsieur Genet, had done his best to keep Monsieur Dupin's vineyard in reasonable shape, but six acres were too much for one elderly man. The vines needed pruning, and weeds were sapping the goodness from the soil. Many of the supporting posts and wires needed to be changed, and the farm machinery required cleaning, servicing, and repairing or replacing.

Ten days went by, and each day was the same. Max would leave the house at first light without coffee and return towards seven in the evening, when he would pour himself a large glass of pastis. First one, then another and frequently a third. Then he and Camille would eat together, drink wine and talk a little before falling exhausted and loveless into bed.

❧

One evening, on Thursday, March 21, Max did not come home.

As Camille was preparing dinner, the telephone rang.

"Hello minou, it's me, Max." His voice was a little muffled. "I'm up near Châteauneuf-du-Pape with Pierre. We have some wine business to finish and won't be back tonight. I'll explain when I see you tomorrow."

"That's a shame. I was cooking you a nice dinner, but it will keep until tomorrow. Just be careful."

Next morning, there was a knock on the front door. It was their neighbour, little Madame Genet, bearing a gift.

"I thought this might be useful," she said. "It's only soap, but it's good soap. *Savon de Marseille*, made by Monsieur Fabre over at Salon, so I thought it would be an appropriate gift for you and Max."

"Why, thank you so much, Madame. That's sweet of you. Won't you come in and see the house?"

While Max had organised the winery, Camille had painted every room, scrubbed and varnished the wooden floors, and hung traditional yellow and blue Souleïado curtains at the windows. And because Van Gogh had painted the originals nearby, she had put up reproductions of the *Café de la Nuit*, *La Nuit Etoilée* and *Le Pont de Langlois* in the bedrooms. For the time being, she had resisted the impulse to hang Leo's compromising photos of her in case they offended Max. She had yet to explain who Leo was. A reproduction of Cézanne's *Sainte-Victoire, Vue de la Route du Tholonet* took pride of place above the fireplace in the sparsely furnished sitting-room.

"It's enchanting, Madame," said the old lady. "I've known this house all my life, and it has never looked this nice."

"Thank you, there's a lot to do, but it is beginning to look a little better, isn't it? Please call me Camille."

The old lady gave the impression of wanting to talk, or at least know everything about Max and Camille, and after a few minutes of pleasantries, the conversation began to flow. Camille found out where the best shops were, when the market days were, and a lot of village gossip. She was delighted by the talkative little Madame Genet and impressed by how sharp she was.

She is like Max in a way. Down-to-earth and unpretentious. Education doesn't make people smart: intelligence is innate.

"Now, have you met Chantal Ebanez yet?" Madame Genet had a twinkle in her eye. "Because she is important to know. She is …"

Their conversation was interrupted by the telephone ringing.

"Yes, hello," said Camille picking up the heavy black receiver, hoping it would be Max, but it was the village telephone-exchange operator.

"I have a call from Ventabren for you, Madame. I'll put you through."

"Camille, is that you?" A thin voice that Camille barely recognised quavered on the other end of the line.

"Yes, this is Camille. Is that you, Bobo? You sound terrible. What's the matter?"

"Oh, thank goodness I've got hold of you. If you are not sitting down, grab a chair and sit down now. I have dreadful news. Bernard is dead. Camille, are you there? Did you hear me? I said Bernard is dead. We found him dead this morning. He died in the night."

Camille pulled up the nearest chair and sat.

"I can't believe it. That's terrible news. And yet he seemed so much better when I last saw him. How are you two doing? Are you all right? How's Maman taking it? If I leave straight away, I can be there by lunchtime."

Camille put down the telephone, sat for a moment, and held her head in her hands.

"I see you have some bad news," said Madame Genet quietly. "I am so sorry. Don't worry. I can keep an eye on your house while you're gone, and you can always leave a message with Chantal. That was her you just spoke to: she's the village telephone operator. She's the one I want you to meet."

"Thank you, Madame Genet, thank you so much," said Camille. "I must write Max a note. He's on his way back from Chateauneuf. I'll be away for a few days with my family until the funeral is over."

To make room in the barn for their cars, Max had pushed the tractor to the side and moved the lighter machinery to the loft. And although she had not used her car for two weeks, it immediately sprang to life.

❧

The sky was heavy with dark, brooding clouds as she drove down the Boulevard Victor Hugo, turned right past the Saint-Paul asylum and began the steep climb up the Alpilles. Moments later fat beads of rain burst on the windscreen and Camille had to grip the wheel and hunch over to peer through the smears from the wipers. For ten minutes she crawled up the hill as the rain hammered on the roof and the small wipers swished back-and-forth at the water, and it was only when she reached the top of the hill that the rain eased and stopped, a weak sun pierced the grey and a patch of blue appeared in the east.

Since they had moved away three weeks ago, she had hardly given Bernard a thought, but the closer she came to Ventabren, the sadder and guiltier she felt. He had been a kind, gentle buffer between her volatile mother and herself, and had kept the peace in the house. She thought back to her time as a little girl when she sat on his knee as he read stories, and the memory evoked his old man smell again; soap and *4711 Eau-de-Cologne*. And she smiled as she remembered how she would keep asking him to tell her how he and her mother met, and how she would laugh with delight when he pulled a face and dabbed at his eyes with a handkerchief.

As she began the descent towards La Fare-les-Oliviers, she reflected on his achievements as a man. Like her mother, he too had been famous, and her eyes filled with tears when she thought of the last time she saw him, so thin and pale, so diminished by his illness. She hadn't cried then but she had seen tears in his eyes when they said goodbye, as if he knew he would not see her again. She wiped away her own tears with her hand, the sky was bright, and the sun was shining again. But as she approached the Chateau de Vaucluse, her heart sank again to see the gates draped in black with silver ropes and tassels. It was sombre confirmation that Bernard was truly dead and a sign she must steel herself to the looming sadness that was waiting.

Above the front door, a gothic shield was being erected with the silver initials B. H. E. de V. with more black crepe with scalloped edges and embroidered bows in silver thread. Memories flooded back to 1955 and the funeral of Bernard's mother, and Camille half-expected to see the old four-wheeled hearse with glass sides and the two black horses with silver harnesses and black feather plumes on their heads that had taken the old lady to the church.

Chapter 10

A Funeral

C AMILLE DROVE HER CAR around the house to the stables and parked in her usual place beside the Alfa. After three weeks in Saint-Rémy, she felt oddly glad to be home and that gave her the strength to brace herself for the inevitable outpouring of emotion her arrival was bound to engender. She gritted her teeth and walked over to the kitchen.

Juliette was talking solemnly to a woman she didn't know, but the moment she saw Camille, she rushed to her.

"Oh, thank the Lord you've come, little one. It was the strangest thing; last night I sat on his bed, and we talked for an hour or more. He was laughing with me and looked stronger and better than he has for a long time. He even suggested we have a Ballantine's together. Then this morning, Nadia took him coffee and he was dead."

Sadness suited Juliette. Her sorrow made her vulnerable, softer, and more beautiful than ever.

"It's so unfair. I'm sure he was saying goodbye to me and knew he was dying. He was young, only sixty-two. It's much too young to die."

Juliette took Camille's hand. "Come on, little one, come and see him."

She dabbed her eyes.

"You may remember when Grandmama died, we stopped all the clocks and covered the mirrors the moment she passed on. And she made me promise to turn the kitchen pots and pans upside down."

"I do, vaguely, but why? Whatever for?" asked Camille.

"Tradition, little one, it's what her family did. The idea is to prevent departing souls from being distracted by earthly concerns such as vanity, time and food. Though of course in her case, it was mainly food."

Camille smiled. "Are we going to do that for Bernard?"

"He made me promise not to."

Juliette smiled at Camille.

Bernard's room was cold and shuttered, and the heavy curtains were tightly drawn so that the only light came from thick candles in tall silver candlesticks on each side of the massive bed.

"Why do you keep his room so dark?" whispered Camille.

"Tradition again. It's more respectful, more dignified."

Bernard was lying on his back wearing white silk pyjamas and was propped up by two embroidered pillows. Nadia was sitting in a chair to the left, dressed in black with sad, empty eyes.

"Hello Camille," she said in a whisper. "I'm so glad you came. It was such a shock. Please don't be upset. He didn't suffer."

Nadia held the family bible in her lap and gazed at his alabaster face.

"I found him lying on his back staring at the ceiling," she said, still staring at his face. "His eyes were wide open, so I closed them."

Cancer had stolen Bernard's hair, and in the dim light, he seemed smaller and thinner than the last time Camille had seen him. His cheeks were sunken and his nose more angular, and by the warm glow of the candlelight, the picture he made was noble and timeless, like a white marble death mask or an old master portrait of a dead saint. His wax hands held his mother's rosary and she stared at him in silence, unable to feel a thing.

This isn't Bernard. This is just his shell. It doesn't even look like him. He's like a flower that has been picked and already wilted. And inevitably an image came to her of Leo on the sofa, eyes staring, dead and tears streamed down her face.

"Don't be sad, Camille. He is in a better place," said Nadia smiling tenderly. "We washed and shaved him and put on his best panamas right after I called you this morning."

She leaned forward and swept an invisible speck off his pillow.

"He looks nice," said Camille, adding, "and yes, I'm sure he's in a better place." She was still thinking of Leo.

For several minutes, the three women contemplated Bernard's remains in silence. Juliette on his right, Nadia on his left and Camille at the foot of the bed.

At long last, Nadia stood up.

"Come on, Camille, let's leave Juliette alone with Bernard."

As they left, Camille turned back for a last glimpse of the dead saint on the bed. If only he looked more like Bernard.

"When's the funeral?" asked Camille.

"Tuesday. The doctor and the undertaker have already been here, and Bernard will stay here until then. It's what Juliette wants. We called the priest first of course, and he recited the traditional Rosary. He even said he would keep reciting it every hour until the funeral if we wanted him to. Both of us persuaded him it isn't necessary."

Gripping Camille's arm, Nadia turned, and a tear trickled down her right cheek. "Camille, there's something I want to tell you in case anything should happen to me."

"Bobo don't talk like that! Nothing is going to happen to you."

"It will, Camille, it will." Nadia's eyes shone with tears. "Something happens to us all in the end, so when my time comes, I want you to know that there is a brown suitcase under my bed with your name on it. It's very, very important."

"Well," said Camille gently, holding Nadia's hand, "if it's so important, why don't you show it to me now?"

Nadia leaned forward and kissed Camille tenderly, pulling Camille's face towards her with both hands. She looked straight into the younger woman's eyes, both faces wet with tears.

"There is a right time for everything, and this isn't the right time. It's because I love you so much. One day you'll understand."

"I love you too," said Camille, and she pulled Nadia closer and hugged her.

After lunch, Camille called the newspapers, and she helped her mother and Nadia write the envelopes for the funeral invitations:

Madame Juliette De VAUCLUSE,
her daughter Mademoiselle Camille DUMONT,
Madame Nadine BEAUSOLEIL,
the whole family and those close to us
have the deepest pain in announcing the death of
Monsieur Bernard Henri Edouard De VAUCLUSE
on March 22, 1968, at VENTABREN
at the age of 62.
The body will leave the CHATEAU De VAUCLUSE
on Tuesday, March 26 at 10.00 A.M.,
for the religious service at the
Church of the Mother of God and Saint Denis
in VENTABREN at 11.00 A.M.,
after which, the body will be buried in the family vault.

It was sad and sobering that Bernard had no children or close family members. Juliette wanted to mention his Légion d'Honneur and many other medals on the invitation, but both Camille and Nadia persuaded her that everybody knew anyway, and it would come across as bragging. Bernard, always modest, would not have wanted it.

At six that evening, Camille telephoned Max. She let the telephone ring and ring until the operator in Saint-Rémy broke in.

"I don't think there is anyone there, my dear."

"Chantal, this is Camille Dumont. I am over near Aix-en-Provence for a funeral. Please tell Max I'll be back on Tuesday afternoon?"

She knew that Max would not telephone her at her mother's house and preferred it that way. But when she called again on Saturday and Sunday and was still unable to reach him, she became concerned. And when Monday came, and there was still no answer, she called Madame Genet.

"Hello Camille, my dear, how are you? Not too sad, I hope? Don't worry about a thing. I spoke to Max yesterday, and he got your messages and will be expecting you tomorrow evening around six. Please don't rush."

Camille's tension drained away. Of course everything was all right. Why had she worried so much?

Since leaving for Saint-Rémy three weeks earlier, her little cottage had remained empty without furniture, so Camille slept in a spare room in the big house. It was cold and damp, and the lumpy mattress had the airless smell of last-century lavender. Tomorrow would be the funeral and she lay curled in a ball thinking of Bernard. And when at long last she drifted off, strange dreams disturbed her.

In the first dream, she threw a shoe under her bed to make sure it came out the other side, and when it did not, she was too scared to lean over and see why. And when eventually she plucked up her courage, she saw Bernard hiding under the bed, holding his forefinger to his lips, and saying ssshhh...

Later that night, she dreamed of Bernard again, and this time he gave her a knife, not a folding-knife like Max's, but a fearsome dagger with a long blade and a white handle. And in her dream, she remembered that Bernard had died and threw the knife away because it scared her. And then the knocks at her bedroom door began, soft and insistent at first, before growing louder and louder.

She woke from her dream with a start, sat bolt upright and listened, but the stillness of the night was broken only by gusts of wind and the rustle of leaves in the trees. She knew she had only dreamed the knocks on her door but found it impossible to go back to sleep after that and lay in the darkness contemplating life and death. But only when it began to get light did she feel safe enough to climb out of bed and get dressed. She put on a black dress and some makeup and went downstairs to the kitchen.

Juliette was already there, sitting alone.

"Good morning, Camille," she said, looking up. "You didn't need to get up this early. The funeral's not for hours."

"I couldn't sleep, Maman. I kept dreaming of Bernard."

"I know," said Juliette. "I've been sitting with him most of the night."

The undertaker and the priest arrived together at eight-fifteen A.M. and took coffee in the kitchen while they discussed last-minute preparations with Juliette. Before long, the first guests began to arrive and those who had known Bernard were invited to pay their last respects before the coffin was closed. Soon more than fifty guests were in the large drawing-room, exchanging anecdotes about Bernard and reminiscing. All, men and women alike, were dressed soberly, and most were old friends, local dignitaries, past comrades, or associates from the Olympic movement. Two maids, local girls brought in by the caterers wearing black dresses and white starched aprons, passed amongst the guests offering coffee and tea, and little orange-flavoured navette biscuits, almond croquettes and small madeleine cakes.

Camille knew few of these people and as Juliette circled among the mourners at one end of the room, she and Nadia did likewise at the other, sharing memories and exchanging pleasantries.

"Good morning, may I introduce myself? I'm Camille, Juliette's daughter. Bernard was my stepfather." And invariably, the response was the same. "Everyone loved Bernard. He was the nicest man I ever met."

Nadia slipped her warm, small hand into hers.

"Come on," she said in a low voice. "I want you to meet someone," and she led Camille over to a tall, thin man of Bernard's age, holding a black silk top hat and standing alone.

"Camille," said Nadia, "I want you to meet my brother Alfons, Alfons Piękny-Słońce."

"Your brother?" exclaimed Camille with surprise. "I didn't even know you had a brother."

"So, this is the young lady," Alfons said in perfect French as he bowed deeply and grasped Camille's right hand and kissed the air above it. "I've heard so much about you."

For a minute, he held her hand and looked intensely at her. "Yes, yes," he repeated several times, his pale eyes moist as he struggled to control his emotions. "I first met Bernard in Paris in 1924, and Juliette in Berlin in '36. I even saw her win her medal," he said with feeling. "She was the most divine, prepossessing young woman I ever saw. Life was very different before the war, you know. People were more adult, more dignified."

He pulled a white handkerchief from his trouser pocket, and Camille saw the flash of a chain and a gold pocket watch. Gently he patted his eyes.

"Alfons has only just arrived from America," said Nadia. "You're tired, Alfons, you must be exhausted, aren't you?"

"Yes," said Alfons, "tired and sad. I was very fond of Bernard. I arrived from New York last night and took the train down from Paris. It was a long journey, more than twenty-three hours altogether. I came as quickly as I could."

At nine forty-five A.M., a cavernous Citroen hearse with a tall black and silver cross on its roof backed up to the front door. The double doors to Bernard's room swung open, the lid was screwed down and six black-suited undertakers lifted Bernard's polished mahogany coffin and manhandled it carefully into the hearse.

Camille and Nadia slipped on their simple hats with short veils, as Juliette donned her black, wide-brimmed hat with a long veil. She wore a black Givenchy suit.

"I have to say it, Maman," said Camille. "You look quite wonderful. Extremely glamorous. Like Jackie Kennedy. Bernard would be proud."

Juliette squeezed her hand.

"I know," she said. "I do my best. But thank you, that means a lot to me."

As soon as everyone was ready, the priest stepped onto the driveway and his long black cassock twisted in the breeze. With one hand clasping his biretta to his head, and swinging a thurible of incense with the other, he led the way down the drive through the gates, chanting the funeral liturgy in Latin:

"*Requiem æternam dona eis, Domine, et lux perpetua luceat eis. Te decet hymnus Deus, in Sion, et tibi reddetur votum in Jerusalem. Exaudi orationem meam; ad omnis caro veniet.*"

Behind him, a hatless acolyte in flowing robes held a candlestick aloft with a symbolically extinguished candle followed by two more black-cassocked priests who, according to tradition, were a young boy and an old man. Then came the grieving members of the family led by Juliette, Camille and Nadia, all three with their tears obscured behind veils. Walking with them was Alfons, conspicuous with his black top hat and round, dark glasses.

Behind them, the Citroen hearse inched along, followed by the six blank-faced pallbearers walking in step. A sea of mourners trailed behind, some wearing uniforms, most dressed in black: dignitaries, distant cousins, friends and acquaintances, all walking in silence with their heads bowed by the weight of their memories or to hide tears.

As they progressed slowly up the hill through the village, the young and old who knew the family joined in. And when they finally reached the church, members of the choir were waiting, and close to two hundred people were amassed before the entrance to bid Bernard farewell.

It was moving and astonishing, and Camille wished Max could have been there to witness the depth of compassion, dignity and respect. During the service, she thought of Max again. Presumably, he had never had the privilege of attending a ceremony such as this. How meagre and empty his philosophy was when compared to the glories of Catholic ritual. She heard his voice in her head again, saying "God is irrelevant."

After a moving eulogy from the priest and the choir's heartrending rendition of *Stabat Mater dolorosa* by Pergolesi, the pallbearers shouldered the heavy coffin from its place before the altar and followed the priest through the north door to the cemetery. Moving carefully along the uneven path, the mourners passed the low wall that separated Protestants from Catholics until they reached the de Vaucluse mausoleum, an imposing stone sepulchre, where the bones of Bernard's dead relatives slept in coffins stacked in tiers underground.

Camille squeezed Nadia's hand and shuddered as the pallbearers lowered Bernard onto a shelf beside his parents and ancestors. The stone slab slid back smoothly into place with a dull thud, and it was over. And a good many onlookers who had muffled their sobs, allowed their tears to flow.

❧

By four that afternoon, when lunch was over and the last mourner had left, there were no more cars in the drive. The canopy surrounding the front door had been removed, and the only traces of the cheerless event were the black drapes on the chateau gates and tire marks in the gravel.

"Please stay a little longer," said Juliette sadly. "Do you have to go so soon?"

Nadia pleaded with her eyes as Alfons towered over her.

"Alfons is staying for a few days; won't you stay longer for him? He is so much fun, and I would love you to get to know him."

"If you can't stay, you must promise to come and see me in New York," Alfons said.

"Now there's a thought," said Camille. "I've always wanted to visit New York."

"Then consider yourself invited. All three of you, if you wish. I live in the West Village and have plenty of room in my house. It's an exciting place, and I would enjoy showing you around."

"That's a wonderful idea," said Nadia. "I'll go and pack my suitcase."

They all laughed.

"I would so love to stay a little longer, but I have to go. I promise I'll be back soon, Maman, Bobo. And as for New York, yes, please. I can't think of anything I'd like better."

Camille stood on her toes to kiss Alfons goodbye.

As she drove through the gates, her burden lifted. She would like to have stayed, but she had not spoken to Max since before she left and was anxious to get home to see him.

Poor Bernard was now simply a memory, alone in the cold underground. And only when she tasted the salt of her tears did she realise she was weeping involuntarily for the first time since she arrived.

Chapter 11

RESTAURANT BAUMANIÈRE

W HEN CAMILLE ARRIVED HOME, Max was at the kitchen table with a glass of red wine, cutting himself a thick slice of fresh bread with his Laguiole knife. He stood up as she came into the kitchen and stepped forward to embrace her.

"Ah, minou, how was it? You must be drained," he said. "I thought of you a lot. I may pretend not to care about dying, but I know how upsetting death can be. I was thinking of making an Aligot for us, like my mother used to make."

"What in heaven's name is an Aligot?" asked Camille, laughing.

"An Aligot? Not very complicated. It's like a Truffade, made with melted cheese and mashed potatoes, but with garlic and cream. The cheese has to be very fresh like curd and I'm not sure where to get curd round here. Basically, it's…"

"Max, thank you, but that's enough. I appreciate the thought and you are right: I don't feel like cooking tonight, so why don't we go to a restaurant? We've worked hard enough." Camille took Max's hands in hers. "Look, these last few days haven't been easy, and I am still sad. A restaurant is exactly what I need. There's one Madame Genet recommends in Maillane called the *l'Oustalet Maianen*. We could go there."

"If that's what you want," replied Max, "but why don't we go to that place in Les Baux, *l'Oustau de Baumanière*? It's supposed to be best restaurant around here. I'll see if they have a table for eight."

"Even better. I've always wanted to go there."

The sun had set, and it was almost dark by the time Max and Camille left their house in the Peugeot. The restaurant was eight miles away on the other side of the Alpilles, nestled below the towering escarpments and ruins of the medieval village of Les Baux. Twenty minutes later, they drew up in front of an imposing stone building with a Roman-tiled roof and a dovecote, where they parked their car between a silver E-type Jaguar and a midnight-blue Mercedes-Benz 250 SE.

"Nice cars," said Max, "there must be money here."

As a hostess showed them to a table by the window in the elegant dining room, they passed photographs of famous guests, who included General de Gaulle and Princess Margaret of England. And Max whispered in Camille's ear.

"I'm not sure this is such a good idea. I'm not comfortable in a place like this. I just hope they didn't see our car." He chuckled.

"Don't be ridiculous," said Camille squeezing his arm. "They don't care what kind of car we have. All they want is our money."

She was delighted that Max had dressed nicely for the occasion and wanted him to be happy and relaxed.

"I love you in a shirt and tie, and they go so well with your long hair. Let's start with a drink, shall we? I can't wait to have a glass of champagne. Won't you join me?"

"You know what I drink," replied Max taking out his blue packet of Gitanes. "I'll have a fée verte."

"Oh, for goodness sake, you have pastis every evening. Max, won't you have something else tonight? It's a special occasion.

"No, I won't, Camille. I don't drink champagne because I don't really like it," Max leaned towards her, his voice sharp-edged and hard. "And for more than one reason."

At that moment, a middle-aged waiter with a professional smile and a gold Dupont lighter sidled up to Max.

"May I?" he asked, as he leaned forward and flicked the wheel with his thumb towards the unlit cigarette that dangled from Max's mouth.

"Would Madame and Monsieur like an aperitif?"

He gave them each a menu Camille's without prices and Max turned to him, smiled, and ordered a glass of champagne for Camille and a pastis for himself.

For a few moments, they sat in silence as they studied the menu.

"So, have you seen anything you like, Max?"

"You choose for me, Camille, but keep it simple. You know me."

"All right, do you think you'd like to start with a *Pissaladière*?"

"That's some kind of tart, isn't it?" asked Max.

"It's a Provençal specialty: a savoury onion tart, cooked with anchovies and black olives."

"I would rather have liver pâté. Don't they have pâté of some kind?"

"They have foie gras and wild boar pâté, *terrine de sanglier aux truffes*."

"Give me that. That sounds more like me."

"The wild boar terrine? And what do you want for the main course?"

"Rabbit? Pork of some kind? I definitely don't want chicken."

"They don't have chicken, though they do have duck. Oh, and they have rabbit, a saddle of rabbit, *râble de lapin farcis aux morilles et au foie gras*. And, hey, you might like this, from your part of the world: *Jarret de porc d'Auvergne cuisson lente, caramélisé au miel de fleurs, parfum d'épices*?"

"That sounds good. I'll try the ham caramelised with honey from the Auvergne."

The waiter arrived with the drinks, and Camille ordered *Beignets d'épinards* to start, followed by lamb, *Côtes d'agneau Champvallon*, for herself. Max asked for the wild-boar terrine and the ham hock from the Auvergne.

"Oh, and bring us a bottle of house red," added Max brusquely.

"Right away, Monsieur."

"Come on," said Camille to Max, "let's drink to our new life." And they clinked glasses.

"To our new life," they said in unison. And Camille added silently, to dear Bernard.

As they waited for their first course, they glanced around at the other customers. Nobody famous, as far as they could tell, but they quickly noticed that they were the youngest couple in the restaurant.

Their well-placed table was beside a floor-to-ceiling window overlooking a courtyard dominated by two huge mulberry trees, floodlit with gnarled branches overhanging circular tables and chairs. Around the walls, small spotlights picked out terracotta vases bearing small olive trees that glowed in pools of light.

"We should come when it's warmer and eat outside," said Camille.

Max nodded.

A different waiter arrived with the wine, a local bottle of *Coteaux-des-Baux-de-Provence V.D.Q.S.* The waiter poured a little into Max's glass, and Camille gazed approvingly at her unusual, handsome man. She recognised the classic gestures of a practiced oenophile who knows his wines from crafting them, not from tasting them in expensive restaurants. Max glanced at the colour, swirled the red liquid round in the glass, inspected it against the light, and unpretentiously, though somewhat noisily, sucked a little into his mouth. He looked up at the waiter.

"Good," he said, "very good."

Camille heard his words again in her head: I am not a complete peasant you know. And indeed he was not.

Their waiter arrived with their appetisers a moment later, served on over-sized white china plates emblazoned with the restaurant crest.

"While you are here, bring me another Ricard," said Max, holding up his glass to the waiter, "a double like the last one, and no ice."

He turned to Camille and said, "This may surprise you, but I have a feeling I am going to enjoy myself tonight. I like it here."

"That's good news," said Camille tenderly. "I'm enjoying it too. I love to think that we own a vineyard in this beautiful part of Provence. I can hardly believe it, can you?"

"I can when I look at these calluses," said Max smiling. "Here, feel how rough my hands are."

Max stretched his large red hands out towards her, and Camille pushed them away. "I like your hands, but please, let's eat."

As they dined, Max became increasingly relaxed and consumed more wine. He told Camille that when he was younger, he believed all restaurants should be utilitarian and serve no other purpose than to nourish the hungry. Elaborate meals, he used to think, were indulgent, decadent and bourgeois. However, he confessed that as he got older, he realised that because humans are fundamentally and irrefutably animals, and every single thing we do and think about is conditioned by our physical existence, we might as well enjoy everything we do, including eating.

"You overthink everything," said Camille smiling, straightening the linen napkin on her lap. "You spent too much time alone in those mountains of yours."

"Not at all, that's the point. All that time alone gave me plenty of time to think, and the silence allowed me to see the truth." Max spread more terrine on a piece of bread. "Which is that every single thing we do, all our thoughts, actions, and instincts are shaped by our need to survive."

"I know, you've told me all this before," said Camille gently.

"That's why we eat, sleep, and make love. To survive! Can't you see that? Our lives are physical. We are animals, so when our bodies are dead, we don't exist anymore! There can be no afterlife! So, because there is no life after death, it doesn't matter what we do. We might as well enjoy life while we are here."

Max picked up his napkin, wiped his mouth, and tossed back the dregs of his wine. Then he grabbed the bottle, tipped last drops in his glass and signalled to the waiter to bring another.

Camille listened quietly and tried to disguise her concern at how much Max was drinking.

"I can't agree, Max," said Camille gravely. "You're arguing for lawlessness; you're advocating anarchy. Society couldn't exist because it's a belief in a supreme being that binds us all together. We have to be accountable for our actions. Your philosophy takes no account of a greater power, altruism, music, or the arts. There can be no glory in a shambolic free-for-all."

Camille stopped mid-thought. "Wait a minute. Are you teasing me? You're pulling my leg, aren't you?"

"Not really Camille. I was just thinking aloud," said Max laughing.

"Okay, that's fine. That's how people articulate ideas. It's at the root of all philosophy. Do you remember quoting Sartre the first time we met?"

Max guffawed. "Of course I do, but to be honest, I know nothing about Sartre. I didn't even know it was Sartre who said that thing about being alone."

"But Max, you are a natural philosopher! You should read Sartre. You would like him. I think you would like Camus or even Nietzsche. Now that I think about it, I know you would love Nietzsche."

Max reached for another cigarette. "Why? What would I like about him?"

"For one thing, he was an atheist. He said that God is dead."

"I agree with him there!" Max roared with laughter and took a deep gulp from his wine glass. "But seriously, Camille, why are you talking about philosophy to me? About Camus and Nietzsche? To impress me? That's what I don't like about rich people. You think yourself superior. You think that because I haven't been to school, I don't know anything."

"Hey, stop right there, Max, nothing of the sort. I'm impressed by everything you know. You know so many amazing things that people can't learn in books, about nature, about life."

"Impressed? You're impressed that I know something you don't know? You don't understand the measure of it, do you, Camille? You people know nothing about anything that really matters. The bourgeois society that you have built, so prim and proper, with the right way to do this and the wrong way to do that…it's nothing but a prison you have created for yourselves! Can't you see that? With stupid rules and regulations written by the rich to keep the poor in their place. You and your kind know nothing about real life, Camille! You're soft and weak…"

Max's voice faded away as two waiters arrived carrying large white plates covered with high silver domes.

In perfect synchrony, the two waiters said: "Bon appétit" and lifted the silver domes.

Camille's rack of lamb was exquisitely presented, with the ends of each little bone embellished by a tiny paper toque. Max's ham hock, caramelised with honey, was served off the bone and decorated with wildflowers and parsley.

"I like the look of this," said Max as he bent over and scrutinised his plate. "Even if it is a toffee-nosed version of real food," he said, turning to Camille, "it certainly looks tasty and, as I said before, we're on this earth to enjoy ourselves, aren't we?"

They both laughed.

For a few minutes, they ate in silence.

"This really is delicious," said Max. "I suppose you were brought up eating this kind of food every day?"

"I certainly was not," said Camille putting down her knife and fork. "And what you don't know is that my mother came from a poor family, not as poor as yours no doubt, but she got where she is today because of her determination and hard work. It was her success that opened the door to a better life."

Max continued to eat as he listened, looking up at Camille as he poured himself another glass of wine. "Then why is she such a snob?" he asked.

Camille laughed. "It's true. She is a snob. I think it's because she isn't a very happy person and clings to the past. She was feted all over France when she won her gold medal at seventeen. Plus, everybody told her how pretty she was. In many ways, it's been downhill ever since. You're a handsome, clever man Max. You may not have had a classical education, but I believe that you could be anything you wanted to be if you set your mind to it. You could be rich, too, if that's what you wanted."

Max bellowed with laughter. "You don't understand anything, do you? I would never want to be part of the bourgeois establishment. I despise it! Let me tell you something about money. There was a time, years ago, when Jews weren't even allowed to own property. In Paris, in Beaucaire, in Saint-Rémy or anywhere in France."

"Ssshhh, Max, not so loud, please," said Camille in a low voice.

"And because," Max continued loudly, "the Christians thought lending money and charging interest was sinful, guess who lent the Christians money and charged them interest? The Jews! They weren't allowed to have shops, so they set up benches in the markets and dealt in money, in gold and jewels. JEWels. Get it?"

Camille leaned forward. "Please, Max, not so loud. People are looking at us."

"I couldn't care less," hissed Max. "What is the French word for a bench, Camille? Banc! Think about it! Banc is the French word for a bench! That's where the word bank comes from! The Jews controlled all the money then, and they still control the money today!"

"Stop it, Max. We all know that the Jewish thing is incredibly complicated, but the Jews are not bad people. They are normal human beings, just like us. People have mistreated them throughout history because they had a different religion that forbade them from marrying Christians. They've been persecuted since Roman times for keeping their traditions, that's all."

"I don't care," shouted Max. "All I know is that they control the money today."

He was about to add something when Camille reached out to take his hand. "Hey, stop that!" she said gently. "You're with me. We are having a nice time. Let's talk about something else. Now, was that good? Do you think you would like some dessert?"

"I don't want anything; I'll have some cheese," said Max testily.

"Me, too," said Camille. "Let's have some cheese."

She pulled back her hand to signal to a waiter to clear the dishes.

Max leaned back in his chair, stretched out his arms, and pulled out another Gitanes from his pocket. Quickly, he lit it with his own flip-top gasoline cigarette lighter.

"Not fast enough," he said, winking at a young waiter who had started towards him.

"Did you see that, Camille?" Max said with a broad grin. "They employ people just to light cigarettes. No wonder it's so expensive here."

When the cheese arrived, it was on a two-tiered trolley with ornate silver handles and a cantilevered glass top that shielded more than thirty kinds of cheese.

"Madame, what may I offer you?" said the waiter opening the glass top. "A little Brillat-Savarin perhaps? Or some Langres or Pont L'Evêque?"

"Have some Cantal," said Max. "That's from my part of the world. And some Roquefort, too. I like Roquefort."

"Yes," said Camille, "I love both. Some Cantal and some Roquefort, and a little goat cheese, a crottin de Chavignol, please?" Max had the same.

"Now Cantal, is real cheese," said Max, as he drained the last of the wine. "You know, minou, my mother used to make Cantal from the milk from our cows. Did I tell you we used to make Cantal cheese? Big fat wheels of it!"

Max gestured with his hands to show the size.

"No, you didn't tell me that, though I know you had dairy cows. I imagine them white, like Charolais."

Max's eyes were half-closed, and he was slurring his words.

"No, no, not Charolais! You disappoint me. You are showing your ignorance. Charolais cows come from Burgundy. We have Salers in the

Auvergne! Huge and deep red, with big horns. I was brought up with them. They were my cows." Max lifted his wine glass to his lips and took a non-existent gulp from the empty glass.

For a while, their waiter had been standing near their table with the check on a silver dish. Sensing the moment, he placed it quietly on the table between them. Max grabbed the waiter by the arm. "Ah, here's a man who looks like he knows about philosophy! I bet you know who Sartre is? Tell me about Sartre!"

Camille leaned forward discretely and took the bill.

"Jean-Paul Sartre, Monsieur? Unfortunately, we've never had the pleasure of serving him here, as far as I know."

"Come on, Max," said Camille rising to her feet. "Let's go." And turning to the waiter, she paid the bill in cash.

"Allow me to escort you, Madame," said the waiter as he accompanied her to the front door while Max fetched the car. "Be careful. He's dangerous, this man," said the waiter.

"What do you mean?" Camille turned towards him, alarmed. "The alcohol, Madame, the alcohol. Be careful," he whispered as he opened the passenger door for her.

Max insisted on driving home, despite Camille's pleas. It was a clear night, but the thin crescent of the waxing moon hung low in the sky, and the road was ominously dark. The yellow headlights of the old Peugeot scarcely pierced the blackness, and Camille held on tightly, closed her eyes and prayed.

"Not so fast, please," said Camille softly. "Please don't drive so fast."

Max paid little attention to Camille and less to the road.

"You're right, Camille! I will be rich one day. You'll see!" Max thundered. "Look! Look at me, Camille! I am the king of the road."

Camille buried her head in her hands, slunk down in her seat, and closed her eyes tighter.

Chapter 12

MOUNTING TENSIONS

··

AT SEVEN A.M., Camille was woken by the tolling of the angelus bell of Saint Martin's church and the din of small trucks and stallholders setting up the open-air market in the Place de la République. As usual, it spilled over to the Boulevard Victor Hugo and up the Avenue de la Résistance as far as the Place de la Mairie [the Town Hall].

Soon the air filled with the sweet-smelling aroma of grilled meats and sausages, and the good-natured banter of the hundred vendors who arrived every Wednesday and Saturday to sell a variety of foodstuffs, including endless kinds of cheeses, butter, milk, cream and homemade mayonnaise; garden-fresh fruit and vegetables; thirty sorts of bread and baked goods; freshly caught fish from the Mediterranean, dried sausages, smoked hams and other cooked meats; honey and jams; and herbs and spices from North Africa. Old posters and postcards, bad paintings and bric-a-brac extended the market, and every week the *Ecrivain Public* [Public Scribe] set up his stall in the most privileged place of all, the steps of the Mairie where he filled in official documents and tax returns for people who could not read or write and helped them with love letters and poetry.

Max came downstairs to the kitchen after ten.

"Any coffee going?" he asked.

"That food was good last night, don't you think?" said Camille, as she poured him a cup. "How's your head this morning?"

"Perfect, no problem at all. Did I drink too much again last night?"

"Yes, you certainly did. Are you going to work today?"

"No, I think I'll take a day off."

"Good idea. You deserve it."

Max sat down at the kitchen table with his coffee and the newspaper, and as Camille prepared breakfast, she reflected on their lives together.

While they still enjoyed each other's company, they spent little time together, had no friends and shared few interests. And the one time they had dined out at a restaurant together, Max had drunk too much and behaved boorishly, and the evening had become less enjoyable as it wore on.

For the first time, the differences in their backgrounds began to trouble her. It was difficult to imagine Max mingling with, for example, the mourners and family friends at Bernard's funeral. Yet, it was because he was so different that she found him attractive but wished he would not drink so much.

Just then, there came a light knock at the front door, and it opened simultaneously.

"It's only me," a small voice called out. "I hope I am not disturbing you."

"That's fine, Madame Genet, please come in. How can I help?"

"I'm on my way to the market and wondered if you wanted to come along?"

"That's very thoughtful of you. Could we say in a minute or two?"

"I'll come back in a few minutes," said Madame Genet as she left the house.

"Don't you see enough of her, the old shrew?" asked Max as he looked up from his newspaper.

"Max, please! She's actually very nice, and it's good to know people in the area."

"I'll tell you something. Her husband told me he could get me a Someca 55, not new but almost, for nine hundred and fifty francs."

"What's a Someca 55?"

"A tractor, we need one for the vineyard."

"Do we really need it? Doesn't the old one in the barn work?"

"Camille, that's more than thirty years old! Anyway, it's too big to go between the rows of vines, though I think I can get a few francs for it."

"We don't have that much money left over from selling the wine." Camille stiffened. "And don't forget, I'm not earning any money, so we need to be careful."

Max's face darkened a shade.

"Hey, I am trying to run a business here. I've already repaired a mass of equipment to save money. If I say we need a tractor, it's because we need one…"

His voice trailed off as Madame Genet called.

"Coming, Madame Genet," Camille said as she turned to Max. "All right, if you really need the tractor, I'll take the money out tomorrow. Let's not fight."

The tractor arrived the following Tuesday. It was not brand new, but in good condition and Camille was happy she had agreed and understood why Max needed it. Without a tractor, it would be tedious and painstaking to walk up and down between the rows of vines, carrying lots of chemicals and pump-spraying the plants by hand. This way, they could save on labour costs and even rent the tractor out to other farmers. Max was clearly delighted and spent the whole day driving up and down between the rows of vines, spraying them with ammonium sulphate.

Each evening, they would sit down to eat at eight o'clock and listen to the news on the radio. The story that evening was that over in America, Martin Luther King Jr. had been assassinated the previous day and that President Johnson was appealing to the American public for unity and calm.

"I feel so sorry for those poor, repressed people," exclaimed Camille. "And just when they had found a voice."

"You think so? Here in France, it's us, it's the working people who are repressed. We're the needy; we're the blacks in this society," said Max reaching for the newspaper. "De Gaulle, Johnson, Brezhnev, they are all the same, riding on the backs of the poor in pursuit of power and money. Look at what's happening in Vietnam. And in Cuba, for God's sake, look what they did to Che Guevara!"

"Don't start on your politics again, please, Max," said Camille with a sigh. "Now, if you get up early tomorrow and finish spraying those vines, we can sell more wine, make more money and you can become finally become a bourgeois."

The frown on Max's weathered face softened, and he laughed out loud as he drained his glass. "Never, Camille, never!"

On Friday, the dry Tramontane wind blew all day, though it was warmer than the Mistral further east, and when Max came home that night, it was earlier than usual.

"That wind! My eyes hurt," he said, blinking, "and look at my arms. They are all red."

He stretched out his arms to show Camille.

"It was probably the fertiliser, not the wind that made them red," Camille said. "Go and have a bath while I pour you a drink and get your dinner ready."

Ten minutes later, Max reappeared, his long hair wet and slicked back. He wore blue jeans and a white cotton, short-sleeved shirt with no collar.

"Now, where's that drink?

For the next few days, Max was relaxed and even-tempered. Just as he had transformed their vineyard in the few short weeks they had been in Saint-

Rémy, he too had undergone something of a transformation since Camille had returned from Bernard's funeral.

Sustained by pastis, Gitanes and plenty of red wine, their passionate but good-tempered conversations and politics were part of every evening meal. Although he and Camille did not differ very much in their attitudes to poverty and injustice, their similar, left-leaning views had been formed under very different circumstances.

Plainly, a crippling lack of resources had fuelled Max's outlook, and a lack of education had nurtured a sense of injustice that now raged against privilege and those wealthier and better educated than he was. And against a society that belittled people like him and treated them as second-class citizens.

Camille had reached her less strident but, nevertheless, firmly held views, despite having had all the benefits Max so despised: material comfort, social position, and private education. Her support for the underdog had come about from an inborn sensitivity kindled by her own, very personal suffering.

Born illegitimately, she had been brought up as a barely acknowledged appendage of a self-absorbed, unusually beautiful mother whose own empty, narcissistic values precluded concern for lesser mortals or even tenderness towards them. That included her daughter, who, to her apparent disappointment, was not as athletic nor exceptionally glamorous as she was. Camille sometimes wondered if her mother had even wanted children. Consequently, she lacked self-confidence and abjured competition, and did not look for company among the privileged.

In rare moments of candour, Camille would concede that the move to Saint-Rémy had been rash and influenced as much by her wanting to leave Ventabren, as a desire to start a new life with Max. It was undeniable that they didn't know each other very well and she avoided speculating about their future as a couple. Yet Camille and Max were oddly suited, and if there was a shadow, it was alcohol.

At first, when they started spending time together, Max did not drink excessively. Once they started living together, however, Camille noticed he already smelled of alcohol before arriving home for his pastis and dinner. She was well aware that many French workmen began and ended the day with a beer or a glass of wine, so she wasn't particularly worried until one evening when Max did not come home at his usual time.

It was Good Friday, April 12 and Camille had decided to cook a special dinner, Max's favourite *andouillette vigneronne*, oven-roasted offal sausage cooked with shallots, white wine, mustard and butter. She had bought the sausage that morning from Jacques, the musical butcher in the town centre famous for singing the praises of his sausages that he made from pork tripe, seasoned, and smoked to perfection. His song claimed they were the best in Provence, and if the words were his, the tune was his take on Verdi's La donna e mobile.

By seven o'clock, everything was ready. A blue and red checked tablecloth, candles and red tulips decorated the kitchen table. Max's Ricard was prepared, and the andouillette was in a cast-iron casserole ready to be heated in the oven. Camille had bought two bottles of 1964 *Côtes du Vivarais* to make a change from their own wine and a large jar of his favourite *Maille* mustard.

Max was not particularly reliable and certainly not a good timekeeper, so when he had not arrived by seven thirty, Camille was not worried. She poured herself a glass of wine, cut herself a slice of saucisson, and broke off a piece of bread. By eight, it was almost dark, and a seed of worry had begun to grow. By eight fifteen, it was darker still and with a stab of panic, she realised that she had only the vaguest idea where he might be. In the barn or the winery? Or up in the vineyard?

Telling herself not to worry, she went out of the kitchen and across to the winery. It was deathly quiet when she pushed open the door and switched on the lights.

"Max, Max, are you there?"

There was no reply. Camille turned and hurried over to the door of the old barn. His car was not there, although the tractor was. Could he be in the vineyard tending to something? Not in the dark—unless he has had an accident and is lying there unable to move. A heart attack!

"Oh, dear God no." She said out loud, fear rising in her breast. "I have to get there."

Her car started at once and hunched over the wheel, she coaxed the little Dauphine up to its maximum, hurling up the twisting lanes to the vineyard, ignoring the mechanical shriek of the small engine, unused to such abuse. Within minutes, she was bumping slowly along the edge of their vineyard, the yellow headlights of the small car barely illuminating the rows of vines. Apart from a few rabbits, there were no other signs of life. She left the engine running and the lights burning and ran through the black rows of vines. Then she stopped, stood still, and listened intently to the thick silence. Nothing. The emptiness, the damp cold of the evening dragged her spirits down.

"Max, are you there? Answer me, are you all right?" she called out in a small voice.

There was no reply.

It wasn't long before she began to scold herself. How stupid I am. When Max comes here, he takes the tractor, not his car. I bet he's already home and is worrying about me.

She headed home in a rush. His car was still not in the barn.

Camille poured herself a glass of wine, sat down, and tried to remain calm. There has to be some logical explanation for all this. Perhaps he forgot to tell me that he was going to Chateauneuf with Pierre again. Yes, that must be it.

To occupy her mind, she switched on the radio to a profusion of bad news. In West Berlin, Rudi Dutschke, leader of a left-wing German student movement, had been killed on his way to get cold medicine for his son, shot three times on the Kurfurstendamm by a house painter. There were strikes in Italy and Poland, the government was… Camille switched off the radio. She needed to hear Max arrive.

She tried to read the newspaper: student protests in Paris against the war in Vietnam; Jim Clark, a famous British racing driver, killed in a crash in Germany. She put down the newspaper. Why was the news always bad?

At nine o'clock, the worry rushed back. Where was Max? What could have happened to him? She refilled her glass as her head began to spin. She broke off another piece of bread and sliced some more cheese.

If he hasn't returned or telephoned by nine thirty, I shall call the police.

At nine thirty, she reached for the phone, but stopped. He'll be furious with me for involving the police if there is nothing wrong. I'll give him another thirty minutes, then I'll call them.

At ten minutes before ten, Camille heard a car outside, and the barn doors open. It was Max, and she rushed out to meet him.

"Max! Where the hell have you been? Do you know what time it is?" Camille's voice was louder and harsher than she meant it to be.

"Hey, what's the matter with you, woman?" said Max chuckling to himself as he lurched towards her.

"Have you any idea what time it is? I have been waiting for you for hours! I thought you'd had an accident." Camille was surprised by the anger in her voice. "You could at least have phoned me to tell me you were running late. I've been waiting…"

Her voice was drowned by Max, who staggered forward to growl in her face.

"Get out of my way, you *vieille taupe!* You don't own me! I'll come back if and when I please."

The alcohol on his breath was overwhelming.

Fuelled by the wine and stoked by worry, Camille was taken over by a woman she didn't know or recognise. With legs apart and hands planted firmly on her hips, she blocked Max's way, summoning up everything her mother had ever taught her about the arts of argument and humiliation.

She thrust her face into his. "How dare you call me a vieille taupe, you uncouth Auvergnian peasant! I prepared a special dinner for you tonight, an andouillette the way you like it and we're not even supposed to eat meat on Good Friday! And you call me a taupe? You're just a…"

Camille was not used to insults and, as she groped for the words, Max's much louder voice interrupted her.

"Taupe? Taupe is too good for you!" he exploded. "Now get out of my way and get me my fucking dinner!"

This man expected her to serve him dinner after he had come home late and insulted her like that? As a child, Camille had learned that arguing with her mother was painful and fruitless, and that it was often more effective to say nothing. Or better still to laugh and pretend she didn't care. But her anger was primitive and animal, an explosive cocktail of conditioning and fear.

As Max forced his way past her, Camille narrowed her eyes, and with acid dripping from every syllable, intoned: "Get your own bloody dinner, you pathetic sham of a man."

It was the way she had overheard Juliette insult Bernard.

Max swung around and grabbed her and gripped her arm with brutish strength. He marched her to the kitchen and sat her down at the table before releasing her arm.

"Get me my fucking dinner!" he bellowed, his face an inch from hers. "NOW!"

He pulled out his chair, sat down, crossed his legs, and poured himself a glass of Ricard as he fished out a loose cigarette from his pocket.

Camille hesitated, wiping the tears from her eyes with her sleeve. Her heart pounded and her chest heaved with short, sharp intakes of air. She looked at the candles and flowers. To deny him would provoke him further, and besides, her arm hurt. Without another word, she lit the candles and meekly put the casserole in the hot oven.

"It'll be a while," she said, as much to herself as to Max, but she could hear him behind her, breathing loudly through his mouth.

❧

It was nearly ten-thirty in the morning when Max finally showed his face, his dishevelled hair and his bloodshot eyes.

Camille was already downstairs, sitting at the kitchen table with a bowl of milky coffee and the newspaper. She had deliberately chosen a cream, short-sleeved T-shirt to show the angry, blue and red swelling on her arm, shaped like the five-finger imprint of a hand.

"You hurt me last night."

Camille turned towards Max to make sure that he could see her arm.

Max's eyes widened when he saw the livid bruise. "My God, I did too. I am so sorry, minou."

Max put his hand out to touch the swelling, but Camille winced and withdrew her arm. "I am sorry about last night. I had one too many... I didn't mean to hurt you."

"One too many?" interrupted Camille. "More like ten too many. You were drunk, Max. I've never seen you so drunk. I wonder how you managed to drive home in that condition."

"I said I was sorry. Can we drop it now?" said Max sharply, as he stared down into his coffee and ran the fingers of his left hand through his hair. "I met a cousin of mine, and we had a few drinks. He told me my mother's sick. I am going to have to go and see her next week for a few days. That all right with you?"

"Your mother is ill? What's wrong with her?" Camille's tone softened at once.

"I don't know. Too much wine probably. Dad says she fell over and hurt herself, maybe broke something." Max continued to stare, head down, at his coffee.

"Who's looking after her now? Do you want me to come with you?"

Camille leaned forward and reached out to touch his arm.

"No, it's okay. My dad is with her for the moment, but he has work to do. That's why they need me there. He found her lying in the kitchen, bleeding from the head."

Max smiled at her weakly.

"Good heavens, that's awful," said Camille. "Will she be all right? How long will you be gone?"

"Not long, I hope," he replied. "They don't have a phone in the house, so I'll have to call you from the village when I know."

"But what about the vineyard? Will it need anything doing to it?"

"No, it'll be all right, just as long as it doesn't freeze or get too hot. Not much we can do if it does. Anyway, I won't be gone long. I should be back in a few days."

After breakfast, Camille helped Max pack a small suitcase and walked to the car with him to kiss him goodbye. She watched and waved as the Peugeot turned out of the barn and took off up the road.

Chapter 13

MAX'S MOTHER

FTER MAX LEFT, CAMILLE WAS TROUBLED. The fact that they had quarrelled the previous night was bad enough, but the conjunction of argument, alcohol and violence was disquieting.

It was Holy Week and on Easter Sunday, April 14, Camille selected a jacket to hide her bruises and joined Monsieur and Madame Genet at Mass.

The neoclassical church of Saint Martin, its rich, bright interior filled with spring flowers, overflowed with young dressed in white and bright colours and the old in their dusty Sunday best. And, when the service was over, the bells rang out to break the silence kept by tradition since Maundy Thursday. And everyone hugged and kissed each other to celebrate.

"The bells are back! The bells are back from Rome," cried one little girl excitely. "Does that mean we can have our chocolate eggs now?"

Camille's life was very different from her time in Ventabren, and a world apart from her life in London. In Saint-Rémy she felt more at ease than she had ever felt in her parent's village. Here, she was accepted for who she was: a simple villager, just another anonymous member of the community.

That evening, Max called.

"Camille, it's Max. Can you hear me?"

"Yes, Max. Where are you? You sound as if you're in a bar."

"I am in a bar, minou, I am in a bar."

"Max, have you been drinking?"

"Yes, I have! That's what people do in bars."

"Max, you are there to see your mother. How is your mother?"

"My mother? She's fine; she's going to be fine."

"So, you're coming home tomorrow?"

Max hesitated as people talked and laughed in the background. "Not tomorrow, not tomorrow. But I'll be home soon. I want to stay a few days to make sure that she's all right." A hoot of laughter sounded near the phone.

"Max, are you sure you are with your mother? Who's that in the background?"

"I told you; I am with my mother, minou. I'll be back very soon, I promise." Another peal of laughter came as he put the phone down.

Camille replaced the receiver and pushed her hair back to the side.

I suppose he has friends up there; anyway, he'll have to be back soon for the vines.

Two days later, Camille was in her kitchen when the barn doors opened, and she heard a car door slam.

"It's me again," Max called out as Camille came out to meet him.

"I was wondering where you were," she said. "How's your mother?"

"I'm fine, as you can see, but my mother is not so well. I'll have to go and help my father again this weekend."

"Really?" Camille replied sharply. "You've only just got back."

"Good God, Camille," said Max impatiently, "do you always only think about yourself? My father has a full-time job trying to run the farm, and he is getting old. He can't look after her and run the farm. I am going to have to help until my mother is better."

Camille took his hand and led him into the kitchen. "I am sorry, Max. You're right. I was thinking about myself. If your mother is ill and your parents need you, do what you must do. I am sorry for being selfish."

And so it continued.

For the next three weeks, Max left on Thursday and came back on Monday. But being so much alone left Camille too much time for reflection. Was living in this small town what she was looking for? Did she want to spend the rest of her life with Max? The bonds of affection and affinity were already fraying.

The difference in their backgrounds was vast, but on the face of it, neither of them cared very much. At least Camille didn't, and if Max did, he never showed it. Their politics were similar and they both preferred simplicity, but there was little empathy at a deeper level, no meeting of the minds. The fact that Max never expressed affection for her was not surprising; he was independent and solitary by nature, although he could articulate his views on life and politics well enough.

Though time passed slowly, Camille was never lonely, and despite being an outsider, she was accepted and welcomed with good grace by the locals. There were times when their kindness and inquisitiveness were exasperating, but Madame Genet explained it away as simple village nosiness; Camille was a stranger, and they wanted to know everything about her.

With Max gone so much, her *Darty Roadstar* transistor radio became her constant companion, and Camille began to follow the news of riots and student agitation in the suburbs of Paris. When, on May 6, university students put up barricades in the street by the Sorbonne, the crisis dominated the news. Molotov cocktails from one side, tear gas from the other, and six hundred arrests. How Max would have loved it. Students and workers against the establishment.

When the French national television and radio stations went on strike, Camille tuned into the uncensored, on-the-spot updates from RTL, the French language offshoot of *Radio Luxembourg*, which had rapidly become the trusted source of news. Every day the tension mounted though the week until Friday, May 10, when it exploded.

A large crowd of students had gathered outside the old Santé Prison on the Left Bank in the 14th arrondissement of Paris, where fellow students were rumoured to be held behind bars. By dusk, their numbers had swollen to ten thousand, offset by an enormous police presence that had difficulty controlling the crowds. More agitated students kept arriving, many wearing motorcycle helmets and by nine in the evening, the crowd had doubled, and the students had built more barricades in the narrow streets near the Sorbonne from chopped down trees and overturned cars.

The reaction of the authorities was predictable. At two fifteen in the morning, Brigades of riot police joined the fray and the students erupted in fury, unleashing an orgy of destruction, smashing windows and setting dozens more cars on fire. Molotov cocktails were combined with cobblestones ripped from the streets to use as ammunition against the police. The police replied with gunfire, and many police and more than a thousand students were wounded.

The next day was Saturday and Camille was in the kitchen listening to journalists discussing the unions' call for a General Strike in solidarity with the students. She was unsure which side to support; her upbringing inclined her to favour the authorities, but her instincts and the rebel that London— and Max—had awoken in her was...

There was a knock at the door.

"Bonjour Madame," said a middle-aged officer of the Police Municipale with a lopsided smile. He had short grey hair, and sported a perfectly trimmed French moustache with waxed, pointed ends.

"Madame Dumont?" He touched the peak of his cap as he spoke.

"Yes? Please come in, officer," said Camille. "How can I help? Is something wrong?"

Camille's first thought was there had been an accident. Her alarm must have been evident to the policeman, as there was concern in his demeanour as he stood at the door.

"Nothing bad Madame, I am sorry to trouble you, but may I speak to… I am told that Monsieur Morel may be in this house?"

Camille's relief was palpable. "Morel? No, I am afraid not. Nobody called Morel lives here, and I don't know anybody called Morel."

"Sorry to have bothered you. We are looking for Max Morel. We were told we might find him here. It's not important. The Mairie was defaced last night, and a witness said they saw him do it."

"What did he do?" asked Camille falteringly.

"Oh, graffiti on the walls, like they have in Paris. *Bourgeois, vous finirez tous par crever de confort* [Bourgeois, you'll all end up by dying of comfort]," the policeman said smiling. "It's not the sentiment we care about; it's defacing public property we can't allow."

"I wish I could help you." Smiling

After the officer had gone, Camille thought dryly that her Max would agree with those sentiments, though it was disconcerting that the police should think to look for Max Morel here.

After lunch, Camille walked up to the butcher under the plane trees on the Boulevard Victor Hugo.

"Bonjour Madame!" called out the butcher.

"Bonjour Jacques," replied Camille, "may I have some lardons fumés, pork shanks, a saucisse de Toulouse and some duck confit."

"Sounds like you are making a cassoulet," said Jacques, reaching for the pork ribs.

"Yes, for Monday tonight. Max is coming home."

"With pleasure, Madame," said the butcher, his red face beaming as he raised a cleaver. Camille was always puzzled how he kept his apron so white despite his bloody profession.

"I appreciate your business. It's an old-fashioned dish, is cassoulet," Jacques continued as he sliced the lardons. "Which version are you making? The Father, the Son, or the Holy Ghost?"

"I am not sure I follow you," replied Camille. "I thought there was only one kind of cassoulet."

"There are three from competing towns in the same region. Each thinks theirs is the best. The Father comes from Castelnaudary, the Son comes from Carcassonne and the Holy Ghost is from Toulouse," the butcher said laughing. "There is not much difference, just a few ingredients."

Camille smiled broadly. "I have no idea which one I am making. I'd never heard that before."

"Sounds to me like you're making the Father, the one from Castelnaudary with beans, duck confit, loin, breast, rinds, pork shanks and onions… Is that it?"

"Yes, pretty much. So, I'm making the Father?" Camille laughed. "I thought there was only one version."

"That's the best one," said the butcher.

On Monday morning, she was surprised by an early call from Max.

"Camille, chérie." He never called her chérie. "Listen, I have a problem. I was drinking last night and had one too many. Anyway, nothing bad, but I am at the police station in Saint-Rémy," he paused, "the thing is I need you to come and collect me. And you'll have to bring some money with you."

"Some money? How much and what for?"

"We have to pay a fine of one hundred and twenty francs."

"We have a fine to pay? For what? That's a lot of money. What have you done now?" Camille's voice rose.

"It's nothing," said Max. "I'll explain everything when you get here."

The police station is off the Avenue de la Libération to the east of Saint-Rémy, less than five minutes by car from Camille's house. She parked her little Dauphine and hurried up the steps of the Commissariat.

Behind the wooden counter, a policeman was seated at a desk typing, stabbing at the letters as he found them, like a chicken pecking grain. The desktop was strewn with papers.

"Good morning, I have come to collect Max Berger," said Camille as calmly as she could.

The officer looked up, a brown Boyard cigarette dangling from his lip. He made a half-hearted attempt to stand and touched his forehead in a laconic salute. It was the same officer with the grey hair and luxurious moustache who had called at the house on Saturday.

"Good morning, Madame. It's Madame Dumont, isn't it? From the other day? You've come for Max Morel?"

The policeman fingered his moustache, tugged out a file, and withdrew a piece of thin copy paper, smudged and blue from the carbon. He ran an inky finger down the list.

"Madame, the man we have here is known to us as Max Morel. You said you didn't know him the other day."

Camille's heart sank. At the same moment, Max called from a corridor on the left.

"Camille, it's you! Thank you, minou, I knew you would come."

She turned in the direction of the voice and spun back towards the police officer. "Tell me, is his name Max Morel or Max Berger?"

"We've always known him as Max Morel."

The policeman called out his colleague. "Jean-Pierre, you can bring Max out now. His fine is being paid."

He turned to Camille and added: "That'll be one hundred and twenty francs, Madame. Thirty-five francs for the misdemeanour of being drunk and disorderly, and eighty-five francs to cover the damage to municipal property. I'll need you to fill out this form and sign the release, here."

He pointed with his blue finger to a space at the foot of the paper.

As Camille signed, she saw Max's detention was indeed for being drunk and defacing the Mairie. So *Bourgeois, vous finirez tous par crever de confort* was him. Of course it was. She should have known. She reached for her wallet and pulled out two fifty-franc and one twenty-franc note.

She looked up to see a second officer approach her. He had the earnest, pigeon-toed gait of an overweight schoolboy and looked too young to be a policeman. On his left, he held the arm of a dishevelled Max, who wore a sheepish expression and a crooked half-smile. His hair was unbrushed, and he had obviously slept in his clothes.

"Ah, good morning, Camille, thank you for rescuing me," he said.

Both police officers stood at the door and watched as Max and Camille left the police station and walked towards the car. On the short drive back, Camille said nothing, though she boiled inside. It could have been worse, but questions eddied and billowed in her mind. What was this Morel business? What was he doing in Saint-Rémy? Where was his car? Why wasn't he in the Auvergne with his mother? Max tried to talk to her but soon realised it was pointless.

Once home, Max headed sullenly for the winery. He needed to check the vats, he said, and start the process of cleaning and disinfection while they were empty. At midday, Camille split a baguette, buttered the inside, and filled it with slices of smoked ham from Bayonne, mustard and sweet pickles. Although still angry, she wanted answers to her questions and took the sandwich to the winery.

She pushed open the door and called out. "Max, I've brought you some lunch. It doesn't mean I'm happy or letting you off the hook, but you need to eat."

"Leave it on the table in the office," came the gruff reply from the top of one of the vats. "I'm cleaning the safety valves."

Camille returned to the house, seething that he hadn't even bothered to thank her. She resolved to try again over supper tonight, and not to let him get away with this.

By seven-thirty, Max had still not reappeared, and Camille returned to the winery to try and smooth things over. She found him asleep in the office.

"Max," she said, "Max, wake up. Two things. Firstly, I've made a cassoulet for us to-night which will be ready in an hour. Secondly, I have to ask you something. Don't get angry. I'm no longer angry with you. I want to understand. That's all."

Max opened his eyes but did not move. He remained slumped forward on the desk, his head resting on his arms.

"So, tell me, what is this Morel business? Is Morel your real name? And what were you doing in Saint-Rémy this weekend? You told me you were going to be with your mother? What happened? Didn't you go?"

And why was there a half-empty bottle of eau-de-vie beside him on the desk? The man was drinking again.

"Max, did you hear me? Who is this Morel person? Why did the police call you Morel? And why didn't you go and see your mother?"

He said nothing and Camille's temper rose.

"Are you listening to me, Max? Are you drunk? Mary, mother of Jesus, you've been drinking all day, haven't you? Didn't you have enough last night, for God's sake?"

"Fuck off and leave me alone," snarled Max. "Leave me alone, woman."

His head still rested in his hands.

Camille bent over and snatched the bottle away and hid it behind her back.

"You disgust me!" she shouted. "You are a liar and a drunk." Bending closer, she yelled in his face: "What is the Morel business all about? Why do the police think your name is Morel?"

With a howl, Max jumped to his feet and grabbed her by the wrists, and with his face an inch from hers, he thundered: "Because my fucking name IS Morel! Max Berger Morel! Is that good enough for you? Now fuck off and leave me alone, woman. I have had enough!"

He let go of her and wobbled towards the door.

Passion and violence are close cousins, and once aroused, each feeds the other. Despite her fine manners and delicate upbringing, the latent beast that resides in all of us burst from Camille, and she rushed after him and struck him forcefully on the back of the head with his bottle of eau-de-vie. Shards of glass flew everywhere, and blood seeped, then dribbled down his neck.

Before Camille could recoil in horror, her man, her lover, barely flinching from the blow, swung round to face her with a snarl and punched his minou in the face, knocking her clean to the ground. Never had she felt pain like that before: intense, excruciating physical pain blended with intolerable humiliation. She fell with a thud, amazed, shocked and semiconscious, but in moments she was up again, running at her man.

"How dare you hit a woman," she screamed. "You pig, you coward."

Launching herself onto his back, she pulled at his hair and reached round to scratch at his face.

"Never, ever hit a woman!" she shrieked, reverting to her mother's way of speaking. "You bastard, you coward, you uneducated oaf, you good-for-nothing…"

Camille didn't see the next blow coming and there was no sign of Max when she woke up. Breathing shallowly and rapidly, she pulled herself up on one elbow to find blood running from her nose and one eye completely closed. Unable to move, chastened and in shock, she tried to catch her breath and calm down, though when the winery door eased open a minute later, she sat up at once, her heart racing.

It was Madame Genet.

"Are you all right? I didn't mean to pry, but I couldn't help overhearing… I am so sorry. He's gone now and I saw blood on him as he drove away. I hope you don't mind if I call the police, I'm so frightened for you."

Camille said nothing, but the tears on her cheeks could not disguise the hurt or her utter and total loss of face.

"It's terrible what he's done. A man should never, ever hit a woman," she whispered.

"When they get drunk, they all do, my dear, his kind," said Madame Genet, "because we let them get away with it."

"Not me. I'm tired of this," said Camille through her teeth.

And the moment she said the words, Camille felt the veil lift, the mantle that had masked the unpleasant truth she had avoided for so long. Max was not right for her. She had always known it but could never bring herself to admit it.

"Yes, call the police Madame Genet," she said. "Please call the police. I am not putting up with this anymore."

Chapter 14

COLD TRUTH

....

SAINT-RÉMY WAS UNUSED to the two-tone sound of a police siren rever-berating off its walls. It was ten minutes after eight, and most people were either at home eating dinner, watching television, or both. But there were few who did not notice the blue lights flash by.

When the police pounded on her door and shouted, "Police! Open up!" Camille sensed a wave of fear sweep over her, and Madame Genet helped her open the door to the same two officers Camille had seen earlier.

"Are you all right, Madame? Did he do that to you? Did he?" The elder of the two policemen gawked at Camille's face.

"I am all right, not perfect, but all right," replied Camille weakly.

Though her nose had stopped bleeding, it was now throbbing and swollen, and her right eye was discoloured and closed.

"Is he here? Is Morel still here?"

"No, he's gone. I'm the neighbour who called you," replied Madame Genet. "I saw him leave in his car."

"At least we know where he lives," replied the older of the two whose name was André. "We'll start by checking there."

"Where he lives?" Camille raised her voice. "What do you mean, where he lives? This is where he lives. He lives here, in this house."

The two police officers looked at each other and hesitated.

"We know him well around these parts," said André. "He also lives over the river, in Beaucaire. Or he used to."

"I'm sure he still does. At least his woman and his children still live there." added Jean-Pierre.

"Wait," said Camille indignantly. "What did you just say? His woman and his children? He told me he didn't have children and his wife died of cancer."

This was not the first time Max had disappointed Camille, but this time was altogether different. This was shattering, totally life-destroying. Their whole time together had been a lie.

"I am sorry we are the ones to break it to you, Madame, but it's true," said the moustachioed older policeman, looking at her with unnerving intensity. "We know him as Max Morel. He used to work at the garage by the bridge in Beaucaire until they fired him a year ago. The police over there know him well too, but he hangs around the bars over here, in Saint-Rémy. And it's not the first time he's been violent, though it's usually related to alcohol or debts."

There was a spark of compassion in his eyes.

"He's not a bad man, but he doesn't fit with the people around here. He's a drinker and can be a bit wild."

"Yes, and cunning, too. He's crafty, crafty as a fox," added the younger policeman, grinning.

"He hasn't hit a woman before, at least as far as we know," continued André, "and I think you should press charges to protect yourself. He needs to be taught a lesson. You seem like a nice lady."

The policeman hesitated and turned to Madame Genet. "He's rough, is Morel, definitely not good enough for Madame Dumont. There are others around here who could help with the vineyard."

"Oh, and if I were you, Madame, I'd get a dog, a big one," added Jean-Pierre. "If you plan on staying, you'll need protection."

So, it was over. Camille's dream had only lasted a few months.

She could already see the I told you so look on her mother's face if she returned to Ventabren. Even Nadia's tears of joy would be embarrassing. No, she would stay here, and the police officer was right; she could find someone to help her with the vineyard. She would not even tell Juliette and Nadia. They had never come to see her anyway, and they need never know that Max was no longer in her life.

Camille did not sleep well that night. Her face was throbbing, and the ache of the new reality numbed her ability to think. She felt deeply sad and alone, and her mind whirled with all the things to be done—annul the contract with Max on the house; have the locks changed; find help with the winemaking; get rid of Max's things. And find a dog.

In the morning, Madame Genet recommended a good lawyer, well respected in the town of Saint-Rémy, and two days later, Camille pushed open a heavy door in a medieval stone wall to find herself in a centuries-old courtyard.

A flight of stone stairs curled up to Maître Courtecuisse's high-ceilinged office, and the moment Camille saw him, she felt reassured. He was an older man with a kind face and long grey hair swept back with pomade. He was wearing a black suit and a white shirt with a stiff collar.

"Bonjour Maître," Camille said as she shook his hand, "I've brought my copy of the loan agreement, and the bill of sale for the house."

He invited her to sit down in a heavy, Napoleon III armchair.

Camille bit her lip as she waited for him to read the documents. He was slow and methodical, and his thoroughness inspired confidence.

The lawyer looked at her over the top of his gold-rimmed glasses. "Did you read these documents before signing them?"

"Yes, I did," said Camille, "at least I read the loan agreement very carefully."

"As you know, these are two quite separate and distinct agreements. The loan is a straightforward agreement between you and Monsieur Berger. That is entirely lawful. Monsieur Berger owes you the money that you lent him to purchase a fifty percent share in your property. However, the second document, the deed of the property, is what concerns me. This was signed at a later date and takes priority over the earlier loan agreement."

The older man looked up at Camille again.

"Are you aware that the deed includes a clause de tontine?"

"No, I don't remember reading that," said Camille. "The lawyer asked us both to sign a bill of sale. He didn't ask us to read anything. What is a clause de tontine? What does that mean?"

"A tontine, dear lady, is something we don't see a lot of these days. It dates back to the seventeenth century. It means that when a property is purchased in two names—a house and a vineyard in your case—by law it immediately becomes the equal property of both signatories. The singular significance of a tontine is that when one owner dies, the surviving owner is deemed to have been the sole owner since the date of purchase. Consequently, nobody else, such as the family of the deceased, may have a claim on the property."

"All right, but our situation is a little different," said Camille. "I paid for everything, and the loan Max signed commits him to repaying half my investment over time. Surely the house and property remain mine until he pays me fifty percent, which of course will be never. And since he is now out of my life and has paid me nothing, can't we simply add a codicil?"

"I wish it were that simple," said the lawyer. "A deed containing a clause de tontine is very difficult to break, and when you signed that deed, your earlier loan agreement became moot in the eyes of the law as far as the property is concerned. Morel automatically became joint owner of the house and vineyard the moment you signed the deed, so from his point of view, he no longer needs to repay you the fifty percent you lent him.

"In the case of a dispute, the only resolution is to sell the property. However, both parties must agree either to the sale or the annulment of the tontine, and I am afraid it is unlikely that Monsieur Berger will consent to the tontine being annulled to please you.

"On the other hand, if you both agreed to sell, he would be entitled to half the proceeds; in which case, you could then invoke your loan agreement requiring him to repay what he owes you. Though, from what I understand, he would be unlikely to honour it. In short, he is more likely to want to retain his interest in the property until one of you dies. And, putting it bluntly, it would be to his advantage if you died first. Of course, if he died first, you would inherit his share."

"But that's ridiculous," cried Camille. "He doesn't have a share. I paid for everything anyway." She sat silently for a moment. "Could I rent out the house and the land to a tenant?" she asked.

"Not without the consent of Monsieur Berger, I am sorry to say. The property is in both your names."

Maître Courtecuisse walked over to put his arm around Camille. "I am afraid there is more. You really should have taken legal advice before signing. Most unusually—in fact, I have never seen this before—the deed includes a paragraph entitled *clause extensive de possession réciproque* [extensive clause of reciprocal possession]. The way this is worded theoretically extends the consequences of the tontine to include not only the house and the land, but everything."

"Everything? What do you mean everything?" whispered Camille.

"I am afraid you are the victim of a dishonourable man, or at least a man who employed the services of a—I do not like to disparage fellow members of my profession, so let me put it this way—an ethically challenged lawyer. He must have counted on you not reading or understanding the deed. This unconventional addition purports to mean that whoever dies last will inherit all the possessions of the other. Accordingly, if he should die first, you would inherit everything he owns. Likewise, if you should die first, he would inherit everything you own, meaning the house, the vineyard and anything else you owned at the time of your death, including all assets, goods, or property you may have inherited from other sources in the meantime."

Camille took a deep breath and bit her lip again but could not prevent a tear from trickling down her cheek.

"Everything I own? I cannot believe it. How could he do that? The bastard, the bastard!" she mouthed the words incredulously. "So, is there anything I can do? Anything at all?" Her voice rose.

"Under French law, there is nothing we can do about the clause de tontine as it refers to your house and the vineyard, I am sorry to say," replied the lawyer, "other than to hope that he dies first. As for the clause of reciprocal possession that covers everything each party owns at the time of death, you could temporarily divest yourself legally of any other assets while we establish whether a court of law would revoke that clause if your heirs were to bring a claim after your death. I believe there is a good chance you would prevail, however, for the moment, there is nothing else we can do. I am sorry to be the messenger of such bad tidings."

When she got back to the house, she and Madame Genet sat down in the kitchen to assess the situation.

"I can't rent this place out, I can't sell it, and I can't leave it empty. I can't do anything without Max's agreement unless I buy him out, and that I won't do. I have no alternative; I'll have to stay here, which isn't so bad because I like it."

Camille smiled at the older lady. "Anyway, I won't be pushed out by him. I'll show him; I'll make a go of it. Could Monsieur Genet help me with the vines until I find someone? And find a dog?"

"Finding a dog will be easy," Madame Genet said. "My son-in-law breeds boxers. I'll ask him if he knows anyone with a mature dog looking for a home. I'll phone him tonight."

❧

Camille had not been feeling well since Tuesday, the day after Max had beaten her and disappeared. Her nerves were still on edge, and her heart and her mind were racing. No doubt typical reactions, she told herself, after the emotional whirlwind of the breakup.

But on Thursday, her discomfort felt different. After eating a simple supper of salad and cheese, accompanied by a small glass of wine, she became light-headed. Then, without warning, she doubled over with a debilitating pain in her stomach, perspiring excessively. All at once, her mouth felt salty and unpleasantly watery from excess saliva, and she spent the rest of the night in the bathroom with empty retching and an upset stomach.

When Friday morning came and she felt no better, Camille knew she should call someone.

"Goodness, you look terrible," said Madame Genet when Camille asked her to come around. "I am going to call the doctor."

The doctor arrived quickly and alarmed by Camille's pallor, tested her reflexes and checked her temperature, pulse and blood pressure.

"I don't believe you have the flu; this looks like food poisoning to me," he said. "Now, tell me exactly what you have been eating."

Camille told him everything she remembered eating, including the cassoulet she had prepared for Max, most of which remained untouched.

"Other than that, I've had been eating much the same as I always do. Bread and butter, chicken and ham, salads, cheese. A glass or two of wine."

"We'll need to test everything," said the doctor to Madame Genet. "Would you please collect the leftovers from the kitchen?"

Turning to Camille, he put his hand on her forehead. "I am certain you don't have the flu, and you definitely don't have a fever. Unquestionably, you have the symptoms of poisoning."

"I haven't been out recently," Camille said, breathing with difficulty, "or even eaten very much. Though I haven't been sleeping well. Could breaking up with my boyfriend have anything to do with it?"

The doctor was looking at his thermometer. "I am not seeing signs of emotional trauma. If you haven't been cooking every day, have you eaten some old food, do you think? Do you have infestations such as rats or mice? Or recently used poison, for example? In the house or in the barn?"

"We don't have mice here, at least not in the house," said Camille. "The barn is not my domain, so I suppose it's possible. I know Max needed poison to…"

Her voice faded away.

"The wine! Of course, the wine! I thought the wine tasted funny. Could the wine be poisoned?"

Madame Genet returned from the kitchen with a half-empty bottle of wine and put it with the food she had found.

"Is this what you were drinking?" Madame Genet held up a bottle, and Camille nodded wide-eyed.

"We'll test the wine first," the doctor said, "and then we'll test the food. Meanwhile, I want you to drink plenty of water, as much as you can, and get lots of rest. Oh, and I'll need a urine sample and for you to shower very thoroughly in case there are traces on your skin. We need to act quickly to be on the safe side. I'll give you some garlic extracts and potassium pills to take now and if you feel any worse, you must call me immediately.

"I am going to the laboratory as quickly as I can. If it turns out you have been poisoned, depending on with what, I shall be back to give you an injection, Prussian Blue or Dimercaprol, and the sooner the better. Meanwhile, Madame Genet, please have a good look around the house and the barn and see if you can find anything else that might have made Madame Dumont sick. Let me know what you find at once, and I'll get back to you when I have the result."

Camille lay in her bed for the rest of the day, attempting to sleep. She had difficulty catching her breath and was racked by intermittent bouts of coughing. She heeded the doctor's advice to drink lots of water but was unable to banish the thought that Max might have tried to poison her.

By the time the doctor returned in the late afternoon, Camille was feeling a little better.

"It's good you've been drinking lots of water because we needed to flush your system. Now, I have to tell you the wine did contain arsenic, certainly rat poison, and it was lucky you didn't drink more. Arsenic can be dangerous, even fatal, and if you don't think it was accidental, you should inform the police."

Madame Genet broke into a relieved smile. "The main thing is that you're all right," said the older lady, before adding quickly, "but I do think we ought to tell the police."

"Only if you are sure it wasn't an accident," replied the doctor. "Camille ingested very little, and we managed to catch it in time."

"Should we test the wine in the winery too?" Madame Genet asked, and without waiting for an answer, she added, "I'll get my husband onto that, and ask him to fit new locks on your doors. Oh, and good news, Camille, Jean found a dog for you. He's five years old, his name is Clovis, and Jean will bring him over tomorrow."

"Well, that's exciting," said Camille brightly. "I've never had a dog before."

Inside, she was confounded by the news. A few days ago, she and Max were a couple, then she learned he had tricked her, today she learned he was poisoning her and tomorrow she would have a dog to protect herself.

By the time the dog arrived, Camille's resolve to stay in the village had increased. Monsieur Genet had tipped away the unsealed bottles in the winery, sent samples from the vats to be tested, and ordered new secure locks for the house, the winery and the barn doors.

Clovis the dog was impressive, with a deep, muscular body and powerful jaws.

"He doesn't look like it," said Madame Genet's brother Jean, "but he's a softie. He may look menacing, but like all boxers, he's super-friendly. And you'll see; he'll be very obedient once he knows you're his boss. But please understand he has been trained as a guard dog and will attack to protect you. Boxers are hearing guard dogs. That means they alert their owners to perceived threats such as the sound of someone at the door or an unusual noise outside. He'll take a few days to get used to his new surroundings, but he'll be very loyal. Make sure you give him lots of love and attention."

Jean paused to pat the dog. "He's not used to living in a house, so I suggest you keep him in a kennel in the courtyard, but it's all right if he sleeps in the house until you find a kennel."

Camille slept better that night, knowing Clovis was there.

Five days later, there was a knock at her front door. It was Monsieur Genet.

"Good morning, Camille. Good news! Let me introduce Serge."

Serge was a gruff sixty-year-old, born and bred in Saint-Rémy, whom the Genets had known all his life. He was short but powerfully built and almost as wide as he was tall. Camille smiled warmly as he gripped her hand with rough fingers, as gnarled as the roots of a vine.

"You can rely on Serge," said Monsieur Genet, his arm around the smaller man's shoulders.

"He'll help you tend the vines. There's a lot to do at this time of the year."

Serge nodded.

"He doesn't talk much, but he's a hard worker. Aren't you, Serge? He'll keep an eye on the rootstock for you and do the weeding."

Serge smiled and nodded his head again. "I'll be doing more than weeding," Serge said in a thick Provençal accent. "The vines need tending, and there are the trellises to check and the wires to tighten. The real work will begin at the end of the summer, with the harvest. And if you need me to make the wine, Madame, I can do that for you, too."

"Well, welcome, Serge. Thank you. I feel sure we are going to get on fine."

She knew she could count on Serge.

Chapter 15

BULLS, FIRE, AND DEATH

···

T HE TEMPERATURE SOARED IN THE MONTH OF JUNE as Saint-Rémy
slipped into a lazy summer of listless days and late-night lingering on
café terraces, with countless carafes of chilled vin rosé and beer.

The heat bode well for the vineyard, and Camille was grateful to the
Genets for finding Serge. She would learn from him and looked forward to
producing her first wine with his help, which she hoped to sell by the bottle
if good enough.

Anger, humiliation, and resolve had helped Camille recover from the
trauma of the breakup and she had heard nothing from Max since May 13.
She enjoyed living by herself, increasingly liked Saint-Rémy, and was falling
in love with the house. The change in circumstances was as an opportunity
to reinvent herself and she decided to take up photography again. And to
reaffirm that this was indisputably her house, she hung Leo's prints in the
bedroom and put Max's few things in the barn.

Two years of photography at the London Polytechnic had taught her to
look for narrative in her compositions and to pay attention to repeating
patterns and complementary colours. And because she had been able to see
London and the British through foreign eyes, she had enjoyed seeking out
and photographing sociological and cultural differences that ranged from
local customs and unusual clothing to strange food and eccentric people,
pubs, red buses and black cabs.

On her return to France years later, she had seen Provence with fresh eyes,
and noticed customs and idiosyncrasies she had not been aware of before.
And it happened again when she moved to Saint-Rémy, where she was
enchanted to find the region steeped in unfamiliar traditions, folklore and
legends.

There was so much to photograph; from gypsies on white horses and
shepherds herding sheep through the streets, to street markets and basket-
weavers, spice-sellers, musicians and poets. As well as constant processions,
festivals and carnivals celebrating the old saint Rémy, wine and olive-oil,
bulls, jazz, the arts, organ music, witches and monsters. And the Saintes-
Maries-de-la-Mer [the Holy Marys from the Sea].

It was a rare opportunity to document the unique heritage of this unspoiled corner of Provence the way Cartier-Bresson might have done and capture what he called decisive moments with a discrete handheld camera. She placed an order for a Leica M4 and everything she would need to make prints in black and white, including a Durston enlarger like the one she had used in London.

Off the kitchen was a scullery with running water and a sink, and once she had painted the walls black and obscured the window with a heavy blind, it made a perfect darkroom.

※

On Saturday, July 13, her order arrived, and Camille spent the day arranging the paper and chemicals and learning to use her new camera. In the evening, she walked up to the Place de la République with Clovis and the Genets to join the crowds and watch one of the weekend celebrations commemorating the storming of the Bastille on July 14, 1789.

"You're going to see something special tonight you'll never see in your corner of Provence," said Monsieur Genet proudly. "Keep watching to your right. In a minute, you will see some horsemen and bulls charging up the street towards us. They call it *Bandido manade l'Amista*."

"What does that mean?" asked Camille.

"Nothing much today. It's the old Provençal language. They're re-enacting a tradition where the matadors used to corral the bulls through the streets from the arenas back to the fields. They aren't allowed to do that today, so they run them into trucks to be taken away. Watch out. Here they come."

The excited crowd surged forward and pushed against the barriers, and the air filled with cheers as approaching hooves thundered down the road. A group of *gardians* on sturdy white horses, snorting and neighing, galloped towards them, corralling a dozen black bulls, chased in turn by young men of all ages attempting to catch their tails.

"Those boys are villagers having fun," Monsieur shouted in Camille's ear. "I used to do that when I was their age."

And then suddenly, it was over. The bulls and horses disappeared leaving the air humming with the excited buzz of the crowd, the thick smell of bulls and swarms of large flies. Immediately, some children lit fireworks, and the loud bangs made Camille jump and Clovis bark.

"There is going to be more of that tonight," laughed Madame Genet. "Let's go and have dinner."

The three of them strolled to the Place de la Mairie, where an open-air barbecue had been prepared in the square, garlanded for the occasion with flags, lights and lanterns strung through the trees. They were about to sit down at a small table set aside for them when more fireworks exploded close by, and Clovis yelped and cowered in fear.

"I am sorry, but I can't do this," said Camille. "I am going to have to take him home. This big, fierce dog is terrified of fireworks."

❧

The following day, the Genets called on Camille.

"We are hoping that you'll join us for tonight's barbecue in the square?"

"I'd love to. I'm sorry about last night. I'll leave Clovis at home this time. What else is planned for today?"

"Well," said Monsieur Genet, "after lunch in the Mairie, the mayor leads a brass band in a procession to the War Memorial where he'll give a speech. It's very near here, in the Place de la République where we saw the bulls last night. We could listen to him if you wish?"

"Let's do that," said Camille. "I'm a taxpayer after all. What happens after the speech?"

"Not much until the other barbecue this evening by the Mairie when the mayor will give another speech—probably the same one—before he invites everybody to raise a glass to La France. And that's followed by dancing and a fireworks display."

"Let's do that one, shall we? Just the barbecue? I don't need to hear both the mayor's speeches."

Camille spent the rest of the day taking photographs before joining the Genets in the evening to walk to the Mairie. The square already thronged with people, and they grabbed three places at a long table.

"What a crowd," said Camille raising her voice and leaning towards Madame Genet. "I love this time of the year. Everybody's so happy."

"Yes, because most of them have been celebrating all day," Madame Genet said with a laugh. "That's why!"

All at once, a great cheer arose from the crowd as two strong young men arrived carrying a roasted sheep hanging upside down on long poles, followed by two more young men with another sheep. They reached the carving tables to more shouts and cheers, and a dozen young villagers began filling wine glasses before distributing plates of lamb and ratatouille to the adults. There was a great deal of friendly banter, merriment and laughter.

A little over an hour later when people had finished eating, the mayor rose to give a short speech to remind everybody why they were there. He spoke briefly about his accomplishments over the past year and his plans for the year to come and invited everybody to join him at eleven P.M. for the official fireworks display in the sports field outside the town. A toast followed to La France and another to *Liberté, Égalité, Fraternité*!

As the cheering died down, the young sprang into action to remove the tables and chairs so the dancing could begin.

"That's it! Time to go home," said Monsieur Genet with his arm around his wife. "Are you staying for the dancing, Camille?"

"By myself? No, I don't think so," said Camille, laughing. "I'll come home with you."

Camille had been reluctant to leave Clovis alone. As she approached the house, she heard him bark unhappily but as soon as he saw her, he rushed to her and wagged his tail.

"My poor Clovis," she said as she bent down to stroke him. "There will be more fireworks I'm sure, so it's best if you sleep in the kitchen tonight."

She poured herself some wine and switched on her new television to watch the repeat of the morning's military parade down the Champs-Elysées, President de Gaulle's address to the nation, and political discussions on the state of the country. Several times her eyelids drooped, and her chin fell forward on her chest, but every time she was on the edge of sleep, another firework exploded and Clovis barked.

At eleven-thirty P.M., the programming on ORTF, the only television station, came to an end, marked by the playing of the national anthem to patriotic imagery. Camille turned off the set and watched the bright screen shrink to a small white circle, pause for a few seconds and fade to black. The crackle of fireworks died down as fatigue, parental curfews, the effects of alcohol and diminished resources reached their natural conclusions, and Camille went upstairs to bed. Sleep came quickly as it did most nights, helped somewhat by the wine.

At close to three in the morning, Clovis began to bark with a deep and loud sound, more urgent and despairing than before. The bark soon altered to an unearthly wail, then a howl. Camille sat straight up in bed, terrified. Never had she heard a noise like that before.

All of a sudden, acrid fumes stung her eyes, and made it difficult to breathe.

"Oh my God," she cried out loud. "The house is on fire!"

She tumbled out of bed and flicked on the light to see smoke seeping under her bedroom door. Her first instinct was to rush down the stairs to reach the outside, but when she pulled the door open, red flames licked the stairs. And from somewhere down there came the spine-chilling screams of Clovis.

She slammed the door shut, grabbed a damp towel to shield her face and rushed to the window for help.

"Help!" she shrieked at the top of her voice. "Help! For God's sake help me. My house is on fire!"

Camille trembled, beside herself with fear.

"Fire! Fire! Fire!" she screamed from the window. "Fire! Fire! My house is on fire!"

In despair, she turned and saw the dense smoke and orange flames glowing through the door and felt herself begin to panic. Dear God, I can't breathe. I am going to die.

She screamed out of the window, again and again. "For God's sake, HELP ME. My house is on fire!!"

As the bedroom door collapsed, thick black smoke billowed into the room and suffocated, choked, and smothered her as it swirled and fought its way through the window to the sky. Then came a shout from below:

"Keep calm, Camille, the Fire Brigade is here with a ladder. They'll have you out of there in a minute." It was Monsieur Genet.

Moments later, barely conscious, Camille was aware of a loud clang as a long metal ladder crashed against her window. Though she was fading fast, she felt the strong arms of a firefighter grab her and carry her semiconscious, down to safety. Through smarting half-closed eyes, she glimpsed the flames shimmer and blaze in her bedroom.

"No, no, no! Clovis! Not my dog, my poor Clovis," she sobbed, before losing consciousness.

"You are in hospital. Now lie still," said the sister when Camille tried to ask her where she was. "You're wearing an oxygen mask because you are suffering from smoke inhalation. You also had a bang on your head, but you are going to be all right, thank the Lord. Your lungs and throat will be uncomfortable for a day or two, but we should be able to take off the mask tomorrow, and you will be home in a day or two."

The sister smiled down at Camille warmly and took her left hand in both of hers.

"Home?" echoed Camille weakly. "I don't have a home anymore, do I?"

Before the sister could answer, a man Camille did not know put his head around the door.

"Good morning, Mademoiselle Dumont, how are you? I am Detective Inspector Dufresne. May I have a quick word?"

The inspector was a short drab man with rimless glasses, wearing a grey checked sports jacket and dark trousers. He clutched a brown leather briefcase in one hand and a sheaf of papers in the other.

"I'm glad to see that you are awake and sorry to bother you so early. I wonder if you could answer a question or two?"

"Very briefly, please," said the sister, removing Camille's oxygen mask.

"Of course, Inspector, how can I help," said Camille with a weak smile as she sat up before blurting out: "Oh no, Clovis! My dog! Wait, wait, my dog was in the house with me! Did you find him? Oh, my poor dog."

"Your dog is with your neighbours. The firemen found him in the cellar pressed against the wall behind the boiler. He's fine but has significant burns and is suffering from smoke inhalation. A fireman strapped an oxygen mask over his face. He's not well but he'll live."

"Thank the Lord for that," said Camille sinking back on her bed.

"It is rare to have a house burn the way yours did, and the law requires us to establish the circumstances of the fire to make sure it was not started deliberately. Are you aware of any reason your house might have burned like that? Were you, for example, stocking chemicals?""

Despite protests from the sister about exhausting herself, Camille told the inspector all she knew.

"No, no chemicals. Just ammonium sulphate in the winery—which isn't flammable—and I had a small quantity of chemicals for my photography; but they aren't flammable either."

Camille propped her herself up on her elbows.

"It's been very hot recently, and everything was very dry. Do you think it could it have been a firework? I can't tell you much else. I turned my light out at midnight and my dog woke me up around three and the house was on fire."

The inspector put down his notes. "We have no idea what caused it yet, but a firework is possible. In any case, the remains of the house are undergoing examination as we speak, and we'll do our best to find out what happened. I'll make my report and let you know what we find."

❧

The next morning, Camille felt stronger and asked if she could go home.

"Please don't think I am prying," the sister said, "but before you go there is something I must ask you. Our vocation demands that we tread a fine line between privacy and health, and I couldn't help noticing you need to urinate frequently."

Camille was sitting up the bed. "Wouldn't that be normal? I am beaten down, after everything I've been through these last two months…"

"Camille," said the Sister, reaching for her hand, "excuse me for interrupting, but I don't think it's that. Do you think," she said speaking very tenderly, "do you think you could be pregnant by any chance?"

Camille's eyes widened and her mouth fell open.

"Pregnant? What a thought! I don't think so. I suppose it is theoretically possible, but I separated from my…er…partner a little over two months ago."

"We can easily find out with a urine test with your permission. It's simple, reliable and painless and it won't take a minute."

Camille's heart sank when she saw what remained of her house. Parts of the roof had burned away, and heavy clay tiles had crashed through the ceiling and brought burning rafters down. Much of the left side of the house had gone up in flames, including the stairs, her bedroom, the kitchen and the darkroom. And practically everything the fire had not destroyed had been damaged by water. Even a part of the barn was scorched, though the fire had not spread to the winery. Camille held her head but could not prevent tears.

Everything she valued was gone: her clothes, her camera and Leo's prints. The camera and clothes could be replaced but losing Leo's photos was devastating. They were all she had left of him.

"You are staying with us tonight," said Madame Genet firmly. "It's not the Ritz, but you are very welcome."

"May I see Clovis?" she asked, spinning on her heel.

"Of course you can. We're keeping him inside for the moment."

"I suppose it had to have been a firework," said Camille as they walked over to the Genets' house. "There were lots of children in the street that night."

"Could be," said Monsieur Genet, "but I doubt a firework would do that much damage. They think the fire started in two places: at ground level and on the roof. I am no expert, but I don't see how a firework could start a fire like that."

Camille stopped and gripped Monsieur Genet's arm. "You think Max started it, don't you?"

They both turned to stare at the remains.

"I don't know, Camille. It's possible. Did you padlock the barn doors that night?"

"I know I did. I checked when I came home. Why?"

Monsieur Genet hesitated. "When the firemen arrived, they had to pull your car from the barn to save it—it still runs, but you'll need to replace two tyres and get the paintwork fixed. But what's more important is that they told me the barn doors weren't locked, that there wasn't a lock of any kind on the doors."

"What do you mean there wasn't a lock? There was a brand-new padlock."

"I know," said Monsieur Genet. "I put on that lock myself, so I know it was a sturdy one. I've searched everywhere but can't find it. And if the barn was open, that means… Let's not worry too much for the moment; there is always an investigation when a house burns down, and they'll find out what happened. I presume the house was insured?"

"It certainly was, as were the contents and the car," said Camille.

❧

That evening, during a light supper with the Genets, Camille said:

"I'm going to have to find somewhere to live. In the meantime, as soon as Clovis is better, I'm going back to my family in Ventabren. My mother will be pleased to see me."

Later that evening, after the old man went to bed, Madame Genet sensed that Camille was troubled and had something else she wanted to tell her.

"What's on your mind, Camille?"

Camille froze. She wanted to confide in Madame Genet, but how could she admit to the terrifying reality that she was expecting a baby by Max? Yet when finally she summed up the courage, she was heartened by Madame Genet's sympathetic words.

"Why that is wonderful; I am so pleased for you!" the old lady said. "Now, you must not worry about Max being the father; he is not all bad. Everybody has good points, and he is a strong, fine-looking man who's intelligent and very good with his hands, and though he may have done things he shouldn't have, not everything was always his fault. The poor man was not brought up to understand the rules of life, or practice kindness and compassion. It would help if he believed, but I'm sure nobody ever taught him about God."

"Thank you, I know you are right," said Camille, not wanting to get into a conversation about Max's good and bad points, much less about his views on God. "You've helped me so much."

Camille trudged upstairs to the Genet's spare bedroom, feeling very low. What a mess her life was in. How could she have been so naïve as to fall for

Max only eight months after leaving London—before she had recovered from Leo. And now, of all things, she was expecting Max's baby. It did not bear thinking about. She felt very lost, dejected and alone.

She closed the door and sat down despondently on the single bed, glanced around the small room and caught sight of her reflection—at least she caught sight of the reflection of an ethereal, monochrome version of herself sitting forlornly on the bed. She gasped and laughed aloud and stared fascinated at the image of her ghostly self. She looked like the theatrical embodiment of a fallen woman, with rumpled hair in disarray and a small white, downcast face. But worse, much worse, were the huge dark circles around her eyes that made her look demented. And to top it all, there was a long purple weal across her forehead.

"I don't believe it! I look like something out of a horror movie," she said out loud and laughed again. "I am the Bride of Frankenstein," she said playfully in a melodramatic, fake Hollywood voice and pulled a ghoulish face. "Peril in Provence, starring Camille Dumont," she went on with a wide-eyed, frightened face, "playing a poor, innocent girl pursued by a psychopath."

The moment the word psychopath entered her mind, it struck her. Could Max be a psychopath? Was it possible? The idea shocked her profoundly, yet she knew the same second it was true. Max must have targeted her deliberately thinking she was rich. The first time they met, she had thought it odd that she didn't need to tell him who she was, where she lived, or who her mother was. He already knew. He must have counted on her being attracted to him and invented the story about his wife having cancer. And to cap it all, she had believed every single thing he said.

Camille stood up and walked over to the open window to stare at the stars in the sky. If it was her money he was after, he would have a long time to wait, she thought grimly. Then stiffened. First the poisoned wine, and now the fire. Maybe he didn't plan to wait. But if he meant to kill her, why set fire to the house? To inherit a burnt-down house and a small vineyard? That made no sense. The whole clause de tontine business suggested his eyes were set on a bigger prize. And Maître Courtecuisse's words came to mind: *if you should die first, he would inherit everything you owned ... including all assets you may have inherited from other sources.* Was Max prepared to wait more than thirty years until her mother died?

Camille caught her breath as she recalled Max's words the first evening at her house: hunters decide what they want to catch and prepare a suitable trap. It's that simple. Of course he wasn't prepared to wait. He must be planning to kill Juliette first. Camille took a deep breath and told herself to think calmly.

So Max is a psychopath, that much is clear. But knowing that both she and her mother were in danger, they could take measures to defend themselves. As Bernard used to say: Praemonitus praemunitus. To be forewarned is to be forearmed.

She glanced at her reflection in the mirror again. She couldn't go home like this. She needed to look good and feel better about herself. Tomorrow, she would have her hair cut, buy some new clothes and trade in her old Dauphine for a new car.

So much for a tranquil life making wine and taking photographs in Saint-Rémy.

※

Camille said her goodbyes to the Genets standing beside a shiny, two-plus-two Renault Caravelle convertible.

"We shall miss you," said Madame Genet. "You look so nice with your new haircut and that pretty dress."

"And your car," added Monsieur Genet. "I've always wanted a red convertible, but Madame Genet would never let me have one."

"Because you only wanted it to pick up girls," Madame Genet replied and wagged a finger at him.

They all laughed.

"I owe you so much; thank you for everything you have done. I'll stay a little while with my mother." Camille leaned forward to embrace Madame Genet. "And once the insurance comes through, I'll come back and rebuild the house."

"I know you will," said the old lady. "In the meantime, we'll take care of everything and forward any letters to you. Now off you go and drive safely."

Once underway, Camille zoomed uphill past Van Gogh's asylum, accelerating to leave her troubles behind. The new car was powerful, chic and feminine, and it incarnated her resolution to make a fresh start. She glanced down at Clovis beside her, and he stared back at her with brown, unblinking eyes. His scars were still pink, but they were healing quickly, and it felt good to have him by her side.

As her journey progressed, she reflected on what to say to her mother and Nadia. Yes, they had been right all along. Yes, her relationship with Max had been a total disaster, and worse than her mother had predicted, unimaginably worse. She knew that. It would be better not to tell them everything straightaway.

Reality only set in when it came to her that she could not avoid telling them she was pregnant. She couldn't hide that or the full weight of the extraordinarily negative turn her life had taken since she had been away. Denial would not make the truth go away. The simple facts were that she had discovered that Max was a psychopath who had deliberately tricked her into falling for him with the intention of stealing the family's money. Worse, he had made her pregnant and threatened her life twice. Even now, she found it hard to believe.

Much better to tell the whole sordid story to her mother and Nadia straightaway. Her mother knew the right people, the police chiefs, the magistrates and the lawyers. Max would be caught and locked up, the deed would be annulled, and the nightmare would be over. As she approached Lançon, she realised that she had yet to tell them that she was on her way home, and she pulled up by the Bar Tabac café beside the Esso garage on the main road.

"Come on, Clovis, my sweet boy," she said, and they walked together over to the café in the hot sun. Briefly, she turned to admire her new car, then pushed aside the thin curtain of coloured strips of plastic that shielded the open door from the flies.

Behind the simple zinc bar, a balding man with his back to her was arranging packets of French and British cigarettes on the lower shelves. Gauloises Bleues and Caporals, Gitanes, Boyards, Marigny, filter and non-filter, in front of Embassy, Rothmans, Players, Woodbines, red tins of Benson and Hedges and the flat white packets of Abdulla No 5. The increasingly popular, more expensive American cigarettes were arranged at eye level: Craven A, Camel, Marlboro, Philip Morris, Lucky Strike, Peter Stuyvesant, Chesterfield and Winston.

The room smelled of beer and tobacco, and the only other occupants were a thin man in his fifties with greying hair perched on a stool sipping Kronenbourg and a sallow youth in black wearing suede shoes with thick soles—brothel creepers Leo used to call them. A jukebox played Nights in White Satin by the Moody Blues, which competed with the noise from a television set above the bar.

"Bonjour Monsieur, may I use the telephone, please?"

The barman turned around from the cigarettes and proffered a token from a wooden box beside the cash register and waved his hand in the direction of a small telephone booth behind a glass door adorned with numerous business cards and handwritten messages advertising taxis, hairdressing, carpentry, piano lessons, used baby paraphernalia, a good time and more.

As she dialled the number, Camille thought about what to say. She was on her way home, she would be there in an hour, there was nothing to worry about. No need to go into details. There would be time to explain everything later.

Three times she got the engaged signal, and on the fourth, the telephone kept ringing and ringing. Where was everybody? Camille checked her watch: it was three minutes after three. As she waited, she watched the television idly through the glass door. Suddenly she saw a photo of her mother on the screen. They were talking about her mother.

She pushed open the door to hear the announcer discussing Juliette Dumont, the heroine of the 1936 Olympics with her gold medal, followed by a clip of her with Prime Minister Léon Blum at the official reception on her return to France. *My God, why are they talking about my mother?*

She put the receiver back on its cradle and hurried over to the bar.

"Why are they talking about Juliette Dumont?" she entreated the barman.

"Didn't you hear? She's dead," he replied matter-of-factly as he dried a beer glass. "They found her dead yesterday. Fell down the stairs or something."

It was not possible. Camille grabbed the bar to steady herself. "Are you sure, are you sure?" she insisted. "That's my mother they are talking about."

The thin man and the youth turned towards her, and the older man stood up and put his arm around her.

"Oh, mon Dieu. I am sorry, my dear, so very sorry," said the barman as tears streamed down Camille's face. "Here, take this."

He reached behind the counter and pulled out a box of Sanys paper tissues.

"Thank you, but no, I am fine," Camille said, weeping. "I must get home as soon as possible."

And she turned and ran back to her car, Clovis bounding on his leash behind her.

Chapter 16

REVELATIONS AND SECRETS

E verything was eerily quiet as Camille drove up to the house, uneasy and apprehensive. She had half-expected to see an ambulance and police cars, or journalists and a television crew. But there were no cars. No unusual activity.

She parked at the front, ran up to the door and pushed it open.

"Bobo," she cried out. "Nadia, are you there?"

At the same moment, Nadia rushed from the kitchen into Camille's arms.

"Oh, thank heavens, you are here. Where have you been? We… I've been trying to call you, but I couldn't get through. Oh, poor Juliette. I can't believe it, it's so awful… And what on earth has happened to you? You look frightful; your forehead is swollen and bruised! Are you hurt?"

"Wait, Bobo, wait. I am perfectly all right. I had a slight accident and banged my head, but I am fine now. Tell me about Maman. Where is she? Tell me it's not true that she's dead!"

"Yes, yes, it is true, poor Juliette. I found her you know, I found her lying on her back on the stairs."

"Oh no! That's terrible. Where is she now? When, when did this happen?"

"Yesterday, yesterday morning. I kept trying to call you but couldn't get through. Where have you been? Why didn't you answer?"

"My phone is out of order," Camille said.

"Oh Lord, I can't tell you how dreadful it was. I found her dead near the bottom of the stairs. She must have slipped and fallen in the night. They took her to the hospital yesterday morning. I can't tell you how horrible it was to see them putting her in an ambulance and pulling a sheet over her. It was unspeakable."

Nadia was shaking as she spoke.

"They said that she had probably been there for a while and must have lost her balance coming downstairs for something—or she could have been on her way upstairs. I don't know. I didn't hear anything. If only I had heard her fall, I might have saved her. Oh, God, I feel terrible. Poor, poor Juliette. I can't believe she's dead."

Camille listened quietly. "How horrible, what a shock that must have been. Do you think she banged her head as she fell?"

"We'll know very soon. At least there was no blood."

Nadia looked at Camille, her wide eyes overflowing with tears. "They'll have to do an autopsy. I can't bear to think of them cutting her up, my poor, beautiful Juliette."

It was later that day that Camille and Nadia found the courage to open Juliette's will locked in the safe in Bernard's room. Somehow, Camille had always imagined that as the only child and with Bernard dead, she might inherit everything from her mother, so it was something of a surprise to read that Juliette had left the house and her possessions to Nadia.

That evening they sat down to eat at the kitchen table. Nadia had prepared a gigot d'agneau with flageolet beans, and Camille opened a bottle of red wine for them both. Clovis sat quietly under the table.

"Camille," said Nadia, "I can hardly bring myself to tell you what a friend to me your mother was. Much, much more than you realise, but the time has come when I must. What I am about to tell you may come as a surprise, but I want you to listen quietly and understand that there are reasons we couldn't tell you this earlier.

"I remember you being surprised when you met my brother Alfons at Bernard's funeral. The truth is that Alfons and I met Juliette for the first time in Berlin in 1936, and when it came time for Juliette to return to France, she invited me to come and stay with her. I liked Paris so much that I applied to study at the Sorbonne, like Alfons."

Nadia stopped talking, sighed deeply, and took Camille's left hand with both of her own. "What I am going to say now may come as a shock."

She let go of Camille's hand to take a deep sip of wine, retook her hand, squeezed it and let it go. "Paris was everything I hoped it would be."

Nadia paused again and studied her wine glass before she turned to Camille and looked her straight in the eyes. "Well, and I don't want to over stress this, but Juliette and I became a little more than good friends, if you see what I mean. We were both very young and there were parties all the time and one thing led to another…"

Camille listened, enthralled.

"Paris wasn't quite as wild as Berlin, but we certainly had our share of fun. Anyway, I was accepted at the university and… you know your father was a professor of sociology at the Faculty of Humanities at the Sorbonne? In any case, he was an extraordinary man and incredibly attractive."

Camille said nothing.

"He even thought of your name. In 1936, Greta Garbo made a film called Camille based on La Dame aux Camélias by Alexandre Dumas. All three of us had a soft spot for Greta Garbo and loved the film, and that's another reason La Traviata is my favourite opera…" Nadia's voice trailed away. "And why we called you Camille."

Nadia's eyes filled with tears again, and she fell silent for a moment. She took both Camille's hands in hers.

"Antoine was a wonderful man and quite a bit older than us, and Juliette and I sort of shared him…"

Nadia paused again and looked down. "Anyway, one day, I became pregnant… And you are the result!"

Nadia stopped talking and watched a wave of astonishment sweep over Camille's face, and her tears begin to flow. "What? What did you just say? I can't believe this," said Camille through her tears. "Are you saying that you are my mother? But why? Why did you keep it a secret? Why didn't you tell me? It's incredible, all this time…"

Nadia was crying too, and for a while, they held each other tightly, rocking gently in a sea of tears.

"I hope so much you can forgive me," she said, her head resting on Camille's shoulder, "but when I became pregnant, I was too frightened to return to Germany. I was only eighteen and Alfons was about to go and live in America. Juliette sweetly said she would help, and although your father was already married, he was supportive too."

Nadia drew back and took Camille's hands again. "So, I decided to stay in Paris. Besides, everybody was so scared of what was happening in Germany."

"Oh my God, I can't believe this. You are my mother? I've always called you Bobo. Where does that come from?"

Nadia laughed softly and looked lovingly at Camille. "My family name was not Beausoleil, but Piękny-Słońce, which means 'beautiful sun' in Polish. At the Sorbonne, I was nicknamed Sunbeam, as Alfons was, and it was Juliette who came up with the name Beausoleil in French. And you who shortened it to Bobo."

"But I don't understand. Why did Juliette have to pretend to be my mother? I even look more like her than you. And where does the colour of my hair come from? Why couldn't you have told me?"

"Camille, there is something else. Your father's name was Antoine Meier. He was a professor of sociology, and yes, as you can guess from his name, he was Jewish, and yes, he had blond hair."

Nadia was looking intently at Camille. "Well," she continued, "although my father was Catholic and we were brought up as Catholics, Alfons and I always suspected our mother was Jewish—incidentally, Alfons confirmed that she was Jewish at Bernard's funeral.

"In any case, back in the 1930s it wasn't easy being Jewish in Germany. If the Nazis labelled you as Jewish, you were treated like a second-class citizen. It was quite different in France when I arrived in 1936 because French Jews were assimilated, and there was no stigma attached to being Jewish.

"There was intermarriage between the Jews and the French, and most Jews thought of themselves as French first. Although it's true that were already nationalists trying to stir things up against the Jews and the immigrants. Personally, I never thought about being Jewish. I had no reason to care if I was. As I told you, both Alfons and I were brought up as Catholics. So, when you came along, you were French as far as I was concerned. Not Jewish, nor German nor Polish, you were French. I was so proud to have a little French girl. And whenever he could, your father would come around and play with you. I still have photos of us all together, which I've kept for you.

"Things got worse when you were less than a year old. In July 1938 thousands of Polish Jews, who had been living happily in Germany for years—like us—were arrested and forcibly taken back across the Polish border. Alfons had warned me it might happen and that if it did, both of us might be classified as Polish Jews. Luckily for us, Alfons had left for America by then, and I was living in Paris.

"Among the Jews sent back to Poland were the parents of a Polish boy who lived in Paris, and in November, he went to the German Embassy and killed a diplomat to draw attention to what the Germans were doing to Jews. And the reaction in Germany was known as Kristallnacht."

Camille stared at Nadia, hanging on to every word. "Yes, we've all heard about Kristallnacht."

"Then you'll know that the Nazis set fire to synagogues and smashed the windows of Jewish-owned shops and homes throughout Germany. Thousands of Jews were deported to concentration camps, and I can tell you, even in Paris, we were terrified. There was no way I could even think of returning to Germany after that. Thank God Alfons had seen it coming.

"Of course, Kristallnacht prompted thousands more Jews to flee Germany, and many came to France. Most wanted to keep their ethnic traditions, unlike French Jews, so not all Parisians were thrilled about this influx of poor, strange-looking foreigners from Germany."

Nadia paused for a moment to take a sip of wine and grasp Camille's hand. "When war was declared in 1939, the French government interned all German-speaking immigrants, and I would have been one of them if they had found me. A year later when the Germans reached Paris, a new French government was installed."

"The Vichy government." Camille said.

"That's right," replied Nadia, "with pro-German people like Pierre Laval in charge who wanted Germany to win. The right-wing press began to print anti-Jewish articles, and Jews were denied important positions. And when we heard they were taking a census of foreigners, Juliette and I decided that I should stay in the apartment and not leave. Then Juliette did the most amazing thing.

"She decided to pretend that you were her child so that we could get food for you, and so it continued through the war. Through her connections, she got ration cards and papers drawn up and officially registered you as her child with a father unknown. You and I wouldn't be here but for her."

Nadia paused and took another sip of wine. "That way, Juliette could take you out for walks and be seen with you. Later on, she managed to get papers for me under the name of Nadine Beausoleil. Hard to believe, but we were helped by a German General we met in a nightclub in Berlin after the Olympics Games."

She paused again, and Camille took the opportunity to ask: "And this General lived in Paris?"

"Yes," replied Nadia, "he was very high up. Juliette met him again by chance when she was working in an antique shop. He came to buy a painting and recognised her. Everybody did, of course. They went to dinner and started seeing a lot of each other after that."

Nadia looked up at Camille. "You can guess what happened next… Please don't criticise her. You have no idea how difficult life was in those days. He was a good person to know, and through him, she got a special ID card that helped her get extra things, ordinary things that were hard to find. You know, like sugar and rice, soap, potatoes and meat. We had nothing, you see. You can't imagine what a difference it made to occasionally have milk and cheese, extra eggs and bread. Even wine and coffee sometimes."

Camille listened quietly. "What happened to my father? Do you know?"

"After the war broke out, we lost touch, but the last news we had was in July '42, just before the Vel d'Hiv …"

"The Vel d'Hiv?" asked Camille.

"Another terrible thing. The Vel d'Hiv was when the Germans arrested thousands of Jewish refugees and herded them into a sports stadium called the Vélodrome d'Hiver near the Eiffel Tower. From there, they were sent to the death camps."

"And you think my father was among them?"

"Oh no, I am sure he wasn't. He was French, remember? The word was that he had been arrested for refusing to wear a yellow star. I tried to find him after the war and discovered he had died in Auschwitz."

Nadia and Camille sat silently for a while until Camille finally said, "I still can't believe that you're my mother. I am very pleased, but I still find it hard to understand why you didn't tell me earlier. That's all."

"We did it for you. Both my papers and yours were false, remember. As a foreigner, I would have been arrested had they caught me, but with Juliette protecting us, we were safe. And then, when the war was over, it seemed sensible to continue in the same way. Many things were still unresolved and unpredictable. For years, old scores continued to be settled, so we decided that it would be better for you to be brought up as a Catholic and as Juliette's daughter.

"And that's what we did. It wasn't easy though; I can't tell you how often I wanted to take you in my arms and tell you. Especially when Juliette was hard on you, but you must understand what she did was for you, for me, for us both. She never had children of her own or got another opportunity to shine after Berlin. There were no Olympic Games in 1940 or 1944, and she was too old to compete in London in 1948. She was truly a wonderful person."

Camille looked at Nadia, her mother, tenderly and smiled.

Nadia had always been there for her. When she was hurt or felt sad, it was invariably Nadia who pulled her tightly against her bosom and stroked and caressed her neck. Juliette had never taken her in her arms.

"So, do I have any other family, any cousins you haven't told me about?"

"That's the saddest thing," said Nadia. "There were some cousins back in Poland, and I tried to trace them but found out they were arrested in June 1939 and died in a concentration camp somewhere."

They both fell silent for a moment.

"Let's talk about other things, Camille. Happier things. I want you to tell me all about your new house, your new car, your vineyard, Clovis and Max."

"Bobo, Nadia, I can't call you Maman yet; I hope you don't mind. It's true, I have so much I want to tell you, but do you mind if we don't do it tonight? You've given me a lot to think about, and I'm emotionally drained. And I hate to mention it, but we are going to have to talk about funeral arrangements at some stage," she said. "Shall we talk tomorrow morning?"

Camille was not inclined to sleep in her own small house that night, even if there had been a bed to sleep in. She kissed Nadia goodnight and hugged her, holding her tightly before walking outside into the clear night with Clovis. He ran around, excited by the new smells. He could sleep in the kitchen tonight, but tomorrow he would sleep outside.

Upstairs in the spare bedroom, sleep did not come easily. It had been a frenetic, emotional day. Camille pictured Juliette tripping and falling in slow motion before she smashed her head on the stone stairs. But why didn't she cry out as she fell? Surely Nadia would have heard her. A darker notion slunk into her mind: perhaps she didn't fall, maybe she was pushed, and only one person had a motive to kill her.

Shuddering, she remembered Max boasting about being taught to kill with his bare hands in the Foreign Legion. It was so blindingly obvious. Max must have killed her, and that meant that she, Camille was next in line. Because what Max did not know was that Nadia had inherited the house and the money.

She lay staring at the dark with her eyes wide open and resolved to tell the police everything in the morning.

Chapter 17

DRAMA IN VENTABREN

···

THE NEXT MORNING, Camille came out of her bedroom and paused on
the landing to picture Juliette leaving her room in the darkness,
tripping and plunging down the stairs. She must have screamed as she
fell; her fall must have made some noise. Downstairs in the kitchen,
Clovis welcomed her and wagged his tail so hard that his whole body swayed
back and forth like a little twist dancer. Camille opened the kitchen door to
let him out and watched him bound away.

She picked up the newspaper, eggs and fresh bread left by the back door. It
felt good to be back.

As she turned the handle on the coffee grinder, the kettle began to boil and
Clovis came running back through the open door, panting heavily. She emp-
tied a tin of Canigou into his bowl and added a little juice from last night's
lamb as he spun impatiently in circles. She patted him briefly, put his bowl
down and watched him guzzle his food. He was definitely on the mend.

Once the coffee was made and breakfast was ready, Camille sat down and
glanced at the newspaper headline announcing that the Casino Municipal of
Aix-en-Provence had been robbed again last night. Disguised as clients, two
armed men created panic by shooting in the air before fleeing with the evenings' takings.

Nadia came into the kitchen.

"Good morning, sweetheart," she said brightly, "how are you today? Did
you manage to get any sleep?"

"Good morning, Bobo," replied Camille, "no, not much. But I thought of
something in the night. When Maman fell down the stairs, are you certain
you didn't hear anything? Not even a faint cry or the sound of her falling?"

Nadia looked at her thoughtfully. "You know, I wondered about that, too.
I am a light sleeper but heard nothing, nothing at all."

Nadia poured herself a large bowl of coffee weakened with warm milk,
spread some butter on a sliced baguette and added some apricot jam.

"I've been thinking," said Nadia. "I've never even met Max, though I did
see him when he worked at the garage, and very handsome he is, too. Now
that you know that I am your mother, would you allow me to meet him?"

The moment had come to tell the truth.

Yes, she had fallen in love, yes, she had made poor decisions, and yes Max had turned out to be less, much less than she had been hoping for. And although they were no longer together, it had not been all bad. She owned a small house, she still had a vineyard producing good wine, and she had learned a lot about life and herself. More challenging to talk about were the details of her relationship, but she knew she needed to tell Nadia everything. Almost.

"This may sound strange," it was Camille's turn to take Nadia's hand, "but the first few weeks were perfect in many ways. Max was fun, hard-working and thoughtful, and I was quite happy. It wasn't romantic bliss, but we got on well and agreed on almost everything, especially politics. As you know, I've always preferred simplicity. But as we got to know each other, he started drinking too much and becoming less caring, and then disappearing for days at a time, claiming he had to be with his sick mother who lives six hours away in the Auvergne.

"Then came May 13. I'll never forget that day. Max was arrested in Saint-Rémy for being drunk and disorderly, and I had to collect him from the police station and pay a fine. I was quite angry because he was supposed to be in the Auvergne with his mother. Once we got home, he went straight to the winery saying he had work to do, but in the evening, he was drunk again, and we had a terrible argument. Well, we started fighting and... and he punched me in the face and knocked me out."

Nadia could not stop herself from interrupting. "He hit you in the face? And knocked you out?" she asked, alarmed.

"I'm sorry to say he did. He knocked me out cold. Luckily, our neighbour overheard us and called the police and..." Camille hesitated, "... and, well, they told me that Max was well known to them and..." She hesitated again before blurting out: "He has a wife and children in Beaucaire."

Nadia's face fell, and her mouth dropped open in astonishment. "I don't believe it," she gasped, squeezing Camille's hand.

Despite desperately trying to hide her despair, Camille's eyes brimmed over and with tears streaming down her cheeks, she went on to explain that this terrible news had been liberating.

"There is more," said Camille through her tears, "and this may come as a surprise. Do you remember that one of the first things you said to me was that I looked dreadful?"

"Oh, my goodness, did I say that? I am so sorry, I didn't mean to hurt you," Nadia protested.

"No, you didn't hurt me at all," said Camille. "It's perfectly true. I know I'm not looking my best. I have also been putting on weight, though not as much as I expect to put on."

Nadia's eyes widened in shock.

"Yes, Bobo, I am expecting a baby," confessed Camille and could not stop herself weeping again.

"Camille, that's marvellous, if very unexpected, and we'll just have to deal with it," said Nadia as she rocked Camille in her arms. "Don't forget, sweetheart, I went through something similar when I had you."

The final and equally fundamental reason that Camille was pleased she had left Max was more painful to explain; that he had duped her into signing a deed that included a clause de tontine, and a condition of possession réciproque which meant that everything she owned was his, and vice versa.

"The Gospel according to John, Chapter 17, verse 10: All I have is yours, and all you have is mine, and in them, I am glorified." There was a faint look of triumph on Nadia's face as she said it. "There, that surprised you, didn't it?"

"Well, yes, it did," laughed Camille. "How do you know that?"

"Needs must, and I was brought up a Catholic, remember," said Nadia. "So it means he would inherit your house and vineyard?"

"Worse than that. The lawyer said that if I were to die before him, he would inherit everything I owned at the time of my death, not just the house and vineyard. And I am sure he thinks that now Maman is dead, I have inherited this house."

At that moment, there was a loud knock, and Clovis charged to the front door barking furiously. Camille and Nadia exchanged glances fearfully, as if it might be Max.

"Now, who could that possibly be?" Camille asked.

Nadia opened the door cautiously to four men: two in police uniforms carrying canvas bags, a tall man in a black suit, and an overweight older man with a kindly, lived-in face who wore a flat cap and a Burberry trench coat.

"Bonjour Madame," said the tall man in the black suit. "May we come in?"

"Bonjour Mesdames, I am Chief Inspector Paquet," the older man in the trench coat said. "You may remember we met a year ago? When you found the owner of the garage dead?"

"I remember you very well. Please come in."

Camille ushered the four men into what had been Bernard's room, and they explained the reasons for their visit.

Inspector Paquet spoke first. "It falls to me to give you the news, and it's not good news as it happens."

He brushed an imaginary speck off his shoulder. "A preliminary autopsy has been completed on the body of Madame de Vaucluse, as required by law in the event of any unnatural or unexplained death, however the pathologist has brought an anomaly to our attention that requires further tests and investigation."

He paused and looked first at Camille, then at Nadia.

"There were bruises on Madame de Vaucluse's neck, head, and chin that could have been caused by falling against the banisters and onto the stairs, but none were serious enough nor symptomatic of the type of injury that could cause death. The pathologist has determined that Madame de Vaucluse's death was due to asphyxia."

Paquet paused to read from the pathologist's report, "…asphyxia caused by decreased oxygen delivery to the brain, either by compression of the cervical blood vessels or by tracheal occlusion."

Paquet looked up at Camille and Nadia as they exchanged uneasy glances.

"While it is within the realms of possibilities that these injuries were caused by the deceased falling down the stairs, the pathologist informs me that Madame de Vaucluse had multiple fractures in the bones in her neck, including the hyoid bone. Now, experience tells us that it is exceedingly rare for a hyoid bone fracture to be caused by blunt trauma. However, a broken hyoid bone is common in victims of homicide by strangulation."

The inspector paused again.

"We are not ruling out an accident, but given the illustrious reputation of the deceased, particular care must be taken in this affair until it can be said with absolute certainty that this was a homicide or an accidental death."

The man hesitated before addressing Nadia and Camille directly. "Given the results, we will need to re-examine the scene of the incident and try and establish what happened."

"So, in other words you now think it was murder?" asked Camille.

"We do not know at this stage," the police officer said defensively. "It is our duty to establish the facts. Madame de Vaucluse may indeed have slipped and fallen on the stairs, but in those circumstances, it is very unusual for the victim to die. We need to complete our investigation with more tests before we can rule out an accident, and we will not be able to release the body until all the facts have been established."

Camille shivered and gripped Nadia's hand.

"If you think it could be a homicide, I know who did it," she said slowly, and all four men and Nadia turned in her direction.

She told her story methodically and deliberately so that the inspector and officers could keep up with their notes. When she had finished, Paquet put down his pad and addressed the two women.

"If it turns out that this individual, this Max Morel, did break into the house, he can't have come in through the front door because, Madame Beausoleil, you told me that you are certain the front door was still locked when your call for help was answered. A conclusion we may draw is that the perpetrator, if there was one, may have wanted to make it appear as if the fall was an accident and not leave any sign of a break-in. But if that is the case, how did he get into the house?

"Please don't touch anything, and I will ask the gentlemen to fingerprint you both, before they dust the windows, the front and back doors, all the locks, and everywhere else. Once we finish, you should check to see if anything is missing or out of place. In the deceased's room, for example. Papers, money, or valuables. And please check the safe, if you have one."

"Before you start, Inspector," said Camille, "about Walter Clément's death a year ago. Did you ever reach a conclusion? Did you establish whether it was murder or suicide?"

"We know that it was murder staged to look like suicide. Clément was nearly dead when he was put in the car, but we don't have the culprit yet."

"May I suggest you look at Max Morel? He took over the garage after Walter died, and I believe he killed him to reach us."

※

That afternoon, the house was swarming with more police and specialists from the Institut de Recherche Criminelle de la Gendarmerie Nationale, taking photographs from every angle, dusting the doorknobs and the banisters for fingerprints, examining the windows and doors for signs of forced entry, and meticulously sweeping the floors for evidence. It was all a little late, but the assumption that it was a routine accident and the improbability that the legendary Juliette Dumont could have been murdered had distracted the officers from being as diligent as they should have been.

When the police finished, Nadia and Camille began their search for missing valuables. There were few places they needed to consider: the sitting room, the safe in Bernard's office and Juliette's rooms.

They found nothing missing.

❧

The following day, a letter arrived from Saint-Rémy forwarded by Madame Genet. It was from the insurance company and addressed to both Camille and Max.

"Here you are," said Nadia. "Open it. I bet it's good news."

Camille opened it and stood still, stunned into silence. "Two checks," she said at last, "one for me and one for Max."

Camille sat down with her head in hands. "That's it! The bastard! That's why he burned the house down."

"What are you saying, Camille, burned what house down?"

"I didn't tell you, did I? Max burned the bloody house down. I couldn't understand it at first." Camille still had her head in her hands. "He burned the house down for the insurance money because he knew the house was in both names."

"Are you going to tell the police?" asked Nadia.

"Oh, I'll tell them, but they won't be able to prove anything. He made the fire look accidental by choosing July 14. That's his specialty, making things look accidental. The investigation they couldn't rule out fireworks. But you are right, dammit, I should add that to his dossier. I have nothing to lose."

Inspector Paquet listened politely. "As you know, we already have a strong circumstantial case against the man. And if we add what you just told me to what we already have, including your mother's demise and Monsieur Clément's death, we have enough to bring him in."

That afternoon, the *Juge d'Instruction* [Examining Magistrate] issued a warrant for the arrest of Max Berger Morel residing at 8 Rue Jean Lestchenko in Beaucaire, Languedoc-Roussillon.

Camille was numb. Back in Saint-Rémy, bruised by the emotional ups-and-downs of the last few months, Ventabren had seemed like a beacon of peace, safety and sanity. Now this. And the awful reality that she, Camille, could have been even remotely responsible for Juliette's death was unbearable. Camille did not sleep well that night, despite Nadia's reassurance she was not to blame.

The following morning she was still consumed with guilt when she reached the head of the stairs. She paused once again and imagined Max breaking her mother's neck like the animals he trapped in the valley.

Camille shook her head and wiped her eyes as she came into the kitchen. She unlocked the back door, let the dog in, and picked up the paper and the bread. She had begun to make the coffee when Nadia entered the kitchen.

"Good morning, my angel," said Nadia picking up the paper from the table. "Oh no, did you see the paper? Did you see this?"

She held it up to show the headline emblazoned across the front page.

MARIANNE ASSASSINEE !
Juliette Dumont, héroïne de 1936 assassinée chez elle !

Camille looked over stunned and stopped grinding.

"How could they print that? Who told them it was murder? Oh, poor Maman, that's sickening! And to think all this was my fault." Her tears gushed as she fell into Nadia's arms.

Less than thirty minutes later, there was the sound of a car on the gravel outside, and Clovis began to bark. Nadia opened the door to a young man with a broad smile and a felt hat.

"Good morning, Madame, I'm from the Sud-Ouest newspaper," he said, tipping his hat. "I wonder if I may have a few words?"

Behind him, a second car was coming up the drive.

"Camille, please send them away quickly, and go and lock the gates. The press will be coming in droves. And put up a notice saying NO PRESS."

Turning to the reporter, she added, "We have nothing to say, nothing at all. We are much too upset and ask you to respect our privacy and leave us alone. Please."

"You realise," Camille said to Nadia a little later, "all this will put more pressure on Max? I know he's planning to kill me. I'm going to ask the police to protect us. If Max could get into the house and kill Maman without breaking in, he could do it again."

"Except this time, we'll be expecting him," said Nadia with a gleam in her eye. "Let me show you something."

Camille followed her upstairs and into her bedroom.

She had always liked Nadia's room, lined with bookshelves awash with biographies of artists and musicians, composers and philosophers. And on a table by the window sat her old Pye Black Box record player, and an LP collection of German and Italian operas, Brassens and Brel, and British and American rock and roll. Most of all, Camille loved the collection of detective novels that Nadia used to read to her, and the four-poster bed with red hangings.

Getting down on her knees, Nadia leaned forward and pulled out a brown leather suitcase from under the bed.

"This is the suitcase I wanted to give you should anything happen to me," she said, opening the lid. Inside were two leather journals, several brown envelopes full of papers and photographs, and a jumble of small mementos from Camille's childhood.

"Here it is. Look at this," Nadia said, unwrapping a black leather holster from a white cloth. Inside was a German officer's Luger P08 semiautomatic 9mm pistol.

"Oh, my goodness! Where did you get that?" exclaimed Camille. "Do you have ammunition for it?"

"Yes, I do," said Nadia. "It was Juliette's. She was given it to protect herself when the officers' Lugers were replaced with Walther P38's. She gave it to me. I've never fired it, though I know how to, and I've got a few boxes of bullets for it. Watch this."

Nadia pressed the release button below the trigger and removed the magazine. Expertly she pressed on the barrel, rotated a small lever on the left, and slid off the assembly.

"I could take it to pieces completely, but I'm not going to now. I used to practice disassembling it and reassembling it all the time because it gave me something to do. And anyway, if you want to keep them functioning, you're supposed to keep them clean."

"Who taught you to do all that?" asked Camille.

"Nobody," said Nadia brightly. "It came with a book of instructions. German was my first language, remember."

Camille concluded that she hardly knew Nadia at all.

"Oh, and I also have this." Nadia had that glint in her eye as she bent down and pulled out a long object wrapped in a soft cloth. "Another souvenir of the war."

Camille unwrapped the bundle and gasped. It was a long knife, an ornamental dagger with an ivory handle and a polished, ten-inch blade guarded by an eagle standing on a swastika.

"That is so amazing," Camille said, trembling. "The night after Bernard died, I dreamed he gave me a knife like that, and I threw it away."

"This isn't a knife, Camille," said Nadia, "this is a German Officer's dress dagger. It's still incredibly sharp. Don't you like it?"

"I do, I do. I find it very beautiful in a macabre way," said Camille. "Where do you think we should keep all this?"

"All right," said Nadia, "I suggest we keep the gun in the drawer of the hall table by the front door, where the phone is. We could keep the dagger with the cutlery in the kitchen—or the safe would be a better place, don't you think?"

"Better keep it in the safe," said Camille. "I don't want to see it every time I cook something. But if Max does come and pay us a visit, he is in for a surprise."

They looked at each other and laughed.

They did not have long to wait. That evening the telephone rang for the umpteenth time that day.

"If that is somebody from the press again," said Camille as she strode towards the telephone, "I am going to give them a piece of my mind."

"Camille, listen carefully," said a voice. It was Max.

"My God, it's you. How dare you call me here!"

"Listen, listen to me, Camille. I can't talk for long. I am sorry to hear about your mother, but I need cash and I need it quickly. By Monday. If you give me thirty thousand francs in cash, I will sign a paper annulling our contract, including the deed, and even give my copy to you. Then I will go away, and you will never hear from me again."

"Are you crazy, Max? Where do you think I can get that kind of money in cash by Monday? It's Friday evening, and the banks are closed."

"You'll find the money, Camille. Bring it to the last confessional on the left in the church Du Saint-Esprit in the Rue Espariat in Aix, at ten minutes past midday on Monday. That'll give you time to collect it from the bank. Do NOT tell the police about this. If you do, I won't sign the paper, and you won't get your deed back. Do not tell anybody about this, under any circumstances. This is between you and me."

Camille put the receiver down and turned slowly towards Nadia. "The bastard wants thirty thousand francs by Monday, in cash. Tell me, where am I going to find that much cash without giving the bank notice."

"Thirty thousand francs?" asked Nadia. "As a matter of fact, I have some cash put aside, a little over twenty thousand. That's a start."

"You think we should give him all that? And what about the police? He said not to tell them."

"Camille, think about it. If the police arrest him before he signs the paper, we will still have the problem of the deed. But if we give him the money, and he gives us the deed, and then the police arrest him, we'll get the deed and the money back. Don't you see? We have to outwit him, that's all."

"Bobo—look, I am still calling you Bobo—you amaze me. First, you produce a gun, then you tell me you have twenty thousand francs in cash, and now you want to outfox the fox."

"Don't forget, we had to think on our feet during the war." Nadia's eyes gleamed again. "Juliette and I outsmarted a lot of people more dangerous and brighter than Max. And remember, Camille, we have an ace up our sleeve."

"And what, may I ask, is the ace up our sleeve?"

"Me!" said Nadia triumphantly. "Me! He's never even met me, so he doesn't know what I look like. Or that I've got a gun."

Camille awoke to the familiar trill of cicadas. How she had missed that gentle chatter swishing in waves up the drive, a syncopated mantra building to a crescendo, falling back to pianissimo and swelling to crescendo again. It was going to be another scorching day.

As she lay listening, she was suddenly overcome with relief. Despite the shadow of Max, despite the death of Juliette, despite all the unpleasantness— or because of it—she felt safe here, and Saint-Rémy had become faded, grey and irrelevant. Blurred and faraway, like a distant memory.

Over breakfast, Nadia and Camille debated as to whether they should tell the police.

"I have a better idea," said Nadia. "Max said we shouldn't, and if he finds out we did, it could make him more violent. Once you give him the money, I could follow him with my gun, and…"

"And what?" interrupted Camille impatiently. "You have no idea what he is like. More violent, you say? How much more violent could he be? He's already killed Maman, and he's tried to kill me, on top of which, if the police are there, and we give him the money in exchange for the deed, we'll have proof that we gave it to him.

"It's the only way."

Chapter 18

GIVE OR TAKE

....

"I'VE VISITED EVERY CHURCH IN AIX," said Nadia, "and I know the Du Saint Esprit well. It's quite pretty and was the first church in Aix to be built in the Baroque style with chandeliers and Corinthian columns."

"I don't need to know that," said Camille crossly.

"Listen to me," replied Nadia. "The point I am making is that the church is small and dingy, so it's dark inside. There is a wide central nave with a narrow aisle on each side and there are only two confessionals."

Nadia and Camille made their way separately to the church, with Nadia preceding Camille by thirty minutes so that she could sit close to the last confessional on the left and pray with her head bowed. The police had pledged to hide discreetly and not make a move until Camille emerged with the signed paper in her hand and gave the signal.

At six minutes past midday, Camille arrived. As a sign of respect for Juliette, she was dressed entirely in black and wore the same hat with a veil she had worn at Bernard's funeral. The church was almost empty apart from a few scattered worshipers and the choir practicing Sanctus-Benedictus a capella by the altar. Nadia was already in place in a pew near the confessionals, transported by the heavenly voices of the choir.

Neither of the confessional's red lights were on, and in the pew ahead of Nadia was a young woman who, like Nadia, was enchanted by the singing. On the other side of the main aisle, two men in dark suits had arrived a moment after Camille. They sank to their knees and prayed. Another man, two rows behind, read the bible.

Camille genuflected, made the sign of the cross, and discreetly made her way up the left aisle of the church. According to custom, she covered her left ear as she passed the first confessional. At the second, she paused, knocked gently at the door and entered swiftly without waiting for an answer.

For ten minutes, nothing happened. Camille waited, barely able or daring to breathe. Then she heard the heavy church door creak on its hinges and the echo of its heavy latch being lifted. But ten more minutes passed without a sign of Max.

Finally, after twenty minutes of waiting, she opened the confessional door and walked over to Nadia and whispered. "No sign of Max. Have you seen him?"

The three male worshipers made their way over to the two women.

"Good morning, ladies," said Inspector Paquet, who was dressed in a dark suit. "Too bad he didn't show up. I've got police inside and outside the church; he would never have got away."

"So, what do we do now?" asked Nadia.

"Nothing. You'll have to wait for him to contact you again," came the reply.

Camille and Nadia were in a melancholy mood as they drove home in their cars that afternoon. Outside the gates, a uniformed gendarme stopped them and saluted as they drove up.

"Good afternoon, ladies. I've been asked to watch over you until eight tonight, after that, a colleague will take over. He'll stay until two in the morning, then another will take the night watch for six hours. You have nothing to worry about. We are in radio contact with the station and will guard you twenty-four hours a day."

"Well, that's reassuring, thank you," said Nadia. "I hope you scare him away."

"Dear God, that's it!" Camille said as they approached the house from the stables. "That's how he got in the house to kill Maman."

"What? What are you talking about?" asked Nadia alarmed.

"The key to the front door of the house. I kept it hanging behind my door in the cottage. I bet he took it."

Taking Clovis with them, they walked quickly over to the cottage and tried the door. It was unlocked, and cautiously they pushed it open. Sensing tension, Clovis emitted a low growl.

Inside, the cottage was much as she had left it, but as Camille feared, the key to the main house was missing.

"You know what that means?" said Camille anxiously. "It means he has the key to the front door. That explains why the front door was still locked after Maman died. He relocked it after killing her."

"We are going to have to bolt all the doors and windows tonight, that's for sure," said Nadia. "And you can sleep in my room if you want to. I'll call the locksmith and get the locks changed."

Late that afternoon the telephone rang.

"Quick, pick it up. It's probably Max," said Nadia.

"Hello?" said Camille hesitatingly.

"Good evening, Mademoiselle Dumont. This is Inspector Paquet. I am so sorry about what happened—or what didn't happen in the church today. As you must have noticed by now, I've arranged to have your house guarded around the clock, and if Morel tries to telephone you, we will be listening. Just be sure to keep him talking so that we can trace the call. Do not worry. You won't see us, but we are there. We will catch this man; I assure you."

Camille turned to Nadia after she hung up. "You know, one thing I'm sure of is that Max is no fool. He may be a psychopath, but he's more devious and craftier than Machiavelli himself. I don't think they have the faintest idea who they are dealing with."

That evening, after a light supper, Camille and Nadia went around the house to ensure that the windows were fastened and the deadbolts on the front and kitchen doors were tightly locked. They debated whether it would be better to let Clovis sleep inside before deciding he should sleep in his kennel outside.

"Listen," said Nadia, "he's a guard dog. If he sees or hears anything at all, he'll start barking, and the policeman at the gate will come running. It's better if he sleeps outside. That's his job."

And with that, Clovis trotted happily off to his kennel and Nadia bolted the kitchen door behind him.

※

When Camille awoke, the sun was streaming through the curtain-less window, and the cicadas were silent. I know what that means, she thought, the Mistral is back. By the time she reached the kitchen, her thoughts had turned back to Max. Nadia was preparing breakfast.

"Where's Clovis?" asked Camille. "Have you let him in yet?"

She opened the door and called his name. "Clovis, Clovis! Come here. Clovis!"

There was no answer. That was unlike him. She called his name again and ran outside to look for him with growing trepidation.

"Clovis, Clovis! Where are you? For God's sake, where are you?"

She heard flies swarming and knew he was dead before she reached the tree, the same tree with the cicadas that Max had shown her a year ago. Clovis was upside down, strung up by his back legs from a branch. His sightless eyes were still open, and Camille wailed when she saw his throat was cut.

Screaming and sobbing inconsolably, she tried to release the poor dog as the policeman came running from the front gate.

"Are you all right, Miss?" the policeman cried.

"What does it look like? He's killed my fucking dog! He's killed my dog for God's sake! Look at it! Didn't you see him, didn't you hear anything? I thought you were supposed to be guarding us."

"Please don't touch anything," said the officer. "I'll call Inspector Paquet from the car."

It was a good hour before Camille was able to calm down, holding her head in hands, pacing up and down. By the time the inspector arrived, a ferocious unshakable resolve, steeled with the daring of Nadia, had set in.

"That bastard. First, he tricks me, then he tries to kill me, then he kills my mother, and now he kills my dog," she growled.

Later that morning, two locksmiths arrived to change the locks on all the doors.

"Make sure you change the lock on the cottage door too," said Camille. "And that every window in both houses locks securely."

By late afternoon, the locksmiths had finished.

"We couldn't match the old locks on the doors, so we replaced them with something stronger and more modern. We've also added a spy hole on the front door, so you can see who is outside. And see this chain? Hook it up before you open the door to anybody. These old doors are very sturdy though, solid oak; you'd need a tank to get through them. We checked all the window frames in the house, and they are oak too and very strong. Most of the locks were working fine and we only had to reseat four of them—just keep them locked and you'll have nothing to worry about. And make sure you close all the shutters at night."

That afternoon, a letter postmarked from Marseille arrived. It was from Max's friend Pierre.

> Camille,
> Call me at Aix 67523 on Thursday morning (August 8) at 11
> or at the latest on Friday morning (August 9) at 11
> It is important.
> Pierre
> P.S. usual conditions apply.

"Does 'usual conditions' mean what I think it means?" Camille asked Nadia.

"It means don't tell the police, and I am not sure we should. They bungled it last time. Let's do as Pierre asks and call him at eleven tomorrow. We'll see what he has to say and decide then. We can't call from the house because the police are listening. Let's call him from the village."

The next day they drove up to the village in Nadia's car, a beige Citroen 2CV. And as a precaution before leaving, she showed Camille how to work the Luger.

"Don't be silly. We won't be needing this," Camille said. "There is no reason for Max to show up in the village."

"You can't be too careful," replied Nadia. "You told me Max is capable of anything and we have to be one step ahead. Anyway, I want you to feel comfortable with it."

The public telephone box was by the Bon Accueil at the top of the village, and they parked the car behind the church and walked. Nadia checked her watch.

"It's almost eleven. You dial, I'll read out the numbers. Here, take this," she said, and handed Camille a token. "I'll listen on the earpiece."

The phone had hardly begun ringing before it was answered.

"Camille? Ah, Camille, I was hoping you would call," gushed Pierre, in a thin metallic voice that oozed insincerity. "It's been a while since we met. Why don't we meet for a drink at Chez Thomé? You must know it. It is off the road behind Le Relais Cézanne in Le Tholonet. You went there with Max. Tomorrow at eleven would be perfect, on the terrace outside. Only you, though, nobody else please." The line went dead.

Camille did not have time to reply or say a word.

As they returned to the house, they discussed whether to tell the police and after decided that they should, Inspector Paquet came around to the house to discuss it.

"We'll check the number you called, though it's certain to be a public telephone somewhere and there are hundreds, if not thousands in Aix and the surrounding villages."

"One thing, Inspector, is that your men must be more discreet this time," Camille leaned forward as she spoke. "Max is a man who knows nature better than anyone, and Le Tholonet is on the edge of the forest. If he could avoid you so easily in the church, even police dogs wouldn't find him in Le Tholonet. I know this man. He will be watching. I am sure he was watching me at the church and will watch me meet Pierre tomorrow. So, if he realises that the police are there…"

Camille paused and looked down at her hands and looked up with fire in her eyes.

"I know he plans to kill me because he thinks I've inherited the house. And for that matter, I intend to bring thirty thousand francs in cash just in case.

It will be hidden in the car, and I won't give it to him unless I absolutely have to."

"Camille," said the policeman. "Promise to only give him the money after he has given you the house deeds. He knows he is a wanted man. We will be watching, and we'll only intervene if your life is in danger. I will go alone to Chez Thomé, that I promise. But I will have reinforcements hidden close by, and they will be armed. Neither Morel nor Paglioni know me, so there is no chance at all I'll be recognised."

Camille looked at Nadia and saw that she intended to be there too.

❧

Pierre Paglioni was already at Chez Thomé, sitting at a small table on the terrace by himself when Camille arrived. He jumped to his feet to shake her hand and pulled another chair out for her.

"Sit here, Camille, sit here," he said as the waitress arrived with two glasses.

"A glass of red wine?" he suggested.

"Where's Max?" asked Camille testily.

"Oh, come on! You didn't think he would show up here, did you?" Pierre replied harshly. "Our mutual friend is angry with you. He made you a serious offer, and he wants this business to be concluded rapidly. He's as tired of this as you are."

"I doubt it," snapped Camille. "And if by 'our mutual friend,' you mean Max. Call him Max. This isn't a game. Where is he anyway?"

"I can't tell you that, but I can tell you that Max is not happy with you. You were stupid to tell the police you were going to meet him in the church. I hope you won't be stupid again this time?"

"No," said Camille grimly, "I will not. I want this thing over."

"That's good; it's better that way." Pierre leaned forward, and lowering his voice said, "As I am sure you will understand, Max is disappointed by what happened in the church. You let him down, and he has raised the price. He will not go through this again. He wants me to tell you that this is your last chance. He now wants fifty thousand francs, or the deal is off."

"Fifty thousand francs? That's a huge amount of money. Where am I going to get fifty thousand?" She paused and looked hard at Paglioni, who stared back at her with his piercing blue eyes.

"If I agree," said Camille warily, "I insist that I give it to him personally, to Max, in exchange for his copy of the deed with my signature on it and a signed codicil revoking it. I won't give any money to you under any circumstances."

Pierre threw his head back and laughed. "Oh Camille, oh Camille! I am only here as a friend, as a friend to you both! As your witness. Remember when we signed that loan agreement last year? When I witnessed your signature for you? Well, you'll need me to witness Max's signature, if you want Max to sign a codicil revoking the contract with you. Don't you think?"

"No," Camille countered, "I don't think. I want his copy of the property deed, the original, back."

"Calm down, Camille, calm down. That's what you'll be getting: Max's copy of the house deed and a signed codicil. In exchange for what we talked about…"

"The money, in exchange for the money," interrupted Camille.

"Yes, in exchange for the money. He wants it in used fifty and one-hundred-franc notes and wrapped in cellophane in a plastic bag, so please respect that. I repeat, wrapped in cellophane in a plastic bag. And if you do, and only if you do, Max is prepared to annul his copy by putting his signature to these words."

Pierre handed Camille an unsigned letter written on a letterhead from Maître Chapuis:

'I, Max Berger Morel, agree unequivocally and unconditionally to the annulment and dissolution of the deed as it relates to my proprietary rights at 10 rue Roger Salengro, Saint-Rémy-de-Provence, specifically as it relates to the clause de tontine and the clause de *possession réciproque* in the attached deed signed in Aix with Camille Dumont on February 27, 1968, and to renounce any claim in perpetuity to the said property, goods, capital, or future inheritance of Camille Dumont with immediate effect.'

"You can read this, but don't touch it. Max will sign it and give it to you with his copy of the deed when you give him the money."

"All right," said Camille after reading it, "in principle, I agree. And after that, he will leave me alone?"

"Yes, he will. He will vanish from your life and never contact you again. He will give you his word."

Camille almost laughed. Max's word?

"So, what's the next step?" she asked.

"It would easier if we could all meet in Aix somewhere, but for obvious reasons, we are not going to be able to do that. What Max suggests is that we meet soon on neutral territory not far from here."

"So, where will that be?" asked Camille.

"I can't tell you that now, but we could begin by meeting here again, at Chez Thomé, next Tuesday at six P.M., and I'll take you to the meeting place in Max's Peugeot. So, bring the money and no friends."

"There is no way that I will be getting in a car alone with you. I will follow you in my car and bring Madame Beausoleil, my mother's friend, who lives with me. She can be a witness if I need one."

"All right," said Pierre, "but we don't want you driving that red convertible. You must drive something less conspicuous, more commonplace. Do you have another car you can use?"

"Madame Beausoleil has a beige Citroen 2CV. Would that work?"

"A 2CV? Yes, that should do it. I may have to see the car first, but it sounds okay. Let's agree to meet again next Tuesday. Come here at five, and don't forget the money."

When Camille got home, she was amused to see Nadia's car drive up behind her with Inspector Paquet's car right behind.

"So how did it go?" asked the inspector breathlessly, running over to Camille. "You didn't see me, but I was right there, in the restaurant, laying the tables and cleaning glasses. I could see you, though I couldn't hear anything you were saying. And, incidentally, did you notice the waitress? She was one of ours, too."

Camille smiled and got out of the car. She had been beginning to lose faith in the pedantic policeman, but once back in the house she explained what she and Pierre had discussed.

"I'm not sure this is a good idea," said Paquet. "If we don't know in advance where you are going, how can we protect you? We can't very well have a squad of police cars following you, and you are not giving me much time to get this organised. At best we can have unmarked cars covering the exit roads and communicate by radio."

"I'm sure you'll find a way," said Nadia.

Chapter 19

CONTENTION

················

Nadia and Camille were up early.

"Have you seen the weather?" asked Nadia. "It's pretty dismal. They said it may rain later."

"Yes," agreed Camille, "I saw that. At least it'll be cooler today."

"I'm excited," said Nadia to Camille as she poured the coffee. "I cleaned my Luger last night and filled up both magazines. That gives me sixteen bullets altogether. That should be enough, don't you think?"

Camille laughed.

"Enough? I should hope so! You amaze me. You're excited? I'm absolutely terrified. You sound as if you are hoping to use that thing," she said. "Please tell me I'm wrong?"

"I've had it for years: it's about time I fired it. I hope I won't have to use it, but I'm prepared to if I have to. Don't forget this is the man who killed Juliette, tried to kill you and killed your dog."

"I know, I know. I feel the same way as you do. But Bobo, bear in mind by even carrying that gun, you will be breaking the law. This isn't 1944. If you shoot him, you'll be in trouble. If you kill him, you'll go to prison. I beg you to be careful, and only use it as a last resort."

"Oh my!" laughed Nadia. "Who is whose mother? Listen, I am supposed to be the wise one, and I promise I'll be careful."

"I spoke to our diligent friend Inspector Paquet," said Camille, "he said we should go straight to Chez Thomé and make sure we are there before six and not to worry about them. Personally, I am scared as hell that Max will try to double-cross us. What happens if he does? What happens if he tries to take the money before he signs the codicil or tricks us some way? We'll be in an even worse position."

"Listen Camille, we've been through all this. That's what the gun is for!" Nadia said, looking up.

Camille opened up a map of Sainte-Victoire and the surrounding region.

"I spent time looking at the map last night," she said. "Come and see this. Here's Aix, and these are the two roads running east that skirt the mountain, one to the north, the other to the south. The D10, on the north side, runs from Aix through the village of Saint-Marc-Jaumegarde and onto Vauvenargues.

"The one on south side, the D17 from Aix, skirts the mountain and passes through Le Tholonet until it peters out in Puyloubier, seven miles further on. Bobo, those two roads enclose the whole Mont Sainte-Victoire reserve. It's an enormous area and includes both the Aix reservoirs, Lac Zola and Lac du Bimont."

"Yes, I get it. I know all this," said Nadia impatiently. "What's your point?"

"The point is you don't know Max. This is the kind of countryside where he will feel at home. Look at this." Camille pointed. "See all the service roads, tracks, and trails running through the reserve? The place is thick with trees. The police are going to need to be on their best game to find Max if he gets away."

"I am away ahead of you, Camille," said Nadia. "Inspector Paquet went through all this with me yesterday. He is hiding unmarked police cars on all the roads leading away from Chez Thomé: if Pierre turns right out of the parking lot to go south, there will be a car to follow him and radio the other cars. If he turns left out of Chez Thomé, which is the most likely, there will be two cars to cover him if he takes the D17 to Aix. If he turns right towards Puyloubier, two other cars will follow him.

"Paquet will be in his white Simca and will follow Max's Peugeot and us in my 2CV at a discreet distance. All the police cars will be unmarked with two policemen in each car, and which ever one sees us first will radio our position to the others, and then follow us inconspicuously until overtaken by another unmarked police car. I think it's a good plan."

It had not started raining when Camille and Nadia arrived just before six P.M. at Chez Thomé, but rain threatened, and the sky was overcast. They were careful not to park near the inspector's white Simca, but both noticed that Max's car had not arrived. They chose a table on the terrace, in sight of the car park, and sat down without talking. After a minute or so, the bartender came over to Camille and asked:

"Excuse me, are you Camille Dumont?"

"Yes, I am," replied Camille. "Is there a problem?"

"No problem," replied the bartender, "a man called Pierre was here earlier and asked me to tell you he can't meet you here. He left this note for you."

He handed Camille a sealed envelope.

"Thank you," said Camille tearing open the envelope. Nadia leaned forward to see it too.

It was typewritten.

```
Camille, a change of plan
1. Go back to your car at 6.15 P.M.
2. TURN LEFT from Chez Thomé and drive to the Relais
Cézanne
3. Turn RIGHT onto the D17
4. After exactly 1.5 km, TURN LEFT at a large sign 'Parc
Départemental de Roques Hautes' and a red sign saying
DFCI
5. Take the RIGHT fork marked by another small red DFCI
sign and follow the track for 400 metres until it forks
again
6. TURN RIGHT, then LEFT, and drive for 500 metres until
it swings sharply to the left and begins to get steeper
7. Ahead you will see a sign that says 'Private Road. No
entry to the public. Service Road. Nature Reserve of
Sainte-Victoire.' Ignore it, and drive straight on
8. Drive for 2.6 km (it's steep in places) all the way
up to the dam at Lac du Bimont
9. Max will be waiting for you on the far side of the
dam.
```

With Camille driving and Nadia reading the instructions, they turned left from the car park in the small beige car towards the D17. There was no sign of Max's Peugeot.

"I hope to God the inspector is on his toes," said Nadia. "This wasn't the plan."

"We have to trust him, Bobo," replied Camille looking in the mirror. "Anyway, I can see his white car. He's following us. Keep an eye on the directions, we turn right here."

Camille turned right onto the D17. After a mile or so, she turned left as Nadia followed Pierre's instructions. Two small DFCI signs, then right again, up the track for four hundred metres until the trail forked again. Right, then left, along the track for five hundred metres, then sharp left until they saw the sign saying 'Private Road. No entry to the public. Service Road.' They sailed on past it and sped north up the incline under mature pine trees in the direction of the dam.

"Don't you love my little car?" asked Nadia breezily. "Did you know it was designed to carry two farm workers and a sack of potatoes across a ploughed field without breaking any eggs on the rear seat?"

"Stop," said Camille, "can't you be serious for a moment?"

"I am being serious," laughed Nadia. "It was, I promise you."

❧

Inspector Paquet had been following Camille and Nadia in his Simca but had been too far back to see them turn off the D17. However, he soon came across another police car waiting in a side road two hundred metres farther down and realised he had missed her, turned around, and headed back to take the track to the dam.

Only minutes behind, he and his driver caught glimpses through the trees of the diminutive car in the distance, bouncing up the trail before it swung sharply left and vanished into a thicket of pine trees leading to the dam.

Paquet's driver drove as fast along the track as the heavy Simca would allow, while the inspector radioed the others to look out for a car exiting onto the D10 in case Max tried to escape to the north.

The Simca rumbled and bounced along the track, until they reached the sharp left where they had last seen Camille. To their surprise a chain was across the road and the beige Citroen 2CV was straight ahead, its engine still running and the front doors wide open. There was no sign of the two women or Max's Peugeot.

Paquet stopped the car and both officers threw open their doors and ran to the beige car with their firearms drawn. It was empty, with only a typewritten note on the passenger seat.

"Look at this," said the driver. "They must be somewhere around here."

"Here, give me that," said Paquet.

```
Camille, a change of plan
1. Go back to your car at 6.15 P.M.
2. TURN LEFT from Chez Thomé and drive to the Relais
Cézanne
3. Turn RIGHT onto the D17
4. After exactly 1.5 km, TURN LEFT at a large sign 'Parc
Départemental de Roques Hautes' and a red sign saying
DFCI
5. Take the RIGHT fork marked by another small red DFCI
sign and follow the track for 400 metres until it forks
again
```

```
6. TURN RIGHT, then LEFT, and drive for 500 metres until
it swings sharply to the left and begins to get steeper
7. STOP when you see a chain across the road by a sign
that says 'Private Road. No entry to the public. Service
Road'
8. Max will be on your right in his car, waiting for you
9. The exchange will take place in the car
10. The road to the right will lead you back to the D17
```

"All right, the note says to meet Morel here! So, where the hell are they?" asked Paquet furiously. "Unless they went with him in his car."

As two of the other police cars pulled up behind the first, the inspector hastily radioed the other cars to look out for the Peugeot coming back down the track to the D17.

"Sir, look at this." Paquet's driver was inside the Citroen. "I don't think this is the right car. This is more like a man's car. It smells of cigarettes and is dirty inside."

"My God, you are right," said Paquet. "Quick, check the license plate. The son of a bitch. He's tricked us. They must have gone straight ahead towards the dam, but how did they get past that damn chain?"

Paquet pointed to the heavy chain across the road. "Sergeant, get a move on, find me a way past that chain."

※

Camille and Nadia urged the little Citroen up the winding, red-earth trail until the incline levelled off and the road crossed a plateau of huge granite rocks, thick scrub and tall pines that led to the blue waters of the Lac du Bimont and the long curving arc of the dam.

"All right, we are here," said Nadia. "This is where it gets serious, so where is he?"

It was not until they were halfway across the narrow top of the dam that they saw Max standing at the far end on the right, by the water's edge. He waved and beckoned to them to drive over and pull up to the right of his Peugeot, which he had parked beside another car.

Max sauntered over to them, smiling. He was wearing a French chore jacket, trousers with pockets, running shoes and two military-style waist packs on a brown leather belt.

"Good evening, ladies! Hello Camille," and turning to Nadia, he said, "and you are Madame Beausoleil? I've been looking forward to meeting you."

Nadia did not answer and hissed to Camille:

"Don't turn the engine off, and whatever you do, don't leave the car."

Max pulled some papers from his pocket and said gruffly: "No, don't turn the engine off. Let's get this over with quickly, shall we? You have the money?"

"Yes, we do," snapped Camille, "but I want to see those papers first and make sure you sign them before we even show you the money."

"Why?" laughed Max. "Don't you trust me?"

"No," said Camille, "I don't trust you, not at all. Once you've signed and dated them, you can give the papers to me, I'll check them, and if you haven't tried to trick us, we'll give you the money then."

"Okay," said Max, "I have no problem with that."

Max straightened out the papers on the front of their car and produced a simple Bic ballpoint pen from a pocket. After twice signing his name Max Berger, he added Morel in brackets.

"Wait, is that the original or the codicil?" asked Camille alarmed. "Do I need a witness for your signature?"

"No need for that," said Nadia. "I'm a witness."

"She's right, Camille; you don't need a witness," said Max.

He leaned forward and passed the papers through the car window to Camille.

"As you can see, this is the codicil Pierre showed you, and yes, it's attached to my copy of the deed. This is your signature. Recognise it?"

She examined it, and looked back at Max.

"All right," she said. "We accept."

"So, where's the money?" said Max impatiently.

"Max, listen. I'll give you the money," said Camille, "though I am giving it on the understanding we never see each other again."

Nadia pulled out a canvas bag from under her car seat and handed it to Camille, who passed it through the open car door to Max.

"Here it is. Fifty thousand francs. Most of it is in used fifty and one-hundred-franc notes, as many as the bank had. They couldn't get hold of anymore in the time, so there are some two hundred and a couple of five-hundred-franc notes in there too. It's all there, wrapped in cellophane. That's what you asked for."

Nadia had been watching the man with narrowed eyes, waiting for an opportunity to use her gun. Leaning against the car, Max took the money out of the holdall, unwrapped, and checked it, divided the sum into two wads, resealed them in the cellophane with broad rubber bands, and pushed them into the waist packs on his belt.

"Okay, close enough," he said, and yanked the car door open. "That's good, so let's kiss and say goodbye, shall we Camille and Madame Beausoleil?" Max leaned into the car. "Or may I call you Barbara?" He added looking at Nadia enigmatically.

Instinctively, Camille leaned away as Max leaned in, and he shoved her violently onto Nadia. Snatching back the deed, he rammed the car lever into gear and wrenched the steering to the right. The little vehicle began to lurch towards the embankment, down to the waters of the lake. Camille struggled frantically to grab the wheel, clawing at Max who was leaning through the door, half-in and half-out. It was Nadia's opportunity. As Max let go and stepped back from the car, she aimed and pulled the trigger. Once, then again and again.

The small Citroen crashed down the rocks and plunged into the water with a splash, remained upright for a moment as if it would float, then slowly it keeled over to the left as water rushed in. A despairing hiss escaped from the hot engine and the little beige vehicle slipped below the surface. Camille's first instinct was to save Nadia, and she tried desperately to pull her through the door, but the torrent of freezing-cold water pressed them to their seats and tipped the car further to the left. For a moment, the whole car shuddered as a pocket of air in the roof tugged it upright before it continued its descent.

Frenziedly, Camille stretched up and yanked back the sliding roof, and with bursting lungs and a ferocious grip on Nadia's arm, they exploded from the car with a cloud of bubbles and hurtled towards the diminishing light. Camille reached the surface with her lungs screaming and struck out desperately for the water's edge, tugging the dead weight of Nadia behind her. She had no thoughts of Max or where he could be, just a blind determination to save herself and Nadia.

Kicking with her legs and towing Nadia, it took every ounce of her remaining strength to grab clutch a branch with one hand and heaved Nadia's limp body up the slope with the other. Half in the water and half out, dismayed by her deathly pallor, Camille hit Nadia between the shoulders with the heel of her hand, pushing, hitting, hammering at her as hard as she could, again and again. There was no response.

"Bobo," she screamed, "wake up, for God's sake, WAKE UP." Feverishly, she tried again with both hands, pushing down in the centre of her back, pumping as hard and fast as she could, two times a second. Ten, twenty, thirty times she pumped. All of a sudden, Nadia coughed, and water leaked from her mouth. She groaned and turned her head.

"Stop hitting me," she managed to say. "You're hurting me. Let me breathe."

Camille would have laughed at her spirit, but she was too relieved and exhausted to think of anything other than their safety. Calmly, Nadia took deep, deliberate breaths until her strength returned and they struggled from the water and crawled up the embankment.

"Oh my God," muttered Camille. "Max! The bastard! He just tried to kill us! I can't believe it. Can you see him? Where the hell is he now?"

They craned their necks to see if he was up there, waiting for them, and at the same moment they heard Inspector Paquet shout: "There they are!" and he clambered down the slope towards them.

"Where is he?" cried the inspector. "Are you two all right? Did you see where he went? Is he in his car?"

Paquet was looking beyond them to their right, and they followed his gaze to see Max's Peugeot half-submerged in the water just metres away, caught by its rear wheels in the brush of some low Kermes oaks and juniper bushes.

"Oh, dear God. What happened? Where is he? Where's Max?" cried Camille.

"We don't know," shouted the inspector. "He could still be in the car. Can you see from where you are? Is he in the car? You two better get up here quickly if he is."

Camille, though breathless, did not hesitate to answer. "Where the hell were you?" she managed to say. "Where were you? Weren't you supposed to be following us?"

As three policemen descended the bank and approached the Peugeot warily with their guns drawn, the inspector's driver and a policewoman helped Camille and Nadia, wet and frightened, up the bank to the police car.

"Morel's not in his car," one of the officers yelled out, "but there is blood in there, on the steering wheel and on the door."

Nadia whispered triumphantly to Camille, "See? I did hit him! I didn't dare shoot when he was in the car with us in case I hit you. God, I hope I killed him."

"My guess is he was trying to get rid of his car so either he's in another car, or he's on foot around here," said the inspector, calling to the two women.

"You two had a lucky escape! So, I did hear gunshots?"

Camille and Nadia looked at each other. Nadia spoke first.

"Yes, it was me," she said shivering. "I tried to shoot him. I didn't trust him and was sure that it was a trap, so I brought along an old handgun I had from the war."

"Bravo! It looks like you hit him," said the inspector. "The question is, how badly injured is he? Do you see where the bullet hit?"

"I have no idea," said Nadia. "It all happened so quickly, but my God, I can't believe I actually got him."

"You two look frozen!" said Paquet. "The ambulance should be here any moment. Do you realise your car went down in water fifty metres deep? You were lucky to escape. They'll have to get your car out, though that won't be easy, but it can't be left in there, polluting the water."

He paused before continuing. "What about the money? Did you give him the money?"

"Yes, unfortunately, yes we did," said Camille as both she and Nadia remembered the deed.

"Oh my God, the deed!" they cried simultaneously.

"He's got it, the bastard; he snatched the deed back after we gave him the money!" said Camille close to tears. "He's won, dammit. He's won. He's got the deed and the money."

Camille held her head in despair.

"It's not over yet," said Nadia.

"You are right: it's not over yet," said Paquet. "He can't be far. I've radioed for dogs, and if he's around here they'll find his scent in a flash—and the fact that he's bleeding will make it easier to find him. You'll see. He won't get very far."

Another police car arrived, and two officers came running over to the inspector.

"No sign of him, sir. We have a car guarding the northern exit to the D10 and another car on its way. We've blocked the road and no cars have gone through. There is no chance he could have gone that way without us seeing him."

"Good. That confirms he has to be on foot somewhere around here."

At the same moment, there was a growl of thunder, the dark clouds broke, and it started raining.

Chapter 20

DASH FOR COVER

....

NADIA HAD MISSED MAX WITH HER SECOND AND THIRD BULLETS, but the first had hit his right hand, although in the fury of the moment he had been more angry than hurt. The pain, while extreme, had not slowed him down. He had underestimated them. He had not expected them to have a gun.

Max watched Camille's car slip below the water then turned and rushed to his car and only noticed how badly his hand bled when he struggled to open the door. Once behind the wheel, he leaned over to twist the key with his left hand, hauled the steering wheel to the right, shoved the car in first gear, jammed the accelerator, released the clutch and leaped out. Like Nadia's little car before it, the Peugeot catapulted down the rocks to the water.

Max dashed back to his second car, a blue Citroen, but knew he was too late when he heard the police cars approach—if he tried to drive away now, they would see him, and the only thing to do was to run. He was ready but had not wanted this turn of events though he relished outwitting the police: this was a chance to use skills honed since childhood and perfected in the Foreign Legion. *Entraînement difficile, guerre facile* [training difficult, war easy]. Without a backward glance, he spun on his heel and raced away east towards the dense brush and thick pines that surrounded the lake and the foothills. He hurtled over rocks and dead branches and charged through the trees and low bushes. Within minutes, he had arrived at the lake's edge where he could either run left and follow the sweep of the west bank as it curled north to form a bay or try and swim across to the south bank.

Max thought quickly. He was already on the north side of the lake, so the police would expect him to head north towards the D10. Yet if he swam across the lake, he risked being seen from the dam and although the black clouds were lower and dusk was fast approaching, he could not wait for the night. It was then that the first drops of rain fell, and Max checked the sky. He looked across at the south bank and guessed it was three hundred metres away.

He unbuckled his belt with the waist packs and spread his jacket on the ground, tore off his clothes and shoes and rolled everything into the coat. He inhaled deeply several times to oxygenate his brain and backed slowly into the water. It was excruciatingly, numbingly cold, but with the bundle balanced on his chest, and his head held as high as possible, he struck out on his back for the other side. It was then that a growl of thunder unleashed the first sheets of rain and by the time he reached the headland, the rain was beating down and spray had obscured the dam.

Though his hand was injured, and he had to leave the car, his plan had worked and now he had the money and the deed, and Camille and the other woman were with the fishes, lying at the bottom of the lake. He would find a phone soon, Pierre would pick him up, and the lawyer would set the wheels in motion. He felt no remorse for Camille. What had happened was her own fault. He had warned her constantly how weak the rich are, how they've lost touch with the way the world works. It's all about survival, he had told her many times. It's dog eat dog. It's every man for himself.

The rain was still teeming down when he reached the other side and he hauled himself wearily up the bank, robbed by the cold water of feeling bar the angry pain in his hand. He moved stiffly towards the trees where a herd of deer taking shelter from the rain bolted and scattered at his approach, and Max collapsed gratefully into the dry foliage of their refuge, still warm and reeking of musk. He lay there breathing heavily, drying, and regaining strength, and by the time darkness folded in, he had pulled on his clothes and was under the leaves, warm and dry, trying hard to disregard the ache in his hand and the unrelenting throb. At least he was safe here. Better rest while he could. He would need all his strength for the chase.

In the faint veiled light of the small hours, pale shades of grey, more greys and black, everything was reduced to shadows and vague ill-defined shapes, and Max slept fitfully, half-awake, half-asleep. As the hours slid by, the persistent dripping from the trees slowed and stopped, and only the sighs of the wind and the rustle of deer moving through the pines disturbed the peace of the night. Presently the low, repetitious croak of bullfrogs started up, soon joined by the call of an owl. The forest was returning to normal, the temperature was rising, and it was time to get moving again. With his injured hand pounding and weeping blood, he wrapped the lanyard around his wrist to form a crude tourniquet and looped it round his neck as a sling. It was vital to get to the village quickly and call Pierre for help. It would be light shortly and the police would start searching with dogs.

Before the first glow of dawn tinged the sky in the east, Max had made it through the dark to the dam and approached the road cautiously. The only signs of police were the lights of a lone police car in the distance to his right, where Camille had gone into the lake. He stole across the road like a shadow to look over the parapet and saw water glistening in a spillway far below: it was the source of the river that flowed down to Lac Zola and Le Tholonet.

At the end of the dam to the right, beyond the police car, the road swung left, prolonging the arc of the dam. The drop from that side to the spillway was not impossibly steep, though it was largely bare granite and would mean having to pass the police. The slope to his left was far steeper and covered with scrub and bent pines, but there was also a footpath that zigzagged downhill to the water.

Max stumbled down the path in the predawn light, slipping on the scree and clutching at the scrub with his one good hand until he made it down to the spillway. From there, he could pick his way over in the dark to the thick vegetation surrounding the source of the river and lower himself into the water. It was fast-flowing and bone-chillingly cold, and he slipped and faltered many times as he waded knee-deep along the riverbed until the valley broadened out, the river widened, and he could climb up the riverbank and push his way through the trees. And by the time dawn yielded to morning and light had spread across the sky, he had left the dam and Lac du Bimont far behind.

He was moving forward rapidly and making good progress when suddenly he froze stock-still. Carried by the wind, though very faintly, he could hear hounds baying with the otherworldly howl that hunting dogs make the first time they detect a new scent. He knew how they raced with their noses to the ground and how tenacious they could be, and that while most dogs lose the scent when their prey changes course, hunting dogs lift their heads, sniff the air, and pick up the scent again. He stood motionless as adrenaline coursed through his veins, paralysed by a primeval fear. Then, just as quickly, the howling on the wind faded into the gurgling of the river and the warble of finches in the brush. Driven by his fear of dogs, Max propelled himself faster and paused every few minutes to listen, but he never heard the hounds again and within the hour he was close to Lac Zola.

His hand, meanwhile, had become stiffer and heavier as he ran and when he paused to examine it, he was stunned by how swollen it had become. He knew that the common weed yarrow helps contain infection and he cast around for some plants. And once he had chewed a handful of leaves, he applied the paste to the wound, picked more leaves to make a dressing and tucked his hand in his shirt.

Forty minutes later he had skirted Lac Zola and reached the old dam that Camille first showed him, and he paused to assess his options. To the left, the ground rose sharply towards a peak of grey rock thrusting through the trees while straight ahead, it dipped to a shallow valley and a canopy of oaks and pines. To the right, was the well-trodden, red earth track that circled down to Le Tholonet, the path through the pines that he and Camille had taken up to the dam. It would be the quickest and easiest, but the risk of someone seeing him was great: even now, there could be people on the path and police out looking for him. He chose the middle, more direct route along the river to the village.

Max slithered down the slope to the water gushing from the dam and he was soon lost to view in the undergrowth. At first, the stream flowed calmly along a fissure in the limestone through a shallow gorge bordered by oaks trees, acacia, and aromatic juniper, and it was easy to stay out of sight. But when the river widened and meandered through a meadow of lavender and grass, Max worried he could be seen. It wasn't long before the river narrowed again and began to flow faster as it approached a ravine and his efforts to follow it became increasingly perilous as the water accelerated towards the village. In places, the water cascaded and pooled in rocks, then plummeted and dashed against the boulders below. The drops were dauntingly steep where the ravine was at its narrowest, and Max scraped against the sides, lost his balance, slipped, and grabbed at branches to avoid falling. At last, the ground levelled out quite abruptly and the river streamed peacefully into a broad basin of calm water bordered by bulrushes and mimosa and shaded by mature Aleppo pines.

Bruised, soaked and exhausted, Max moved forward warily to assess the change in surroundings, and found a wall and sluice gates that dammed the river and divided it into streams. Two stone conduits channelled the water for ten or so metres through an arch-shaped gap in the ruins of a crumbling Roman aqueduct, whereafter the larger stream became a river again, and tumbled down a cliff as a waterfall to flow calmly into Le Tholonet. The other, smaller stream poured into a cavernous wooden pipe.

It was a chance to pause and catch his breath, and Max dropped to his knees and drank deeply. He had lost all feeling below his right wrist, and the wound felt stiffer than ever, and when he washed the blood off, he was stunned to see how swollen it was and that the bullet had gone through his hand. It was now leaking serous fluids and the red of the flesh was dull, but he couldn't begin to look for a phone until dark and he had to find somewhere to hide.

The old Roman aqueduct looked promising. In places the mortar had crumbled and left gaps between the stones, and Max clambered to the top to the old watercourse to find it warm and full of leaves. It was an ideal place to hide, made better by a panoramic view of Le Tholonet over the tops of the trees. To the right was the back of the Chateau du Tholonet just two hundred metres away, and straight-ahead cars were plainly visible driving past the Le Relais Cézanne. Once dark, it should be simple enough to slip down to the village and find a house with a phone—for whoever had dammed the river and cut the arch through the aqueduct, had also built steps leading down to the chateau car park. Max began to relax. He could hide here safely out of sight. He removed the waist packs, and despite the deafening clatter of the cicadas in the trees, he was soon fast asleep.

It was early evening when the cicadas ceased their relentless chant and Max woke up with a start. The temperature had dropped, the light was waning, and he looked at his hand again. The deep red of the wound was browner now and it was oozing foul-smelling pus and with a pang of fear he realised it could turn gangrenous. From his perch above the trees, he started a feverish search for a house or a shop that might remain dark after the sun set, and he was scanning the village when a tide of golden light washed silently over the rooftops. As darkness fell, a daisy-chain of streetlights turned on in succession to join the strings of coloured lights of the restaurants; and one by one the shops and houses switched their lights on until the entire village was lit.

Max had singled out a house as a potential target but changed his mind when he saw the lights go on in the chateau. He could see through the windows that the building was a business; and if it were a business, the employees would leave soon and there would be telephones, water and something to eat. He waited impatiently for the workers to leave and thirty minutes later, the last light went out, a man left the building and departed in the remaining car.

Max scrambled precariously down from his hiding place and crept down the steps to the car park to steal silently over to the door. He ran the fingers of his good hand around the lintel to check for an alarm and examined the lock with his lighter. Seconds later the door swung open, and he found himself in an anteroom with benches and lines of coat hooks. A second door led to a larger room with tall windows that his lighter showed to be an old-fashioned kitchen with a yawning fireplace and stone floor.

Ravenous and short of breath, Max made straight for a large American refrigerator in a corner of the room and opened the door to find an array of different foods including a plate of cheeses, a full baguette, a slab of butter and some Bayonne ham wrapped in greaseproof paper. There was also an earthenware dish containing pâté, an open bottle of white wine, two bottles of mineral water and five bottles of beer.

Max propped the door open to provide some light and took the bread and pâté over to a table where he found a half-full bottle of red wine and two wine glasses. Despite not feeling well, he couldn't prevent a euphoric hoot of laughter: the only thing missing was a waiter. As he reached for the red wine, he knocked the bottle over and it fell to the floor and smashed. Cursing, he lurched back to the refrigerator, grabbed the white wine, and drank deeply from the bottle. Before very long, he had finished all the bread, the paté and the wine, and was on the point of returning for some cheese when he remembered he needed to phone. He stood up unsteadily and found his way through a door to an office with several rows of desks. And on every desk was a telephone directory, a pile of papers and a telephone.

Max grabbed the nearest handset.

"Hello?" he said. "Hello?"

There was no answer, and it dawned on him that an operator must control the phones through a switchboard, and he moved on through the darkened building to the main entrance. On the desk of the receptionist sat a large black box with a handset, earphones and a series of lights and switches.

Max picked up the handset, hoping to dial Pierre directly.

"Good evening," said a female voice, "we are working late tonight?"

"Yes," said Max weakly, "we're working late. Would you put me through to Puyloubier 3897?"

"Hold the line, please," said the voice. Several clicks followed before a long repetitive tone.

"There's no answer, dear," said the voice after a while. "Do you want to leave a message with me?"

Max thought a moment. "No… Well, yes, yes, I would like to leave a message, please. Would you say that one of the brothers-in-arms needs help as soon as possible? Meet him at the aqueduct above the Chateau du Tholonet and bring a medicine chest with bandages and penicillin. Again, it's very urgent. Come as soon as possible."

"That doesn't sound good. Is everything all right? Would you like me to call an ambulance?" the voice asked.

It took all of Max's remaining strength to reply politely: "No, please don't. Everything is fine, thank you. Just tell him it's for an injured dog by the old wall, behind the chateau. It's for an injured dog."

"I'll keep trying until eleven tonight," the voice continued, "I go off duty then. If I don't get through, you can always dial the police directly if you need to. In any case, Giselle comes in at five in the morning, and I can leave the message for her. Will that be all right?"

"It will have to be," said Max feebly. "Of course, thank you, that'll be fine."

Max made his way back to the kitchen, deeply worried he had been unable to speak to Pierre. He took another handful of ham and cheese, left the building the way he came in and relocked the door. The moon had risen, and the sky was bright, but his back and his neck hurt, and his vision was blurred. It took all his strength to climb the steps and he had almost reached his hiding place when he felt an overpowering urge to vomit and threw up everything he had eaten by the wall.

Pierre will be here soon, he kept repeating to himself, as he heaved himself up to his hideout. Pierre will bring penicillin and bandages, and everything will be all right. His heart raced and he shuddered at the thought he could lose his hand. And he recalled the legendary episode of 1908 they used to talk about when a snowstorm surprised the Foreign Legion in the mountains of Morocco late at night; thirty-nine died and twenty-two had limbs amputated.

Chapter 21

DEAD OR ALIVE

....

AMILLE AND NADIA WERE UNABLE TO HELP THE POLICE. They had no idea where Max went after he tried to kill them. They did know, however, that a major manhunt was underway using dogs and all available resources, and that Paquet had promised to double the police guard at the house until Max was caught. They didn't even know if Max knew they were alive so as the wind died down and the cicadas were settling two days following the terrifying events, Camille was nervous when there was a knock on the door of the Chateau de Vaucluse. She peered through the peephole but was unable to see who it was. She hooked the chain into place and opened the door a crack.

"Who is it?" she called.

"Good evening, Mademoiselle Dumont. It's me, Inspector Paquet."

Camille unhooked the chain and opened the door.

"We have good news for you. We have found Morel!"

"You've found Max?" repeated Camille excitedly, and she called over her shoulder to Nadia.

"Bobo, did you hear? They've found Max!"

Camille led the way to the kitchen, where Nadia joined them.

"Please," she said, "pull up a chair. Tell us everything."

The policeman sat down and fumbled for his notebook and set it on the table in front of him. "Let's see. We knew he was wounded, of course, though we didn't know how badly. The bleeding should have made it easier to track him, but if you remember it started raining almost immediately and by the time the dogs started searching, there wasn't much blood left to find. As you know, his Peugeot was half in the lake, but the dogs picked up his scent inside another car, a blue and white Citroen, nearby. We think he planned to use that car to get away, yet at the last minute he ran away on foot. Why? He must have seen us coming, so the question was, where did he go?

"We decided he must gone north towards the D10 and set up roadblocks that we manned all through the night. The next day at dawn we started searching with dogs but that's a huge and very dense area and if they may have caught his scent for a bit, they lost track of him very quickly. None of us thought that he would make his way back to Le Tholonet. However, we were wrong because at midday today, we had a breakthrough when someone reported a break-in at the chateau."

Camille and Nadia stared at him, captivated.

"The Chateau du Tholonet?" Nadia sounded disbelieving. "What was he doing there? Oh, Inspector, what about the money? Did he have the money with him?"

"Don't worry about the money for the moment," the inspector said. "The important thing is that Morel won't trouble you anymore: we have him in a safe place, in hospital in Aix."

"So, what happened?" broke in Camille. "What's he doing in hospital?"

"He's in a bad way. Not in good health to put it mildly."

Inspector Paquet looked down at his notebook and continued. "At twelve-forty-five P.M. today, we had a call from the manager at Canal de Provence over in Le Tholonet. You may know them. That's the company responsible for the reservoirs and canals in the area. They are the owners of the chateau."

Paquet looked up at Camille. "At lunchtime someone realised that a lot of food was missing from the fridge, and they started accusing each other." The inspector chuckled. "Then someone noticed a broken bottle of wine under the kitchen table and realised the white wine was empty too. To cut a long story short, after some discussion, the receptionist volunteered that someone was working late last night. She knew that because, Giselle, the village tele-phone operator, had asked her this morning how the dog was doing."

"The dog, what dog?" interjected Camille.

"Ah-ha," said Paquet, "someone tried to call a number from the chateau last night about an injured dog."

Camille and Nadia looked at each other, puzzled.

"It seems someone left a message with the operator that said something to the effect 'bring bandages and penicillin to the old aqueduct as soon as pos-sible for an injured dog.' They realised then that someone unauthorised had been on the premises, so they called us at the station. It wasn't hard to put two and two together. We had the dogs with us, and we weren't far away, so we got there very quickly. We knew it could only be Morel."

The inspector looked up at Camille.

"Do you know the old Roman aqueduct? It's a local beauty spot they call *Le Bout du Monde* [The End of the World]. Very picturesque, with the ruins of an old Roman wall and a pond that supplies water to the fountains of the chateau. Anyway, the dogs were onto him in a flash."

"So, he was hiding there?" asked Nadia, engrossed.

"The dogs tracked him from the chateau, across the car park, and up the steps to the Roman aqueduct where they went crazy by the wall. He had vomited on the ground, which is what the dogs found first, and we found him lying in a hollow at the top of the wall. We thought he was dead at first, he was in such a mess. But the medics told us he was breathing, and he was semi-conscious when we eventually got him down. But he was in a terrible state."

Paquet looked at Nadia. "You shot him in his right hand, Madame Beausoleil. The bullet went right through the palm and made quite a hole."

"Good." Nadia said grimly.

"For the record, I'll need to know what kind of gun you have and where you got it?"

"It was a Luger P08 semiautomatic. Given to Juliette de Vaucluse by General von Schaumburg in Paris during the war. I don't have it anymore; it went into the lake with my car."

"A Luger P08, eh? I'm impressed," said Paquet. "That's quite a weapon, and historic too. Pity it's gone in a way. As for Morel, the wound must have slowed him down quite a bit because it was severely infected. We got him to the hospital as quickly as we could, where they told us he was suffering from sepsis. A few more hours and he would have died."

Paquet looked down at his notes. "Morel contracted gangrene from a bacterial infection aggravated by the sudden stoppage of blood flow. Probably waterborne. That's what the surgeon told us."

"Surgeon, did you say?" asked Camille.

"Yes, I did say surgeon. They amputated his right arm below the elbow this afternoon. He is very sick, and they are not sure they can save him."

"My God, Max dead? I can't believe it," said Camille.

"I didn't say he's dead. He's in a bad way. He knew he was in trouble, though, because of what he did to his arm... I hesitate to tell you the details."

"Oh, go on," said Nadia. "We're big girls; we can take it."

"If you insist," continued the inspector. "Morel knew he was seriously ill because he had tied a cord below his elbow to make a tourniquet. His idea was to try and...try and cut his hand off with a knife. And he almost succeeded. You know there are two bones in your forearm? He managed to cut through the smaller of the two, the ulna, but couldn't cut through the radius bone and tried to break it with a rock. He didn't succeed though, poor fellow and made a terrible mess of himself. He had passed out when we found him."

"Dear God, that's repulsive. Though I don't feel the least bit sorry for him," said Camille, shuddering as she pictured him sawing through his arm with his Laguiole knife, the same knife she had used to slice cheese and dried sausages. "I can hardly believe it's over, that he's finally caught. Do we know who Max was trying to call?"

"Yes, we do," said Paquet. "The number belongs to a nursing home for sick and wounded soldiers of the French Foreign Legion over at Puyloubier, the other side of Mont Sainte-Victoire. For the moment, we don't know if his message got through."

"That's interesting? Why would he call them?" asked Camille.

"We are not sure yet, but they stick together, the ex-Legionnaires. But there are other things we don't understand," said the inspector, "including the blue Citroen he hoped to get away in. We established that it was sold for five thousand francs three months ago, and registered in Calvi, in Corsica. Now, how did Morel find the money for that car?"

"You still haven't mentioned our money," said Nadia. "Did you recover it yet?"

Paquet seemed less sure of himself. "Now that's the curious thing, there's no sign of it yet. We searched everywhere: both his cars, his clothes, all around the wall. But a large sum of money like that doesn't evaporate. We will find it."

Paquet looked down at his notes again. "The only things he had on him were a ten-franc note, two fifty-franc notes, a packet of Gitanes, a lighter, his pocketknife and the lanyard he used as a tourniquet ... oh, and some food he took from the chateau."

"Okay," said Nadia, "so which hospital is he in?"

"Don't worry about him. After they cut his arm off, he was transferred to the Centre Hospitalier Montperrin near the station because it is safer there," said Paquet, adding, "It's a very secure facility where they treat the mentally deranged."

"Well, that's good news. It sounds like the perfect place for him," said Camille.

The month of August continued wet and cold, and the first days of September were no better, and for the first time since Juliette had died, the atmosphere in the Chateau de Vaucluse approached normality. With Max safely under lock and key and his name rarely mentioned, Juliette became the principal subject of discussion. She would have been fifty on September 24, and Camille and Nadia were anxious to make arrangements for her burial. However, following the inconclusive autopsy, they were still waiting for her body to be released. Camille refurnished her house by the pool, and Nadia, after some hesitation, moved into Juliette's room. And life was made easier, thanks to the tidy sum that Nadia inherited.

One evening, they were in the kitchen sharing a German dish that Nadia had prepared; Kartoffelpuffer potato pancakes served with applesauce, sour cream, smoked salmon and onions.

"My mother would make this, and I used to love it, but I haven't made it for years. Juliette didn't like German dishes very much." Nadia looked affectionately at Camille.

"I always wondered about the mystery of your upbringing," said Camille. "I used to think that you were brought up in the Var, in Salernes, which was how you knew Maman."

"That's what everybody was supposed to think," said Nadia. "But no, I was brought up in that wild city of Berlin, at least it used to be wild before the war."

"Ah, the wild city! Yes, I'd like to hear about that!" Camille said laughing. "Though to be honest, I can't say I have ever thought of you as very wild."

"What do you mean?" Nadia looked at Camille with her hands on her hips and pretended to be offended.

"Bobo, if I dare say so, as far as I know, you've never even had a boyfriend, not counting my father."

"Oh Camille, there is so much about me you don't know. I repeat, I was brought up in Berlin," Nadia laughed, "and as you know, it was a crazy place before the war, particularly when I was growing up."

Nadia hesitated before continuing, and refilled Camille's glass. "For your information, we partied all the time and did some scandalous things by the standards of today. Nudity and homosexuality, for example, weren't as shocking they are today. Berlin was a very open city: some boys preferred boys, and some girls preferred girls and as a matter of fact, I was one of them."

Camille threw back her head and laughed. "Good for you! Of course, you already told me that's how you and Juliette met."

"Yes, dear Camille, we were a thing, but we both liked men too. And when you came along, you were our baby. Mine and Juliette's. You were the glue that held us together all those years. I loved Juliette from the moment I met her when we were seventeen, and if she was sometimes a little short with you, I think deep down she was jealous of the bond that you and I had, as mother and child."

"Oh my goodness, this is going to take some digesting. But I can see you now, the wild young thing in Berlin, in dubious nightclubs, smoking joints and getting drunk."

"I take that as a compliment. Better than being the boring old woman I am now, who has never had a boyfriend. Thank you for that."

"Oh, I'm sorry; I didn't mean to hurt you." Camille said quickly.

"You didn't, Camille. But you were wrong about me smoking joints and getting drunk. I suppose some people did, but I was a bit young for that. But you're right. There was a lot of partying in those days that included drinking, smoking and drugs."

"Drugs? Weren't all drugs illegal? I thought the Nazis banned drugs," said Camille.

"Yes, they did at first. Drugs were considered a sign of moral decay when Hitler became Chancellor of Germany in 1933. I was only fifteen then, but I can tell you drug-taking definitely continued behind the scenes in private and in nightclubs."

"And you took part in that?"

Nadia laughed. "Yes, I did, a little bit. Cocaine was frowned on as being American, but it was easy to get and lots of artists and musicians used it. After I left Berlin at the end of 1936, the Nazis even permitted speed, amphetamines, to be sold on the streets as antidepressant, happy pills."

Camille reached over and filled their glasses with wine.

"Thank you, Camille! Since we are talking about debauchery, you've never told me about your debauched life in London. From over here, swinging London sounded pretty wild, too."

It was their last secret. Camille had both longed for and dreaded this moment. Nadia was much easier to talk to than Juliette had ever been, and certainly less easy to shock. She had spoken in generalities of her life in London many times, including working in photography with Leo. But she had never mentioned Leo's death.

"Do you realise I've been back for almost two years? God, time flies. But yes, I suppose I did have a wild time in London in a way—at least it was wild compared to Provence."

Camille smiled and took a sip of wine. "As a matter of fact, looking back, I had an amazing time in London, and like everybody else, I experimented in every way. I've already told you about Leo, haven't I?"

"Yes, very much so. We chatted about him when we went to see the Antonioni film, the one that won first prize at Cannes."

"Blow Up? Yes, that whole film just about sums up my time in London, except for how it ended."

"I don't remember the ending."

"Mimes in the park pretending to play a tennis match. My ending wasn't nearly so mysterious, though someone did die."

"Who died?"

Camille hesitated and was silent for a minute, as her eyes welled with tears. "Leo," she said eventually, swallowing hard. "Leo died. And it was my fault."

Ten minutes later, after more wine and tears, Nadia had heard the story of the calamitous evening, starting with the stereo headphones, the Beach Boys and the Stones, the decision to take LSD together, the wine and the sleeping pills. And the horrifying moment when she found Leo dead.

Nadia was holding Camille's hand. "So why do you blame yourself, why do you say it's your fault?"

"Because I was a coward," she said through her tears. "Leo said I should let the sugar melt in my mouth, but I crunched mine and swallowed it because I was frightened. I hoped it wouldn't have the same effect."

"But you still took LSD, and you still had a trip. And it wasn't the LSD that killed him anyway, was it? Wasn't it the mixture of wine and sleeping pills?" Nadia said gently.

"I don't know, I don't know. I should have stopped him drinking so much; I should have stopped him from taking those pills."

"Look Camille, sweetheart, it was NOT your fault. Accidents happen. Did you ever think he didn't suffer? Perhaps he died having the most wonderful, gentle trip, skipping through a meadow with you."

Camille laughed through her tears. "That's a sweet thought. Thank you for that. It does make me feel a little better."

The next morning they had a familiar visitor.

"Good morning, ladies," said the inspector carrying a cardboard box, "may I put this somewhere?"

"You can put it on the kitchen table if you wish," said Nadia.

"I thought you would like to be brought up to date. First, Madame Beausoleil, good news regarding your car. They fished it out of the lake along with two bicycles, a stolen motorbike and a washing machine. Not that you'll ever be able to use it again. No sign of the documents you mentioned, but they found two purses with your driving licenses and keys, which may be useful."

Paquet opened the box and pulled out Camille's and Nadia's bedraggled, water-stained handbags.

"And the money?" asked Nadia. "Please tell us you've recovered the money?"

"No, not yet, but we retrieved something else interesting on the floor of the vehicle, which you may be pleased to recover," Paquet said. "Would this be yours by any chance?"

He winked as he handed the Luger to Nadia. "It hasn't suffered much. Now put it away somewhere safe, and I'll pretend I haven't seen it."

Nadia's jaw dropped with delight, astonished to get her gun back. "I will, I will," she said. "I'll clean it today and put it away. Thank you so much."

"So," said Camille, "what news of Max?"

"Morel? Looks like he'll recover, minus an arm obviously. He's still under a twenty-four-hour police guard and will be appearing in court the day after tomorrow to be officially charged with murder and attempted murder. But don't worry; he's safe where he is, and there's no doubt that they'll put him away for thirty years. Or worse."

Paquet drew his forefinger across his throat in a macabre gesture.

"Don't tell me what you mean by worse," said Camille. "I don't want to know. Did you ever hear back from the Foreign Legion at Puyloubier? Do you know if anyone got the message?"

"Yes," said Inspector Paquet, "not only do we know that someone picked up the message, but we have also established that Morel's friend Paglioni, as an ex-Legionnaire himself, was working there then. They are a tight bunch and stick together and we haven't been able to find any trace of Paglioni so far. We think he took the ferry from Marseille to Corsica the afternoon of the day we found Max—as you probably know he is Corsican, so we'll have problems finding him over there."

"One more question." Camille looked at Nadia and then at the inspector.

"Does Max know we are still alive?"

"I don't think so, not yet," replied Paquet. "But he's bound to find out soon."

Chapter 22

CONSEQUENCES

M AX WAS FORMALLY REMANDED IN CUSTODY and charged with the attempted murders of Mademoiselle Camille Dumont and Madame Nadia Beausoleil and the premeditated murder of Madame Juliette de Vaucluse née Dumont. Although also suspected of murdering the old garage owner, Walter Clément, charges were not brought for lack of evidence and reasons of expediency.

The violent nature of the accused's crimes and the national renown of Juliette Dumont meant there was a risk of public disturbance so the trial on the first charge was arranged at the earliest possible date commensurate with jury selection and the completion of the pre-trial examination of the case against Max that included a judicial review of Inspector Paquet's evidence of Max's guilt, and interviews of the two other witnesses, Camille and Nadia in the presence of the *Avocat Général* [Chief Prosecutor], the presiding judge and Max's court-appointed defence lawyer.

The date chosen for the first trial was Tuesday, September 24. A second trial for Juliette's murder would follow consecutively with new judges and a new jury, who would be honour-bound to avoid reading and talking about the first case until both trials were over.

Tuesday, September 24, 1968.

Max Berger Morel was brought before the *Cour d'Assises* [Criminal Court] in the Palais de Justice in Aix-en-Provence to answer the charge of attempted murder before the principal witnesses for the prosecution: Chief Inspector Paquet, Nadia Beausoleil, and Camille Dumont who was alarmed to be called as a key witness. At five months pregnant, her belly was starting to show, and she dreaded being asked who the father was.

"Nobody knows you are pregnant," Nadia had said, "and if you wear a loose-fitting dress and a thin coat, nobody will notice anything. Wear black. It's both appropriate and slimming."

Mother and daughter parked their car in the Place de Verdun opposite the Palais de Justice, close to where Camille had parked her car seven months ago when she had signed the ill-fated document in the office of Maître Chapuis.

Holding hands, the two women walked resolutely between the white marble statues of long-dead lawyers, up the stone steps into the vast colonnaded lobby of the Law Courts. After registering with court officials and being greeted by the Avocat Général, they were shown to an area reserved for witnesses off the main courtroom, where Inspector Paquet, smart in his Gendarmerie officer's uniform, was waiting. All three were instructed to remain there until they were called and forbidden to discuss the trial or talk to other witnesses.

The two witnesses for the defence, Max's common-law wife and Pierre Paglioni, were scheduled to speak after the prosecution made its case and were instructed to wait in a separate room off the courtroom to prevent them from hearing the testimony. At least Max's wife was, and Pierre would have been, but the police had been unable to find Paglioni and a warrant had been issued for his arrest.

The cathedral-like courtroom was wood-panelled and divided like a theatre with a stage at one end for the judges and jury, an area in the middle reserved for the lawyers and witnesses, and a large auditorium for the public that already brimmed with journalists of all descriptions as well as amateur sleuths, law students, and energised, excited spectators anxious to see and hear Max, the alleged killer of Juliette Dumont.

Under the high ceiling and below a bank of small windows stood the raised podium for judges and juror's, with a throne-like chair in the middle reserved for the presiding judge, the Président of the Court, who represented *L'État* [the French state]. On each side of the Président's chair, a black-robed associate *Assesseur* judge [Magistrate] was already seated, with five jurors on one side and four more on the other.

On the far left, to the Président's right, the Avocat Général sat solemnly in his red and black robes at the end of the podium. As the chief representative of Société, the French people, his role was to lead the prosecution and ensure that the laws of the French Republic were applied fairly.

At the opposite end of the podium sat the black-robed *Greffier* [Clerk of the Court], whose job it was to transcribe everything. And at a desk just in front of him, sat the stern looking *Huissier* [Court Bailiff], there to police the process and make sure court procedures were followed correctly.

Below the judges' podium, the witness counter symbolically separated L'État from Société—the republic from the people—with the latter represented by lawyers for the prosecution on the left, and by lawyers for the defence on the right, all of them already poring over papers. And with their backs to the public sat another row of expert witnesses.

The prisoner's dock was to the right of the defence and as the moment approached for the trial, a small door opened in the wall and the enthusiastic chatter of the public hushed to a murmur as everyone craned their necks to see Max enter the dock escorted by two gendarmes. His hair was cut very short and his right arm—or what was left of it—was bandaged in a sling. He appeared strong and defiant. He was neither manacled nor handcuffed to show that he had yet to be proven guilty.

Moments later, another door opened behind the podium and the Président entered wearing a red and black silk gown trimmed with white ermine and carrying a black velvet hat. Everyone rose to their feet. The Président signalled the court to sit and placed his hat on the counter in front of him, and after ensuring that the accused had legal representation, he summarised the proceedings for the day. The Huissier then read the charge out aloud and called upon the Avocat Général to present the case for the prosecution.

"Monsieur le Président, judges, ladies and gentlemen of the jury," the lawyer began, "today we will show you irrefutable proof that the defendant attempted to kill Madame Nadia Beausoleil and Mademoiselle Camille Dumont in pursuit of a disreputable attempt to defraud the family of Juliette Dumont. And when we have finished, we will have proved beyond any reasonable doubt that the defendant is guilty as charged.

"Let me take you back to the Olympic Games in Berlin in 1936. France won seven gold medals that year, including one gold medal for swimming, which was won by seventeen-year-old Juliette Dumont, the second-youngest athlete in the history of the Olympics to win a gold medal. She became instantly famous in France, indeed the world over, and turned many peoples' heads with her beauty, including the head of a ten-year-old boy living on a farm in the Auvergne: Max Berger Morel, who you see in the prisoner's dock today."

The Avocat Général looked over his glasses at Max.

"Nothing wrong with that, you may say. There must have been thousands upon thousands of young children who cheered on Mademoiselle Dumont in 1936. But Morel was not like other children. His enthusiasm gave birth to an obsession, an unhealthy, unnatural obsession for Juliette Dumont that consumed him over the years. He was still obsessed with her in 1943 when she married Bernard de Vaucluse, the owner of the Chateau de Vaucluse in Ventabren and heir to the de Vaucluse fortune. The wedding was a beacon of light in those dark days, and it made national news: and seventeen-year-old

Morel added many more newspaper cuttings to the collection he started in 1936.

"We know all this because the police inquiry, led by Chief Inspector Paquet, recovered two boxes from Morel's home that have been placed on the Exhibits table in front of me. The boxes contain ninety-six newspaper cuttings concerning Juliette Dumont, starting with photographs of her winning her gold medal in the 1936 Olympic Games. The last one, from June 17, 1967, was a photograph that appeared in the La Provence newspaper. Imagine keeping thirty years of newspaper cuttings about one person.

"Now, why? Why does someone start such a collection, you may ask? There must be a reason. Admiration? Naturally. There was much to admire about Juliette Dumont, and perhaps it started like that, but in the accused's case it was not just admiration. There was something else, less commonplace, more sinister. Morel was an only child brought up in a region where people like to hunt, where hunters learn to stalk their prey using guile and subterfuge. Many hunters keep reference books and notes on the wildlife they hunt. Morel kept cuttings about Juliette Dumont, and I suggest that Morel's collection was based not on admiration, but on envy, on bitterness. For Juliette Dumont represented everything Morel didn't have and despised: status, beauty, high society, fame and money. All passports to a world he loathed."

Again, the Avocat Général altered his stance to gaze at Max, paused and looked down at his notes:

"You see, Morel developed a plan, a long-term plan to defraud the family of Juliette Dumont. He had discovered that the arrangement that bound his grandparents was not marriage—they were never married—but an old-fashioned legal arrangement called a tontine. What is that I hear you ask? A tontine, dear members of the jury, is an ancient, little-used legal device based on trust, used by country people. It was the invention of an Italian banker to raise money for King Louis XIV; an ingenious, if cynical, scheme for borrowing large sums of money from wealthy investors by offering them high returns. For as each investor died off, the interest due on his loan was shared among the surviving investors. And when the last investor passed away, the capital reverted to the crown with no more interest payments due. It was a system that pitted investor against investor, and each had an interest in the others dying before him, and that, of course, was an incitement to conspire, manipulate and murder, and by the end of the eighteenth century, Signor Tonti and his invention were disgraced.

"However, tontines didn't fall out of use. In fact, to this day they are used legally, though rarely, to simplify property ownership. It works like this: if an unmarried couple signs a tontine to buy a house together, the couple will jointly own the house until one of them dies, regardless of who actually paid for it. The survivor will be deemed to have been the sole owner of that property since the date of purchase, preventing anybody else—the family of the deceased for example—to have a claim on the property. In other words, whoever dies last wins. A sacred trust between two people until one of them dies. If you die first, what was yours will become mine. And vice versa."

The Avocat Général peered over his glasses at Max again and turned back to the jury.

"And the jury should know," he said slowly, "that a tontine is legally irrevocable without the written and notarised consent of both parties."

The lawyer paused again for effect.

"On Friday, June 16, 1967, Monsieur Morel was fired from his job at a garage in Beaucaire. The following day Madame Juliette de Vaucluse was invited to open a new Euromarché supermarket in the town of Les Milles and Morel added a new cutting to his collection: yes, it was the photograph cut from La Provence newspaper. I suggest it was losing his job that provoked him to implement his plan, a plan that he been brooding about and refining for years, his plan to get his hands on the de Vaucluse family fortune."

He turned to study the jurors.

"But how? How could a simple, uneducated man such as Morel possibly manage that? He knew that Madame de Vaucluse lived in the village of Ventabren and six weeks later he started a job working as pump attendant and general mechanic at the only garage in Ventabren. Fortuitously—for him—the owner needed someone to take over the garage because three weeks earlier, her husband had died under suspicious circumstances at the garage."

The imposing lawyer swung round again, red and black robe flapping, looked over his spectacles at Max, and turned back to the jury with a dramatic flourish of his attorney's robes.

"Remember, this man is a hunter, a predator," he said, waving his forefinger, "and he moved fifty miles from his home to the village of Ventabren, to a garage less than a mile from the Chateau de Vaucluse, the home of Bernard and Juliette de Vaucluse, Nadia Beausoleil, and Camille Dumont. I am persuaded, I firmly believe, he moved to be close to his prey."

There was a murmur of excitement from the audience.

The Avocat Général went on to recount how Morel waited passively for a de Vaucluse family member to come by, like an animal waits for its prey, and on August 3 Juliette Dumont's unmarried daughter, Camille, stopped by to fill her car. It was the moment he had been waiting for. Morel turned on the charm and a week later, he was buying her drinks in Aix-en-Provence.

"Now, nobody should judge Mademoiselle Dumont. Morel is not unattractive and, I am told, he can be charming. I can't answer to that, but what I do know is that he is a cunning man and for the next five months he played the role of her suitor. Generous and attentive, a veritable Romeo until he was sure he had captured her heart. Which was when he launched the second phase of his plan and suggested they buy a small house and a vineyard together in Saint-Rémy-de-Provence."

The Avocat Général looked around the courthouse.

"He had no money, but Mademoiselle Dumont trusted him and agreed to lend him half the purchase price. And why not? The property would remain hers until he paid his share, and the loan would be underwritten and safe-guarded by a legal contract."

Once again, the Avocat Général glanced at Max who had leaned forward in his chair and was staring at the floor.

"The loan agreement Morel arranged to be drawn up was entirely legal—and remains valid to this day. On December 16, 1967, Morel signed it readily, eagerly even, because he knew by doing so, he would inspire Camille Dumont's confidence. He signed it because he had no intention of honouring it. He had his eyes on the deeds of the house which they would both sign on February 27 of this year because Morel knew, because Morel had made sure, it contained a clause de tontine. Whoever dies last wins."

The tall prosecutor paused for effect and the counsel for Max's defence leapt to his feet.

"Objection, your honour."

"Objection sustained" replied the Président at once.

"However," continued the Avocat Général, "this was a tontine with a differ-ence. At Morel's request, his lawyer had added an additional clause, wrapped in legalese, a clause de possession réciproque, a devious clause designed to broaden the effect of the tontine to include not only the house and the land, but everything Camille Dumont and Morel possessed at the time of the death of either one of them. So not just the house and the vineyard, but any-thing and everything else each of them owned at the time of death. So that included all assets, goods, or property—and this is a key point—inherited from other sources.

"Simply put," continued the Avocat Général, "if both Monsieur and Madame de Vaucluse had died after that document was signed, and Mademoiselle Dumont had inherited everything, Morel would have expected to inherit the entire de Vaucluse fortune at the death of Camille Dumont.

"That was Morel's plan. And as destiny would have it, Bernard de Vaucluse passed away less than one month later from cancer of the prostate, on March 22, 1968. Sad news for everyone, except Morel. He was one step closer to his goal."

The red-clad lawyer stood and looked at Morel for a moment, then swung around to look at the Président of the court.

"Monsieur le Président, I would now like to call Mademoiselle Camille Dumont, daughter of Madame Juliette de Vaucluse, to the witness stand."

There was an audible drawing-in of breath from the audience. They were about to hear from the victim of the attempted murder, the daughter of the murdered celebrity Juliette Dumont.

Camille entered the courtroom conscious of the public gaze and walked confidently up to the witness stand. She stared straight ahead, without a glance at Max and told the court in a quiet voice how she had lived in London for six years before returning to Ventabren in November 1966 for personal reasons. She was still feeling vulnerable when she first met Morel at the garage in early August 1967, but she found him interesting and charming and enjoyed his company. As she got to know him better, she realised that he was an unusual man and was impressed by his encyclopaedic knowledge of nature. He could be caring and attentive, and she had no doubts about him when five months later he broached the question of them buying a property together. She believed in his integrity and trusted him totally when he volunteered to get a contract drawn up to safeguard a loan, a contract that she read very carefully.

"When the moment arrived to pay for the house, I admit I did not read the deed, which was of course a terrible mistake. In my defence, I should add that I was in the presence of Morel's lawyer who did not invite me to read the deed, so I assumed, stupidly, that it was a straightforward bill of sale—which is what the lawyer called it. I know I should have taken legal advice, but I was naive and trusting, and unaware of the existence of such a thing as a tontine, let alone the significance of a clause réciproque in the deed. So I signed it."

"Everybody understands you made a mistake," said the Avocat Général. "Would you please describe to the court what happened after you bought the property and moved in together."

Her voice faltering, Camille pushed her hair from her face and spoke briefly of their move to Saint-Rémy and how they were content, if not ecstatic, at first but how Max changed after Bernard's funeral. He had always like to drink, but it was then that he started drinking more and disappearing for days at a time, claiming he had to look after his sick mother.

She described how her world fell apart on May 13 when she was physically assaulted by the person she thought she loved, only to discover days later that Max had a common-law wife and children living nearby. And how devastating it had been to conclude that she had been deceived from the beginning and the whole affair had been a sham. Finally, after describing her fruitless efforts to have the tontine annulled, and how the house was burned down on July 14, she broached the dramatic moment following her return to Ventabren. Until then, she had kept her composure, but her voice broke as she described the moment she learned that her mother had fallen down the stairs and been pronounced dead.

"Thank you, Mademoiselle Dumont," said the Avocat Général. "We may need to call upon you later in the proceedings. Please stay in the courtroom. Meantime, I would like to call the second witness in his role as chief investigator, Chief Inspector Paquet of the Criminal Brigade of the County Gendarmerie of the Bouches-du-Rhône."

The public leaned forward to watch the ponderous Chief Inspector arrive and walk up to the witness bar. Paquet looked directly at Max and stared at him for several seconds without speaking, then slowly turned and looked around the room.

"Monsieur le Président, ladies and gentlemen of the jury," he began, "unfortunately I never have the good fortune to meet Madame Juliette Dumont personally, but like so many people present here today, I held her in very high esteem. Today, September 24, she would have been fifty years old and since I am fifty-two years old, I remember her winning her gold medal very well. And like many young French people at the time, it had a huge effect on me. I admired her, not just for what she achieved, but for her beauty and her grace. She was a normal girl from a normal family, and she inspired us all. In fact, like many young men at that time, I idealised her and, I confess, absurdly, I used to dream of meeting her, even marrying her…"

Paquet paused as the audience broke into laughter,

"… you may laugh, but I was not alone. Such was the influence that Juliette Dumont had on the French people at the time. She was, and I say this with pride, my heroine, the people's heroine, a true heroine of France. You might even say my admiration veered on obsession, like Morel here. He too was obsessed. Yet, my obsession—if that's what it was—did not make me want to harm her. Or to steal from her. Quite the contrary."

Paquet paused and wiped his brow with his right hand. He gripped the witness bar as he recalled the dismay at the entire police station when they heard the news of Juliette Dumont's death. Two days later, he had the painful duty to communicate the findings of the autopsy to her daughter, Camille Dumont. And it was she who suggested that Morel could be a person of interest. By early afternoon, he had a copy of Morel's police record, including the report of Camille's assault, and a warrant was issued for Morel's arrest.

"He knew we were on to him because a day later, he tried to get thirty thousand francs from M'selle Dumont in exchange for annulling their agreement. We nearly trapped him then, but he got away."

As Paquet spoke, Max feigned boredom, leaned back in his chair and gazed at the ceiling. But when he closed his eyes and pretended to sleep, the Huissier admonished him for his impudence and lack of respect.

The court listened spellbound as the policeman described Max's second attempt to extort money from Camille. How they followed Camille and Nadia through the nature reserve of Sainte-Victoire, and their dramatic escape after Morel forced their car into the lake. The audience remained captivated when Paquet explained how the police hunted Max with dogs until a tip led them to the Chateau du Tholonet, where they found him near death after failing to cut off his own hand.

A psychological expert spoke next in defence of Max, about his lack of education and poor upbringing in the mountains of the Auvergne. He stressed how he had effaced his early troubles with the law by serving in the French Foreign Legion and described the difficulties ex-soldiers face when they try to re-join society.

The counsel for the defence called for the positive testimony of his common-law wife who forgave him for his bad behaviour, pleading that although he had faults, Max also had good qualities.

"And what would those qualities be?" asked the Président of the Court, leaning towards her as she steadied herself at the witness bar.

"He's a knowledgeable man, your honour. He has a real brain. He knows more about nature than anyone has a right to know," she pleaded, "and if he has done wrong, it was only because he wanted to better himself."

"Madame, please stop there," the Avocat Général interjected. "This court is not concerned with the accomplishments or domestic intentions of the accused. All that interests us is whether he broke the law."

Last to testify was Nadia, whose lively testimony corroborated Camille's and Paquet's accounts of the hunt. And then came the moment everyone had waited for: the chance to hear Max reply to the charge spontaneously, as was his legal right, before being interrogated by the Président the court. Through-out the trial, Max had, by turns, looked smug, bored and defiant, even wink-ing once at a female juror.

Now, all eyes were on Max as he stood up with his police escort.

Max began by proudly describing how poverty had given him a sense of resilience and shaped him as a man.

"Inspector Porky here," he said, looking at Inspector Paquet, "wouldn't last a day in the wild without a hot meal and a dab of Brut Cologne." Despite a titter from the audience, neither Camille nor Nadia, nor the judges smiled, and his disrespect earned him another reprimand from the Huissier.

"You are to take the court seriously. Do you not understand that you are accused of attempted murder? This is your opportunity to prove your inno-cence, your opportunity to deny the charges or prove extenuating circumstances."

"I deny the charges because I don't recognise the right of the court to judge me," replied Max testily. "For over six hours, I've been listening to this waste of time and resources. You, Monsieur le Président, in your red silks," he said looking to his right at the podium. "You're supposed to represent the people of France, yet you look more like a king to me. Not that I've ever seen a king of course," he added, making the audience laugh.

"You, Monsieur le Président," he said as he pivoted back to him, "only rep-resent the privileged! You don't care about the poor! I, too, am a citizen of France but I don't believe that you speak for, or give a damn about, people like me. The French Revolution was about new ideals—Liberty, Equality, and Fraternity or death! What did we get? Not liberty, certainly not equality and no…"

"Now that's enough," intervened the Huissier sharply, as the Avocat Général stood up. "Any more of that and you'll be taken down to your cell."

"No," said the Président. "Let him continue. That way everybody can learn the true character of this man. Continue Morel but think before you speak and be warned that everything you say is being noted by the court and may influence the jury in their deliberations."

Max continued in a loud voice. "France is supposed to be a democracy. Government by the people for the people. But here in France, it isn't the people who govern; it's the rich and powerful who govern, and they delib-erately keep the poor down!"

Max looked directly and glared at the Président. "And why do they want to keep us down?" he asked the audience. "Very simple! Because the rich are scared of us! We outnumber them thousands of times over, and they are frightened of another revolution! So, they stifle us with taxes and rules to keep us poor and in hardship, as meek as a herd of lambs. I believe in freedom, real freedom and freewill. I believe in a country where no one is forced to do anything, because when the free stand together, the will of the people is unbeatable. Strength through unity. We need real liberty, real equality and real fraternity in this country. Or death. As it says in the Declaration of the Rights of Man of 1789."

With a nod to the Huissier, the Président brought the court to order.

"That is enough!" he bellowed. "We have all heard enough of your anarchist, dangerous drivel. If you cannot confine your remarks to the matter in hand, you will forfeit all privileges. I will ask you one last question. What do you say in your defence to the charge that you attempted to murder Mademoiselle Dumont and Madame Beausoleil?"

"I don't deny it," said Max angrily as the spectators gasped. "It's obvious that whatever I say, you will find me guilty. So yes, I admit it; I did try to get rid of them."

The crowd erupted in low cries and loud gasps, and the Président raised his voice once again.

"Quiet! I will not tolerate this noise! The court has noted that the accused has confessed to the charge of which he is accused, and the jury will duly take note of that in its deliberations on the sentencing."

In a loud voice Max added: "One more thing, the charade that you have planned to follow this one, on the other charge. I am going to save you the trouble. Chalk me up for that one, too, while you are at it."

Once again, the crowd shouted and gasped in astonishment, and everyone started talking at once. And once again, the Président raised his voice.

"Quiet! I say, quiet!! Monsieur le Greffier, I trust you noted what the accused said?"

The Président waited for the court to quieten down before continuing. "Morel, am I correct in understanding that you are not only pleading guilty to the charge of attempted murder for which you are in court today, but you are also pleading guilty to the charge of the murder of Juliette Dumont?"

"Yes," said Max defiantly. "Yes, I am. Because whether I am guilty or not, you will still find me guilty because I am poor, and Juliette Dumont was rich and famous. And I do not want to go through this humiliating circus again just to please the media and you."

"Monsieur l'Avocat Général, what do you say?" asked the Président.

All eyes turned to look at the tall, thin figure in red and black, who took off his glasses and looked up from reading a piece of paper.

"On behalf of the Minister of the Public and the Prosecution, given that the accused has admitted the charges of murder and attempted murder to the assembled court, we ask for the maximum sentence permitted by law."

"In that case," said the Président, "I declare today's proceedings closed. And given that the accused has admitted his guilt on both charges, we will not go forward with a second trial. Instead, I will invite the jury to begin their deliberations on the sentencing on both charges when we reconvene at nine o'clock in the morning."

When the court reconvened the following day, the Président addressed the jury.

"The accused is recorded as having admitted his guilt to both charges, and the Huissier will now advise the jury of the penalties prescribed by the law for his crimes."

The Huissier stood up and turned to face the jury. He spoke slowly and clearly. "Under Article 221-2 of the Criminal Code, the crime of intentional homicide preceding another crime, the purpose of which is to prepare or facilitate a crime, is punishable by life imprisonment which can range from a minimum of twenty years of incarceration," the Huissier paused and looked up at Max, "to the death penalty."

There were wails, gasps and boos from the crowd, and several people shouted, "Shame! Shame!"

As the Huissier demanded order in the court, the Président raised his voice, and Max appeared worried for the first time. "I remind the court that a decision on the sentence must be taken by a majority, and at least eight votes are necessary to pronounce the maximum sentence, the death penalty."

After which, the nine jurors and the Président and the two Assesseur judges retired to the windowless jury room to consider the maximum sentence required by the chief prosecutor, the Avocat Général.

Nadia turned to Camille. "Let's stretch our legs. They won't be back for a while. It's a terrible thing, the death penalty, but the punishment must fit the crime. Though here we are in 1968 and armed robbery is still punishable by the death penalty in this country, in theory, at least. And I can't agree with that."

"Good God, I had no idea," replied Camille. "Since when?"

"Since 1950. They changed the law following a rise in armed robbery after the war."

"Bobo, I just don't know where you learn this stuff."

Nadia laughed.

Soon after four in the afternoon, the bells began to ring in the lobby outside the courtroom, and ushers called people to their seats. The jury was due back imminently with their decision on the sentence.

"Please sit," said the Président of the Court.

"The ladies and gentlemen of the Jury, as true representatives of the people of France, have made their decision, which is incontestable, that is to say, there is no right of appeal to the sentence. Before proceeding, I certify that, according to the law, all the members of the jury were asked if there were extenuating circumstances to justify the crimes of the accused. I can confirm that all twelve jury members voted in the negative.

"Subsequently, according to established procedure, a secret ballot by unanimous vote has found the defendant to be guilty on all charges, and by a vote of nine to three, the maximum sentence as requested by the Avocat Général was affirmed. That is to say, according to Article 12 of the Penal Code, the defendant will suffer the penalty of death by decapitation."

There were loud intakes of breath and howls from the audience, and as more people shouted "Shame," another shouted: "the Sixth Commandment. Thou shalt not kill." And still another shouted: "you cannot efface one crime by committing another."

As the Huissier demanded order in the court, all eyes turned to the dock where Max remained expressionless though Camille could see he had understood the gravity of his situation. The Président of the Court declared the proceedings closed, and Max was taken to a cell in the ancient prison behind the courts to remain behind bars in solitary confinement, under surveillance day and night, to prevent any attempt at escape or suicide. He was unable to appeal his sentence because it could only be reconsidered on legal grounds and was told that his only chance of avoiding the death penalty was if Général de Gaulle, the Président of the Republic, chose to examine his case and grant Max a pardon. He had six months to decide.

After a month in the Aix prison, Max was transferred twenty miles away, to the larger, more daunting prison of the Centre Pénitentiaire de Marseille des Baumettes in the bustling port city of Marseille.

Chapter 23

A BLACK MISTRAL

D ESPITE THE INITIAL EUPHORIA FOLLOWING MAX'S CONVICTION, it was not easy for Camille and Nadia to accept that it was over, much less to celebrate.

It was a relief not to see police cars outside the house and know that Max was in prison, but they both knew that Max wanted them dead, a grim truth confirmed by a package in the mail containing a bird skull, an empty tin of rat poison and some newspaper cuttings of the trial. From whom they never knew. Pierre? Max's parents? His wife? Accomplices? Camille never found out, and she and Nadia shrugged it off.

Since the trial was now over, Juliette's body could be released, and Camille and Nadia arranged for a cheerless and intensely private funeral at the church in Ventabren where Juliette joined Bernard in the family vault. Meanwhile, the International Olympic Committee and the Féderation Française de Natation arranged a grand memorial service in Paris appropriate to Juliette's status, with ministers and Olympic officials, athletes, and television stars competing with each other to sing Juliette's praises. Neither Camille nor Nadia relished the thought of more attention from the press and declined to make the trip to Paris. Besides, Camille's pregnancy was well advanced, and her baby was due in February.

In the Chateau de Vaucluse, both Nadia and Camille felt Juliette's loss acutely, and they adapted slowly to life without her. Camille moved from her cottage into Juliette's apartment off the kitchen to be closer to Nadia in the house, and instead of replacing her lost little Citroen, Nadia began to use Juliette's Alfa Romeo.

"You don't think she would mind, do you?" she asked Camille. "You know how she loved that car."

"Why would she mind?" asked Camille. "She's dead. She isn't going to be driving that car or any other. In fact, she would probably be thrilled to know you are driving it. Much better than selling it or letting it rot in the garage."

Early December was dry and sunny, but two weeks before Christmas, the wind intensified, and the temperature dropped sharply. And when the rain arrived from the northwest, Camille knew that what the locals call *un mistral noir* [a black Mistral] was on its way.

The black Mistral had been blowing for three days without letting up, and Camille was in the kitchen preparing lunch when she was startled by a voice behind her.

"Mmm, that smell's good, Camille. What are you cooking?"

Camille's blood ran cold, and she stiffened with fear in mid-motion, like the prey of a predator when it's trapped. She spun around furiously to see Max standing by the door from the hall. He was wearing blue jeans and a denim jacket. And his hair was very short.

"Dear God, you scared me! How dare you! You pig! How the hell did you get in here?"

"Through the front door. Don't you ever learn? You never lock it, Camille. I've told you many times not to be so trusting." Max whistled. "Good God! Look at the size of you! You've been putting on weight! Who's the lucky guy?"

The sight of him standing there, sneering at her, daring to insult her brought it all back. Indignant, angry and more than a little scared, she said through clenched teeth:

"What are you doing here? Aren't you supposed to be in prison? You'd better get out of here now or..."

"Or what? You'll call the cops? Come on, Camille, there are no cops around here anymore. They think I'm in prison, remember?"

"There will be when they realise you've escaped. This is the first place they'll think to look."

"I won't be here long enough. I'm only staying a few minutes," said Max.

"What are you doing here anyway?" said Camille angrily, her hands on her hips. "What do you want from me?"

"Don't pretend you've forgotten. We have a score to settle, unfinished business, remember?"

"If it's money you want, I'll give you some cash if you go away. How the hell did you escape?"

"Yes, of course it's money I want. Why else do you think I came here?"

Max moved a step closer to Camille, who looked around for a means to defend herself.

"Stay away from me! I don't want you in this kitchen. What I'd like to know is how you escaped? And why you're not in a prison uniform?" As Camille spoke, she was thinking frantically that she must keep him talking, that she must humour him. Nadia would be home soon.

"How did I escape? Thanks to this! I was supposed to visit the hospital for the surgeon to look at it."

Max waved the stump of his right arm at her. And Camille recoiled at the sight of the soiled bandage oozing yellow fluids and plasma.

"Look at this. Go on, Camille, take a good look! Making sure my arm got reinfected, that's how I got out."

Max sounded increasingly angry as he talked.

"Can you believe they want you to be healthy when they cut your head off? They don't want people to die before they kill them, so they send you to a doctor if you're sick! And you know what? They even gave me these threads to look nice for the hospital visit. Not too bad, eh? Very thoughtful of them."

"Stop! You disgust me, Max!" said Camille, trembling. "I have some cash in the safe. I'll give it to you if you swear to leave me alone."

With her pulse and her mind racing, she led the way through the hall to Bernard's old room. The curtains had remained closed for weeks, and the room smelled stale and musty. Camille switched on the light and walked over to Bernard's bureau, now clear of papers. She pushed the heavy chair to one side, and crouched behind the desk, aware of Max watching her. Methodically, she turned the dial on the old safe; centre on zero, then two 360° turns to the right, back to seven, forward a full turn to zero and back to nine.

"I can't believe you still have that old safe. You should get a new one. A child could open that thing."

On the top shelf were two bundles of banknotes, and on the lower shelf were some beige folders and piles of papers. And under them was Nadine's German officer's dress dagger. Camille pulled out the bundles of notes.

"What are you, Camille? A drug dealer, or something? What do you need all this cash for?"

"Not your business Max. Just take it and get out of here."

"I will, I will," said Max reaching out for the money. "You are right. I do have to get out of here. I have a car waiting outside."

He made as if to leave the room before turning back. "There's one more thing before I go. You didn't forget, did you? Oh, Camille, did you forget our agreement?"

He pushed the money into his jacket pockets, and stood still for a moment, staring pensively at the ground. Then he slid his hand into the back pocket of his jeans. "This is the difficult bit."

Max looked at Camille with an uncharacteristically remorseful look, which alarmed her.

"I'm sure you have worked out that I still have my copy of the deed, and know I'll inherit everything if you die, including this house? You do know that, don't you?"

For a moment, Camille saw a flash, a faint glimpse of the old Max.

"I liked this place the first time you showed it to me, remember?" Max went on. "But I could never see myself living in a chateau. But now, I am beginning to think I would like it. Ironic, isn't it? Me, as a rich bourgeois, living in a chateau. Wasn't that what you always wanted? Me to be bourgeois?"

Max paused and forced a smile. "I know I should have arranged for you to have an accident. I know that. I did think of taking you with me and leaving you in some remote place with broken legs like the girl in the old newspaper, remember? But I don't have time for that, and anyway, it's far too complicated."

Max looked sourly at her again. "So, what the hell am I supposed to do with you, Camille? They want to guillotine me! Guillotine me, do you hear? Do you understand they want to cut my head off? It won't make any damn difference whether I kill you or not. They are going to try and put me to death anyway.

"But what I will tell you is this. Where I'm going, I'll need money, if I get there. So, I'm sorry; I have no choice. I have to go now, so let's get this over with, shall we? There's no other way."

Max took a step towards her and pulled a switchblade from his back pocket and pressed the button on the handle: a razor-sharp, six-inch blade snapped out and locked with a metallic clunk.

"How do you like the knife?" he asked, looking down at it approvingly. "It's called a stiletto siciliano. Pierre gave it to me. I think I like it even more than my old Laguiole, don't you? It's better for a man with one arm."

Without another word, Max lifted his head and looked at Camille with blazing eyes and lunged straight at her. Petrified, Camille put her arms up to defend herself and tried to push him away, but the knife cut her left arm, sliced her hand, and slipped down to her belly.

"Wait, stop, oh please God no!" screamed Camille as she fell bleeding to her knees and tried to scramble behind the desk. "This is your baby I'm expecting, for God's sake," she shrieked. "Who will look after him if you kill me? Please, please, Max, kill me but don't kill your baby."

For a second, Max looked shocked and stopped short.

"My baby? That's a surprise! But you know what? I don't care, Camille. It doesn't change a fucking thing. I need money, not babies, where I am going."

"Going somewhere nice and hot, I hope?" said a voice from the door. "Like hell, for example?"

It was Nadia standing in the doorway with the Luger in her hand, pointed directly at him.

"Jesus, not you again, you bitch," said Max, as he pivoted and rushed at her with the knife.

"It's the bitch again," said Nadia acidly.

She pulled the trigger, and the 9mm shell detonated like a crash of thunder. Max kept moving towards her with the knife, but there was an odd look in his eyes and a stain spreading on his jacket. Before Nadia could pull the trigger again, Camille had leaned over and grabbed the dagger from the safe and hurled herself at Max, and in exquisite slow-motion, she buried the steel in his side.

It was otherworldly and surreal, and disconcertingly gratifying to watch the blade slice through the denim, cut through the *epidermis*, plunge through the *subcutaneous* tissue, cleave the *latissimus dorsi*, and, slippery with blood, sever the *superior mesenteric* artery and come to rest deep inside the large intestine.

Camille fell back, stunned at what she had just done.

Still holding the dripping dagger, she stared mesmerised at Max as he tumbled to the floor, the blood pumping and gushing from his side. He gasped and tried to steady himself, and his breath came in short, shallow gulps.

"There, Max," she said, dazed and panting heavily. "Damn you! You asked for that."

At once, all the tension drained away and she gazed dispassionately at Max, bleeding to death on Bernard's oriental rug. She looked at him calmly and indifferently, as if the trauma had allowed her to shift her point of view from leading protagonist to that of a detached observer, indifferent to the physical and emotional ordeal. And then, light-headed, she became aware of a cloying warmth on her thighs and looked down to see her dress soaked with blood. She understood it was not Max's blood but hers, and it was coming from the wounds to her arm and hand, and where Max had cut her belly.

"Bobo," she whispered, "please help me. I don't feel well. I feel faint."

"Oh my God, look at you," said Nadia leaping forward. "My poor baby. Don't move. I'll call an ambulance and get some bandages. Stay awake, and whatever you do, don't close your eyes, don't sleep and don't try to move."

Nadia raced to the phone on the hall table and dialled the emergency number. "We have an emergency at the Chateau de Vaucluse. Please hurry ...yes, yes...Ventabren... Send an ambulance and the police."

Max, his head on the rug and his eyes half-closed and unblinking, tried to turn and look at Camille.

"You did it, Camille. You got me," he managed to wheeze.

Camille, her body trembling and weak from loss of blood, felt no anger and looked back at him calmly without malice.

"Fuck you, Max. You tried to kill me." She leaned over to whisper in his ear, "But this is it, it's curtains for you. You are dying Max. I'm not sorry it ends this way. But as you always used to say: it's dog eat dog."

Max murmured something inaudible before his eyes blanked and glazed over, and his life ebbed away.

"He's dead, Nadia," said Camille quietly, as Nadia came back into the room. "Please hurry, I may not be far behind."

"Good riddance to him," said Nadia. "It's you I care about. The ambulance will be here in a minute."

As swiftly as she could, Nadia dressed Camille's left arm and hand, and wrapped the bandages tightly to slow the bleeding. It was not easy to staunch all the blood seeping from the wound to her belly. Neither of them mentioned the same terrifying thought in their minds. Would Camille live? Would the baby survive?

"They will be here any moment, sweetheart," Nadia said calmly. "Just keep still. You're feeling faint because you've lost a little blood. Once the ambulance arrives, you'll be fine."

Abruptly the sound of an urgent car horn came from outside the house, and a moment later, the front door burst open, and a voice yelled: "Come on, Max, let's go! The police are coming. We have to go!" It was Pierre.

"Max is going nowhere," said Nadia, as she leaped to her feet and grabbed the gun. "Your friend is dead."

She held the Luger with two hands and pointed it directly at Pierre, who stood transfixed in the hall, gaping at his friend and Camille lying there, their blood flowing and intermingling on the floor.

"Stay exactly where you are," Nadia said. "Do not move an inch. The police will be here in a minute."

Keeping her gun trained on Pierre, she turned to check on Camille and saw a smile flutter in her eyes as they both heard the police arrive. Then Camille's eyes closed, and she slumped over to her side.

Camille's life hung by a thread when she was rushed to the main hospital in Aix where, following a massive transfusion of blood, they were able to stabilise her. Even so, despite their best efforts, the doctors were unable to save her baby.

"You lost too much blood," said Nadia holding Camille's hand. "And they told me that even if they had saved the baby, it would have had damage to its little brain. I am not sure if you know this, but the knife also penetrated the baby's back so he might have had other physical problems. It was probably just as well."

Camille looked up from her bed. "He? Did you say 'he'?"

"Yes, I did say 'he.' You would have had a little boy."

"God, that hurts to know the gender. But I suppose you're right, it's just as well he didn't make it. He would have been a permanent reminder of Max, and God knows what he might have turned into. A little terror in all likelihood."

They both laughed.

Chapter 24

The Last Secret

··

HE FIRST FEW DAYS OF 1969 WERE BITTERLY COLD, and the thermometer plunged to -12° Celsius [10° F], and the chilly weather persisted through the spring. Yet from morning to night, the sun shone every day in a brilliant cerulean sky. It was the kind of weather that endeared Provence to Camille, unlike the mild, grey winters of London.

On January 10, Camille was allowed home from the hospital on condition she returned three times a week for physical therapy. Her scars would be a permanent reminder of Max.

On February 28, the inspector came to visit.

"I'm pleased to see you looking better," Paquet said, shaking Camille's hand. "I have news for you." Paquet was carrying a large cardboard box that Nadia suggested he put on the kitchen table.

"Because of that infamous clause de tontine that caused you so much trouble, you ended up inheriting Max's possessions. Not that he had much, though you may find one or two things interesting.

"I'm sorry it has taken so long, but the law moves slowly, and Max's status as a convicted prisoner complicated the procedure. Plus, we had to consider the rights of other claimants and his common-law wife. He also had some debts, which won't surprise you, but you saw for yourself that a tontine is impossible to break and trumps all other rights. So, the law decided this belongs to you."

Paquet open the cardboard box, to reveal the two shoeboxes of newspaper cuttings from the trial, seven old books, numerous artefacts and oddities, Max's Laguiole knife and a small, battered leather case.

Camille forced a smile and made it clear that she had no interest in keeping anything, least of all the Laguiole knife.

"Don't be too hasty," said the inspector. "You might want to keep the newspaper cuttings about your mother as well as one to two other things. We've looked into his background to match his profile to unsolved crimes and know more about Morel now."

Camille looked up from the box. "Before you tell us what's in the box, you never told us how he escaped from prison?"

Paquet smiled knowingly, gratified by the expectant faces of his small audience.

"Did I never tell you? He planned it all. He deliberately infected his arm—you both saw that—and was in league with Paglioni, of course, though essentially it was incompetence of the part of the hospital security staff. Their excuse was they didn't expect to have a problem with a sick, one-armed man. Anyway, Max disabled his guard in the washroom, and walked out of the hospital wearing a doctor's coat. Simple as that, and Paglioni was waiting in a car."

"You could never underestimate Max. He was strong, very strong," said Camille, shaking her head. "What else did you find out?"

"For a start," Paquet replied, "Morel's father was not a farmer, but a coal miner who died of silicosis in 1941 in Alès, about ninety miles northwest of here. Though he did spend his childhood on a mountain farm in the Auvergne, which belonged to his maternal grandparents. He was born illegitimately when his mother was sixteen, and it was his grandparents who brought him up. They never married and joined by a tontine.

"We found no trace of his mother. She may be alive, but we doubt it. She may have died in the war. In any case, we established that Morel went to school for the first time at fifteen in Clermont-Ferrand in late 1941, and his school records show that he was bright but very headstrong, and difficult to discipline."

Paquet paused and looked at Camille. "He probably saw a German for the first time one year later when they came south in 1942. In any case, when they arrived in Clermont-Ferrand, the Gestapo arrested all the foreign Jews, and most of the French Jews fled— and Morel broke into a house left behind by a Jewish family and stole their car, and doubtless other things.

"He was caught and lucky not to be sent to work in Germany. He wasn't imprisoned either, no doubt because the prisons were full. So, they offered him the chance to join the Avant Garde, the junior section of the Milice Française. You know what the Milice was all about?"

"The Milice? Wasn't it a French, pro-German organisation, formed to fight the French Resistance?" Camille suggested.

"Exactly. An unpleasant group of people. Opportunist, fascist, anti-communist and anti-Semitic, and like Morel, most of them were young and poorly educated." Paquet continued. "The Resistance thought of the Milice as worse than the Gestapo because they were traitors, which is what they unquestionably were. Being French, they knew the local towns and countryside, and could understand all the slang and different dialects."

Paquet pushed the leather case towards Camille.

"Go ahead, unlock it." The inspector said.

Nadia clicked the releases on the two catches and opened the lid. Inside were Max's waist packs still on their leather belt, a large brown folder, a tin box and Max's cigarette lighter.

"The waist packs are empty," said Paquet hurriedly, "and I'm sure you have no use for them, but I have something here you'll be pleased to see."

Paquet bent down, opened his briefcase, and removed two thick envelopes.

"Your money or most of it. We finally recovered it from Paglioni. He sang like a bird when we offered him leniency in exchange for information. He told us he got Max's message early in the morning and left to help him straightaway, but when he found him on the Roman aqueduct above the chateau, he couldn't wake him up. And seeing what a mess Max had made of himself, he decided he had to be dying, so he left him there and took the money. There's a friend for you. Incidentally, Paglioni also told us that Max was not in the Foreign Legion for five years as he claimed. He said he helped to get him in, but Max was discharged a year later. Here, look at this."

Paquet opened the brown folder and removed a small booklet.

"We got hold of this after his trial," he said. "It's Max's military record, his *Livret Militaire* from 1947. At twenty-one, he was dismissed without honour. What is surprising is that they accepted him in the first place. They would have had many other applicants to choose from at the time."

The burly policeman licked his thumb and flipped the page in his official notebook.

"There are one or two other things that may interest you. Let me show you."

Paquet tipped the contents of the folder onto the table.

"Look at this," he said, picking up a travel document. "It's an unused ferry ticket from Marseille to Oran, Algeria dated Friday, August 16, 1968. It means he was planning to go there in the other car after you gave him the money in Le Tholonet. And look, here are some newspaper cuttings about the death of Walter Clément, the owner of the garage where Max worked."

"I told you Max killed him," said Camille.

"I know you did Camille, and we agree with you, but it's too late now. Incidentally, did you know that Clément was German? His wife told us that he was an ex-Prisoner-of-War who stayed on in France after the war."

"Okay, I didn't know that. So, what's in the tin?"

Paquet leaned over and picked up the small tin. On the lid was written *Gargarisme du Luchon.*

"Nothing special about the tin, just an old box of throat lozenges," he said, as he pried the lid open and tipped several war mementos onto the table. They included a few old Vichy aluminium coins, two empty bullet casings, several military brass buttons and a small photo. As well as a Milice beret badge and a Milice lapel pin.

"All right," said Nadia picking up the photo. "This looks like him in this group of Miliciens. He was basically a Nazi if he was a member of the Milice. No wonder he had a thing against Jews."

"Oh, there is no question he was a member, but we can't prove it because the Milice destroyed all their membership records after D-Day," said Inspector Paquet.

"There is one more thing I want to show you."

For a fleeting moment, the inspector appeared uncomfortable, and he looked first at Camille, then at Nadia. And then, like a country magician saving his best trick until last, he produced a small, battered notebook from inside his blazer pocket. And when he used two hands to hold the small book, they knew it was important.

"Before I get to it, could I possibly have something to drink?"

"With pleasure, Inspector. Would you like a glass of water? Or something a little stronger?"

"Wine? A glass of red wine would be perfect. What I am about to say is off the record."

"Inspector Paquet! I am shocked! You are drinking on duty!" Camille laughed as she gave him a glass of wine.

"I did say off the record," Paquet smiled sheepishly, "which technically means I'm off duty, so if I'm not working, I can have a drink."

Paquet took a sip of the wine and held the glass up to the light. "This is good wine, singularly good, thank you. What I want to show you is this."

He held up the small notebook.

"Amongst Max's possessions was this notebook. He started taking notes soon after he became a member of the Milice in January '44. It's not Molière, but it makes interesting reading. I have read every word and it wasn't easy if you look at writing."

Paquet cleared his throat and looked down at the journal.

"Most of what he writes is of no interest: what time he got up, what he had for breakfast, that sort of thing. But intriguingly, he occasionally writes about tasks he was given. And there was one task of particular interest to him as well as to us."

Paquet looked up at Camille and Nadia before he continued.

"He was asked to help uncover the identity of a member of the French Resistance known by the codename of Barbara. He was particularly interested because this Barbara was thought to associate with Juliette Dumont. And, as we all know, he was obsessed with Juliette Dumont and knew a lot about her."

Paquet paused again and took another sip of his drink.

"The point is we already know from other sources that the Gestapo and Milice were interested in Juliette Dumont, either because they suspected her of helping the Resistance or because of her connection with this Barbara. Or more likely both. Now, how do I put this? It occurred to me that you, Madame Beausoleil, being so close to Madame de Vaucluse, might have come across this mysterious Barbara? As I said, this is off the record, just out of interest."

As he was talking, Paquet pulled out a small black and white photograph of two women walking together in the sunshine.

"This photograph was among Max's possessions. From the vehicles and the clothing, it was taken during the war, and judging from the buildings and the café terraces, they were somewhere in the South of France. In Aix perhaps, or Marseille. If you turn it over, you'll see someone has written 'Juliette Dumont and Barbara(?)' in pencil on the back. It certainly looks like Juliette Dumont, but do you recognise the other woman, Madame Beausoleil?"

Both Camille and Nadia studied the photo, and there was a long silence before Camille finally answered.

"Well, I don't want to put the cat among the pigeons, but I think the other woman looks like you, Bobo. And when you mentioned Barbara, Inspector Paquet, it reminded me of something I have been trying to remember ever since Max attacked us. Nadia, why did Max call you Barbara, before you shot him?"

There was another long silence before Nadia replied.

"Yes, I agree the photo looks like me, but that doesn't mean it is me, or that I am Barbara," said Nadia defiantly. "But what I want to say this. The war finished a long time ago, almost twenty-five years. If Max was a member of the Milice, he was lucky he survived as long as he did. The Milice were traitors. After Paris was liberated in August '44, being cowards, the Milice ran away. A few escaped to Germany, but many more were imprisoned or murdered by the Resistance. And when the war was over in 1945, more were thrown from windows or found floating in rivers. They got what they deserved."

The inspector took another sip from his glass.

"I wonder what Max was doing with the photograph, and where he got it from?"

He picked up the photo again and studied it. "I suppose it's possible he spotted Juliette in the street by chance and took a picture of her. I think it more likely the photo was taken by someone spying on her or her companion. In which case the photo was taken by a photographer working for the Milice."

"You think Madame Beausoleil was Barbara," Camille said, looking piercingly at the inspector. "You do, don't you?"

"I don't know. It's not important today, but yes, I think it is possible."

Inspector Paquet looked at Nadia. "Perhaps you don't want to talk about it. If so, I completely understand. I was a young policeman back then and I don't like talking about the war. We did many things I'm not proud of."

Nadia looked at them both and said defensively. "There was nothing I did that I am not proud of."

There was a moment's silence as Paquet and Camille sensed she wanted to add something. They looked at her expectantly, and Nadia picked up the photo again.

"All right," she said, "I'll tell you. Firstly, yes, that photo is of Juliette and me, and it was taken in September 1943, in Marseille. And yes, I did take part in the Resistance, and yes, my codename was Barbara.

"As Camille knows, I was born in Germany and came to France in 1936 when I was eighteen. Once the war began, I desperately wanted to do something to help, and since I speak four languages—German, Polish, French, and English—I had something to offer. Through Juliette, I made it known to Bernard that I was anxious to help but I didn't take part in any missions until early 1943."

"Stop." Camille looked at Nadia in surprise. "Did you say Bernard? What did he have to do with it?"

"You didn't know, did you? How could you? Bernard lived here all his life and knew many influential people around here, and, like countless other people, was eager to help. Two friends of his, Henri and Nancy Fiocca, had a business in Marseille, and they set up an escape route to help Allied soldiers and airmen get to Spain. Bernard would arrange false identity papers and find places for them to hide, and a network of people, including his wife Nancy, escorted them from Marseille over the Pyrenees to Spain."

"Good God, I had no idea. He never mentioned it," exclaimed Camille. "Did anybody ever hide here, in our home?"

"Oh yes, many times," replied Nadia.

"That's amazing. So, Juliette was in the Resistance too?"

"No. She wanted to be, but she was too conspicuous, too well known, so she helped look after our guests and hid them in the house. And in answer to your next question, in the attic above the stables."

"So, what did you do?"

"There were many girls like me who spoke several languages, all of us very young, and the younger we appeared, the less likely the Germans were to suspect us. My first missions were as a simple courier, dropping off messages, that sort of thing. Later on, I got to escort British and Polish airmen to Spain for the Fiocca Pat O'Leary line."

Inspector Paquet listened quietly. "Those were terrible times, but they brought out the very best in some people and the very worst in others."

Paquet drained his glass and looked at Nadia.

"May I ask you if that Luger you have was really given to Juliette Dumont by General von Schaumburg?" asked Paquet.

Nadia put her head back and laughed. "No, Inspector Paquet, it was not. I took it from a dead German as a souvenir of the war. We all did when we could because we weren't given arms—but we had to know how to use them, and we were trained to use Lugers, Walther P38s and British Sten guns. It was only towards the end of the war that they allowed us to carry firearms, and that was just on sabotage missions."

"And what about the dagger?" asked Camille.

"That was a souvenir, too. After the war, they were highly prized and lots of people collected them."

"Then it didn't belong to General von Schaumburg?"

"I never said it did. No, just a souvenir. Sorry to disappoint you."

There was a long pause.

"Well, at least I now understand why Nadia was so good with that Luger," said Paquet looking at Camille.

"Another glass of wine, Inspector?"

As Camille refilled the policeman's glass of wine, she said slowly: "Do you think it possible, that Max meant to kill Barbara that night, and not Juliette?"

"We'll never know," said Nadia, "but yes, I thought of that, too. It definitely is possible."

In early July, a letter arrived from New York.

"It's from Alfons," said Nadia. "I wonder what he wants."

She stood in the kitchen and read it silently.

"Well, I am not sure what to make of this," she said, turning to Camille. "Alfons wants us to come and stay with him. He says he was shaken up last week at a demonstration at the Stonewall Inn in the West Village where he lives, and it made him think about his mortality."

"Nadia, that was not a demonstration; that was a full-blown riot. It even made the French newspapers. Was he hurt?"

"No, I don't think so, he says shaken up—a bruised ego probably."

"The Stonewall Inn is a queer bar, for homosexuals. How did he, of all people, get involved? I thought he was much too proper for that. Don't tell me my uncle Alfons is queer, is he?"

"You don't know Alfons, sweetheart."

"So, you mean he is queer?"

Nadia put her hand out and touched Camille's cheek.

"I can't say if he is or he isn't," Nadia whispered theatrically with a smile. "It's my last secret."

The END

THE FRONT COVER

The front cover of this book was inspired by the iconic **Gitanes Cigarettes** packet featuring a flamenco dancer with a tambourine, dancing through wisps of smoke. The designer of that packet was the celebrated French designer Marc Ponty (1924-1972) who won a competition to redesign the new packet in 1947, following increased competition from American cigarettes after the Second World War.

With my hat off to the skill of Ponty (and apologies to him), I changed the profile of the dancer to make her look more modern and put a dagger in her hand—the profile of which came from a real German officer's dagger kept as a souvenir from the war.

The French word *gitanes* of course means *gypsy*, and I felt the reference to Gitanes was justified as Max liked to smoke Gitanes and the gypsies are an important part of the culture in that part of France: in Beaucaire, in the Carmague and above all in Saintes-Maries-de-la-Mer, where the centuries-old annual gathering of gypsies from all over Europe takes place every May.

Author's note

The idea for *Secrets from a Stranger* was inspired by real places and real events including, to some degree, my own life. For I lived in Berlin in my teens, where I was lucky enough to swim, and even compete on occasion, in the Olympic pool where Juliette would have won her gold medal. Alfons' house was where my family lived and I used to swim and play tennis in Nadia's club.

Born in Britain, I worked in advertising in London before moving to Paris where I developed a passion for France, for history and for the visual arts. In fact, central Paris was my home for more than twenty years, and I lived in several different arrondissements, including the left bank and the Marais—which was then much less grand than it is now. Many of the now-renovated, historic town houses, were still sub-divided into small apartments as they had been following the Revolution, and the area was still known as the Jewish quarter, and it was there that many Jewish refugees were lodged in the 1930s.

To paraphrase Baudelaire, I was permanently drunk on the beauty of the city's architecture, the weight of history and the very Frenchness of it all. And naturally I got to know and love the south of France too, including Aix-en-Provence and Saint Rémy.

I now live in in the United States, in the vibrant city of Miami after living in Princeton and New York—another wonderful seductive city full of surprises, and perhaps where Camille will have her next adventure.

Meanwhile, I hope you enjoyed reading this book as much as I enjoyed writing it.

If you want to keep in touch, please visit my website at www.davidnewtondunn.com and use the contact page, and leave me your email address.

David (Nick) Newton Dunn.
Miami, 2021

Printed in Great Britain
by Amazon

83703596R10161